PRAISE FOR

DRACUL

"The prose is modern, energetic, and easy to read. *Dracul* reveals not only Dracula's 'true' origin, but Bram Stoker's as well. More than just a Dracula novel, it's a great addition to the entire vampire genre."

—*SF Reader*

"The narrative moves fairly quickly, pulling readers into this thrilling tale, with twists that keep the pages turning, even late into the night. . . . A strong pick for fans of classic gothic tales, such as *Dracula*, but also good for anyone who appreciates gripping historical novels, including those by Carlos Ruiz Zafón." —*Library Journal* (starred review)

"A big book that will no doubt be a hit among monster-movie and horror lit fans—and for good reason." —*Kirkus Reviews*

"Bram Stoker fans and scholars will find this a satisfying exploration of his legacy." —*Publishers Weekly*

"Sheds light on the original characters and author. Adding just the right touch of suspense increases the pace and ratchets up the tension."

—*Booklist*

"A terrifying and compelling prequel that reveals how a young Bram Stoker confronted evil to craft a masterpiece." —*Library Journal*

"A compelling, deep, dark drama about Dracula's origin. Even I had to keep the lights on when reading this book!"

—John Saul, author of *Suffer the Children*

"An exhilarating fever dream of creeping dread and dark adventure. Reading *Dracul* is like stepping into a time machine and traveling back to a shadowy landscape ruled by nightmares. I devoured it in two sittings and was delighted and chilled with every turn of the page. You will be, too." —Richard Chizmar, coauthor of *Gwendy's Button Box*

"Whatever fiendish bargain Stoker and Barker struck to resurrect the voice of Bram Stoker with such authenticity and aplomb, it was worth it, at least to their mere mortal readers. *Dracul* is a genius and fevered nightmare of Gothic madness, each page seeping with ominous dread and escalating horror. It is a prequel more than just worthy of the original novel—it is sure to be an undying classic of its own, haunting, terrifying, and entertaining generations to come." —Eric Rickstad, author of *What Remains of Her* and *The Silent Girls*

ALSO BY DACRE STOKER

Dracula: The Un-Dead

The Lost Journal of Bram Stoker: The Dublin Years

ALSO BY J. D. BARKER

Forsaken

The Fourth Monkey

The Fifth to Die

The Sixth Wicked Child

DRACUL

DACRE STOKER

and

J. D. BARKER

G. P. PUTNAM'S SONS
New York

PUTNAM
— EST. 1838 —

G. P. PUTNAM'S SONS
Publishers Since 1838
An imprint of Penguin Random House LLC
penguinrandomhouse.com

Copyright © 2018 by Dacre Stoker and J. D. Barker
Penguin supports copyright. Copyright fuels creativity, encourages
diverse voices, promotes free speech, and creates a vibrant culture. Thank
you for buying an authorized edition of this book and for complying with
copyright laws by not reproducing, scanning, or distributing any part of
it in any form without permission. You are supporting writers and
allowing Penguin to continue to publish books for every reader.

Drawing on the book spine, detail of "Celtic snake knots" by Matilda Stoker,
copyright © 2013 by Bram Stoker LLC, courtesy of the Stoker Family Collection

The Library of Congress has catalogued the
G. P. Putnam's Sons hardcover edition as follows:

Names: Stoker, Dacre, author. | Barker, J. D. (Jonathan Dylan), author.
Title: Dracul / Dacre Stoker and J. D. Barker.
Description: New York: G. P. Putnam's Sons, [2018]
Identifiers: LCCN 2017052374 | ISBN 9780735219342 (hardcover) |
ISBN 9780735219366 (ebook)
Subjects: LCSH: Stoker, Bram, 1847–1912—Fiction. |
Vampires—Fiction. | Horror fiction.
Classification: LCC PS3619.T645 D7 2019 | DDC 813/.6—dc23
LC record available at https:// lccn.loc.gov/ 2017052374

First G. P. Putnam's Sons hardcover edition / October 2018
First G. P. Putnam's Sons international edition / October 2018
First G. P. Putnam's Sons trade paperback edition / October 2019
First G. P. Putnam's Sons special value edition / January 2021
G. P. Putnam's Sons special value edition ISBN: 9780593331194

Printed in the United States of America
1 3 5 7 9 10 8 6 4 2

BOOK DESIGN AND MAP BY MEIGHAN CAVANAUGH

For further information, please contact bramstokerestate.com.

For all those who know
monsters are real.

———— ◆ ————

How these papers have been placed in sequence will be made manifest in the reading of them. All needless matters have been eliminated so that a history may stand forth as simple fact. I have collected these documents and organized them from those involved with their knowledge and desire to share what occurred—a bleak and formidable time. Interspersed, you will find my narrative to create a whole.

Take from this what you wish.

———— ◆ ————

Dublin

Swift's Hospital
Dr. Steevens' Hospital

Trinity College

Dublin Castle

St. Stephens Green

Marsh's Library

43 Harcourt Street

ARTANE

Artane Castle

Artane Lodge

Carolan's

Marino Crescent

CLONTARF

Church of St. John the Baptist

BRAM STOKER'S DUBLIN
AND CONTEMPORARY EUROPE

DRACUL

PART I

I am quite convinced that there is no doubt whatever that the events here described really took place, however unbelievable and incomprehensible they might appear at first sight.

—Bram Stoker, *Dracula*
Taken from the recently discovered original preface, which was extracted prior to publication.

I heard a strange, shrill laugh, like the sound of a glass bell—it was her voice—I still shudder at it, this voice was not human at all.

—Bram Stoker, *Makt Myrkranna*

NOW

———❖———

Bram stares at the door.

Sweat trickles down his creased forehead. He brushes his fingers through his damp hair, his temples throbbing with ache.

How long has he been awake? Two days? Three? He doesn't know, each hour blends into the next, a fevered dream from which there is no waking, only sleep, deeper, darker—

No!

There can be no thought of sleep.

He forces his eyes wide. He *wills* them open, preventing even a single blink, for each blink comes heavier than the last. There can be no rest, no sleep, no safety, no family, no love, no future, no—

The door.

Must watch the door.

Bram stands up from the chair, the only furniture in the room, his eyes locking on the thick oak door. Had it moved? He thought he had seen it shudder, but there had been no sound. Not the slightest of noises betrayed the silence of this place; there was only his own breathing, and the anxious tapping of his foot against the cold stone floor.

The doorknob remains still, the ornate hinges looking as they probably did a hundred years ago, the lock holding firm. Until his arrival at this place, he had never seen such a lock, forged from iron and molded in place. The mechanism itself is one with the door, secured firmly at the center with two large dead bolts branching out to the right and the left and attached to the frame. The key is in his pocket, and it will remain in his pocket.

Bram's fingers tighten around the stock of his Snider–Enfield Mark III rifle, his index finger playing over the trigger guard. In recent hours, he has loaded the weapon and pulled and released the breech lock more times than he can count. His free hand slips over the cold steel, ensuring the bolt is in the proper position. He pulls back the hammer.

This time he sees it—a slight wavering in the dust in the crack between the door and the floor, a puff of air, nothing more, but movement nonetheless.

Noiselessly, Bram sets the rifle down, leaning it against his chair.

He reaches into the straw basket to his left and retrieves a wild white rose, one of seven remaining.

The oil lamp, the only light in the room, flickers with his movement.

With caution, he approaches the door.

The last rose lay in a shriveled heap, the petals brown and black and ripe with death, the stem dry and sickly with thorns appearing larger than they had when the flower still held life. The stench of rot wafts up; the rose has taken on the scent of a corpse flower.

Bram kicks the old rose away with the toe of his boot and gently rests the new bloom in its place against the bottom of the door. "Bless this rose, Father, with Your breath and hand and all things holy. Direct Your angels to watch over it, and guide their touch to hold all evil at bay. Amen."

From the other side of the door comes a bang, the sound of a thousand pounds impacting the old oak. The door buckles, and Bram jumps back to the chair, his hand scooping up the leaning rifle and taking aim as he drops to one knee.

Then all is quiet again.

Bram remains still, the rifle sighted on the door until the weight of the gun causes his aim to falter. He lowers the barrel then, his eyes sweeping the room.

What would one think if one were to walk in and witness such a sight?

He has covered the walls with mirrors, nearly two dozen of them in all shapes and sizes, all he had. His tired face stares back at him a hundredfold as his image bounces from one looking glass to the next. Bram tries to look away, only to find himself peering back into the eyes of his own reflection, each face etched with lines belonging on a man much older than his twenty-one years.

Between the mirrors, he has nailed crosses, nearly fifty of them. Some bear the image of Christ while others are nothing more than fallen branches nailed together and blessed by his own hand. He continued the crosses onto the floor, first with a piece of chalk, then by scraping directly into the stone with the tip of his bowie knife, until no surface remained untouched. Whether or not it is enough, he cannot be sure, but it is all he could do.

He cannot leave.

Most likely, he will never leave.

Bram finds his way back to the chair and settles in.

Outside, a loon cries out as the moon comes and goes behind thick clouds. He retrieves the pocket watch from his coat and curses—he forgot to wind it, and the hands ceased their journey at 4:30. He stuffs it back into his pocket.

Another bang on the door, this one louder than the last.

Bram's breath stills as his eyes play back over the door, just in time to see the dust dance at the floor and settle back down to the stone.

How long can this barrier hold against such an assault?

Bram doesn't know. The door is solid, to be sure, but the onslaught behind it grows angrier with each passing hour, its determination to escape growing as the dawn creeps nearer.

The petals of the rose have already begun to brown, much faster than the last.

What will become of him when it finally does breach the door? He thinks of the rifle and the knife and knows they will be of little use.

He spots his journal on the floor beside the basket of roses; it must have fallen from his coat. Bram picks up the tattered leather-bound volume and thumbs through the pages before returning to the chair, one eye still on the door.

He has very little time.

Plucking a pencil from his breast pocket, he turns to a blank page and begins to write by the quivering light of the oil lamp.

THE JOURNAL *of* BRAM STOKER

———◆———

The peculiarities of Ellen Crone. That is, of course, where I should start, for this is as much her story as it is mine, perhaps more so. This woman, this monster, this wraith, this friend, this . . . being.

She was always there for us. My sisters and brothers would tell you as much. But how so, is where inquiries should lie. She was there at my beginning, and will no doubt be there for my end, as I was for hers. This was, and always shall be, our dance.

My lovely Nanna Ellen.

Her hand always reaching out, even as the prick of her nails drew blood.

MY BEGINNING, what a horrid affair it was.

From my earliest memories, I was a sickly child, ill and bedridden from birth until my seventh year, when a cure befell me. I will speak of this cure in great length to come, but for now it is important you understand the state in which I spent those early years.

I was born 8 November 1847, to Abraham and Charlotte, in a modest home at 15 Marino Crescent in Clontarf, Ireland, a small seaside town located about four miles from Dublin. Bordered by a park to the east and with views of the harbor to the west, our town gained fame as the site of the Battle of Clontarf, in 1014, in which the armies of Brian Boru, the High King of Ireland, defeated the Vikings of Dublin and their allies, the Irish of Leinster. This battle is regarded as the end of the Irish–Viking Wars, a bloody conflagration marked by the death of thousands upon the very shore over which my little room looked. In more recent years, Clontarf found itself the destination of Ireland's rich, a holiday setting for those wishing to escape the crowds of Dublin and enjoy fishing and strolls across our beaches.

I romanticize Clontarf, though, and in 1847 it was anything but romantic. This was a period of famine and disease throughout Ireland that had begun two years prior to my birth and did not find relief until 1854. *Phytophthora infestans*, otherwise known as potato blight, had begun ravaging crops during the 1840s and escalated into an abomination in which Ireland would lose twenty-five percent of its population to emigration or death. When I was a child, this tragedy had reached its peak. Ma and Pa moved us inland in 1849, to escape hunger, disease, and crime; and the fresh air, it was hoped, would avail my poor health, but all it brought was further isolation, the sounds of the harbor sought by my young ears falling more distant. For Pa, the daily walk to his office at Dublin Castle only grew as the world died around us, a damp web of grief lacing over all that was left.

I WATCHED ALL THIS transpire from my attic room high atop our home, known as Artane Lodge, as nothing more than a spectator, relying upon the tales of my family to explain everything taking place beyond our walls. I watched the beggars as they ravaged our neighbors' gardens of turnips and cabbage, as they plucked the eggs from our chicken coop, in hope of staving off hunger for one more night. I watched as they pulled clothing from the rope-strung laundry of strangers, still damp, in order to dress their children. Despite all this, when they were able, my parents and our neighbors opened their homes and invited these less fortunate inside for a warm meal and shelter from the storm. From my humble birth, the Stoker family motto "Whatever is right and honorable" was instilled in me and guided all in our home. We were by no means well-off, but our family fared better than most. In the fall of 1854, Pa, a civil servant, was toiling in the chief secretary's office at Dublin Castle, as he had for the thirty-nine years prior, having begun in 1815 at only sixteen years of age. Pa was substantially older than Ma, something that did not resonate with me until I was an adult. The castle was the residence of the Lord Lieutenant of Ireland, and his office handled all correspondence between English governmental agencies and their Irish counterparts. Pa spent his time cataloging these communications, ranging from the mundane day-to-day business of the country to official responses on topics having to do with poverty, famine, disease, epidemics, cattle plagues, hospitals and prisons, political unrest and rebellion. If he wished to ignore the problems vexing our time, he could not; he was deep in the thick of it.

Ma was an associate member of the Statistical and Social Inquiry Society of Ireland, a major force in the food drives and relief efforts of Dublin, a post previously reserved only for men. Not a day would pass when she wasn't haggling with a neighbor for milk, only to trade it with another neighbor for cloth. Her efforts kept food on the table for our large family and helped to feed countless others who crossed our threshold in these times of need. She held our family together—and as an adult, I see that now, but my seven-year-old self would have testified otherwise. I would have told you she locked me in my room, trading my happiness for isolation from the world's ailments, not willing to allow even the slightest exposure.

Our house stood off Malahide Road, a street paved with stone extracted from the quarry near Rockfield Cottage. I was confined to the attic, its peaked windows my only escape, but I could see much from such a height—from the farmlands around us to the distant harbor on a clear day—even the crumbling tower of Artane Castle. I watched the world bustle around me, a play for which I alone was the audience, my illness dictating my attendance.

What ailed me, you wonder? That is a question with no real answer, for nobody was able to say for certain. Whatever it was, my affliction found me shortly after birth and clung to me with wretched fingers. On my worst days, it was a feat for me to cross my room; the effort would leave me winded, bordering on unconsciousness. A mere conversation drained what little energy I possessed; after speaking but a few sentences, I often grew pale, and cold to the touch, as sweat crawled from my pores, and I shivered as my moisture met the seaside air. My heart would sometimes beat fiercely in my breast, irregular, as if the organ sought rhythm and could not find it. And the headaches: they would befall me and linger, day upon day, a belt tightening around my head at the leisurely hand of a fiend.

I spent the days and nights in my little attic room, wondering if my last dusk had just passed or if I would wake to see the dewy dawn.

I was not entirely alone in the attic; there were two other rooms. One belonged to my sister Matilda, eight at the time, and the other was occupied by our nanny, Ellen Crone. She shared her room with Baby Richard, my recently born brother and her most pressing charge.

The floor below mine housed the home's only indoor privy as well as my parents' room and a second bedroom occupied by my other two brothers, Thornley and Thomas, nine and five, respectively.

At the ground level could be found the kitchen, a living room, and a dining room with a table large enough to seat the entire household. There was a basement as well, but Ma forbade me from ever descending those steps; our coal was stored down there, and exposure to its dust could consign me to my bed for a week. Behind our house stood an old stone barn. We had three chickens and a pig there, all tended by Matilda from the time she was three years old. In the beginning, she had named the pigs, but around her fifth year she realized someone was switching the larger sows for smaller ones at least twice a year. By her sixth year, she realized those same pigs went to the butcher and found their way onto our supper plates. She stopped naming them then.

Over all of this, Ellen Crone watched.

THE JOURNAL *of* BRAM STOKER

————◆————

Where to start? There is so much to tell and precious little time to tell it—but I know when all things changed. By the time one particular week came to a close, I would be healed, our dear Nanna Ellen would be gone, and a family would be dead. It started innocently enough, with a little eavesdropping. We were but children—me, seven; Matilda, eight—and yet that fall season was never to be forgotten. And it began with only two words.

October 1854—"Buried alive," Matilda said again, her voice low. "That's what she said. I heard her true."

Although she was one year older than I, I spent many of my waking hours in Matilda's company, particularly when I found myself confined to my room, as I was today. We were standing at my window, and Matilda was pointing towards the harbor. "Ma said the man was diseased, and when he pled for help, the men who answered only dug a hole in the earth and pushed him in. What type of person does it take to do that? How could others participate in good conscience?"

"Ma said no such thing," I told her. Following her finger with my eyes, I tried to see through the fog rolling off the water.

"She did. If you ask her about it, I am sure she would deny saying it, but she told Pa when he returned home from work not more than twenty minutes ago. I came to you straightaway."

I tried not to smile, for I knew Matilda only spun such a tale in order to boost my spirits, but the corners of my mouth rose nonetheless, and she smacked me on my shoulder. "Now you're mocking me." She frowned, turning from the window.

"Where did you say this happened?"

She didn't answer, staring instead at the far wall.

"Matilda? Where did this occur?"

With a deep sigh, she returned her gaze to the window. "At the cemetery behind Saint John the Baptist Church. She said they buried him amongst the suicide graves."

"Suicide graves?"

Matilda grew frustrated. "I've told you about them before; they're hidden at the far east end of the cemetery, just beyond the wall, in constant shade. Anyone who takes their own life is buried there, as well as thieves and criminals and the like. There are few markers or crypts, mostly just raw earth covering hundreds of dreary graves. It's not consecrated ground, either, so the buried will never know peace. They spend eternity damned."

"So why bury a sick man there?"

"You mean, why was this *particular* sick man buried alive there?"

"If they buried him alive, he was, in fact, murdered," I said. "He would be entitled to burial as anyone else, in blessed earth."

"You cannot hide a body amongst the common graves, but bury him amongst the suicides and he will never be found."

A coughing fit came upon me then, and I turned my head away until it dispelled, then said, "If Ma knows of this, she would tell the authorities. She would make it right."

"Maybe the authorities already know and they simply don't care. One less sick man walking the streets may not be of concern."

"What did Pa say of all this?" I asked her.

Matilda crossed the small room to my bed and settled down on its corner, her finger twirling around her long, blond locks. "At first, he was silent, considering the story. Then he said, 'Things are even worse in Dublin,' before returning to the newspaper, giving it not another word."

"I don't believe any of this; you're just spinning tales again," I said, the smile edging my dry lips.

"It's true!"

"What is true?"

We both turned at once to find Nanna Ellen standing in the doorway with a lunch tray in hand. She entered the room with a skillful grace, sliding across the floor more than walking, her steps silent and sure, and placed the tray on my night table.

Matilda's eyes met mine and silently told me not to say a word about our conversation—not that I had any intention of doing so. "Nothing, Nanna."

Nanna Ellen's eyes narrowed as she stared first at me, then at Matilda, and back again before returning to the tray and pouring a hot cup of tea. "The talk between you two is horrid. Men buried alive in unmarked graves? *Really*. This is not the topic of adults, and most definitely not suitable for the likes of you. And why are you even out of bed? You're going to catch your death standing near that window. And then what? I suppose we'll have to dig a little hole amongst the suicide graves and plant you along with the other sick." She gave Matilda a wink. "Think you can find time in your busy day of gossip to show me where to find this place and possibly fetch a shovel?"

I scurried back to my bed and found my way under the covers. "You wouldn't," I said.

Nanna Ellen tried to hold a straight face. "I most certainly would. I've got my eyes set on this room of yours; mine is getting a bit cramped with the baby in there." She picked up the little bell from my night table and gave it a ring. "There would be no more of this, then, would there? Sounds like a perfectly happy world to me."

I tried to pluck the bell from her fingers, but she proved too quick for me; my reach only found air. "You know I don't like to use that; Ma insists that I do."

"So you don't believe me, either?" Matilda frowned.

Nanna Ellen placed both her hands upon her waist and sighed. "I do not believe for an instant that the good people of Ireland would stand by and watch as a living man was pushed into an open grave to be forgotten. I think your imagination is getting the better of you. I'm sure you heard something, but it was not that. Maybe your time would be better spent in the kitchen helping your mother with dinner rather than skulking around corners to glean conversations not meant for your young ears."

"To be sure, she said exactly that." Matilda pouted.

Nanna Ellen sighed and sat on the edge of the bed beside me, her slender fingers reaching out for my forehead. I shrunk back at her touch, her skin like ice.

"You have a fever again, young man." She poured water from the pitcher on her tray into the basin beside my bed and moistened a cloth, wrung it out, and placed it across my scalp. "Lie back," she instructed.

I did as she asked, then said, "Gray."

"What?"

"Your eyes—today, they are gray." And they were, too, a dark gray, reminding me of the thick storm clouds that had filled the harbor's sky only two days before. "Yesterday, they were hazel. And, the day before that, they were blue. What color will they be tomorrow?"

She looked down upon me with these eyes and tucked her curly blond hair behind her ear. Most days, she wore it up, but today it was down, hanging just below her shoulders.

. . .

I HAVE OFTEN REFLECTED on the beauty of Ellen Crone. At the age of seven, I had no such thoughts; but as an adult, I cannot deny her allure. Her skin glowed, flawless as a fresh coat of snow, not a single blemish or line, not even around her eyes or mouth. When she smiled, the whiteness of her teeth astounded. We often joked about her age—she along with the rest of us. She joined our household in October of 1847, only weeks prior to my birth—right after Miss Coghlan took leave due to health issues, explaining the arthritis in her hands had made the act of caring for a child unbearable. Miss Coghlan had been with the family through the births of both Thornley and Matilda and had been expected to stay another year or so, long enough for Ma to find a replacement. Her early leave-taking came at a difficult time; Pa spent most of his hours at the castle, due to the start of the famine, and Ma was in no condition to interview replacements, being only weeks away from my birth. Ellen appeared as if sent by God—through word of mouth alone, she had heard about potential employment and arrived on our doorstep with nothing more than a small bag in her possession. She claimed to be fifteen at the time, an orphan who had spent the past five years in a household looking after the children of her providers—a boy and a girl, aged five and six—only to lose the entire family to cholera the month before. The mother of the house had been a midwife, and Ellen explained she had aided her with dozens of deliveries; she would be willing to offer her services in exchange for lodging and a small stipend for a short period of time, at least until after my birth, while Ma had time to recuperate. Ma and Pa had no other alternatives available to them and they welcomed Ellen Crone into our home, where she immediately became indispensable.

My birth in November of 1847 was a difficult one. I was born breech, the umbilical cord wrapped around my neck, at the hands of my father's cousin, a prominent Dublin doctor, who believed I was stillborn since I did not utter a sound. Uncle Edward Alexander Stoker declared that no heartbeat was found beneath my blue skin. But Ellen insisted I was alive, snatched me from him, and went to work breathing for me, her lips on mine for nearly three minutes, before I finally coughed and joined the world of the living. Ma and Pa were amazed, and Uncle Edward claimed this was nothing short of a miracle. Ma later told me she was sure I was dead in the womb because I rarely kicked; as a mother of two, she had real experience to draw upon and she felt certain. For that reason, she hadn't allowed Pa to settle upon a name. It wasn't until I was breathing and proven alive that she agreed to the name Abraham, my father's namesake, and took me into her arms for the first time.

In later years, Ma told me Nanna Ellen had looked worn and haggard that night—appearing as if she, too, had given birth and that it had taken every ounce of her strength. The moment I was tucked safely at Ma's side, Ellen had retired to her room and did not emerge for nearly two days, much to the dismay of Pa, who spent hours at her door in an attempt to coax her out, as he needed help with both the children and Ma. For those two days, Nanna Ellen went unseen; she finally emerged on the third day without a single word about the episode, and simply returned to her household duties. Pa would have sacked her had he a replacement, but there was none.

In those first three days, my condition only worsened, and Pa feared I would not live another night. My breathing came in short gasps and became choked with fluid. I had yet to cry, and my eyes were unresponsive to any stimuli surrounding me. I would not take the breast. I would not eat at all. Ellen moved my cradle into her own room and remained with me for all waking moments, forbidding the others from seeing me—she insisted I needed rest. They reluctantly obliged, and on my fifth day, around two in the morning, my cries rose through the house for the first time, cries loud enough to wake Matilda and Thornley, who also joined in with cries of their own. Pa helped Ma to Ellen's door, and when she opened it with my little form swaddled in her arms, everyone knew the danger had passed and I would live. Ma said Ellen looked far older than her years at that moment, worse than she had after my birth, worse than she had ever appeared since. After handing me to Ma, Ellen Crone continued down the stairs and out the front door into the dead of night. She did not return for two full days.

When she did return, she was her youthful self again, cheeks flushed with color, eyes radiant blue, and with a smile on her lips for the ages. Pa didn't scold her for leaving this time, for my condition had worsened while she was gone, and somehow he knew she could help me as she had on both occasions prior. He returned my cradle to her bedroom, and there it remained as Ellen locked the door with the two of us secured inside. She would emerge with my health waxing and hers waning. This pattern would repeat dozens of times in those early years—she would nurse me back to health, then vanish for a few days only to return in good health and take charge again. What transpired behind her closed door was never revealed, and Ma and Pa did not ask, but her eyes told the tale—the deepest blue when her health proved strongest, pale gray shortly before she would take leave.

I STARED UP into those now gray eyes, knowing she would be leaving again soon.

"Perhaps you should focus on your own health and not these imaginary shadings in my eyes, which are no doubt just reflecting my clothing. Perhaps if I don a red dress, they will flame as red as Mr. Nesbitt's down the way after a night at the pub?"

"You'll be leaving again soon, won't you?"

At this, Matilda perked up. "No, Nanna. You mustn't! You promised to sit for me so I can draw your portrait!"

"But you have dozens already—"

"You promised." She sulked.

Ellen went to her and ran a finger over her cheek. "I will be gone only a day or two, at most. Don't I always return? And then I will sit for you for yet another portrait. While I'm away, I need you to look after your brother and help your mother. She has her hands full right now with Baby Richard. Do you think you can keep house in my absence?"

Matilda nodded reluctantly.

"Okay, then. I best return downstairs and begin preparations for dinner." She placed her chilly hand upon my forehead again. "If you don't improve, I will have to call upon your Uncle Edward."

At this, my stomach twisted into a knot, but I said nothing.

MATILDA WATCHED Nanna Ellen leave, then scuttled to my side. "I need to show you something."

"What?"

Her eyes drifted to the open door, then to her sketchbook, which she had left on the dresser when she first entered. Crossing the room, she closed the door, holding the knob to ensure the drafts of our home didn't seize the door and slam it shut. She retrieved her pad and returned to the bed. "Do you consider me a fine artist?"

"You know I do." This was no embellishment. From the time she was three or four years of age, it was obvious she possessed a skill unmatched by other children her age. In recent years, her drawings and paintings proved to be on par with many adults held in high regard. To prove it, Ma had commissioned a friend to show one of Matilda's paintings to a wealthy art lover in Dublin. She had not told the friend it was the product of a child; she had simply said the painting was a prized family possession she wished to have appraised. The man had offered ten shillings for the piece, but Ma had declined, saying the painting was simply too treasured, one which they could not part with.

Shortly after, Matilda was accepted into an art school in Dublin.

I COULD TELL by the expression on her face, though, she needed fresh praise. "You are a *fine* artist. Truly!"

Matilda narrowed her eyes, then patted her sketchbook. "What I am about to show you must remain between you and me. You must promise you won't discuss this with anyone else."

Before I could answer, a coughing fit came upon me, burning within my chest with each husky gasp. Matilda quickly poured a glass of water and held it up to my lips. I drank eagerly, the cold liquid quenching my raw throat. When the fit finally ended, I simply said I was sorry. Matilda ignored this, as was her way when it came to me being sick; I don't recall a single time she actually acknowledged my illness. She again tapped her pad, this time with impatience. "Promise me?"

I nodded my head. "I will not tell a soul."

This appeared to be enough, for she flipped open the cover of the pad and thumbed through a number of pages before settling on one in particular. She held the picture up to me. "Who is this?"

"William Cyr." He was a farmer over the hill in Puckstown, and the sketch showed him tending his fields.

She flipped to the next page. "And this?"

"Surely that is Robert Pugsley," I replied. He was riding atop his mobile butcher wagon.

"How about this one?"

"Ma."

"And this?"

"Thornley tending the chickens."

"This?"

I studied the image for a moment—a woman of seventeen or eighteen, but not one I recognized. "I don't believe I know her."

Matilda stared at me for a second, then flipped to the next page. "How about her?"

Another girl, a little older than the last. She seemed vaguely familiar, but I could not place her face. I shook my head.

Matilda showed me pictures of three other women, the oldest no more than twenty. This last had been painted with watercolors; the image was vibrant, a living being captured with such detail it seemed I could reach out and touch the paper and feel the warmth of her skin. I did not recognize these women, though, which seemed odd; I knew most of the residents living near our home, and Matilda wasn't permitted to venture far from our door unless in the company of an adult.

"You don't know any of these women?"

I turned back through the pictures, taking the time to study each more closely. I could not place a name with the faces. "I don't. Perhaps you met them at the market or in town with Ma, someplace without me?"

Matilda shook her head slowly. She leaned in close and whispered at my ear. "They're all sketches of Nanna Ellen."

I frowned and returned to the sketchbook. "But they look . . . they look nothing like her."

"They all look nothing like her and yet they all look exactly like her. I could show you a dozen others, but none would be familiar to you."

"I don't understand."

"I don't, either." She lowered her voice again. "It seems whenever I draw Nanna Ellen, the resulting picture looks nothing like her. I cannot capture her no matter how hard I try; her image eludes me."

I didn't know what to say to this, so I changed the subject. "What more have you learned of Thornley?"

Because I rarely left my room, I depended on Matilda for household gossip, and it was rare that she disappointed. Although Nanna Ellen was the focus of her sleuthing, my brother was a close second, and she could often be found lurking in his shadow.

"Oh, Thornley." Matilda turned the page of her sketchbook to one filled with text. "Last night, I saw him leaving Nanna Ellen's at nearly two in the morning."

"Why would he be in her room?"

Matilda tapped at her pad. "That's not all. He was fully dressed, and after he left her room, he didn't go back to his own; he went outside."

"In the middle of the night?"

"In the middle of the night."

"What did he do out there?"

Matilda frowned. "I don't know. I lost sight of him near the barn. But he was out there for nearly twenty minutes, and when he came back in, he was filthy."

"Did he see you?"

"Of course he didn't see me."

"So this is what? The third time?"

She shook her head. "This is the fourth time in as many weeks that he has snuck out like this. If he does it again, I plan to follow him."

"You should tell Ma."

She wouldn't. I knew she wouldn't. The way she closed her sketchbook and left my room in a huff told me so.

My fever worsened. By the ninth hour of that night, my body screamed with pain and my bedsheets were drenched in sweat. Ma sat at my side with a bowl of water in her lap and a damp cloth to wipe the sheen from my forehead. At one point, I fought her. I was so chilled, the cloth felt like ice against my skin. My arms flailed to bat her away. It was then that Thornley and Pa came into the room, holding me down, pinning my arms and legs at my sides. My moans echoed through the house, guttural sounds more like those of a wounded animal than a child.

Down the hall, I heard Baby Richard crying out from Nanna Ellen's room, and Ma asked Matilda to see to him. I remember her protesting though her words escape me. She didn't want to leave my side, but Ma insisted. She wasn't permitted to bring the baby into my room for fear of his catching whatever ailed me. I think we all knew this to be illogical—my illness had persisted for years and no one else in the family had contracted it—yet we all seemed to be agreed it was best not to risk a contagion with the infant.

Matilda rushed from my room, and I heard Pa cursing Nanna Ellen for taking leave only hours earlier. They depended on her, and she was needed now more than any other time, and yet she was gone, leaving for reasons known only to her. In my fevered mind, the sketches Matilda had shown me glowed: dozens of women all blurring into one, resembling Nanna Ellen for a fraction of a second before breaking apart into the pictures of strangers, women of various ages and appearances, all different, all the same. Their eyes went from the black-and-white of a pencil sketch to the most vibrant blue found only in oils, peering at me through a veil of swirling darkness. I could hear Nanna's voice, but she sounded so far away, as if she shrieked from across the harbor and the fog devoured her cries. Then her face was but inches from mine, her full red lips moving to speak but uttering no sound. A moment later, Ma was back, wiping it all away with that icy cloth, and I wanted to swat her away but my arms no longer obeyed. All went black, and I felt as if I were falling down a well, the world vanishing above me as I was swallowed by the earth, my back on fire as I raced towards Hell. I heard Ma calling my name, but I was so far from home I knew I would be scolded if she learned I had left the house at all, so I said nothing; I only closed my eyes and waited for impact as I fell into the abyss. I imagined this is what it was like to be pushed alive into a suicide grave. I awaited the smothering dirt, poised to die beneath its blanket of filth, left to the eager worms and maggots of the earth.

"Bram!"

MA CALLED OUT TO ME from the the top of the hole, but I remained silent. It wasn't until the third time I finally tried to answer, but my voice failed me. The heft of so much soil on my chest expelled what little air I could muster, only a muted grunt escaping my dry, chapped lips. Around me, dirt fell, raining down in giant clumps, battering my frail body. A crowd gathered at the top of the hole; although I couldn't see anybody, I heard them—shouting and screams, crying, even cackles— first two voices, then four, then a dozen more. I could not keep track, for they were everywhere and yet nowhere, ungodly loud but invisible to me all the same.

Then there was one.

I looked up into Ma's eyes, red and clouded. She held the damp cloth inches from my face and froze as my eyes fluttered open and found her. I was back in my little attic room, back in my bed, wondering if I had left at all.

"He's awake," she said in a hushed tone to someone across the room.

I tried to turn my head, but my neck ached so; I feared the movement alone might sever my head from my body. It felt as if a dozen blades made of ice pressed into my skin. "Cold . . ."

"Shhhh, don't speak," Ma said. "Your Uncle Edward is here; he is going to help you."

Edward's face appeared above me, his wispy gray hair disheveled and falling over round glasses. He pulled a stethoscope from around his neck, inserted the earpieces in his ears, and pressed the metal bell-shaped resonator to my chest—this, too, was icy against my bare skin and I tried to shake it off, but Pa and Thornley held me fast.

"Still yourself," Uncle Edward ordered, his face creased in a scowl. He listened for a moment before turning back to Ma. "His heart rate is highly erratic, and the fever has escalated to the point of hallucination. Without treatment, the fever could result in permanent damage . . . hearing impairment, lost sight, perhaps even death."

I listened to this as if an observer, unable to interact. I watched Ma exchange a worried glance with Pa as Thornley simply peered down at me.

"What do you suggest?" Ma asked of Uncle Edward. Her voice, usually confident and steady, now wavered.

Uncle Edward's eyes fluttered over to mine, then returned to Ma. "We must lessen the tainted blood; only then will his body find the strength to fight the infection and begin to heal."

Ma was shaking her head. "The last time only worsened his condition."

"Bloodletting is the only treatment called for by such a case."

I tried to break free of their hold, and nearly did, for they were distracted by their discussion and had lessened their grip, all but Thornley, who squeezed my arm with such force at my attempt I thought his fingers would break the skin. He frowned at me while mouthing, *No*.

Blackness slipped back over me like a cloak, and I fought to retain consciousness. They continued to speak, but the words became foreign to me, a language I did not speak. Then my body began to shake with a chill so great I felt as if I had plunged into a frozen lake. From the corner of my eye, I watched Pa nod his head.

Uncle Edward removed his glasses, wiped them on his shirt, then replaced them on the bridge of his nose. He opened his bag, a satchel of the finest brown English leather, and removed a small white jar with tiny holes in its lid. He pried it open, its rubber stopper emitting a pop as he did so, then retrieved a pair of large forceps from his bag.

I tried to squirm again, but all strength had left me. I watched as he dipped the forceps into the jar and extracted a large leech—nearly three inches long. It wiggled grotesquely in the forceps's grip, its body twisting this way and that, as Uncle Edward carefully lowered the creature towards my foot.

Just before the leech disappeared from my line of sight, I spied the jaws of the eager sucker opening and closing with appetite as it neared my flesh. Ma looked away, her eyes pinched tightly shut, and Pa, although having grown pale, watched nonetheless as Uncle Edward placed the leech on my foot. I was cold, but the leech was colder still, nearly as icy as Uncle Edward's stethoscope. I imagined the invader's tiny mouth fastening itself to my flesh, its rows of sharp little teeth gnawing, burrowing deep, as it began to feast on my blood. I saw it growing rotund as it engorged on my essence. I was trying to block the putrid spectacle from my mind when I saw Uncle Edward's forceps return with another leech, this one meant for my shoulder, then another after that, and another after that.

I closed my eyes in hopes of finding the embracing grave of sleep.

VOICES SHOUTED ALL AROUND ME. I could hear Ma and Pa, Matilda and Thornley, and even Uncle Edward. I tried to make out the words, forcing my ears to hone in on one particular voice or another, but they made no sense. When I tried to open my eyes, I observed only the thick tar of nothingness, as deep and forbidding as the bogs behind our home. I found myself drowning in it.

For the briefest of seconds, I saw Matilda standing at my side, her face puffy and shining. In that instant she saw me, too, for her eyes grew large, and her mouth opened long enough to speak my name, crying out loud enough to garner the attention of the others in the room; they looked first at her, then down at me. I spotted Ma running towards the bed from the far corner, and Pa leaning over me on one side and Uncle

Edward leaning over the other. Uncle Edward waved a long metal thermometer around and barked something at Thornley, but everything said after Matilda cried my name became lost language. I tried to force my eyes to lock onto Matilda's, to hold her gaze as if squeezing her fingers in mine, but her sweet face faded away. Nothing remained but a shadow, then nothing at all.

"Everyone out!"

I heard the words, but they came to me from a great distance, barely audible over the cacophony. There was so much tumult around me that I believed I was hearing all the sounds in creation at one and the same time; every hiss, utterance, squeal, and cry in the known universe in unison, each subsequent outburst louder than the last. So loud it wielded wondrous pain, agonizing blades stabbing into my ears—and if I tried to comprehend what I heard, I knew it would render me insane.

"I want this room cleared now!"

It was Nanna Ellen. I knew it was her, somehow, even though the voice was not hers but was instead a wail, a banshee shrieking into a storm-filled night.

AT THAT POINT I must have succumbed to the blackness, for an instant later I found myself alone. Ma and Pa had vanished, as had Matilda, Thornley, and Uncle Edward. If Nanna Ellen remained, I did not see her; indeed, I did not see much of anything. All I saw were tiny pricks of light piercing the now fading black. For the first time, I noticed a smell, a musty odor much like a root cellar at the tail end of winter when only the rotting husks of summer's bounty remain, blanketed in mold and feasted upon by the insidious inhabitants of the dank dirt.

"Nanna Ellen?" I whispered her name. So sore was my throat that I took my next breaths in tiny gasps, my eyes tearing from the effort.

Nanna Ellen did not answer, yet I somehow knew she was in the room with me. I felt her presence in the murky darkness. I called out her name again, this time louder than the first, bracing myself for the inevitable burn in my throat that came with the words.

Again, she did not answer.

I was cold, and I began to shiver again despite thick quilts piled high around me. Pa had installed a small stove in the corner of my room to provide heat and it had burned merrily when the others had been here. But now, the stove was dark, the logs gray with cold dust and ash, as if weeks had passed since the last fire had graced the iron.

Something stirred behind me to the left, and I twisted awkwardly in order to gain sight of it. My neck ached with the effort, and I tried to ignore the hurt, squinting against the pain. If this was, in fact, Nanna Ellen, she moved far too fast for me to spy even a glimpse of her, for by the time my eyes found the spot where I thought she had been, there was nothing there but the corner of my dresser and the specter of my coat hanging on a peg on the wall. The garment moved slightly, a fact not lost on me. My windows were all closed tight, so there was no wind to speak of; something else caused the coat to shudder.

"Why are you hiding, Nanna Ellen? You're frightening me." The moment I said this, I wanted to take it back. Pa would have scolded me for displaying any sign of fear, let alone announcing it, but the words were out before I realized I should have stifled them.

When there was no response, I fell still, forcing the shivers from my body long enough to draw in a breath and listen to the room around me. As I drew in that breath, I heard someone else do the same; this time the sound emanated from my right, nearest the door. I swiveled my weighty head that way, but still I saw nothing; the faintest of lights was crawling in from the hallway under the door, but it seemed to die at the threshold as if held at bay by the much stronger darkness dwelling within. I expelled the air from my lungs and again a similar sound crossed the room, the sound of someone breathing in sync with me.

The moment I held my breath, my unbidden companion did likewise, as if engaged in an unsettling game of mimicry.

I turned back to my bedroom door, to the sliver of light piercing the dark at the bottom. I thought I saw shadows moving through that light. I pictured Matilda with her ear pressed against the door and listening intently, her feet shuffling side to side as she heard nothing, then closing her eyes and hoping the loss of one sense would strengthen the other.

I caught movement to my left and forced my head to turn back towards the small stove. This time I saw Nanna Ellen; she was bent over the hearth, stoking the logs with the iron poker. They crackled and popped under her touch, and for a moment I caught sight of a single orange ember. Rather than adding kindling to coax the flames, she stirred the small hot spot and dispersed the glowing fragments of wood until they glowed no more.

"I'm cold, Nanna Ellen. Why are you putting out the fire?" The breath from my words lingered in the air above me, a mist of haunting white.

Nanna Ellen glanced up at me for the briefest of seconds, then she was gone. I wasn't sure if this was a trick the mischievous shadows were playing on me or if I had blacked out again, but in that very instant she seemed to have vanished from sight. I caught a glimpse of her eyes before she disappeared, though, and they were glowing the brightest of blues. I found it odd that I could make out her eyes with so little light in the room, but I had had no trouble seeing them, and there was a part of me that thought she wanted me to see them. Along with her eyes, I spied a smile edging across her red lips. And there was even a laugh, brief as it was, the only sound.

When fingers brushed my cheek, I nearly jumped from my bed, and my head spun around to meet them. Nanna Ellen sat in the chair Ma had occupied earlier, her hand advancing to my forehead. I felt no heat from her touch, no warmth at all. She might as well have touched me with a stick of kindling or the point of a knitting needle. When she pulled away, I expected to see a gloved hand, but such was not the case; her fingers were bare. I marveled at how they looked, the flesh creamy, fresh as a babe's, the nails long and perfectly kept. They were not so much the hands of a worker as those of a royal. Even my own hands at the tender age of seven bore the hallmarks of labor, and I was much more sheltered than any other child my age. I did have a small scar on my left hand just below the forefinger that had never quite healed properly. I had caught it on the sharp edge of a window frame downstairs when I was a young boy. The ragged metal had cut right through my skin, sending forth a fountain of blood. I did not cry when it happened; Ma marveled at this, praising my bravery in the face of such injury. She bandaged the cut as best she could, but the wound had been deep and probably would have benefited from stitches. I share this anecdote only because Nanna Ellen's hands bore no such scars, the cuts and scrapes of everyday life.

Nanna Ellen caught me staring at her hands and withdrew them from sight, brushing the hair from my eyes. "You have worsened substantially; you're delusional, caught up in the fever. Does it hurt?"

I tried to nod my head, but the ability to move had abandoned me again. To keep my eyes open was painful, but I did so anyway, unable to turn away from her.

"It must hurt."

I thought she meant the fever, but then I realized she was looking down at my arm. With all my strength, I raised it. I spotted three leeches below my elbow and at least two others above. All were plump from their ghastly feasts. The largest, which was near my wrist, looked about to burst. Its oily body churned, pumping my skin with ferocity. There were no less than six on my other arm, and I knew Uncle Edward had placed them on my legs and feet, too.

Tears began to well in my eyes, and Nanna Ellen brushed them away with a cold fingertip. I then watched as she brought that finger to her lips and tasted the salty drop. Soundlessly, she then lowered the same finger to the writhing back of the fat leech at my wrist and pressed down on it. The little creature shuddered, then caved in upon itself, going from plump and moist to dry dust right before my eyes. Then it was gone, leaving nothing behind but a smudge on my skin and the small red hole from which it had fed. Nanna Ellen's finger came away red with blood: my blood.

"Do you trust me?" she said.

I forced a nod, unable to speak.

"You shouldn't," she replied.

NOW

Bram glances up from his journal. He heard breathing; thick, ragged gasps, followed by a huff of air against the opposite side of the door. The petals of the rose fluttered silently over the stone floor. One petal broke away. Black with rot and shriveled with decay, it skimmed across the floor and landed at Bram's feet. The remainder of the rose had not fared much better; he would have to replace it soon.

The breath comes again, long this time, an exhale from monstrous lungs.

It sounds like a horse or a large dog, but that cannot be right, for he knew there was no such animal here. Yet he hears it, each inhale and exhale louder than the last. He pictures huge nostrils, those of a Great Dane or mastiff, at the base of the door, inhaling with such force and purpose that it could identify everything in the room from scent alone.

Bram sets the journal on the floor, stands, and crosses the room to the door.

The presence on the other side must know he is near, for the breathing ceases momentarily, then resumes again, this time with more haste. Bram lowers his face to the floor and tries to look under the door, but there is little space, only a hair's breadth between the stone floor and bottom of the thick oak barrier. Then comes another exhale, and Bram shuffles back; the air is hot and filled with moisture, and the dampness brushes against his cheeks as it rushes past, followed closely by the most abhorrent of odors. His eyes water just at the scent of it, and he tries to back away farther still, until his legs clatter against the chair he had occupied moments earlier. The stench enfolds him, and he wants nothing more than to leave. Instead, he rises and goes to the window and sticks his head out into the cold night air, taking it in until the stink washes away from his nose and lungs.

At the door, the breathing continues, louder still.

Bram reaches into the pocket of his coat and retrieves a small vial and holds it up to the flickering light of the oil lamp. Vambéry had filled the vial, along with four others just like it, only two days earlier from the font at St. John the Baptist. Two are gone now; after this one, only a single vial will remain—and Bram will have no means to get more. Carefully, he removes the stopper and crosses the room.

Again, the presence on the other side falls silent for a second as he approaches, then resumes its rhythmic breathing. A low growl follows, then a scratching at the stone, a single, tentative scratch, as if its maker is testing the strength of the stone beneath its feet.

Bram kneels at the door and cautiously tips the vial, spilling the holy water in a straight line, from one end of the threshold to the other and back again, until none remains. The slate seems to drink it up, for the moment it makes contact the liquid vanishes, leaving nothing behind but a thin trail. Behind the door, the creature scuttles back. Then comes the deep wail of a great wolf.

THE JOURNAL of BRAM STOKER

———◆———

October 1854—I woke to muted light, gray beams of sun streaming in through my three windows and flooding my little attic room with a glow that was neither daylight nor dusk. I assumed fog had rolled in off the harbor; this time of year, it was known to do so. There was a moistness in the air, too, and although someone tucked the bedsheets in around my entire body, they did little to fend off the bite of the sea as it snatched at me.

The birdsong told me it was early morning. It hurt to open my eyes, but I did so anyway. The bowl that Ma had used to moisten my brow sat on the table at my side along with the cloth, but the chair beside my bed was vacant. I expected to find Ma there, or Matilda, but neither occupied it. I was alone in my attic room. If Uncle Edward was still in the house, there was no sign of him. His bag was gone, and along with it the horrific jar of leeches. I brushed the bedclothes to the side and forced myself to sit up, holding my arm up to the light. Marks began at my wrist and worked up to the shoulder of both arms, dozens of three-point punctures. I found similar marks on my legs, beginning on my thighs and continuing to my feet. How many leeches had he used? I could not help but wonder. I thought I might be ill but forced myself to choke back the vomit.

Although I was cold, it was not the cold I had known the night before while fighting the fever. In truth, I only assumed it was the night before, for I had no way of knowing for sure. The last time I succumbed to such a violent attack, I slept for three full days before regaining consciousness and rejoining the living. When I awoke after that episode, I was famished, as if I hadn't eaten in days. What little energy my body typically harbored had abandoned me; I could barely sit up, let alone stand. This time I felt weak, to be sure, but not as weak as I had on that previous occasion. In fact, it was the opposite, like I could climb out of the bed and venture across the room, if need be—as if I had emerged from a great sleep—a bear emerging from hibernation and returning to the world.

I reached for the little bell on my night table and gave it a shake. Ma appeared at my door moments later, a breakfast tray in hand. "And how are you feeling this morning?" she asked as she settled the tray on the table beside me. "You gave us quite a scare last night. Your fever exceeded all others in recent memory; I honestly feared you were in danger of combusting while you slept . . . your skin was so hot."

"What of Nanna Ellen? Is she here?" I said in a voice not quite my own.

"She is indeed." Ma's eyes glanced down the hall to Ellen's door. "What do you recall of last night?"

I tried to remember the events of the night before, but it was a dismal blur at best. I vaguely recalled my fever growing worse, then little more until the arrival of Uncle Edward. "Uncle Edward bled me."

Ma sat on the edge of my bed and folded her hands in her lap. "That he did, and a good thing, too; the fever had taken a deep hold on you, and if he had not arrived when he did, there's no telling what would have come of you. Edward is a blessing on us all, and you owe him quite a debt. I expect you to tell him so when next you see him."

"But it was Nanna Ellen who really helped me, was it not?"

Ma shuffled where she sat, her fingers twisting nervously together.

"Your uncle is to thank for your recovery, nobody else; it was his competency that put an end to your fever. To say otherwise is nothing more than conjecture, and I will hear no such talk."

Her eyes fluttered back to Nanna Ellen's closed door down the hall. "I'm beginning to wonder why we allow that woman to remain in our house, disappearing for days at a time and returning according to her own timetable and whim. I require someone dependable when it comes to tending to you and the other children, not an unpredictable, flighty vagabond. I plan to speak to your father about her; perhaps a change is overdue."

She was clearly aggravated, and I did not wish to agitate her further, so I changed the subject. "Is Uncle Edward still here?"

"He left with the rising sun, I'm afraid. He slept downstairs for a few hours but was due back at his work in the early hours and could stay no longer. He was kind enough to check back in on you once before he left and told me your condition improved greatly—a miraculous recovery, he said." Ma turned and over her shoulder loudly announced, "Matilda, your brother is awake!"

Matilda poked her head around the corner of my door; she had been standing there the entire time.

"Why, you little snoop!" Ma exclaimed. "I'm going to take Bram's bell and tie it around your neck!"

Matilda blushed. "I wasn't snooping, Ma."

Ma tilted her head. "I am to believe you were just standing in the hallway outside your brother's door simply because it is a comfortable place to rest your feet?"

Matilda opened her mouth to speak, then thought better of it.

Down the hall, Baby Richard began to wail, and Ma pursed her lips. "That child will be the death of me. Stay with your brother for a moment."

With that, Ma left the room, and Matilda took her place on the edge of the bed. Reaching for the breakfast tray, she plucked up a piece of toast and crammed it in her mouth, then handed the remaining slice to me. The bread was slightly stale, and I wasn't very hungry, but I ate it anyway. When I was sure Ma was out of earshot, I spoke in a low voice. "What happened with Nanna Ellen last night?"

Matilda, too, looked down the hall for Ma before responding. "You don't recall?"

I shook my head, my neck stiff and sore. "She came back early to help me, did she not?"

Matilda whispered, "Nanna Ellen walked you back from the Gates of Hell last night and rescued you from the Devil's touch. Of this I am sure."

"But Uncle Edward—"

"Uncle Edward tried his best, and your condition worsened with each passing hour. But Nanna Ellen . . . she somehow . . ."

"Somehow what? What did she do?"

The wounds from the leeches began to itch, and when Matilda saw me scratching them, she held both my hands in her own. "What she did took place behind closed doors, but when she emerged an hour later, it was clear your fever had broken and the danger passed, but she spoke nothing of her methods, despite Pa's and Uncle Edward's queries. Instead, she walked from your room to her own and closed the door without so much as a single word. Uncle Edward beat on her door for nearly five full minutes before finally giving up and returning to your side only to see what Ma and I were already seeing; the sweats from your fever were gone and you were resting peacefully in this very bed—still and quiet, only the rise and fall of your chest to tell us you were still amongst the living." Matilda glanced at Nanna Ellen's closed bedroom door. "She rests in there still." She leaned in close. "I saw Thornley bring something to her after she left your room. A large bag. Something inside was moving. She opened before he knocked, opened it only enough to take the bag, then closed the door behind her."

"That is ridiculous."

"That is what I saw."

"You must have been dreaming."

She defiantly crossed her arms. "I saw it."

I examined the wounds running the length of my arms, turning them in the light.

"Does it hurt?" Matilda asked.

I was sore, and I knew from past experience it would take days before I would heal, and I told her so, although the wounds seemed to be healing faster this time, already scabbing over and itching something fierce.

Her voice dropped even lower, to a hush barely heard above the birdsong outside. "There is more. When Nanna Ellen first arrived last night, when she shouted for all of us to leave your room, she looked like herself: a young, healthy woman. But when she emerged from your room, she was anything but; it was like she aged a dozen years in those minutes she was in here. Her face had gone pale and dry, her hair limp and brittle. And her eyes were those of an old woman. I caught a glimpse of them as she shuffled to her room, but only a glimpse, for she turned away and shielded her face behind the shadows as she rushed past and closed her door on us."

"What color were they?" I asked her, already knowing her response.

"Blue as the sea when she entered, the deepest gray when she left."

"So, it's happening again?"

Matilda nodded.

MA RETURNED WITH a glass of claret and handed it to me. "I nearly forgot: Uncle Edward said you are to drink this the moment you awake."

I was not typically fond of claret. I didn't develop a taste for wine until later in life, but I knew from past experience the drink would quicken the return of my strength—what little I had in those days anyway. I took the glass in hand and forced the liquid down without so much as a single breath between gulps. The wine was warm and dry and not entirely horrible to my young palate, but alcohol nonetheless, and I quickly felt the effects wash over me. I returned the glass to Ma, who eyed me curiously. "You must be dehydrated; I thought I would have to fight you to get it all down. After witnessing that, I'm beginning to wonder if perhaps this sickness of yours is nothing more than a hangover, that you have been sneaking off to the pubs at night." She said this with a twinkle in her eye. I knew it was in jest; I couldn't help but smile at her.

"How else will I ever perfect my game of cribbage?"

This earned a laugh, and she ruffled my hair. "That sense of humor of yours is going to get you in trouble one day, but it's good to hear its return. I was quite worried last night. That may be the worst you have ever been." She placed her hand on my forehead. "The fever seems to have broken, though. You're still a little warm to the touch, but nothing like earlier. I could have boiled a pot of water on that head of yours."

"He does have a big head," Matilda chimed in.

I swatted at her and missed, nearly knocking the tray off the table. Ma plucked my hand from the air and held it in her own, her eyes filling with tears. "I prayed to the Lord above all day and all night that your suffering would come to an end, that your illness would finally abate. Let us hope Uncle Edward chased the demons from you."

I knew he had not. While I felt better, I could sense the illness brewing within me, dormant for now but prepared to return. The achy feeling in my bones, the fatigue and light-headedness; it had been subdued, nothing more.

"He hasn't told yet, Ma," Matilda pointed out, once again perched upon my bed.

"Perhaps we should give him time to regain his strength, young lady."

"If he doesn't tell now, he'll never remember," she replied.

Ma knew this to be true, a fact that she reminded us of. "Dreams are much like the sand in an hourglass, lessening with each passing second, until the last grain disappears down a hole and is lost forever in the dark."

For as long as I could remember, the three of us shared our dreams, recounting them to one another to the best of our recollection. I would sometimes record them; I kept a journal at my bedside just for this purpose. I would write them down the moment I woke, knowing if I waited even a little while, they would fade, just as Ma always told us they would, and the details would become increasingly difficult to pluck from memory. I hadn't yet taken the time to transcribe last night's dreams, and I wasn't sure I wished to. Unlike regular dreams, fever dreams were extraordinarily vivid. Matilda knew this, which was why she prodded me with such insistence now, and while a normal dream really did fade shortly after awakening, fever dreams burned into the mind. I didn't even want to close my eyes for fear of returning to that ugly blackness which had engulfed me amidst the worst of last night. I remembered being buried alive so clearly that I could taste the dirt and hear the worms as they burrowed inches from my head, hungrily awaiting the rank meal I was to become.

"I . . . I don't want to," I protested sheepishly.

"Was it frightful?" Matilda inched closer, her face beaming. "Oh, do tell, Bram!"

My eyes drifted from Matilda to Ma, then back again. Ma had once told me if we speak of the Devil in our dreams, he loses his power to harm us. So, with a sigh, I told them of my burial; I recited all I could recall. When it was over, I realized Matilda had drawn closer while Ma looked on without a word.

"Was your grave amongst the suicides?" Matilda asked.

At this, Ma frowned. "What do you know of the suicide graves?"

My sister's mind tried to calculate a way to expand on this without betraying the fact that she had been listening in on what was no doubt a private conversation between Ma and Pa, but before she could bring forth some elaborate lie, Ma spoke again. "You were eavesdropping on your father and me yesterday, were you not?"

"I was only walking past and may have heard mention of suicide graves, but I did not continue listening; that would be wrong."

"Yes, it would be very wrong."

"Did the men in town really bury a man alive in the graveyard?" I asked.

Ma drew in a deep breath. "If it's true, Horton Lowell and the constable found no evidence of it yesterday afternoon when they went out to the old graveyard after hearing talk of the burial in town. I have no doubt the story was simply the product of someone's overactive imagination, passed from one gossip to the next, until it garnered a life all its own." She turned to Matilda. "Gossip is not a slight bit better than eavesdropping, and I best not find you doing either in the future or you'll catch a switch on that pasty white backside of yours."

I laughed, which quickly turned into a cough. Ma poured me a glass of water and I drank it eagerly. My throat felt raw, as if I had chewed on stones and swallowed the bits.

Ma continued. "The famine has taken a toll on many of our countrymen. In Dublin, the sick and homeless are dying in the streets. The poor are robbing the poor. Men who once worked their own fields are begging on corners in order to scrape together food for their families. Don't ever underestimate what a man will do to put food into the mouth of his starving child."

"Pa says it's getting better," I said.

"Sometimes I think your father prefers to believe the rhetoric preached amongst the aristocrats at the castle. They want us to believe the famine is coming to an end, so they stand around telling one another it is, but speaking of such things does not make them fact." Ma looked down at her hands. "I think things will get far worse before they get better, so when I hear that a sick man was buried alive, I don't dismiss it as fiction straightaway; I know firsthand what evil men will do when frightened. When I was a little girl and cholera ran rampant, I witnessed men do far worse than bury a single sick soul."

"Was cholera worse than the famine?"

"I don't know if one death is better or worse than another, Matilda. Both kill without prejudice."

Matilda spoke, her voice thin and sheepish. "Is that what will become of us here? Is everyone going to die?"

"The famine is different, Matilda. There is sickness, yes, but nothing like cholera. Most of the ill you behold are suffering from starvation and dehydration, men drinking themselves into a stupor, having failed to provide for their families. It is horrific, to be sure, but a very different beast." She patted our knees. "Enough of this talk; we have much to do today, and I have a feeling Nanna Ellen will not be offering her help."

The three of us glanced down the hall to Nanna Ellen's sealed door. Ma stood. "Matilda, be a dear and gather today's eggs."

My sister wrinkled her nose. "It's Thornley's turn!"

"Your father sent him to the Seaver cottage in Santry for a load of peat for the fire. We're nearly out, you know, and the nights are soon to grow frigid with the approach of winter."

Matilda eased off the bed and thumped down the hall without another word.

Ma placed her hand upon my forehead and smiled. "God has smiled upon you, my little man."

My eyes remained fixed on Nanna Ellen's door, the images of last night still playing in the theater of my mind.

· · ·

SEVERAL HOURS LATER—"What is Nanna Ellen doing?" Matilda asked.

I stood on my toes and peered out my window to our backyard. "She's taking down the laundry from the line."

As I stood there, I realized I felt much better today. Although the telltale ache in my bones remained, my illness had somewhat retreated. Weeks would sometimes pass without my rising from bed. I remained in bed so much, I sometimes developed sores, and my muscles atrophied from lack of use. Ma often worried I would develop an infection and cleaned the sores as best she could, then dressed them in sphagnum moss she kept on a high shelf in the kitchen pantry, away from Pa's eyes, a bit of folk medicine no doubt spurned by the modern doctors in our family. As for my muscles, there was little to be done. On many days, I was simply too weak to leave my bed. At Ma's coaxing, I would try, but my body just didn't possess the strength, and I would lie there, turning every few hours with her help to prevent the bedsores from getting worse.

Today proved different.

Much like the small marks left by the leeches, the bedsores that had riddled my pathetic flesh just yesterday were now dry and faded and itched like the dickens. Gone, suddenly, were the open, pustulating wounds that had been a part of my life for as far back as my memories went; they seemed to be fading as the day went on, healing with incredible dispatch.

I felt stronger, too. There was an energy present inside me now that had been absent in all the previous days, a real strength. At this point I had been out of bed for nearly two hours. Two hours on my feet! I begged to tell Ma of this, but Matilda told me not to; she thought it best to keep this secret between us.

I stood at my little attic window and watched Nanna Ellen as she worked her way down the clothesline, plucking the pins and carefully folding each article of clothing before depositing it in the basket at her feet. She had been down there for ten minutes now and was nearly half-way through the load. I searched for the signs of age Matilda mentioned, but I found it difficult to get a good look at her face. She wore a scarf over her head tied under her chin, and the green-and-white cloth shielded her from view. She seemed to be moving slowly, as if in pain.

"How long before she finishes?"

"Ten minutes," I replied. "Possibly less."

Thornley returned on the back of a wagon full of peat from the Seaver cottage, and both he and Pa began unloading the payload and carrying it down to the cellar while the driver eyed the thick storm clouds rolling in off the harbor. Thornley was covered in sweat, his face black with dirt and mud.

Matilda bounced off my bed and made her way to the door. She pressed her ear against the wood and listened to the hallway. "Ma and Thomas sound like they're down in the kitchen. Richard must be sleeping."

"If you go in Nanna's room, he will wake, and Ma or Nanna Ellen will come running," I pointed out.

"I won't wake him; I can be quiet as a church mouse."

"You shouldn't go in there; she'll know."

"How will she know?"

Below my window, Nanna Ellen nudged her basket farther down the line with the tip of her shoe.

"She'll know."

"If she leaves the line, come and get me. You can be my lookout."

I shook my head. "If you're going, I'm going with you."

"Come, then; enough of this lollygagging."

Matilda twisted the knob of my door and pulled it into the room, mov-ing just fast enough to keep the hinges from squeaking, something they were known to do. With a quick glance up and down the hallway, she crossed the threshold and tiptoed down the corridor, carefully avoiding the two boards near the stairs that always groaned underfoot. I followed only a few feet behind her when I realized this was the first time in nearly three months that I had left the room of my own volition. Pa sometimes carried me downstairs and perched me in the kitchen or on the sofa in the sitting room, but I rarely took these steps on my own. With my last attempt, I had made it only as far as the staircase before gripping the banister and dropping to the floor in utter exhaustion. Pa forbade me from leaving my room after that episode, fearing I might tumble down the stairs and break one or more of my already brittle bones.

As we passed the staircase, I realized I wasn't the least bit tired. In fact, I felt the adrenaline surging through my body, a burst of energy. Every sight and sound seemed enhanced. I heard Ma speaking to Thomas in the kitchen, every word as clear as if they were standing in the very next room. Was this odd? I did not know. After all, Matilda had heard them from my room with the door shut. Still, this seemed peculiar to me.

Matilda reached Nanna Ellen's door and pressed her ear to it.

"She's still downstairs. Hurry."

"I'm listening for Baby Richard."

I closed my eyes and listened, too, envisioning the room on the other side of Nanna Ellen's door, the tiny space she called home. "He's sleeping. I can hear his breaths."

Matilda eyed me for a moment, my claim suspect, before twisting the knob. This door did squeak, and both of us cringed with its retort. Downstairs, both Ma and Thomas laughed at something. My eyes met Matilda's; if they heard the noise, they thought little of it, there being no break in their conversation. This was followed by the clang of pans. Matilda slipped through the door into the maw of Nanna Ellen's room, her hooked index finger beckoning me to follow.

. . .

NANNA ELLEN'S room wasn't large; in fact, it was smaller than mine. Rectangular in shape, with a ceiling that sloped down towards the window, it was no more than ten feet wide by eight feet deep. While I imagined the window looked out over the back fields, I could not be sure because the glass had been covered by a thick blanket, tacked to the frame at all four corners. Light attempted to squeeze around the edges of the blanket, but little penetrated, leaving the space in relative darkness. I could see the outline of Matilda standing over the small crib in which Baby Richard slept. She adjusted his blanket and held a finger to her lips.

I nodded. My eyes adjusted to the lack of light.

Nanna Ellen's bedroom was sparsely furnished. A wardrobe stood against the back wall. There was a small desk to the right of the crib, upon which rested a few sheets of paper and a quill pen. On the left stood a lone table, with washbasin and towel. Her bed was neatly made, with a night table beside it, bare save for an old oil lamp and a newspaper. Upon closer inspection, I realized the basin was dry as a bone. Dust had gathered at the bottom. "This is odd," I whispered.

Matilda came over and ran her index finger along the inside edge. "Maybe she washes downstairs?"

I found a bedpan tucked in the far corner beside the basin; it, too, appeared unused. I moved it aside with the toe of my foot, revealing a ring of dust where the base had been. Matilda and I glanced at each other but said nothing. When Matilda tended the bedpans, Nanna Ellen always told Matilda she would see to her own.

It was then that I spotted our footprints on the floor, a simple trail leading from the room's entrance to where we currently stood. A thin layer of what could only be dirt covered the hardwood, disturbed by our tracks. Although thicker in some spots than in others, it seemed to cover all of Nanna Ellen's room; filthy, as if the room had not been swept in some time.

"She'll know we were in here for sure," I said, more to myself than to Matilda.

"Keep looking; we'll figure something out."

"What are we looking for?"

"I don't know. She has lived here all this time, and we know so little about her." She reached for the doors of the wardrobe and pulled them open quickly, attempting to surprise whatever awaited her inside. Five dresses hung neatly from hangers, and a small box of undergarments resided at the bottom and to the right. I turned away shyly.

Matilda giggled. "Poor little Bram, afraid of a few pairs of knickers?" She held up a pair and motioned as if tossing them to me. I took a step back, and she dropped them back in the box, then knelt down beside it and began rummaging through the rest of the contents. "A lady always hides her most precious of items amongst her knickers because no man would dare search such a spot."

A moment later, she stood.

"And what," I asked, "did you find amongst her knickers?"

"Nothing."

I walked over to the desk and picked up the topmost sheet of paper. Blank.

Matilda snatched the paper from my hand, held it up to the sparse light creeping in from the hallway, then carefully placed it back on the stack. "Keep looking."

I made my way over to the night table. Like the washbasin and bedpan, the oil lamp also appeared to be unused. The font was dry, and when I smelled it, not even a hint of oil was present, only a musty odor like that of a box sealed up and long forgotten, then opened for the first time in ages. I told Matilda, but she waved me off, lost in her task.

The newspaper was yesterday's edition of the *Saunders's News-Letter*. The headline was printed in bold black block letters—

FAMILY MURDER IN MALAHIDE

A barbarous and cruel murder was committed under circumstances most revolting in Malahide on Friday night about the hour of two o'clock a.m. The victims being Siboan O'Cuiv, mother of the deceased children, the eldest son Sean, five years old, and his sister Isobelle, a child about two years of age. The third child, a daughter, six-and-a-half-year-old Maggie, managed to escape the assailant, and it is she who alerted James Boulger, Constable in Charge of the Church Street Barracks, who happened to be passing convenient to the place, when their attention was attracted by a child fleeing the house.

Constable Boulger then entered the house and heard the moans of Patrick O'Cuiv, who was bleeding profusely from both arms. Constable Patterson entered the bedchambers to find a mother and two young, helpless children lying dead in their beds. Mr. O'Cuiv was near death himself, as he had lost a significant amount of blood. He was taken by carriage to the Richmond Hospital.

"Did you see yesterday's paper?" I asked.

"No, but I heard Ma and Pa discussing it over dinner. They said the constable's office believes Mr. O'Cuiv tried to kill his entire family because he couldn't afford to feed them, then turned the knife on himself but was unable to finish the job. If not for little Maggie, he surely would have completed the task and they'd all be dead."

"Where is he now?"

"The Church Street Barracks, I suppose. They patched him up. Should have left him to bleed to death in a bath of salt for such a crime," said Matilda.

The O'Cuiv family had visited for dinner not more than a month ago. The meal had been anything but extravagant, yet they had been grateful nonetheless; little Sean helped himself to no less than three servings, and his little sister said few words, as she was too busy chewing on a cut of bread the size of her head dipped in Ma's chicken gravy. His wife had been understandably quiet—accepting the graciousness of strangers was a most humbling experience, one many would not consider if not for the stomachs of their children aching for food. She had eaten in near silence, responding as Ma and Pa asked her various questions in the course of conversation, but she never offered more than a response to what was asked of her before returning to her meal, her eyes flitting from her children to her husband and back again. I tried to recall whether any tension had been evident between the two adults. Nothing came to mind, though; they seemed cordial enough, victims of the famine, nothing more.

"Do you think Pa could ever do such a thing?" I had asked the question before I realized I had allowed the words to actually pass from my lips, and I felt my cheeks flush.

"Oh, heavens no! First of all, Pa would always find a way to feed us. But even if he couldn't, he is not one to give up, and what Mr. O'Cuiv did is nothing but giving up. Rather than find a solution to the problem at hand, he surrendered like a coward. Pa could never do that. If he tried, Ma is likely to smack him with a skillet."

I knew she was right, but even at such a young age I also understood how easily a problem could envelop someone, isolate them from the rest of the world until it seemed nothing else existed. My own isolation had taught me so. "How do you suppose he did it without waking the others?"

"Will you stop? We need to keep looking around. We haven't much time."

"He killed his wife and three of his four children before Maggie escaped," I pondered.

"At two in the morning—they were probably all sound asleep."

"But to sleep through it? Maybe the first victim, but the others? I find that hard to believe." I returned to the paper and scanned the remaining front-page headlines. "Who is Cornelius Healy? I know that name from somewhere."

"Mr. Healy? He runs a farm for the Domvilles, I think. Why?"

"Listen—"

LAND MANAGER KILLED
IN ALTERCATION AT FARM
AT SANTRY HOUSE

Possible Murder—On Friday evening, a man by the name of Cornelius Healy, the land manager for the Domville family of Santry House, was involved in an altercation with one of his employees. A fistfight ensued as a result of a dispute over the employee allegedly stealing grain to feed his family.

The worker was punished by a caning at the hands of Mr. Healy. Upon release from his bounds, the worker responded by attacking Mr. Healy with his bare hands. The other employees urged on the fisticuffs, as Mr. Healy and the punishments he meted out were apparently not popular with the other farm laborers. Witnesses were not forthcoming with the name of the worker but did tell the police that Mr. Healy slipped, fell, and hit his head on a rock, which caused his death and resulted in the attacker making his quick departure. A full investigation will follow.

"He doesn't sound like a very nice person. What kind of man canes someone who is only trying to feed his family?" Matilda said.

"When was the last time there was a murder in Clontarf?"

Matilda shrugged.

"Now two murders in one day . . ."

"If you continue this, I'm going to take your copy of 'The Murders in the Rue Morgue' and bury it out in the pasture. Focus your sleuthing skills on the task at hand; we haven't much time."

She was right, of course, but I told myself I would research this matter further when the time presented itself.

Matilda leaned against the wall, peering behind the wardrobe.

"What are you doing?"

"I see something behind here, attached to the back." She closed one eye, squinted the other, trying to get a better look.

I leaned in from the other side. I could see it, too. "Give me a hand; let's pull the wardrobe a bit away from the wall."

Together, we both wrapped our fingers around the right side and gave it a tug. The heavy cabinet groaned against the floor. Matilda froze. "Do you think someone heard that?"

I listened carefully. I could still hear Ma in the kitchen. "I don't think so."

Matilda returned her attention to the wardrobe, squeezing her hand into the opening at its back. "I think I can reach it."

I watched the lower half of her arm disappear. It came out with a thin leather satchel.

"What is it?"

A worn string held the satchel shut. She twisted the fastening free and opened the flap, then reached inside and extracted the contents.

Maps.

"Put them here, on the desk."

"They're very old," she said, spreading them out. "The paper is crumbling at the fringes."

"How many are there?"

Matilda turned through the maps, careful not to damage them. "Seven. From all over Europe and the United Kingdom. There's Prague, Austria, Romania, Italy, London . . ." Her voice trailed off.

"What is it?"

"This one is Ireland."

"What is that mark?"

She studied it closely. "Clontarf. The mark is at Saint John the Baptist."

I turned through the others. "They're all marked. The U.K. map has two—one near London and another at someplace called Whitby."

She was frowning. "They're so old; some of the borders are wrong. They look hand-drawn. I don't recognize the language."

My arm began to itch. "I think we should put them back, before someone comes up."

She ignored me, flipping through the maps, reviewing each one, studying each line, memorizing everything.

"Matilda?"

She held a finger to her lips.

The last map.

"All right," she said softly, more to herself than to me.

She put the maps back into the satchel.

"Make sure they are in the same order."

"They are."

Matilda retied the string and placed the leather satchel back behind the wardrobe, attaching it to a small hook I hadn't noticed before. "Help me move it back," she said, gripping the side of the cabinet.

Together, we moved the wardrobe back into place, lifting it as much as we could to keep from making noise again.

"There may be something else. We need to keep looking," Matilda said, turning her attention to the desk. She began rifling through the drawers.

I turned back to the bed.

A thick goose-down quilt covered the small frame, and a single feather pillow sat propped up at the head. The wooden frame was similar to my own, a simple structure with shallow-carved adornments and stained a forbidding brown. I leaned in close and sniffed the quilt—my nose buckled, and a loud sneeze forced its way out.

"Bram!"

I covered my nose and tried to hold back the second one, but it came with more force than the first.

"Somebody will—"

I sneezed a third time, my eyes filling with tears. When a fourth began to tickle at my nostrils, I found the strength to stop it as Matilda came towards me and smothered my face in a handkerchief. I waved her off and stepped back, my eyes locked on the quilt. When I began to lean in close again, she tried to pull me back, but I shook her off. This time I didn't inhale; rather, I gleaned a better look. The quilt was covered in dust. Not a thin layer, but the kind of dust you find coating forgotten furniture in an attic. Dust like this didn't just appear; it accumulated over time due to disregard and neglect.

"How often would you say Nanna Ellen remakes our beds?"

Matilda thought about it for a second. "Every Saturday, without fail."

"Then why not her own?"

The question hung in the air, for neither of us had an answer. "For that matter, where does she sleep, if not in the bed?"

She had a wooden chair at the desk. With a stiff back and arms, it wouldn't allow for so much as a slouch. I could not imagine anyone attempting to sleep in it.

"Maybe she sleeps on the floor," Matilda offered. "My friend Beatrice once told me her father sleeps on the floor all the time due to a nagging pain in his back. The wooden floor is the only surface that provides relief."

"I don't think Nanna Ellen has a bad back."

"Where, then?"

The dust on the floor was thickest at the bed.

I don't know why I noticed it; maybe because I was simply looking down. At the bed frame, it wasn't just dirty; the dust was piled high against the base. It looked as if someone had swept the room repeatedly against the bed rather than to the center of the floor, where it could be picked up. It reminded me of the mounds of dirt washed against the side of the house by rain, climbing against the walls in an attempt to enter. Wasn't that the goal of dirt? To get inside and reclaim what is ultimately the property of the land?

I reached down and lifted the corner of the mattress.

Nanna Ellen's bed was constructed in the same manner as my own. Under the blankets and sheets was a mattress stuffed with goose or chicken feathers, no more than five inches in thickness. This was a luxury for most, one we were quite grateful for. Pa's position granted access to some of the finer things, and while my parents did not splurge on much, proper bedding was something they fervently believed in. They felt that without a good night's rest, we would fail at our next day's endeavors, and that that failure would, in turn, lead to the lackadaisical inertness they witnessed in so many of our countrymen. Whether or not this was true, I did not know. But as someone who had spent a substantial portion of his life in his bed, I was grateful for the comfort.

Beneath the feather mattress of my bed was a box filled with straw. Each spring, the old straw would be removed and replaced with fresh from the fields behind Artane Lodge. We packed it in tight, and the box, at nearly two feet in height, was the perfect foundation. Beneath Nanna Ellen's feather mattress lay a similar box, but as I pulled the mattress aside, it wasn't straw I found but dirt, thick and black. Centered in the dirt was the concave impression of a body.

"She sleeps in that?" Matilda breathed the words. "But why?"

I didn't answer her, though; I was too busy watching the worms as they wiggled out to greet us, slinking over the putrid soil from within the bed's bilious bowels.

It was Matilda who spoke first, her voice quavering. "We need to get out of here."

My eyes remained fixed on the bed, though, on the outline of Nanna Ellen's body pressed into the moist soil. The stench, of death and decay, was nearly overpowering, as if a body, left to rot in the earth, had recently been uncovered by the gravedigger's shovel. White maggots joined the worms, fluttering to the surface with excitement and vigor, their little bodies writhing. My mind went back to the last time I had seen such a sight nearly a year earlier. Thornley had been working in the fields at Artane near the barn and ran behind the house. I was having a day better than most, and Ma carried me downstairs to the sofa in the sitting room. When he barged in, his face flush and dripping with sweat, he could barely speak. He had run so hard that his breath deserted him, and it took him a moment to regain his voice. "You've got to see this," he finally said between gasps. "Behind the barn."

He was eight at the time, and I was only six, but the excitement in his eyes lit a fire within me and I wanted to see whatever it was he had found. I wanted to see it then and there, and an energy surged through me, enough to help me to my feet. I could walk, but not well, so he threw my arm over his shoulder and helped me tackle each step. Faster than I could have moved on my own but slower than he would have hoped, we left the house and crossed the field to the barn, located on the east side. A large structure built to hold more than a hundred cows and nearly a dozen horses and sundry other livestock, the barn towered over most on the property, casting a shadow of immense proportion over the surrounding land. Together, we made our way around the south side and towards the chicken coops. Before we arrived, I sensed something was wrong, for the chickens were emitting the most awful reports. Their normal *bawk, bawk, bock* had been replaced by nervous clucks and squeals I would never imagine coming from fowl. As we neared, I noticed the muddy ground was littered with brown and white feathers and streaks of red that thickened around the coops themselves.

"What happened?" I asked.

"A fox, I think. A fox did this. Or maybe a wolf. Something got inside the coops and killed six of the hens last night," Thornley retorted. "Take a look."

The stench hit me then, the coppery odor of spilt blood and torn flesh. "I don't want to."

"Don't be a ninny."

"No, take me back home."

He wouldn't, though; he kept dragging me closer. It didn't matter that my feet stopped moving as I dug my heels into the dirt; he was much stronger than me, and pulling my frail body along was little chore for him. Before I realized it, we stood beside the open door of the coop, and my eyes couldn't help but land on the shredded bodies of half a dozen hens. A cloud of flies buzzed over the coop, thick and gloomy, as they landed on the knotted flesh and picked at their repast. Tiny maggots dotted the exposed meat; newly hatched and hungry, they tumbled over one another in quest of their next bite. Bile engorged my throat, and before I could turn away the vomit sprayed from my mouth across the carnage.

Thornley laughed. "When Ma serves you chicken tonight, I just thought you'd like to know where it came from. Fresh from the slaughter."

"BRAM, WE NEED TO LEAVE!" Matilda insisted in a loud whisper, tugging at my arm.

"I don't understand," I responded quietly. "She cannot possibly—"

"Now!"

Matilda tried to pull me towards the door, but I remained firmly in place. My eyes returned to the dirt on the floor, the way it formed a small hill as it tried to climb the sides of the bed. Then I understood. When Nanna Ellen swept her room, she swept the dirt towards her bed rather than away from it or into a dustpan. Was it deposited back on the floor as she climbed in and out of the bed frame?

I turned back to the floor and studied the footprints trailing from the door and around the room, the many little footprints—the prints of children—none large enough to have been produced by an adult.

"She doesn't leave footprints."

Matilda turned from the door and faced me. "What?"

"The tracks on the ground, they all belong to us. See how tiny they are? Nanna Ellen is small, but her feet are still larger than ours. She hasn't left a single print. Remember how the dust was when we first walked in? A thin coat spread evenly and undisturbed?"

With that, Baby Richard began to stir in his crib—I had forgotten he was in the room with us. Matilda went to him. His little feet began to pump, and his blanket fell away. Richard's face contorted, and for one brief moment the room fell into complete silence; then his mouth opened and unleashed a wailing shriek loud enough to be heard throughout the entire house. Matilda scooped him up and held him to her chest while gently rocking back and forth.

I quickly returned the mattress back to its original position, careful not to touch the dusty quilt.

Ma appeared at the door. "The lungs on that child will wake the dead! You didn't wake him, did you?"

Matilda shook her head, and, without missing a beat, let slip a lie. "We were in Bram's room when he started crying. I didn't know where Nanna Ellen went, so I figured I would check on him. I think he requires a new nappy."

Ma wasn't listening to her, though; she stared at me. "Bram! You're out of bed!"

When I started to cross the room, she rushed towards me and wrapped her arm around my back in an effort to help, but I shook her off. "I can do it on my own, Ma. See?" And I did just that, walking from the side of the bed to the door. I'd be lying if I said it was easy; the effort was enough to bring a sheen of sweat to my brow, but I truly felt much better than I had in recent memory. My muscles wanted to work, but, after years of atrophy, the movement was difficult.

Ma's eyes teared up. "Well, I'll be . . ."

"It's all right, Ma. He can do it," Matilda exclaimed.

Ma waved her off and took me in her arms. "Thank your lucky stars for Uncle Edward. God bless him!" She squeezed me in a hug that nearly lifted me off the ground. Beneath the sleeves of my nightshirt, the leeches' bites itched.

"How this woman keeps a clean house yet sleeps in such a mess, I'll never understand." She glanced around the room in disgust. "Out with the two of you."

· · ·

THERE IS SOMETHING I did not tell Matilda that day, something I kept
to myself all this time and will take to my grave. As I stared down at the
dirt in Nanna Ellen's bed, as I watched the worms and maggots wiggle
about, as I took in the scent of death, I was not as repulsed as she, as I
should have been. Instead, it seemed vaguely welcoming—instead, I
stood there and fought with all my strength the urge to climb inside
and lie down.

EVENING—I couldn't recall the last time I had sat at the dinner table
and taken my evening meal with the rest of the family. Had I ever?
My illness had dominated my life for so long, all I could remember
were meals in my room, brought to me by alternating members of the
family. This made me feel like a burden upon them, a chore to be accomplished. At first, when Ma brought me down, I wasn't sure even
where to sit. There were seven chairs around the large wooden table,
six of which had place settings. Had Matilda not nodded towards the
chair to her right, the one lacking a setting, I would have continued
standing there like a fool in front of my family, observing them.

I took the seat Matilda indicated, and Ma handed me a plate and uten-
sils. My fingers fumbled with the fork. As I glanced around the table, I
could tell the others were uneasy as well. My little brother Thomas sat
across from me and stared. Every few minutes, his finger would slip
into his nose to pick at something I dared not consider, and Matilda delivered him a swift kick under the table. He frowned at her and continued his unholy quest. Ma sat to my right, oblivious to Thomas's and
Matilda's activities as she was preoccupied with Richard, who was securely fastened into a high chair at her other side. His food had already
been served, and Ma attempted to spoon mashed potatoes into his

mouth only to watch him spit the pale mound back out and rub it into his lap.

Pa sat opposite Ma on the long end of the table. I don't think he wanted to draw attention to me; instead, he opted to pretend there was nothing abnormal about my presence. For this, I was grateful. Aside from Thomas's overt stares, the others attempted to conceal their sense of wonder. On more than one occasion, I caught each of them glancing my way, but nothing was said about it.

Then, however, Thornley mentioned it outright, his bluntness over-powering. I asked him to pass the bread, and he responded with, "Finally gave up on dying to see what was going on in the rest of the world, huh?"

With this, Ma shot him her angriest look. "Your brother has been quite ill, and I think you should be grateful your Uncle Edward restored him to us."

"I think as long as he is cooped up in that room of his, he is not down here helping with the chores. Seems like he suffers from nothing more than laziness," Thornley replied.

Pa raised his eyebrows but added nothing to this thorny exchange; instead, he unfolded today's newspaper and scanned the headlines.

Thornley was only two years my senior, but to me he seemed much older. He was bigger, too, towering over me by at least six inches. While I was slight and thin, his build was bulky due in much part to the work he did to help Ma and Pa around the house. He tended to most of the animals and the yard, toting lumber and such. This made for a strong boy; even at nine years old, he was larger than others his age and he knew it. Thornley was always quick with a jab, whether verbal or physical.

Nanna Ellen appeared with a large stewpot and set it at the center of the table, then began to fill our bowls one at a time, beginning with

Thomas. When she got to mine, Matilda nudged me under the table. I did not peek over at her, though. If Nanna Ellen knew we had been snooping around her room, she said nothing about it. She came in after tending the laundry and proceeded to put away the clothing without even the slightest acknowledgment of our violation. Even when she deposited my laundry in the various drawers of my bureau, she did so without a word. Her head hung low, and her face remained obscured by her scarf.

Nanna Ellen handed me my soup bowl, and I took it from her without meeting her eyes, even though I could sense them on me. It was only when she reached Pa that I dared to glance at her face. Matilda had been right. Nanna Ellen looked as if she had aged in the past few days; her skin was pale and gray, devoid of the shine normally blossoming at her cheeks. The strands of blond hair that poked out from around the scarf appeared dry and brittle. She tried to tuck them back under the scarf, but they fell back out, dangling over her face.

"You don't seem well, Ellen. Do you need to rest?" Ma said from across the table as she dabbed Richard's cheeks with a napkin.

Nanna Ellen offered a weak smile. "I believe I picked up a cold, is all. I'll be okay. I'll lie down after dinner and nip it in the bud. I've never been one to let some illness hold me down."

Thoughts of her bed popped back into my mind, the little worms and maggots sifting through the dirt. I could picture her lying on top of it all, her deep gray eyes wide open in a blank stare as these earth creatures slowly fed on her flesh. The leech bites across my arms began to itch, and I fought the urge to scratch at them. One was visible at my wrist, and I couldn't help but glance down at it, now nothing more than a little pink circle, healed nearly to the point of invisibility. I noticed Matilda eyeing me, and I pulled the sleeve of my shirt down over the mark and waited for a kick under the table that never came.

I took a bite of my bread, and Pa cleared his throat. "Aren't you forgetting something?"

I surveyed the piece of bread in my hand, then looked down at my soup, unsure of what he meant.

Thornley snickered.

Pa frowned at him before returning his gaze to me. "A civilized family says grace before they eat."

I had taken my meals in my room for so long, such things escaped me. I put the bread down beside my bowl, pressed my hands together, and closed my eyes.

"Perhaps you should speak aloud," said Pa.

I opened my eyes. A smirk washed across Thornley's face, and I felt my cheeks flush. "Yes, Pa." I tried to recall the last time I had said grace and simply couldn't. My mind went blank, and I found myself staring down at my soup bowl.

Pa looked to my sister. "Matilda, remind your brother what it is to say grace."

Matilda sat up straight in her chair and clasped her hands, her voice loud and ringing through the room. "Bless, O Lord, this food for Thy use, and make us ever mindful of the wants and needs of those less fortunate. Amen."

"Amen," I said with the others, my voice cracking and a little higher than I would have hoped.

Pa gave her a nod and returned to his newspaper.

I didn't reach for my bread again until I saw Ma buttering hers. "Any word on Patrick O'Cuiv?" she asked.

Pa shook the paper and flipped it back to the first page. "Oh yes, apparently the plot has thickened substantially. Listen—"

MASS KILLING IN MALAHIDE
FATHER SUSPECTED OF
SANTRY ESTATE MURDER

Patrick O'Cuiv was found near death by police authorities at his residence in Malahide; suspicious circumstances are suspected, as he was found not alone in his home but in the company of his wife and two of his three children, all dead in their beds. When informed of the state of his family, he turned hysterical and had to be restrained in his grief. Facts have surfaced that Mr. O'Cuiv was the employee involved in the fistfight with the deceased land manager Cornelius Healy of Santry Estate.

Ma shook her head. "That is terrible. So not only did he kill his family but his employer as well?"

Pa shrugged. "To me, the death of his employer appears to be nothing more than an accident. A man at the end of his rope in a desperate situation. The situation came to blows, and Healy paid the price. He won't be missed; the man was an ostentatious snoot who liked nothing more than the sound of his own voice and the clinking of coin in his pocket. He could have spared some grain, but instead he beats a man attempting to feed his family. He met with God's wrath, nothing more. But this business with O'Cuiv's own family, that I find tragic." Pa paused for a second, retrieved the pipe from his breast pocket, and began to pack the bowl with tobacco from the little brown bag he always kept on his person. "Even without hope in sight, I cannot imagine a father willing to take the lives of his own wife and children when faced with the inability to provide."

Richard began to fuss, and Ma reached over and stroked his hand. "Perhaps he was already at a low then and couldn't bear to face a worse place after killing his employer. After all, if an employed man is unable to feed his family, what is an unemployed man guilty of murder to do?" Richard let out a burp. Ma frowned. "Any mention of their daughter? The one who escaped?"

"Nothing today."

"I wonder who took her in. I don't think the O'Cuivs had family in the area. I believe Siboan O'Cuiv said her family resided in Dublin, but I could be mistaken."

"I imagine she is being well looked after."

"Maybe she can stay with us," Matilda suggested. "I wouldn't mind a sister."

Pa peeked across the table over his pipe but said nothing.

Ma patted her hand. "I have often told your father that very thing! We ladies are far outnumbered in this household. If the Good Lord doesn't see fit to bless this family with another daughter, maybe we should consider recruiting one."

"Do you think she saw what happened?" I asked.

Pa let a small ring of smoke drift from his lips, then said: "She most likely saw it all; why else would she run? Such a thing leaves a mark on a child, one that can never be wiped or washed away. She'll awaken twenty years from now with those images in her mind. To witness your own father take the lives of your mother and siblings, that is an unimaginable atrocity from which there is no escape. I can only hope she one day finds a happiness strong enough to balance out the evil that man committed."

From the corner of my eye, I watched Nanna Ellen take her seat before her own bowl of soup. Her hand shook slightly as she lowered her spoon into the broth and raised it to her mouth. Although her lips parted, the soup never passed them. Instead, I watched as she lowered the spoon back into the bowl. A moment later, she repeated the gesture, the soup never entering her mouth. Matilda was watching her, too, and when she looked across the table at us, we both turned away—I fumbled with my own spoon and nearly dropped it to the floor.

Nanna Ellen slid her bowl forward. "I believe this illness truly has gotten the better of me; please excuse me." With that, she rose from the table and ascended the stairs without so much as a glance back.

LATER—"What is she doing?" Matilda whispered as I crept back into my room, carefully closing the door behind me.

"I couldn't hear anything," I said softly.

Matilda sat on my bed, sketchbook in hand, carefully re-creating the maps from Nanna Ellen's room. How she recalled them in such detail, I'll never understand.

"Maybe she's sleeping," Matilda said without looking up.

After dinner, Matilda and I had returned to my attic room, the eyes of the others on our backs as we ascended the stairs. Although they were my family, I was an outsider amongst them. In truth, I don't believe they ever thought I would survive my first year, much less my first seven. They thought I was to die—perhaps not today or tomorrow, but sometime soon, and that prevented them from getting too close. Even Ma, who spent much of her time with me, did so at a distance—an unspoken chasm between us always. I rarely saw Pa, and Thornley avoided me entirely. And so a sense of relief hung in the air as I excused myself to head back upstairs, but beneath that relief lingered dread: the good days, we all seemed to silently sense, are always followed by the bad.

"She's not sleeping." I pictured her sitting on the edge of the bed, the mattress pushed aside and her fingers sifting through the dirt beneath, the warm dampness of it inching up her arm, a welcoming thing. "Have you ever seen her eat?" I asked.

"She eats dinner with us every night."

"No, I mean have you ever really *seen* her eat?"

Matilda thought about this for a second. "I . . . I don't know. I suppose not, but I've never paid much attention. Are you implying that she doesn't?"

"She *pretended* to eat tonight."

"She didn't feel well. You, of all people, know what it is like to try to eat when you are ill. Perhaps she feigned it to spare Ma's feelings. She probably doesn't want her to believe she didn't like the soup."

My arm itched, and I scratched at the tender flesh.

"Let me see that," Matilda said, setting down her sketchbook and reaching for my shirtsleeve.

I pulled away. I wasn't sure why, only that I didn't want her to see. I felt as if nobody should see. That if someone did, only more questions would be raised. Questions I could not answer.

Matilda stared at me. "Bram!"

"It's disgusting, Matilda. I don't want you to."

"I've seen your leech bites before. Come here."

Again, I pulled away, backing up until I found myself at the wall.

"What has gotten into you?"

I shrunk back against the frigid wood, prepared to push her away, wanting to squeeze through the plaster and siding to the icy air, then—

"She's outside," I said softly.

"What do you mean?"

"Nanna's outside."

Matilda went to my door and edged it open only enough to peek into the hallway. "How could she be outside? She hasn't left her room. We would have heard her."

"I don't know, but somehow she's outside."

"How do you know?"

I opened my mouth to answer, but nothing came out. I was not sure how I knew, only that I did.

I crossed the room to my little window and stared out into the darkness.

A crescent moon dangling in the sky offered the thinnest of illuminations, bathing the world in nothing but faint outlines, silhouettes, and shadows. The tower of Artane Castle was barely visible in the distance, lost behind rolling hills and farmland dotted with the small homes of our neighbors. Beyond that were the hazel and birch trees of the forest, their inky branches scratching at the night sky in anticipation of a pending shower. I stared out upon all this with awe, not because I had never seen it before but because I shouldn't be able to see it now, not with so little light. Yet I did. I could see all of it.

"There!" I pointed north towards the tower of Artane Castle, just beyond the barn.

Matilda joined me at the window and peered out. "I don't see anything."

"She just passed the pasture. She's coming up on the Roddingtons' home. Looks like she is wearing a black cloak with the hood pulled up over her head."

"If she's wearing a hood, how can you be sure that is even her?" Matilda leaned out the window now, her eyes squinting.

"That's her. I know it is."

"I still don't see anything."

I tugged at her arm, pulling her towards the hallway. "Come on; we must hurry."

"Where are we going?"

"I want to follow her."

Matilda planted her feet firmly on the floor. "Do you realize what Ma and Pa would do to me if they found out I let you out of this house?"

"Then we shouldn't tell them," I replied. "Come on."

NOW

Bram shuffles back from the door. The silver cross in his hand grows hot, burning his flesh, the edges becoming sharp as blades. He drops it. His palm bubbling with blisters, the creases filling with rich blood seeping from a dozen cuts.

When a single drop of blood drips to the stone floor, the room goes silent.

Bram hears his breath as he draws air into his lungs, watches it expelled: a thin white mist. Then the creature crashes into the door with indescribable ferocity. Bram watches the door bend towards him; he watches as the bolts securing the heavy iron hinges spring and rattle against the frame.

A howl, deep and guttural, bellows out so loud Bram has to cover his ears. His injured hand closes tight as blood splashes out onto his hair and cheek. This seems to excite the monster even more and it takes another leap at the door, heavier than the last.

Bram plucks a rose from the basket behind him and slides it across the floor to the foot of the door. It lands beside the dried-out husk of its predecessor, and although vibrant and scented only a moment earlier, instantly begins to fade. Before his eyes, the petals twist in on one another and curl, the edges turning first brown, then black, as they wilt and shrivel up.

Bram tosses another rose, then a third, this final flower not fading at all.

The howl comes again, this time subdued and muted. Bram braces himself for another bang on the door, but it doesn't come. Instead, there is the scratching of a great paw being dragged across the door, from its very top, at nearly nine feet, all the way to the bottom.

The wolf's cry is quickly answered by the cry of another wolf, this one at some distance, somewhere far off in the woods. Then another wolf also howls in reply.

Bram climbs to his feet and crosses the room to the window.

The moon fights the storm clouds for space in the night sky, peeking out briefly before getting lost behind them yet again. Even in the dim light, he can make out the outline of the distant forest. The branches are woven together so thickly it is a wonder anything might pass through them, whether in flight or afoot—but he senses life within those trees, the many eyes glowering at him, as he looks down upon them.

When the moon reappears, Bram holds his hand up to the light. The wound is gone now, the flesh mended, leaving behind no trace of the injury but for the dried blood that paints his palm.

Outside the window, a stone gargoyle stands sentry. Thick talons holding firm, wrapped around the intricately carved limestone. Round black eyes seem to leer out over the fields, forest, and cliffs at the distant ocean. He could picture the gargoyle sweeping down from the wall and alighting on the back of its prey, digging its talons into the wretch's bone and muscle so quickly there would be no time to cry out; there would only be death.

The moon grows brighter still, and Bram looks up, watching as the clouds part in a peculiar fashion. Rather than just drifting past, they split at the center, with some moving to the left and others to the right as if the moon blew them apart. The light of the moon falls on the gargoyle and casts an immense shadow of its beastly shape on the wall inside the room. As Bram watches, the shadow's head seems to turn, and its wings seem to stretch: the beast waking from a long slumber. The toes of the shadow's feet twitch and spread as the creature grows larger still and appears to step from its stone perch. Bram turns to look at the actual gargoyle outside his window, where it sits, unmoving and lifeless, as it has for centuries. The moon remains fixed, yet the shadow appears to be walking across the room, looming larger with each step. Bram stares as first one clawed hand and then the other tracks across the wall, crawling across stone, mirrors, crosses, inspecting the surroundings.

Bram reaches out and snatches one of the crosses from the wall, holding it between himself and the shadow. "Behold the Cross of the Lord! Begone, you!" he shouts. "God the Father commands you! The Son commands you! The sacred Sign of the Cross commands you! Leave this place, you unholy beast!"

This does nothing.

The shadow pauses at a large ornate mirror in the corner, then continues across the room, brushing every surface and object. When the wraith reaches the roses, it hesitates and shrinks back, carefully avoiding the blooms, before moving on to the chair and Bram's Snider–Enfield rifle lying on the ground beside it. Bram watches in awe as the shadow's molten blackness rounds the corner and continues along the wall—an impossibility, Bram knows, for the light of the moon can do nothing more than shine through the open window. Yet the creature stands there, a shadow amongst shadows, continuing to explore the chamber. Then he recalls the oil lamp and realizes the creature has somehow abandoned the concealing shadows of the moonlight and taken up its investigation by the light of the flickering oil lamp without so much as a pause between the two, a dance amidst the gloom. As it reaches the final corner, having come full circle, the shadow leaves the wall and oozes over the floor, expanding, until it comes upon the large oak door, where it then stops and falls still.

This isn't right, Bram.

The voice startles him, for Bram thought he was alone, and with renewed vigor he scans every inch of the room, the cross held up high as he rotates slowly in place, his own reflection staring back at him from the many mirrors adorning the walls.

"Show yourself!" Bram commands.

At his feet, the shadow stirs, rising from the floor to the door, growing until it nearly touches the ceiling.

"This is sorcery, nothing more. I will not stand for it!"

The shadow spreads its massive arms until they embrace the walls on either side, then grow longer still as they stretch around bends, encircling the room.

If you let me go, you won't have to die.

It is then Bram realizes the words came to him not from the large shadow before him or the creature trapped behind the door, nor from anywhere within the chamber; instead, the words echo within his mind as if his own thoughts had found voice.

The voice is neither male nor female but something in between, a strange mixture of high and low tones, sounding more like many voices than one in particular.

The hands of the shadow return to the door and trace its edges, translucent black-clawed fingers slithering over the frame and thick metal locks with the fluidity of molasses. When they reach the roses at the bottom, though, they carefully go around, rather than passing over them; either afraid or unable to touch them, like the roses in the basket.

Bram crosses the room, snatches another rose from the basket, and thrusts it out at the black specter. The shadow melts to a point of light as Bram finds the wood of the door with the rose clenched in his fist.

When he pulls back, the point of light disappears, swallowed by the shadow.

"I am not afraid of you!" Bram says in a voice that doesn't sound as strong as he hoped it would.

With that comes a laugh, a laugh of ungodly volume, a laugh composed of the screams of a thousand tortured children, and he steps back, nearly tripping over the chair.

I will gut you from groin to gullet and dance in your ruins as the blood bubbles from your lips if you do not open this door!

The shadow's hands again begin to spread over the walls, wrapping around the entire room, encircling him. The pointed nails of its talons lead the way as the shadow spreads over the room, creeping over every surface, mirrors and crosses alike, until it fills nearly every inch of space.

Bram runs to the window and slams the shutter. Then he goes to the oil lamp and blows out the flame, plunging the room into total blackness, a room so dark no shadow could live.

THE JOURNAL *of* BRAM STOKER

October 1854——Matilda and I left my room and descended the stairs with as much stealth as we could muster, pausing only at Nanna Ellen's room to open the door and ensure she was, in fact, gone. We found her window to be open wide and the room empty, save for Baby Richard sleeping soundly in his crib. I lowered my candle and pointed to the floor—the various tracks and prints we left earlier were gone but the dirt remained, spread smoothly over the surface once again. Her bed was made. Matilda nodded silently and crossed the hallway to the stairs, motioning for me to follow. I gently closed Nanna Ellen's door and caught up.

The hour was late, nearly eleven, and Ma and Pa had retired to their bedroom. If Thornley and Thomas had not yet found sleep, they made no sound to reveal that fact; their room was silent, and no light pooled from under the door. Our house was utterly quiet, and every sound we made seemed amplified—from the creak of the boards underfoot to the click of the front door's lock disengaging the front door. I was sure someone would hear us and come to investigate, but they did not, and within moments the two of us stood outside.

"If that was her," Matilda said, "she has gained a few minutes on us. Where do you think she would be heading?"

As I stood before our house, anxiety washed over me, and I leaned back against the door. I hadn't been outside in years—I remember how Ma held me tight as she carried me to the side of the house on a beautiful spring day to lie in the grass—I couldn't have been more than four years old at the time. I remember the vivid color of that April day, the bright scents, the warm breeze. I also remember how terrified I had been when she went back into the house to fetch a pitcher of water. She had been gone only a minute or so, but in that brief time the earth around me seemed to grow wider, the house looked as if it was moving farther and farther away until it was barely visible, and the sky hovering above seemed ready to fall. I wanted nothing more than to go back inside to the safety of my little refuge, to escape this endlessly empty place before it devoured me. When Ma came back, I told her my illness had returned and the aches and pains were too much. The truth, though, was that I simply couldn't stay out there. She only stared at me, a defeated look in her eyes. When I had begun to cry, she relented and picked me back up and carried me into the house. Until the episode with Thornley at the chicken coop, I would not venture outside again.

Even in the heavy darkness of this late hour the open space grew around me, much too big for a little boy to wander. A vast wilderness that could swallow me whole and leave nothing behind. I wanted to turn back, but I knew I could not.

I drew in a deep breath as Matilda reached for my hand. "We will do this together," she told me.

I wrapped my fingers around hers and felt her warmth drift through me, bringing with it a sense of calm. I summoned my strength. "We mustn't let her slip away."

My eyes drifted to the walls of Artane Castle in the distance. All but the tower was gone, the rest nothing but ruins. The tall monolith reached for the glowering sky and scratched at the clouds, imposing a shadow, long and wide, over the surrounding fields. I knew it had been built by the Hollywood family but knew little else of its history. Much of the stone had been carted away and picked clean over the years. Aside from the tower, only a handful of crumbling walls remained with a small cemetery nestled in the back.

We had been forbidden to enter the castle.

Matilda must have sensed my thoughts, for she squeezed my hand. "She went to the castle, didn't she?"

"I think so."

"But how could you know?"

I didn't answer her. I didn't have an answer. Much like I knew Nanna Ellen somehow left the house and stole outside, so, too, I simply knew she'd gone to the castle. I did not know her purpose, but I was certain she had gone there. I was dead certain she was there right now.

"Come on," I said, tugging Matilda's hand.

Matilda let out a labored sigh and faced the ruins. "Lead the way."

The moon hung low in the sky and offered only scant light. Although Matilda struggled seeing through the gloom, I had no trouble, and I led us through the quiet town, past the fields, towards the forest and the ruins of Artane Castle. Our home seemed so small behind us that I had to turn away out of fear of the anxiety rearing its ugly head again and preventing me from venturing farther. This time it was Matilda who was pulling me along.

As we neared the tower, the weeds and trees grew thicker. Soon we found ourselves pushing through chest-high coltsfoot and scutch grass. I searched for some kind of path but found none and cursed myself for not bringing a billhook. I had watched Thornley use such a blade to clear the arbor of some spent vines, and although I had never handled anything like it, I felt I could have sliced through this jungle with ease.

While Matilda seemed to be growing fatigued behind me, I became stronger with each step. Part of me wanted to run, but we needed to be cautious; Nanna Ellen might be close by, and we dared not allow her to see us.

I had never been this near to the castle. The tower was far larger than I expected, at least twenty feet wide, maybe more. The stones which made up the façade were enormous gray limestone squares, perfectly stacked, with little gaps between, a marvel of engineering for its day. After hundreds of years, parts of the structure still appeared as if they had been built yesterday. Moss crept up its sides, covering nearly the entire north side from ground to crown. I couldn't help but gaze up to the top of the tower, dizziness washing over me for standing so close.

There were three windows on this side, none within reach. Archers once perched there, I imagined, picking off enemy soldiers.

When the entrance came into view, Matilda and I crouched low in the tall weeds.

"Is she in there?" Matilda asked, shivering.

The October air had indeed grown chill, and although I wore my wool wrap, my skin still prickled with gooseflesh. Matilda had donned a wrap as well, but the temperature dropped with each inch of the moon's ascent, and even the warmest of garments could only hold it at bay for so long

"I don't see her," I replied.

"Is she in there?" Matilda repeated with a frustration in her voice.

I hadn't told Matilda outright that I sensed Nanna Ellen's presence, but I had not exactly hidden the fact, either, and while she may have doubted it earlier, her words now suggested she doubted no more. I myself could not explain how or why I was able to do such a thing, yet there it was, a strange tugging, as if a cord had been tied to Nanna Ellen and she was pulling me along behind her. That pull was accompanied by what could only be described as a tickling at the back of my mind, and as I grew closer to her, that tickling redoubled. It wasn't uncomfortable; quite the opposite—I found it soothing. This force wanted me to be close to her.

I faced the tower, my gaze tracing the tall formation from bottom to top, pausing at each of the windows not because I could see inside but because the openings somehow made it easier to feel inside. When my eyes reached the top, sight no longer necessary, I closed them and focused my mind on Nanna Ellen. I gripped the invisible cord and pulled myself along hand over hand until I was no longer in the field at the base of the castle, but floating first through the air, then passing through the thick limestone walls to the interior of the building to a winding set of stairs running along the far wall, to Nanna Ellen descending them. I saw her buttoning her cloak as she took the steps, then pulling the hood over her head. She didn't do this out of protection from the cold but because she didn't wish to be recognized

"She is coming out," I told Matilda. While I heard myself saying the words, it seemed as if I weren't the one saying them. It felt more like I was standing at a distance, watching a boy who looked like me speaking. "She's coming out *now*."

With that, my eyes snapped open, and I pulled Matilda to the ground as Nanna Ellen stepped from the gaping door of the castle out into the night. She was dressed as I had seen her from my bedroom window: a flowing black cloak buttoned at her neck fell nearly to her toes, sweeping over the crackling autumn leaves with a grace that made it appear as if she were floating just above the ground. I pictured her floating exactly like that back in her room at the house, somehow drifting over the floor's dirt rather than traipsing through it as Matilda and I had. The tugging sensation I had experienced, the tugging that drew me to her, was strongest now, so strong I worried I might be pulled to her side. My left hand squeezed Matilda's fingers while my right dug into the earth at my side in hopes of finding purchase.

Nanna Ellen paused for a moment at the castle's yawning mouth, glanced both left and right, then pressed forward down a thin, winding path into the forest. I did not dare speak until she disappeared from sight. "Do we follow her?"

"Into the woods?"

"I'm not sure that we should." I had never been in the woods before. This was, in fact, the farthest I had ever been from the house. To venture into the woods in the dead of night was foolish. But the cord that tied me to Nanna Ellen grew taut, and I wanted to go, I needed to go, even though I knew it to be the wrong course of action. Yet with each passing second, I felt Nanna Ellen drifting farther away.

For the first time, I wondered: If I can feel her nearby, can she feel me?

"I want to know where she's going," Matilda said. She shivered again, and I knew we must move.

I nodded; there really was no other answer but to follow.

We stood, and I led Matilda from the weeds to the mouth of the castle. If the air was cold outside, the air drifting from the castle was colder still. I gave its wide doorway a quick glance, then pulled Matilda down the path into the woods, leaving our world behind.

NANNA ELLEN moved fast.

Only minutes had passed since she disappeared from view, but it felt as if she had journeyed for miles. The cord that bound us was unraveling, yet I grasped it, with little regard for the distance growing between Matilda and me and home. Matilda was silent beside me, her fingers wrapped in mine, as she accompanied me down the narrow, winding path.

All around us, the ash trees loomed. Most of their leaves had been shed, but the bare branches left behind were so thick that the moon had to fight to find the ground. Between the ash, rusty willow trees filled the gaps with thick gnarled boughs dotted with catkins. Weasels ran along them, eyeing us curiously, and I spotted no fewer than three owls studying us from above.

Moss grew on nearly every surface, creating a blanket of green over the large boulders and roots. The ground was damp, so much so that my shoes sunk in slightly, a sucking sound accompanying each step. We would need to wash them thoroughly upon our return home; if Ma saw our shoes in such a state, she would surely figure out where we'd been— and, like the castle, these woods are forbidden. And what would she say to me about being so far from my bed?

"Can you see where you're going?" Matilda asked.

"You cannot?"

Matilda shook her head. "I can barely see *you*."

I thought she was jesting, but the look on her face told me otherwise; her eyes were wide, her face pale with fear. She didn't see the little animals scurrying about around us or the dark beauty of this place; her worried gaze was fixed on me.

I glanced around at our surroundings and realized I saw nearly as well as I did in full daylight. Even in the shadows at the base of the trees, I had no trouble spying the grubs feasting on rotted wood or the worms writhing in the black soil at our feet. I could even see tiny black ants crawling up the moss-riddled trunk of an elm tree nearly ten paces ahead of us.

"We need to keep moving," I told her. "Just stay close."

As we pressed on, a thin mist began to fill the air, and a stray wind drifted through the forest—initially only a mild breeze, but a few minutes later it gained strength, and a gust tore past us. The collar of my coat flapped against my cheeks, and I pulled Matilda closer. She wanted to go back, I sensed that much, but she would never speak the words aloud; her will was too strong. I often heard the fall winds whistle past my room, but I had never once stood in their midst; I found it exhilarating. The forest was alive around us; from the creatures to the swaying trees, I felt the forces of nature in the night air, the delicate balance of life and death.

The mist grew heavier as we continued down the path, swirling around us on the tail of the wind. It wasn't long before even I had trouble seeing more than a few feet in either direction. The mist reeked of dampness and the briny sea, no doubt the peat that flourished in abundance in this region and the harbor not so far off. I filled my lungs, breathing better now than I could ever recall.

I couldn't help but laugh—and the moment I did I regretted it, for Matilda stared at me as if I were a loon.

"It just feels good to be outside, that's all," I said, more to convince myself than her, but neither of us believed it. Something had changed within me; both she and I were aware of it, and it was then that I saw something in my sister's eyes I never hoped to see, something no brother ever hopes to see—

Fear.

Whether fear of me or fear of what she felt had altered within me, I could not be sure.

Her eyes squinted against the strengthening wind, and this time it was she who turned away and pressed on down the path with me in tow, her once-warm hand now clammy.

We continued on for nearly twenty full minutes, our feet digging into the muddy earth with each step as the wind struggled to hold us back. The forceful gale howled at us as it weaved in and out of the trees, a demented specter no way bound to this earth. From high and low the air cursed, pushing and pulling with such fearsome force I nearly lost my footing more than once; if not for Matilda at my side, I would have surely fallen.

Was the forest trying to turn us around?

I wanted to dismiss the thought, but it grasped my mind and held firm. Could a forest prevent someone from entering? I thought not, for even though a forest does live, it lacks consciousness or free will.

With that, the wind kicked up around us, and Matilda stumbled; I pulled her close and kept her from the mud at our feet, nearly falling in the process.

And if a forest couldn't prevent someone from entering, what about something dwelling within it?

The cord that bound me to Nanna Ellen suddenly grew taut once again, and I knew she was close.

A break in the mist revealed a large clearing before us. We came upon this place so fast there was little time to react. I pulled Matilda to the ground with me. She let out a soft cry, but my hand cupped over her mouth before any sound escaped. With my other hand, I pointed.

Nanna Ellen stood about twenty feet in front of us beneath a large willow tree. Twisted branches reached not only towards the sky but also out over the green peat-filled waters of a bog that began at the tree's base and disappeared somewhere in the distance, the edge lost in the thick mist. Moss dripped all around, the brown of the tree trunk nearly lost beneath.

It was then that the wind ceased. Although I heard it howling through the trees at our backs, this place somehow escaped its wrath.

Another owl stared down at us from high above, eyes big and black, glistening in the thin moonlight.

Nanna Ellen had her back to us, and I watched as she removed her hood and let her hair tumble to her shoulders. Something was wrong, though. Her hair was not the curly blond locks so familiar to us; instead, it was wiry and gray, and even at a distance appeared brittle and thin, patches of scalp clearly visible.

If Nanna Ellen knew we were there, she paid us no mind. She reached up to the clasp at her neck and unfastened the cloak, allowing it to puddle at her feet. She wore a thin white nightdress beneath, and nothing else. Her arms and legs were exposed, and I nearly gasped aloud. Her flesh was old and wrinkled, hanging limply from the bones and covered in the deep-blue veins of a much older woman. If I didn't know better, I would have thought her to be a grandmother of seventy years or more instead of the young woman I had known my entire life.

Matilda saw, too, for the mist had retreated to the nether reaches of the bog, and she clutched my forearm so tightly that I thought her nails would draw blood.

Nanna Ellen stepped from her cloak and walked into the waters of the bog. At first, the water only reached her ankles, but then she seemed to find a steep drop, and within a step it flowed past her knees; another step, and it found her waist. The white nightdress ballooned around her as she ventured yet another step, then another. With the next step, water embraced her shoulders, yet she continued forward. A moment later, she was gone, her head disappearing beneath the surface. The bubbling water had closed over her, leaving nothing behind save a thin ripple playing over the surface.

Beside me, Matilda drew a deep breath.

I scanned the surface of the calm water, awaiting her reappearance. For an anxious minute, I watched, then another minute. I began to get nervous, for nobody could hold their breath for so long. When a third minute passed, I stood and stepped forth from concealment into the clearing with Matilda at my back.

"Has she drowned? Has she taken her own life?" she asked.

I shook my head, even though I had no answer to offer. I could no longer sense Nanna Ellen's presence. She hadn't swum away; the bog was large, but not so large we would not see her break the surface at some point.

I looked out over the bog for any sign of life and found none. The location she went under was still. A thick layer of peat covered the surface, sealing the water from the night as if nothing had ever disturbed it. The remainder of the bog was much of the same. Had she come up for air, surely we would have spied her, but there was no sign.

"Should I go in after her?"

"You don't know how to swim," Matilda pointed out. "And neither do I."

I quickly made my way over to the willow tree and plucked a dead branch from near the base. Nearly six feet long and about an inch thick, it snapped off with little effort. I returned to the shore of the bog and used it to stir the surface of the water where she had disappeared. The peat moss was thick at the surface, and I thought the stick would break under the pressure, but it held. I forced the moss aside. The water underneath was opaque, black, more like oil than water, and each tap of the stick sent out slow ripples in all directions.

"Can you see her?" Matilda asked. She stood on her toes, trying to peer out into the water, but with little luck.

Although she was a year older, I was taller, but my height did little good here. I saw nothing beneath the surface. "How long has it been?"

Matilda said, "Five minutes, maybe more. I'm not sure."

"Maybe I should try throwing in a rock?"

"What good will that do?"

"I don't know." A dragonfly began buzzing around my head, and I swatted it away.

"That couldn't have been her," Matilda said.

"It was her, I'm sure."

"That was an old woman."

"It was her."

I reached to the ground and picked up the cloak. "This is Ma's cloak. See this tear?" I pushed my finger through a small hole in the right sleeve. "She told me she caught it on the cellar door about a month ago."

Tears began to well in Matilda's eyes. "I don't want Nanna Ellen to die."

"I don't think—" The dragonfly returned and flew directly into my eye. I slapped the air but missed. When a second flew from the woods at our left and darted between us, I ducked out of the way, my hand covering my injured eye. I turned to find Matilda fighting off three more.

Across the bog came a buzzing noise. Faint, but quickly growing in intensity. I peered into the haze at the far end and didn't spot anything at first; then the white mist parted, and a black cloud came bellowing out from the center. The hum grew louder as it approached.

"What is that sound?" Matilda asked, slapping at the dragonflies circling her head. Two more joined the original three, and four others darted past me on the left. One landed in her hair, wings flapping incessantly as they became entangled. She cried out in disgust and tried to pull the insect free.

My eyes fixed on the black swarm drifting over the bog. Hundreds more, possibly thousands. I snatched the dragonfly from Matilda's hair and thrust it to the ground, grinding it into the dirt with the sole of my shoe, before I pulled her from the water's edge. "Come on, we need to go—"

As we darted back into the woods with the swarm at our backs, I spotted something out of the corner of my eye that haunts me to this day. A hand reached up from the bog, snatched a dragonfly from the air, and returned to the water.

I SAT UP IN BED. I was somehow back in my bed, the room's dark marred only by a sliver of moonlight. I couldn't recall returning home; the memory of the dragonflies was still fresh in my mind. I could still smell the bog, the musky scent of the peat-filled water.

I crawled out of bed and went to the window.

I was wearing my nightclothes yet had no recollection of changing into them.

Staring out into the night, my eyes found the tower of Artane Castle and the forest beyond. I tried to peer past the forest to the bog on the other side, but the distance proved to be, even for me, far too great.

Had I dreamed it?

· · ·

MY ARM began to itch.

It was then that I spotted my shoes in the far corner beside the dressing table, caked with mud, glistening in the dim light. I had just started towards them when her voice scraped against the silence.

"You should not leave your room, Bram, not at night. Bad things happen to little boys who wander the forest in the dark."

I spun around, expecting to find Nanna Ellen standing behind me, but all I found was my closed door and the twisted sheets of my bed.

"The forest is full of wolves. They'd tear the flesh from your bones. They'd dig their muzzles into your belly until their hungry tongues found your heart and liver, then they'd gobble them with a smack of their lips. At last, they'd suck your eyes right out of the sockets. Have you ever seen a vulture do such a thing? It's an amazing thing to witness. Just a quick little pluck, and there is nothing left behind but a gaping black hole."

NANNA ELLEN GIGGLED, a childish little laugh reminiscent of Matilda playing hide-and-seek, in the moments before I discover her beneath the bed. She always hid beneath the bed.

I pivoted full circle, my mind taking in every inch of my room, my eyes able to see perfectly even in the dark. There was no sign of Nanna Ellen.

"You have to be quicker than that!" she said.

A hand tapped the back of my shoulder, and I spun around again, ready to face her, yet there was nobody there.

"Stop this game!" I said.

"Shhhh," she whispered at my ear. "You don't want to awaken the family!"

I swatted at the sound as I had the dragonfly at the bog, but my hand found only air.

"It's good to see you with so much energy! A week ago, you couldn't stand there without help. Yet tonight you ransacked my room, sneaked outside, and ventured a great distance from home and back, without the slightest sign of exhaustion. If I didn't know any better, I would say your Uncle Edward cured you with the tricks in that black bag of his!"

I dropped down to the floor and searched under my bed. Finding nothing, I darted across the room to my cupboard and pulled open the doors, expecting Nanna Ellen to come rushing out, but I found nothing inside except my clothes hanging above and my Sunday shoes side by side below. "Where are you?"

"I'm right here!"

Another tap on my shoulder.

This time I spun around in the opposite direction and simultaneously reached out with both hands. For a fleeting second, my fingertips slid across flesh, but she was simply too fast—gone from my grasp before I even got a look at her.

"Almost had me! My oh my, you are fast!"

Her skin was clammy, as if I had brushed a corpse. A shiver walked my spine, and I wiped my hand on my shirt, attempting to rid myself of the ghastly sensation.

"What was it like? To be covered in leeches? Could you feel those nasty little creatures sucking the blood through your pores? Your fever was so great I bet you didn't even notice their tiny little teeth gnawing through your skin, did you? They looked like plump apples when your Uncle Edward finally peeled them away and dropped them back in his jar. He swore they pulled the illness right out of you, and I guess he was right; look at you now!"

"I know it wasn't my uncle who cured me," I said in a voice so low I wasn't sure she heard me.

"No? Who, then?" she replied. "Because you look much better now than you have in all your days. I wouldn't venture to say you've been cured, but you look much better, much better by far."

"You asked if I trusted you, and I said I did."

"Did I?"

"Then you did something to me."

Again, she laughed. "Something, yes. Maybe. Maybe I did."

I paced the chamber, my eyes sweeping over every shadow in search of Nanna Ellen. Her voice seemed to be coming from all around me yet from no direction in particular. She was close, though; I could feel her nearby. That cord which bound us together was pulled taut. I closed my eyes and focused on that image now, reeling in the line through sheer willpower, forcing the distance between us to close.

Nanna Ellen let out another laugh, this one so loud I was certain the others would be shaken from their slumber. "Perhaps your young age plays a part, but I have never seen someone accept and attempt to master a new skill so easily. Maybe it's because adults lose the ability to imagine, to believe in that which is unknown. Children accept a mystery as fact, and move past it as clear as day, giving it nary a second thought. Nonetheless, I am impressed by you, young Bram."

I pulled the cord tight, but it was still to no avail. Like her voice, she was all around me yet nowhere, a wraith loose in the void.

My arm itched, and I fought the urge to scratch it. "What did you do to me?" I regretted the words the moment I uttered them, for I wasn't quite sure I wanted the answer.

"Well, I walked you back from the Gates of Hell last night and rescued you from the Devil's touch, of course. Is that not what your sweet sister said?" The words came so close at my ear I swore the warmth of her breath touched me. This time I didn't turn, for I knew she would not be there. I remained still, my mind focusing on the cord, attempting to reel it in a little closer. I took a step towards the window.

"Oh, you're getting warmer! Red rover, red rover, send little Bram on over!"

The leaded glass window rattled as thunder rumbled somewhere off in the distance. The first drops of rain found the glass and ticked against the pane, first only a few, then the sky opened up and it came down so heavy the world washed away.

"What were you doing out at the bog? We saw you go into the water and you didn't come back out."

"Yet I am here."

"Are you?"

I reached for the window latch and gave it a twist, then pushed the window out into the night on squeaky hinges. The rain felt like ice on my skin, yet I welcomed it, for like stepping out into the forest earlier, being touched by nature reminded me that I was, indeed, alive.

"Careful, Bram. You'll catch your death!"

I wanted to believe that I could no longer get sick, that whatever Nanna Ellen did to me cured me of all my ailments, but even as the thought entered my mind, I felt the tickle of a cough at the back of my throat. The ache in my bones that had followed me my entire life was there, too, although not as strong as before; the pain remained, a reminder that my sickness wasn't gone but resting, preparing to return. "I know I'm not better, not completely."

At this, she did not respond.

I scratched at my arm, unable to ignore the incessant itch any longer.

Then I thrust my head out the window into the pouring rain and glanced side to side and up and down, my eyes squinting through the downpour at the walls of our house. I didn't know why I thought I would find Nanna Ellen clinging to the worn stucco, but I did think just that. Yet I found nothing but the rain-drenched roads, and I pulled myself back inside.

"I thought you said I was getting warmer?"

"I did, but now you are so very cold."

Nanna Ellen dropped from the ceiling.

I spotted her out of the corner of my eye and tried to sidestep her, but she came down too fast, unnaturally so, as if she weren't falling but had pushed off from the ceiling with tremendous force. As I tried to move out of the way, I watched her come at me, her arms and legs outstretched like a spider pouncing upon some unwitting prey. Her eyes were no longer the pale gray of the woman we spotted out at the bog, nor were they the blue I remembered most, but the fiercest red, burning through the otherwise dark room.

"Bram!"

The call of my name came as if from a great distance, as if I were at the bottom of a well, and someone shouted for me from the mouth of the hole high above.

This place was so dark not a glint of light survived, and it was filled with the stale odor of rot. When I tried to move, I found my muscles no longer worked; I was trapped within a lifeless body.

The dirt of my grave, packed good and tight.

I saw it all again: Nanna Ellen coming at me, dropping from the ceiling, covering me and pinning me to the floor beneath her weight.

Then she breathed in my ear, "Sleep, my child."

With that, all was lost, and I knew no more.

"Bram!"

I heard my name again, this time much closer than before, and with it came a red light, faint but quickly growing in intensity as it either approached me or I approached it; I could not be sure, for I felt like I was in motion while at the same time the room was in motion around me, carrying me from this place to that.

My body shook, and my eyes snapped open. I found Matilda hovering over me.

As she came into focus, strength returned to my arms and legs, and my entire body came to life all at once, flailing this way and that, then finally pushing off the top of my bed with such power I left the surface altogether, hovered in the ether for a brief moment, then came crashing back down.

Matilda stared at me, her mouth agape, and I suddenly grew both embarrassed and afraid all at once.

"DID IT HAPPEN?" I asked.

Before I finished the sentence, Matilda was nodding her head. "The last thing I recall is running from the dragonflies in the forest. Then I awoke in my bed with the light of morning against my cheek. I do not know how we arrived home, and I don't remember getting undressed or crawling into bed. Yet I awoke in my bedclothes, tucked in under the blankets as I would any other night. At first, I wasn't sure, either, but I found my coat covered in burrs from the forest." She paused, then frowned. "You're bleeding—"

"What?"

She wiped at the corner of my mouth with her finger. "It's dry. A few hours old, at least. I don't see a cut, though; only a little dried blood. Did you bite your tongue?"

"Maybe," I said, although I felt no pain.

"What is the last thing you remember?"

I thought about this, for I, too, remembered running through the forest in an attempt to escape the dragonflies. I also remembered the hand reaching up from the water of the bog and snatching one of the flies midair. The hand was fat and wrinkled like a prune, as if it had spent an eternity beneath the water. And the way it grabbed that dragonfly! I was reminded of a frog's tongue striking out lightning fast.

But then I was home, back in bed—the time transpiring between these two events utterly lost to me.

And then there was my encounter with Nanna Ellen.

"You must tell me what you remember," Matilda said, as if divining my thoughts.

So I did; I told her everything.

When I finished, she was not staring at me with the disbelief I expected; instead, her face only deepened with concern and worry. "I found your window ajar when I came in. Look, the rainwater is still puddled beneath . . ."

Ma would have sealed the window before going to bed; she always did. Even during the most stifling of months, she shut my window and locked out the night air for fear of me catching a cold, or worse. My ailment simply wouldn't tolerate such conditions. I had opened the window last night, just as I remembered.

"So why don't we remember coming home?"

Her question lingered in the air, for neither of us had an answer.

Matilda's eyes shifted; she looked down at my arm. I scratched at it, in an absence of mind. I stopped and tried to move my arm under the blanket. Matilda would have none of it; she grabbed my arm and pulled it towards her. "You've been scratching at this since you got better; you must let me see!"

I pulled the arm back with such force my hand cracked into the headboard with a loud thwack. So loud, in fact, I would not have been surprised to find a crack in the oak. Yet my hand seemed fine, unmarked. I quickly tucked it under the blanket.

Matilda stared at me in awe. A few days ago, she was much stronger than me—easily able to hold both my arms back with a single hand, as she had done on so many occasions, yet now I pulled away from her with such ease.

"What has become of you?" she said in a low voice. "Did she do this to you?"

I did not respond; I simply didn't know what to say.

"Let me see your arm, Bram."

BENEATH MY BLANKET, my arm began to itch again, not a little itch like that brought on by a spider walking across your forearm but the kind that would be brought on by a dozen fresh mosquito bites. I tried to ignore it, but it grew fiercer. I rubbed my arm against my torso, but this did little good. Only my nails would appease the itch.

Matilda said, "You're twitching, Bram. Let me see. You can trust me."

I could take no more, and I pulled the arm out from under the blanket and scratched through my nightshirt with enough force that had I been dragging my nails across the surface of a table I surely would have left gouges. When the itch finally subsided, I reached for the cuff of my sleeve and tugged it up with one quick motion, my eyes fixed on Matilda.

My sister stared down at my arm, at my pale flesh. She drew closer, then closer still. When she finally spoke, she kept her eyes fixed on the appendage. "I don't see anything."

"No, but you should. The last time Uncle Edward bled me with leeches, the welts they left behind remained for nearly two weeks. First, as red blotches, then blotches surrounded by black and blue. Eventually, they scabbed over and began to fade. Only two days have passed, and there is no sign of what he did, only this incessant itching."

"Maybe he did something different? Maybe he didn't leave them on quite as long?"

I was already shaking my head. "I healed faster. I know I did. Then there is this—"

I pulled up the sleeve on my right arm and showed her my wrist. Like my left arm—and my legs, for that matter—all signs of the leeches were gone. My flesh was smooth and pure as the day I was born, all but for my right wrist.

Matilda took my hand in her own. The two small pinpricks of red glistened, scabs freshly scratched away, two tiny marks about an inch and a half apart, just below the wrist bone over the vein—the itch greatest here most of all.

Neither of us heard Ma come in and stand in the doorway until she spoke. "Have you seen Nanna Ellen? Her room is empty, and all her belongings are gone."

MATILDA AND I bounded from the bed and raced down the hall. I heard Ma's gasp as I ran past her—she was staring at me, at just how quickly I moved. I reached the door of Nanna Ellen's room before Matilda and stared.

The floor was spotless; all the soil we found yesterday had vanished—not just swept away, for that would have left traces, but as if it had never been there. The window that had been covered was now bare, and light was streaming in, washing over the space. It seemed like a different room, no longer the void we had found yesterday, but instead a simple, empty chamber. Soft cooing emanated from Baby Richard, who was observing us intently as we stepped inside, both his tiny little hands clutching his elevated foot.

Nanna Ellen's desk was vacant, the papers gone. Her wardrobe stood open, stripped of clothing. Matilda and I both turned to her bed—perfectly made, the sheets pulled tight. I walked over and lifted the mattress, expecting to find the bed frame filled with dirt as it had been, but instead the space was full of fresh hay, as it should be.

"It's gone," I muttered.

"What's gone?" Ma replied from the doorway.

I glanced to Matilda, who was subtly shaking her head.

I returned the mattress back to the frame. "I meant *she's* gone. I misspoke."

"Did she say anything to either of you? Anything at all that would explain where she would go? Or why?"

"Nothing," we both replied simultaneously.

Ma eyed us with that look every mother seems to have perfected, the one that says *I know you're lying. And if you don't tell me the truth right this instant, I will pull it out of you.*

"Did she leave a note?" Matilda asked.

"She did not," Ma replied. "Of course, that would have been the proper thing to do. For that matter, she should have told me directly if she wished to leave our employ. To sneak off like this in the middle of the night without so much as the courtesy of a parting conversation is not like Ellen. We brought her into our home. For seven years, we provided her with food, shelter, and employment. I find it outrageous that she would pack up her things like this and depart. What am I to do without her? I cannot be expected to run this household and watch after five children on my own. Where am I to find a replacement? What could possibly have driven her to this?"

"Maybe we should go to the train station? She may still be there," Matilda pointed out. "Or perhaps the docks?"

"When did you see her last?" Ma asked.

Matilda appeared to think about this for a moment, then said, "She went to bed after dinner. She said she was not feeling well and wanted to get some rest."

"Should we check the hospital?" I offered.

Ma ignored my suggestion. "And you, Bram? When did you last see Nanna?"

"At dinner," I said, hoping my eyes would not betray me.

Ma stared at me for a moment, and I thought for sure she saw through my lie. Then she let out a deep breath. "Matilda, I'm going to need you to watch Baby Richard. I'll ask Thornley to go into town with me and try to find her. I doubt she's gone very far, not if she's ill and carrying all her possessions."

"What shall I do, Ma?" I asked of her. My arm began to itch again, and I fought the urge to scratch.

"What am I to tell your father?" Ma pondered aloud, ignoring my query. "After seven years, she just up and leaves . . ."

I watched her turn and head back down the stairs, then I went to Nanna Ellen's desk and began rifling through the drawers.

"What are you looking for?" Matilda asked.

"I don't know, anything. How could she clear out all her worldly goods like this without anyone noticing?" I discovered nothing in the desk and crossed the room to the wardrobe. Leaning in, I began running my fingers along the inside surfaces. "She must have left something behind."

"She left because of us, didn't she?" Matilda asked.

I paused. "We weren't meant to see her."

"I'm going to miss her," she said, and her lower lip quivered.

"Matilda, she's some kind of monster!"

"She never hurt us."

"You saw her walk into the bog and not come back out," I countered.

"I thought I did, but that doesn't make it true. Nor does it make her dangerous," she replied. "The mist was so thick, and we were cold and tired; maybe we just imagined we saw her going into the bog. We don't know for sure that was even her."

"She was wearing Ma's cloak."

"So you said."

In my mind, I again saw her dropping from the ceiling, her eyes flaming red. I pulled the sleeve of my nightshirt up and pointed at the two red marks. "What about these?"

Matilda's face grew firm. "Do you know for a fact she was the one who did that to you?"

"Of course; I saw her. She—"

"You saw her drop from the ceiling and pounce on you like some wild beast. I know. That is what you said, right? Just for a second, let us accept that something like that really did happen. She flew through your room and landed atop you. Did you see her attack your wrist?"

"I—" I had not, and I stopped myself before I admitted as much to Matilda. "If not her, who then?"

"And if it was her, how exactly did she do it? Am I to believe she bit you? She bared her fangs and pierced your flesh like a wild dog?"

"Yes," I said in a voice that did not sound convincing even to me. Finding nothing in the wardrobe, I sat down on the edge of the bed next to my sister.

"Bring her back, Bram. I want her back. I don't want her to go. I love her."

"We need to go to Artane Castle, to the tower."

MA AND THORNLEY didn't return until nearly suppertime. They had found no sign of Nanna Ellen in town, and none of our neighbors had seen her. She was simply gone.

We awaited nightfall, for all in the house to give in to slumber; then

Matilda and I crept silently from our rooms, down the stairs, and to the front door of the house, as we had the night before. The wind was still, hauntingly so, as we stepped out of the house and I gently closed the door behind us. We crossed the fields at a run, doing our level best to keep to the shadows and avoid those places where we might be spotted.

Matilda uttered not a word as we went, which I found troubling. Under most circumstances, it was difficult to prevent her from chattering, particularly when nervous. I glanced at her from the corner of my eye and found her brow furrowed, her gaze riveted straight ahead. I could not expect her to believe what I had told her about Nanna Ellen; even after what we had already seen, it was too fanciful. Yet I wanted her to. I didn't want to be alone in this pursuit. She witnessed Nanna Ellen walking into the bog, just as I had. She witnessed Nanna Ellen disappearing beneath the surface of the bog, and remaining submerged far longer than any normal person could, just as I had. Matilda hadn't seen the hand emerge from the water and snatch the dragonfly from the air, but that didn't make it any less true.

When I glanced back up, we were approaching the coltsfoot and scutch grass, made worse by the brambles and vines that surrounded the castle on all four sides. Matilda's gaze was still fixed ahead. When she finally did speak, she whispered, "Can you still feel her?"

"So you believe that, but not what happened in my room?"

"I—" she stuttered. "I don't know. Maybe. I'm not sure, I don't know."

"I have never lied to you, Matilda. Why would I make up such a thing?"

Matilda let out a sigh. "She was—*is*—our friend. I've known her my entire life; you have known her your entire life as well. She has never harmed us. She has done nothing but care for us as if we were her own children." She paused for a second, her mind searching for the right words. "The way you described her, you made her out to be a monster.

A thing of nightmares, dropping down upon you in such a horrid manner, and to what end? She tells you to sleep? Look at you. You have not left that bed in months. I don't recall a time when you ever left the house without assistance, and yet within one day's time you go from the brink of death to a fitness that rivals my own. Is she responsible for this? If yes, why would she wish you harm?"

"I don't know that she meant to harm me."

"And your arms," Matilda went on. "For the wounds left behind by the leeches to disappear so, it isn't possible. Yet it happened. I presume they are gone from your legs as well?"

I nodded.

"How?"

"I wish I knew."

The itch was there, though, always there. I found myself scratching at my arm even now.

"And that incessant itch?" Matilda stomped ahead. "I don't understand what to make of any of this."

I dropped my arm to my side and chased after her, pushing through the thick weeds.

Matilda stopped and stared up at the castle looming ahead against the night sky. "You didn't answer my original question."

"What question?"

"Can you feel her?"

I fell still and peered up at the forbidding castle. The weathered stones dripped with ivy and moss. As I focused my eyes, I spotted tiny ants crawling over the surface, skittering this way and that, unnaturally active considering the frosty air, with a purpose known only to them. There were spiders, too, hundreds of them, spinning their wicked webs amongst the leaves of ivy in hopes of snaring flies. I witnessed all of this, and knew Matilda had not. She stood at my side, shivering in the chill air, staring up at the castle's vacant windows.

I closed my eyes and thought about Nanna Ellen. I didn't feel the cord binding us as I had on the previous night, let alone the tug that came with it. I felt abandoned at this thought. She had abandoned my family, this was true, but I had somehow believed she had not abandoned me. She was not there, though, and I felt nothing.

I shook my head.

"Well, come on, then," Matilda said, following the perimeter of the square tower around to the front and its large arched entryway.

The opening was nearly twelve feet in height and eight feet in width and reeked of damp earth and mildew. I spied a mouse in the far corner; it stood on its hind legs and stared back at us defiantly, trespassers upon the creature's domain. I watched it scurry away and disappear into a fissure in the stone. At one point, a large door had stood in this very place, but it had long since rotted away. A few decomposing scraps of wood still littered the ground, feeding the termites. The remains of a large metal lock, kicked aside ages ago, rusted away against the left wall.

To the left of the tower entrance stood the only other portion of the castle to survive intact: a single-story square building nearly eighty feet in length and thirty feet in depth with walls that had once stood at least fifteen feet tall but were now nothing more than a crumbling ruin. The roof of this sorry structure was long gone, and trees and weeds now grew in what had once been the great hall. Thornley used to spend a great deal of time here when he was younger, playing. He would come here alone after completing his chores and remain for hours on end. He called this place the Castle of the King. Matilda would tease him by calling him the King of Crumble Castle, before he had chased her away.

Matilda and I stood there, two tiny figures lost against the giant gaping mouth of this place. Then we took each other's hands and stepped into the blackness, leaving the forest behind.

NOW

―――――――◆―――――――

Nearly an hour passes before Bram musters the courage to bring flame to the wick of the lantern and cast light once again about the room. When he finally does, he does so with bated breath as the oil lamp comes to life, at last forcing the shadows into retreat.

Bram waits for the shadow creature to return, but it does not. Nor does anything stir behind the door. Instead, the chamber falls into utter silence, so much so that Bram finds himself opening the shutters in hopes of admitting a hint of the natural world. As he does so, he leans out the window, breathing in the bracing night air. He finds the moon has edged farther along its path; nearly half of the night now behind him.

Returning to the chair at the center of the room, he sits and pulls from his coat pocket a small flask. He shouldn't drink, he knows, particularly on a night like this, but as the adrenaline leaves his body he suddenly feels uncomfortable and needs to warm up. Bram twists off the cap and brings the flask to his lips; he savors every drop of the plum brandy as it warms his gullet and settles in his stomach. Then he twists the cap back on and drops the flask into his pocket before taking up his rifle, which he holds at the ready, the barrel angled towards the door.

The last rose he had placed at the threshold of the door is now nothing more than a tangle of rotted black on the stained stone. If he didn't know the dried-out husk had once been a rose, he would not have been able to discern as much. He considers replacing it but changes his mind; a quick inventory revealing he has only four roses left. The holy water is nearly gone, and he has spent the last of the communion wafers making the paste he used in an attempt to seal the door. It has done little good; the evil inside has caused the mixture to dry and turn to dust. Even now, as he stares at the door, a chunk of wafer falls from the top left corner and cracks on the floor in a bit of dust. Another chunk falls after that, and soon another. It will not take long for the rest of the wafer paste to come down; then there will be nothing holding that door closed but the large metal lock across its midsection and the rose at its foot.

BRAM'S EYES grow heavy, and he shakes his head.

Sleep calls to him, a siren's song.

I won't hurt you, Bram. It was wrong of me to say I would.

The voice comes to him again from somewhere deep within his own head. Not the thick and heavy voice from earlier, but a soft and child-like voice, female, the voice of an angel.

Bram ignores her, unwilling to acknowledge anything at all.

It is cold in here, Bram. And lonely. I have never been in such a dismal place. If you open the door and let me out, there is so much I can share with you. Knowledge of things so incredible you will not believe they are true until I show them to you; then, you will never deny them again.

Bram sits up straight in the chair and raises the barrel of the gun; it had begun angling downward. Holding up such a weighty weapon is growing difficult for his fatigued hands.

You wish me to show you these things, do you not, Bram? Give you the answers to the questions you have asked your entire life? You know you do. Why else would you write of such things? These events from your childhood—they are significant, to be sure—your adventures with your sweet sister. How is Matilda? I miss her so.

The voice changes then, morphing to a slightly deeper voice, a familiar voice, Matilda's voice.

You wouldn't treat me this way, would you? Lock me away in a room and hope for death to steal me away in the middle of the night? Ma would be so displeased with you, treating a lady in such an ill manner. Imagine what Pa would do if he found out! Oh, he would take you over his knee and switch your bottom like you were still a child. He would send you crying to your room, your little attic, the source of so many adventures in later years, but also a place of so much sickness at the start. I'm so glad you're writing about those times, all those memories. I remember all as if it were yesterday, and I find the need to point out that you omitted a lot. I know you are rushed, but a good storyteller never leaves gaps, and I think it would be in your best interest to go back and think about what you left out. Better yet, I could help you! Open the door, and I will pore over every page with you and help you recall it all. Remember the hand in the bog? Would you not like to know who that was? You assumed it was Ellen, but are you sure? I could tell you. Wait—I could show you! I could take you there by holding your hand, and together we can walk up to the shore of that bog and peer into the murky depths with fresh eyes. We could revisit the castle, too. Imagine what it would be like to return there and tell your childhood self what you know now! Can you picture such a thing? We could kneel down at the water's edge and take hold of that hand and pull her close, pull her out of the water. Then we could let her sink her teeth into the fleshy part of our forearms and drink. Is that not what you crave? It would make the itching stop. I guarantee it.

Bram reaches into the basket, picks up another rose, and hurls the flower at the door. He watches it hit the wood, then slide down as if hovering in the air, riding the dust, floating to the stone.

A laugh erupts from behind the door, a laugh so loud the rifle slips from his hands and clatters to the floor. Bram scrambles to snatch it back up and aim the barrel towards the laugh.

You're getting careless, Bram. You forgot to bless your flower; must be the fatigue setting in.

Bram watches in horror as the petals of the rose fall away, one by one, leaving nothing but a thorny stem. The entire mess grows black before his eyes and crumbles away. Behind the door, the laugh comes again, then a loud bang on the door. More of the paste around the edges falls to the ground with the blow, and Bram feels his heart sink as he drops back into the chair.

The laugh fades away, and again the room fills with silence followed by the voice in his head, his sister's.

I used to love picking flowers in the commons outside our home in Clontarf; do you remember? We had a park right outside our door, and the harbor beyond that, Artane behind us. Ma used to take me for walks along the shoreline. We would picnic and watch the ships drift in from the sea. Those were special times. Of course, you were already ill, even back then. You were nothing but a thin wisp of a boy, so frail you looked as if a tumble from your bed might be the death of you.

I remember Nanna Ellen tucking you in each night and telling you a story. Sometimes she would let me sit in, but even if she didn't I could hear her from my room and I would listen to every word. Does that bother you, Bram? Does it bother you I eavesdropped on your private moments?

Bram says nothing.

Her stories were so enthralling; I couldn't resist. If you ask me, they were wasted on you. Half the time, you were in such a fevered state you didn't know where you were, let alone able to offer the attention they deserved. And even on those rare nights when you did listen, you would drift off to sleep long before the story was complete. I would be willing to wager you never once heard the end of one of her stories. I did, though. I learned how they all end. Every last one of them. That night when she pounced on you from the ceiling? I know how that story ended. Would you like me to tell you?

Bram takes a deep breath in through his nose and lets the air back out through his mouth. Sleep tries to capture him, his eyelids threatening to surrender. He stands away from the chair, takes three circuits around the room, then sits back down. He wants another drink of the brandy, but that isn't wise; brandy will only make him more tired.

"There you go again, drifting off to sleep in the middle of a story."

This time the voice is that of Nanna Ellen, exactly as he remembers her from his childhood. And the voice doesn't sound like it is inside his head anymore; this time the voice comes from behind the door, muffled by its thick oak.

"I didn't want to leave that night, I really didn't, but you and your sister gave me little choice. You should have never gone into my room. You had no business in there, in my private space. I would have never entered your bedroom like that, unbidden. I would never have considered rifling through your belongings like a common thief rifling through a victim's possessions. I loved you—you, and your sister, too."

Bram feels his eyes drift shut, and he forces them open and sucks in a deep breath. The musty air is so thick with dank dust, it tickles at the back of his throat. He reaches into his pocket, pulls out the flask, and allows himself another drink.

"You're sitting here as an adult because of me, Bram. You know that, right? I could have left you to die that night, but I didn't. I saw what mischief your witch doctor of an uncle was conjuring and I stepped in to quell it, your mother and father be damned. You have no idea what kind of trouble that brought on me, do you? I did these things because I loved you, I loved you as my own. I still do."

Bram ignores her. The brandy muffles her voice, if only for a little while. It clears the fog in his head and brings warmth to his tired bones. He returns the flask to his pocket.

"Do you remember all those days we spent in your room, just the two of us? Lying atop your bed, telling stories. Oh, how we laughed! I'm sure I scared you, too; some of those tales were quite wicked! Remember the Dearg-Due? You were in a bit of a fever when I told you that one."

The word is familiar, but he cannot recall the story.

"She was trapped in a room not unlike this one and look what happened to her. Look at what happened to the people who put her there. Oh, I would hate to see you suffer such a fate. If you open the door, you'll never have to worry about these things. I can keep you safe."

Another chunk of the blessed wafer paste falls from the edge of the door and cracks into a dozen pieces on the stone floor. Bram barely notices, though; his only thoughts are of sleep, how much he wants to and how he cannot succumb—a battle waged behind heavy lids.

"Perhaps you should take a nap. Just a short one. Just enough to cleanse your thoughts. I'm sure after you wake you'll realize what a horrible mistake you've made. Go ahead and close your eyes; I'll watch over you. It will be like when you were a child."

The rifle slips from Bram's hand and clatters to the floor at his feet. He thinks about picking it up, but his arms seem so heavy, the gun seems so heavy, his eyelids so . . .

"Sleep, Bram, sleep. I've got you."

THE JOURNAL of BRAM STOKER

<hr />

October 1854—As we stepped inside Artane Tower, I immediately noticed a dip in temperature. Matilda's hand trembled in mine, and I knew she noticed, too. The entranceway opened onto a large square room, at least twenty feet across, with stone steps, narrow and steep, protruding from the outer walls and held in place by nothing more than strategic placement. To peer upwards proved dizzying, and as I did so, my body wobbled. There was no banister, only the smooth steps, each being only a treacherous two feet wide, with some even less so, chipped and cracked by time and lost to age, and with each step's corners pointed in shape to accommodate the upwards circling of the stairs. And there were more steps to climb than I dared count; I did not want to know how many. Although two of the windows we had spotted from outside were visible, the third was not. I suspected the staircase ended with a chamber at the very top overlooking the Artane Valley and surrounding forest. The tower was originally designed for defense, and such a position would be advantageous, allowing for a view miles around.

Along the walls, candles burned at every seventh step, their flames an unnatural hue of blue. I stepped to the first of these to get a closer look. The flame danced at the wick and seemed to bend towards me as I approached. I found this to be particularly strange since there was no breeze in this place to speak of. Yet, as I moved my hand closer to the flame, it bent to greet me. And when I moved away, the flame moved in concert, resuming an upright position. Stranger yet, a blue flame usually indicated great heat, but there was no heat, no warmth at all, as if I were watching the image of a flame rather than the actual flame itself.

"She must have lit this candle recently; I see no evidence of melted wax. They haven't been burning long," Matilda pointed out from my side.

She was right. Not a single drip of wax leaked down the side of the candle, nor was there any buildup at the base. Either a candle burned here for the first time or someone had cleaned the candleholder before lighting this one.

Once again, I closed my eyes and reached out to Nanna Ellen. She had to be close—yet I felt nothing, no sign of her at all.

When I opened my eyes, I found Matilda standing on the eighth step, shuffling her feet tentatively against the crumbling stone. The step seemed to be holding up under her weight. "I think it's safe."

As she spoke these fateful words, something large and black came down at us from the top of the tower, falling with such speed and purpose I barely had time to react before it swooped past and then circled back up. Matilda let out a startled scream and fell from the staircase towards the stone floor, and I darted towards her in an attempt to break her fall. The two of us landed in a heap at the bottom.

"Are you hurt?" I asked.

She rolled off me and climbed back to her feet. "I don't think so. What was that?"

I stood and brushed the dust from my coat. "I think it was a bat. A very large bat."

"You're bleeding."

I followed her eyes to the palm of my hand, where crimson from a cut about an inch long shimmered in the pale blue light. I gently touched my palm with my other hand. "It doesn't hurt; I don't think it's very deep."

I pulled a handkerchief from the pocket of my trousers and wrapped it around the wound as a makeshift bandage.

The large bat came back down, first circling high above, then diving directly between us. Both Matilda and I reared back, dodging the creature as it passed less than a few inches from our eyes. I watched the black bat soar back up, then alight upon a wooden beam about ten feet above our heads that ran the length of the tower. The vile creature glared down at us with beady red eyes. The image of Nanna Ellen again popped into my head and I shook it away.

I expected Matilda would wish to leave, but instead she again grasped my hand and started up the steps, pulling me behind her. Undeterred by the bat.

I stood still. "What if it swoops down again when we're way up there?" I asked, pointing at the staircase far above our heads. "A fall from that height would most certainly mean death."

"Then, perhaps, we shouldn't fall," she replied.

I remained still.

Matilda tugged at my hand. "We will watch it closely. I was spooked once; I will not be spooked again."

A mouse scurried past our feet and came to a halt between us and the entrance to the tower, a mouse so plump it could easily be mistaken for a rat. It was nibbling at something, but I couldn't make out exactly what. As if to prove her point, Matilda didn't flinch at the sight of the rodent; she stood firm.

I nodded my head, took a deep breath, and the two of us began to ascend the steps. With this, the candles seemed to brighten.

WE REMAINED CLOSE to the walls, our hands groping for anything resembling a hold in the jagged surface of the stone. Here, the steps were no more than a foot wide, the surface of each perfectly smooth, worn by time and the countless feet that had trod upon them through the generations. Ascending, I kept a wary eye out for the bat. The creature, monitoring us intently from its perch, took flight as we passed and landed upon another beam just above our heads. The flutter of its wings echoed off the ancient walls, filling the chamber with what sounded like a hundred bats beating against one another. Passing the bat for the second time, I heard the chitter of tiny teeth and was reminded of the mouse we saw earlier.

I dared not glance down; the stone floor was at least twenty feet below us now. With each step, I heard tiny little pieces of loose rock slip from under our feet and hurtle to the ground. Matilda squeezed my hand in hers, then let go. The next step was less than six inches wide, nothing more than a nub of rock protruding from the wall. She tentatively placed a foot upon it, quickly shuffled past to the next full step, then waited for me to do the same. I took a deep breath and followed behind her, careful to place my foot precisely where she had placed hers. As we climbed, we realized some of the steps were loose, and although none of them broke away from the wall, a fair number felt like they might.

I looked up. "Halfway there," I mumbled.

The bat must have taken offense at my words, for it fluttered to life and circled past us, cutting so close I felt the wind of its wings on my face as I ducked a moment before it would have collided with me.

Matilda let out a soft shriek and dodged the bat, too, her hands gripping the wall to keep from tumbling. I thought it would fly by again, but it did not; instead, the creature landed at the top of the steps above a large oak door.

"It's blocking our path," Matilda said.

"It will let us pass," I replied, not quite sure how I knew this, only that I did. There was something else. Although I could not sense Nanna Ellen nearby, I was certain she had been here. She left her essence on each step, on each handhold along the wall, her very breath hanging in the air. I was certain she had been here recently, as recently as this very night. Again, I wondered if she could sense me, too, if this strange bond was mutual. And if she could, indeed, sense me as I did her, did she have the ability to mask this sixth sense we shared and somehow hide from me at will? It would seem so. This thought brought on a shudder—I saw her once again, catapulting towards me from the ceiling, only this time we weren't in my attic room, we were standing right here on these steps—I pictured her falling towards us from the top of the tower, her arms and legs outstretched, grabbing at both Matilda and me as she fell past, pulling us with her to the depths below.

"Keep moving," Matilda said. I looked up to find her nearly ten steps ahead of me, almost to the landing at the top, with the bat perched a few feet above her head.

I reached for the stone wall and started up after her, mindful of each step and careful not to slip on the loose stones. We made quick work of the remaining steps and found ourselves at the top, facing a large iron-banded oak door. As we neared, the bat took flight yet again, perched on the windowsill across from us. As I watched, another bat landed beside it, then a third—each larger than the last, their size shaming the size of the diminutive mouse below. Little chirps came from the trio, and they glowered with beady red eyes, long white teeth dripping saliva on their shuffling claws.

Matilda eyed them anxiously, but I refused to display fear; instead, I turned my back to them and took in the large door.

It must have been nine feet wide, and it appeared to be carved of a single slab of oak, improbable as that may be. Large iron bands wrapped the surface at the top, bottom, and again at the center, and in the middle appeared to be an ancient bolt-hole for some type of lock. I found it strange that such a door would lock from the outside rather than the inside and couldn't help but wonder what might warrant such a thing.

I reached for the bolt and pushed it aside. The metal did not squeak, as one would expect of a contraption as old as this, but instead it slid effortlessly aside, finishing with a distinct click as some unseen cylinder disengaged. With this uncoupling, the door pushed in just a hair, now free to swing on its sturdy hinges. A heavy, malodorous air seemed to exhale through the gaps, the foulest of stenches—and a gag escaped my throat. Beside me, Matilda turned away, pressing the sleeve of her jacket over her nose and mouth, her eyes watering with the wicked scent of it. I had smelled death before, and this was such a scent; stagnant and impure, the odor of a long-rotten thing locked away in a small place, contaminating the air around.

With her free hand, Matilda did what I could not and pushed on the door, sending it swinging into the room.

Although a window occupied the far wall, someone had bricked it over, sealing out the night, and the moonlight, too, but this was of no matter for the walls were lined with the same candles we found along the staircase—their flames burning bright and dancing upon the wicks. Again, I noted the lack of fresh wax; the candles burned yet they didn't become spent. They didn't expel smoke or scent, they just gave off an odd blue light.

I think Matilda expected to find Nanna Ellen, because she burst into the room with a quick step, prepared to surprise anyone who may be standing inside. We encountered no one, though.

With the opening of the door, the nasty air rushed out at us as if freed from this place for the first time in centuries. Beneath this odor, I also detected a deep, earthy scent. The room was larger than I had expected, at least twelve feet across, and completely round except for the door. The ceiling climbed to a height of at least ten feet, dominated by a large canopy of stone bricks supported by thick wooden beams much like the ones we encountered in the staircase.

The cobwebs and dust were so thick a hundred years could have passed since the last time someone stepped foot in this place, had I not known otherwise. I thought of Nanna Ellen's room and the dirt on the floor, how she left no footprints while Matilda and I left so many.

I knew Nanna Ellen had been here, because at the center of the room was a large wooden crate, about three feet deep and almost as wide and of a length that rivaled Pa's height. The top had been pried open and set aside, and it was from here the malignant odor emanated. Dirt covered the floor, much like Nanna's room.

AT FIRST GLANCE, the crate struck me as peculiar. Spiderwebs filled the room; they dangled from the ceiling and walls as thick as the canopy of an old weeping willow in the deepest bog. Even as we pushed the door farther into the room, webs broke free and fell to the floor with tiny eight-legged creatures scurrying for shelter the moment they recovered, taking refuge amongst the thick plumes of dust and grime. How had someone gotten such a large box up the stairs?

Matilda, still shielding her mouth, walked with caution into the room, her eyes fixed on the large crate. She circled carefully at a distance of a few feet, then approached, waving away the webs nearby. As she peered over the edge of the crate and took in the contents, her face creased into a frown; then she shook her head and stepped back again, a scream coming from her, but muffled by the sleeve of her coat.

"What is it?"

She grew pale, and for a moment I thought she might give in to nausea, but she fought off the sensation. Unable to speak, she pointed to the crate opening, her finger trembling before her.

I wanted to turn back. I wanted to take her by the hand and rush back out the door, down the steps and across the fields to our house, where I would climb back into the safety of my bed and pretend this was nothing more than another bad dream—but I knew I couldn't do that. We had braved the night to come to this place, to search for Nanna Ellen, to get answers, and I had to remain steadfast and courageous.

I forced my feet to move, for they did not wish to do so. I coaxed them into the room one step at a time until I found myself standing beside the large wooden crate. I felt Matilda's hand on my back and nearly jumped at the touch. My head spun around to face her only long enough to see her mouth the word *Sorry*. Then I turned back to the crate, leaned over it, and peered inside.

Dirt filled the crate to the rim—the same disgusting earth we found under Nanna Ellen's bed, crawling with earthworms as thick as my finger, slithering through the black and over and under one another before disappearing back into the dirt. Peppering the surface were hundreds of maggots, their tiny white bodies glistening with slime under the flickering blue light of the candles. As grotesque as this sight was, it was not the reason Matilda screamed, for this was not the worst thing in the box—not the worst by far.

Near its center, barely visible under the thick layer of earth, rested the mutilated carcass of a cat. Its throat had been violated with a ragged tear, the pink muscle and yellow fat beneath exposed to the air, causing the carcass to brown and dry just the slightest.

As I stared past into the dirt, I realized the feline was not alone; nearly a dozen dead rats also dotted the black earth, their fur so filthy I could barely distinguish them from the dirt. The smell should have repulsed me, but I found the scent oddly calming.

When my arm began to itch at this thought, I took a step back to find Matilda staring at me. "Did Nanna Ellen slaughter those animals?"

In my mind, I saw her glaring down at me from the ceiling, her red eyes glowing with hatred and hunger, and I knew that she could do such a thing, even if I didn't want to believe it. Then a worse possibility dawned on me. "You said Thornley passed a bag to Nanna Ellen in her room, a bag containing something alive . . ." I let the word hang, unwilling to complete the thought aloud.

"Thornley wouldn't do such a thing," Matilda insisted.

I thought of the chickens at the coop, the excitement in his face. *A fox*, he had said. *A fox did this*.

"What purpose do these serve?" Matilda pointed at the crate's lid, leaning against the side. "The top is riddled with holes. For air? Maybe the animals were meant to live inside that box and didn't survive the journey."

"It's filled to the rim with dirt. Nothing was meant to live here." I knelt down beside the crate and inspected the lid closely. Nails peppered its edges, but even though they appeared to be thick, the nails did not protrude to the other side as one might expect; they had been cut off. Fake nails, in other words. Providing only the mere illusion of nails. On the inside of the lid, I discovered six small hasps. I stood and took a look at the crate again.

"Those latches are designed to hook over these staples. I think the lid is designed so someone can lock it from the inside. The false nails give the appearance of being sealed by a hammer, but of course that is not the case."

"That makes no sense."

"Does any of this make sense?" I replied, gesturing around the room.

"Look at your hand," Matilda said in a low breath.

The handkerchief I had wrapped over the wound earlier had fallen away, revealing my palm.

"The cut is gone."

I held my hand to the light, trying to hide the slight tremor that started at my pounding heart and worked its way down my arm. The skin had healed; there was no sign of the injury. "It was a small cut," I heard myself say, knowing the words meant nothing even as they slipped from my lips.

Matilda took my hand in hers, turned it over, then back again. "It was bad enough. There is no sign remaining. Nothing at all."

I shook her off.

She frowned. "We need to talk about this."

"Not now."

"What did she do to you?"

"Nanna Ellen might return at any moment."

"I thought you said you couldn't feel her presence anymore. How do you know she was here at all?"

"We saw her here yesterday," I replied.

"Bram, you must be truthful with me. Can you tell? Was she here on this night?"

I had no reason to deceive her. I nodded. "In this very room, yes. As recently as the past hour."

I watched Matilda glance around at the many cobwebs and the thick dust, and I understood what thoughts raced through her mind. "I'm not sure how she moved about without disturbing anything, but I am certain she did, in much the same way she moved about her own room without leaving a single track in the dust and grime."

I turned back to the crate as something else caught my eye, something beneath the dirt. Before Matilda could stop me, I reached back and brushed the dirt aside carefully with my fingertips. When they found cold white flesh, I pulled back. "Oh no."

Matilda grasped my shoulder and peered down into the crate. "Is that her?"

Our eyes met, my heart beating wildly.

I reached back for the crate, and Matilda grabbed my wrist. "Don't—"

I reached back inside anyway, digging at the dirt, brushing it away, uncovering—

"It's a hand," Matilda said.

As I dug farther, as I neared the wrist, the bony white arm I found—

Matilda turned her head and gagged. I nearly did, too, at the sight of it, at the torn skin and muscle, at the bone protruding and splintered—the hand had been severed at the forearm and buried in this box, in the dirt.

"Not Nanna Ellen's," I forced out, for this was clearly a man's hand; much too large to be that of a woman, although the long, thin fingers were smooth. Not a man who worked the fields, but perhaps one who sat at a desk. The fingernails were abnormally long, protruding over the fingertips maybe half an inch and filed to sharp points.

"Is there more buried in the box?" Matilda said beside me. "Did she kill a man and place him here?"

"There is something in the man's grasp," I said.

I pried the fingers apart one at a time, all dry and brittle, afraid they might snap off, soon revealing the hand's palm and the shiny object at its center. "It is a ring," I said, plucking it out.

Matilda stepped closer as I held the ring up to the light. It was a thick band, a man's ring, wrought of silver or white bronze, I could not be sure.

"That seems old," Matilda said.

I twisted the ring between my fingers. The detail was extraordinary. The sides were intricately carved with various symbols I did not recognize, two on either side of the wide shoulders, which depicted what appeared to be a family crest. At the very center on the head of the ring was the image of a dragon surrounded by a multitude of diamonds so small they seemed more like a glittering of dust than individual stones. The dragon's only visible eye glowed a bright red, a ruby of some sort.

The ring was clearly ancient, but the workmanship rivaled that of the best modern craftsman; I had never seen anything like it.

"May I see?" Matilda asked.

I set the ring in her open palm, and she raised it to the nearest candle, peering at the inside of the band. "There's something written here . . . on the inside."

"What does it say?"

"*Casa lui Dracul.*"

I thought I saw one of the fingers twitch when she uttered these words.

That was when we ran.

PART II

The world must bow before the strong ones.

—Bram Stoker, *Makt Myrkranna*

NOW

Bram wakes with a start. His body jerks up with such force he nearly tumbles from the chair—his journal falls to the floor.

How long had he slept?

Minutes?

Hours?

He cannot be sure.

He turns to the window.

Although the moon is still high in the sky, it has clearly moved farther to the east. Light spills from the surface, only to be diffused by thick gray storm clouds rolling in from the distant mountains. But the moon has moved; of this he is certain.

Bram's rifle sits on the ground at his feet, and the door—

The door stands open!

Bram scoops up the rifle as he stands in one fluid motion, his heart pounding wildly in his chest.

The door is not open much, only an inch or so, but open nonetheless. The paste he used to seal the opening litters the ground in tiny piles of dust and broken chunks. The remains of the last rose he placed are there, too, a decayed ruin.

He slowly approaches the door, his palms sweating on the rifle barrel and grip.

A scratching at the stone floor on the other side. Then the voice comes, feeble and thin, his mother's voice.

You don't want to hurt me, do you, Bram? Put the gun down before you hurt me. I need your help; I don't feel well. Please hurry.

The scratching grows louder, more frantic, tiny nails tick-tick-ticking against the stone.

Bram falls still, his eyes drifting from the door to the basket of roses, the three remaining blossoms. He forces himself to advance towards the door.

It itches so. I never would have expected it to itch so bad.

Holding the rifle with his right hand, he reaches for the corner of the door with his left and pulls it towards him. The heavy oak swings lazily on tired hinges, the scrape of metal on metal squeaking under the strain. The odor from within wafts out at him with such strength he nearly swoons—a horrible stench full of death and rot, a scent all too familiar to him.

At first, he perceives nothing in the gloom beyond. Then he spies the eyes, two eyes of fiery red, staring back at him from the depths. Perhaps they are inching closer, for they seem to wax brighter, and he fights the urge to step back and slam the door. Instead, he raises the barrel of the rifle and points at the pair of orbs, forcing his aim to remain true even though his arms and hands shake in rebellion.

I don't want to die, Bram, says the voice of his mother.

Bram pulls the trigger, and the butt of the rifle kicks back into his shoulder as the projectile rockets out in a cloud of smoke.

He hears a yelp from within, and the glowing eyes bounce up as the bullet strikes home.

That is no way to treat your mother, Bram.

The voice is no longer that of his mother but has morphed into his father's thick Irish brogue. Then comes a growl as the red eyes rush at him, tearing through the gloom with incredible dispatch. In the moment before the monster leaps, Bram catches sight of a large gray wolf bounding from the shadows. He tries to jump out of the way, but the creature proves too fast; the wolf projects itself off the stone floor and catapults through the air, plowing into him with such force he falls back hard against the ground and slides across the chamber, the enormous beast's thick paws pressing into his chest. He looks up at its giant snout, dripping with saliva and acrid gore, as the animal releases a howl loud enough to shake the walls before biting Bram's neck, the wolf's white teeth tearing through flesh as if it is nothing but paper. Warm blood sprays through the air, and Bram tries to scream, but not a single sound escapes—

His eyes snap open, and he falls from the chair onto the hard stone floor, a guttural noise escaping his lips as he does. With both hands, he pushes at the wolf, only to realize there is nothing there. Bram twists and jumps to his feet, pulling the bowie knife from the sheath at his side and slashing at the air, only to find he is alone.

He spins around and faces the door, ready to strike there, too.

But the door is closed.

With his free hand, he reaches up to his neck and finds no wound.

Bram sucks in a deep breath.

A dream.

He goes to the door and inspects the gap. Most of the paste along the perimeter remains intact, and the last rose lies in a withered heap as he remembered; at least that much is true. Judging by the moon, the hour is no later than three o'clock.

If he had been tired before, he finds himself wide awake now, and without hesitation he reaches for another rose from his basket, remembers to bless it this time, then places it before the door.

A stack of letters stick out from the corner of his bag, and Bram picks them up and returns to his chair. The first is written by Matilda, but there are others.

Bram reads Matilda's letter, then reads it again, before slipping it into the pages of his journal, between pages previously written upon, and once again begins writing by the pale light of the oil lamp.

He has so much more to tell. And so little time to tell it.

LETTER FROM MATILDA
to ELLEN CRONE,
DATED 8 AUGUST 1868

———— ❖ ————

My dearest Nanna Ellen,

Or should I call you Ellen? I am, after all, an adult now. Can
you imagine? All grown up, twenty-two years of age. A spinster!
Sometimes I find it hard to believe how the years have flown. Where
to begin? I know some may find it silly to write a letter to a recipient
who will never read the words, but so much has transpired since you
left us, much weighing heavily on my mind. And may I say, I miss
you so? Somehow, through it all, I miss you.

Never far from my thoughts, regardless of how hard I have tried to
forget you.

Oh, now I ramble. That is not my intent. I suppose I am a bit
flustered at the thought of committing these words to paper, for to
do so makes them more real, but do so I must. To think and write
of all that transpired is an admission to myself, acceptance of what
occurred. I am certain you would have me believe the shadows of my
childhood imagination have simply been aggrandized over time, but I
know that such is not the case. These years of reflection have given
me the perspective to untangle the truth from fancy. I may not

know you in the way Bram knows you, but, believe me, I know
you well.

As hard as I have tried to forget the events of your final days in
our home, the memories refuse to let go. They sit in a small room at
the back of my mind, and when the door is about to close on them,
when the last bit of candlewick is about to be snuffed out, they come
pouring forth. I have had dreams, both night terrors and the wakeful
sort, and sometimes the memories scream out in the middle of the day,
drowning out all else around me.

Where did you go?

What became of you?

For years, I wondered if you really walked into the bog and
disappeared beneath the water or if that was just a conjecture of my
childhood's imagining.

Then there was that crate, that horrid thing in Artane Tower, and
its grotesque contents, the sight of which burned into my mind's eye.
Weeks passed before I found myself able to sleep through the night
after finding that box.

We told them everything. We had to.

We fled the tower—we could have killed ourselves scrambling
down those steps—and back home as if riding the very wind. We
woke Ma and Pa straightaway. We told them of our findings between
labored breaths. Realizing the hour and the fact that we had been out
was enough to give them quite a shock, but we went on anyway. Bram
and I did not care about any punishment that awaited us; this tale
seemed far bigger than the consequences of our transgression. We
told them everything. How we found the soil in your bed. How
we observed you eat—or, truly, not eat. We even told them how we
followed you and how you disappeared into the bog. But most of all,
we told them about the crate in the tower and the severed limb lying

within. Ma and Pa listened in silence, their eyes bouncing from Bram to me and back again as the words poured out, and when we finished, they watched us in silence still. Ma spoke first, her words short and thick with sleep. She turned to Pa and patted his arm. "Perhaps you should go and have a look, Abraham."

Still wrapped in our coats, Bram and I both nodded our heads vigorously at that suggestion and leapt from their bed towards the door. Pa did not follow, though; instead, his head fell back upon his pillow. "In the morning," he said. "We'll go at first light."

"We need to go now, Pa! She may still be close!" I cried out.

Pa raised a weary hand and pointed at the window. "It's raining. We're not going outside and traipsing across creation in the middle of the night while it's raining. Your brother shouldn't even be out of his bed. Both of you, return to your rooms."

They were too sleepy to wonder what on earth had propelled their sickly boy from his bed—looking back, perhaps they thought *they* were dreaming.

I was willing to brave the weather; I am certain Bram was, too. I attempted to argue, but Pa was snoring a moment later, oblivious to my words.

Ma pointed towards their bedroom door and mouthed, *You heard your father. To bed with both of you.*

At my side, Bram said nothing. He tugged at my hand and simply nodded.

Neither Bram nor I slept; we did not even take the time to change into our nightclothes. We spent the remainder of the night sitting upon his bed in silence. At dawn, the two of us were standing at the door to our parents' bedroom, unwilling to risk Pa slipping out without us in tow. He rose with a grunt, told us to wait for him in the kitchen, and went about his morning routine.

When he appeared in the kitchen, there was a scowl on his face. "Dirt inside her bed, you say? I found nothing of the sort. Her bed is filled with hay, same as yours."

I opened my mouth, ready to tell Pa that you somehow removed the soil yesterday when you left, but before I could speak, he started towards the door.

"Take me to this place in the tower; show me what you found."

When I saw the look in Bram's eye, my stomach sank, for a realization came to me, same as him—you removed the dirt without anyone the wiser, the tower room would also be cleared.

I considered telling Pa it was all a lie or possibly a dream that felt too real, but one that we now knew to be false, but I could not bring myself to do it. I needed to see for myself. I rose from my chair, donned my coat, and walked out the door towards the fields of Artane, towards the castle. For the first minute or so, I was not even certain that Pa and Bram followed me. I was unwilling to turn, and so determined to see this through I would have gone it alone. They had followed me, though, and together the three of us crossed the muddy fields to the tower rising from the edge of the forest.

Pa was nearly out of breath by the time we reached the top of the stairs; but it was Bram's condition that concerned him. That worry seemed to overshadow all else; he did not comment on the dilapidated state of the structure or the possible risk involved in climbing to the top. When Pa pushed open the heavy door, emptiness screamed out at us.

We found nothing inside.

The tower room was empty.

Not even our own footprints littered the dusty floor, the space appearing as if it had been empty for hundreds of years, and smelling just as deserted.

How did you do it?

How did you hide everything?

So many questions, and now you are gone. You have been gone for so long.

I imagine you are wondering about Bram.

You left him in such a state.

You left us both in such a state.

That was a long time ago. Somehow, Ma and Pa seemed to forget all that, and despite their conventional ways, allowed me to travel to Europe without them. I recently returned to Dublin from Paris.

Oh, Paris, what a beautiful city; I wish I had been able to stay. I spent my days at the Louvre and my nights along the banks of the Seine. There were restaurants and shops offering the most extravagant of things—none of which I could afford, mind you, but a girl can look. I was there to collect an award, the Young Artist's Award for Painting from Life. You always encouraged my drawing and my art; I thank you for that, you and Ma. If you had not encouraged me, there is no telling whether or not I would have pursued the desire to create all these years. Perhaps I would still be sketching, but I surely would not have possessed the courage to exhibit my work. This particular painting is an oil of a woman with flowing blond hair and the most beautiful blue eyes. When they asked who modeled for it, I told them it was not any single woman but the combined images of many women. This was not the truth, but it was not wholly a lie, either. You see, I based the sketch for the painting on the drawings I did of you when I was a little girl. Dozens of pictures, all of the same woman, yet not the same. I was always perplexed by this. To this day, I cannot capture your likeness on canvas. The women I draw are all beautiful, but they are never you, not quite, not even today. If I were to send this letter, I would include one, but, alas, it will not be sent.

I am rambling again.

Bram.

Let me tell you about Bram.

He has grown into a fine young man!

There is not a time he walks down the street and does not turn the head of a lady. He is tall and strong, a star athlete, by all accounts, at Trinity College—rugby, racewalking, rowing, gymnastics. I do not believe there is a sport he cannot master. He has had not a hint of illness since he was a child, since you . . . you . . . What did you do that night?

What did you do to my brother?

Is he still my brother?

He does not speak of it.

Not a word.

From the moment we returned to the castle tower with Pa through today, it is as if none of the events of those days took place.

Uncle Edward healed him.

Uncle Edward and his leeches.

That is what he tells anyone who asks; Ma and everyone else back up this story.

We know differently, though, do we not?

You and I?

If you had not come into our lives, would I have Bram today?

Is he even my Bram? My brother?

I have seen you, you know.

Just recently in Paris. I was on the Champs-Élysées, and I saw you standing beneath the awning of a small patisserie. Your hair was styled differently, but even from across the street I knew it was you. I tried to cross over to you, but the crowd was so thick at that time of day I lost you amongst the rushing Parisians.

Did you see me?

Did you run from me?

If I showed one of my drawings to the people in that crowd, would they have recognized you and pointed in the direction in which you had gone? Or would they have simply shaken their heads and continued on their way? I bet the latter.

Where have you been? Where did you go? Where are you as I write this today?

Thornley is teaching medicine now! Everyone says he will go far, and I know he never intended anything else. He graduated from Queen's College in Galway and studied at the Royal College of Surgeons. He has been a surgeon at Dublin City Hospital, teaches at Richmond Hospital, and spends much of his time at Swift's Hospital for Lunatics, a particular fascination for him. He stays busy—too busy. A far cry from delivering live packages to you during the night.

Dick is following fast on his heels, eager to study medicine after Rathmines School. I suppose he is still Baby Richard to you, considering he was only two years old when last you saw him.

Thomas has action in his bones. He has his sights set on joining the Bengal Civil Service the moment he graduates from Trinity next year, can you imagine? Pa says he will have a lot more studying to do before he sits for the Civil Service exam, but Tom is not thinking about that. You would not know him, of course. He was nothing but a wee lad when you ran off into the night and abandoned us. And Margaret and George had not even been born yet!

It was all so long ago, and yet it seems like the night before last. I cannot imagine where you went, what you have been doing.

Was that you in Paris? Perhaps I must admit to myself it was not. After all, you looked as if you had not aged a day. Better, actually, than that last time I saw you. Perhaps you found Ponce de León's precious fountain and drank from its waters? Girls should not keep such secrets but should share them with each other, do you not think? You always had the most beautiful skin, rivaling that of the purest ivory.

There I go again!

Blabbering on and on.

I know you want to hear about Bram. He was always your favorite, was he not? It is okay, you can tell me; I would not take offense. Of all my siblings, he has my heart as well. He has always been Ma's pet, but probably not Pa's. If Pa has a soft spot, it will be for Thornley and Dick, doctor and doctor-to-be—following in the footsteps of all the other Stoker doctors. Bram tries to please him, and he seems to be following Pa's wishes, but he and Pa do have their differences and have not seen eye to eye recently.

Pa encouraged Bram to sit for the Civil Service exam, which he did. His score was second highest, so he got one of the five open jobs in Petty Sessions at Dublin Castle. He began in the Fines and Penalties Office, and he hates it so!

He claims the boredom is so thick in Petty Sessions it can be seen floating through the air in an attempt to escape the castle, a cloud of gray and muck. He came home yesterday and claimed

to have stepped in some boredom on his way out, catching it
before it could slip beneath the threshold and get lost in the streets
of Dublin.

You and I know Bram would rather be at the theater day and night,
rubbing elbows with the actors and stagehands. He would be happy
to sit in the cheap seats and watch the same show over and over
again.

Of course, Pa is sure the stage is populated by "ne'er-do-wells," and
as much as he enjoys a highbrow performance, he thinks theater work
is not acceptable—he remembers the old burlesque shows and assumes
Bram would get in with a bad crowd. No son of his will work in the
theater!

So many men are out of work—is not Bram fortunate to have a path
laid out for him at Dublin Castle? With his education, there will be
regular promotions and raises. And let none of us forget, Pa started at
Dublin Castle at only sixteen, and he had to work and save for almost
thirty years so that he could afford to marry and provide for Ma. And
isn't Bram thankful? He should be thrilled to follow in his father's
footsteps!

Those conversations make Bram long for his sickbed again.

Oh, my Bram.

You would be proud.

Pa will not hear of him working in a theater, but Bram has found
another way to be involved. He writes reviews of performances in the
Evening Mail. Ironically, an unpaid position, but of course Bram takes it
very seriously. He works much faster than the other clerks so he has
time to write reviews and keep up his journals on the castle's clock,
with his boss none the wiser.

This seems to keep Bram's literary urges at bay for now.

Bram and Pa sometimes even attend theater together! Bram has turned Pa into his sounding board, analyzing every nuance ad nauseam. Of course, Pa thinks Bram will be satisfied to go on that way, but I do not think it will be enough. As soon as Pa relents, or if he turns his back, we will see Bram run for the stage.

You clearly know something about acting, don't you?

How much of what we witnessed was really you and how much was left to acting?

Is your name Ellen Crone or is that just a stage name conjured up by you to suit the play? One you shed the moment the final curtain fell?

Did you love us at all?

So many questions and no means to ask them.

Well, I have much to do today. I have caught you up. This useless letter, never to be posted, but complete nonetheless.

As you can see, we do not need you. We never needed you.

But I would still like to talk to you.

Where are you?

Affectionately yours,
Matilda

THE JOURNAL *of* BRAM STOKER

8 August 1868, 5:31 p.m. — I felt the need to put pen to paper simply to record the oddity of what I just witnessed. My flatmate, the illustrious William B. Delany, thinking he was alone, stood silently in the corner of the common room of our flat, located at 11 Lower Leeson Street, and plucked a plump black fly off the fireplace mantel and dropped it in a glass jar, trapping it inside with a cork-rimmed lid. While on the face of it this is odd behavior, I will be first to admit to doing the same at one point in my life, but I find it important to reveal I was probably eight or nine years old at the time and had seen my brother Thornley ensnaring hapless insects the year prior, and would be party to Thomas harvesting such in the years after. It is not so much the act of trapping a fly I found strange; it is the fact that a grown man, at the ripe old age of twenty-two, would partake in such behavior that seemed more than a little peculiar to me.

Delany was turned at an angle and did not see me enter the room. I can't help but wonder if he would continue upon his quest to trap this flying pest if he knew I was watching; I am inclined to believe the answer to that question is yes. The image of determination on his face, the utter focus with which he acted, told me it was a bad day to be a fly on our mantel.

So, capture the fly he did.

I would like to say this was the extent of the oddity I decided to commit to paper, but, alas, would that really be enough? What really grabbed me as I witnessed this endeavor was that the plump little fly was not alone in that jar; he had company.

An embarrassment of riches, when it came to company.

The jar, being about five inches tall and three inches wide, appeared to be full of flies. How many, you ask? So many that there was little room to spare.

Memo for story: "I once knew a little boy who put so many flies in a bottle that they had not room to die!"

I dared approach just a little closer, and his eyes were so fixed on his prize he still did not notice me. He watched his latest captive as it climbed over the fallen soldiers who had been deposited on this baleful battlefield before it. A couple of times, it tried to rise up out of the jar only to bounce off the lid or the glass walls and land on its many legs, then regroup and try again.

With my closer vantage point, I was aghast to discover at least a third of the other flies were still living, some moving slower than others but alive nonetheless. Most either could no longer take to air or had surrendered to their fates.

"Willy? What have you got there?" I said the words softly; I did not wish to startle the boy but startle him I did, and he fumbled with the jar for a moment before it escaped his grasp. I dove and snatched it midair mere inches before it would shatter on the wooden floor.

"Give me that," Willy said.

I rose to my feet and held the jar up to the light. "I don't believe we're permitted to own pets here. Did you ask our landlord before bringing these little guys home?"

"I'm writing a paper on Francesco Redi. I need them for an experiment."

I returned the jar to him and felt the immediate need to wash my hands. "What kind of experiment?"

Willy rolled his eyes. Those of us of lesser intelligence tended to insult his self-assessed superior intellect with silly questions. "Redi is often considered the founder of modern parasitology. Prior to a paper he published in 1668, it was believed maggots generated spontaneously. He proved they actually came from the eggs of flies. For my paper, I plan to document the life cycle from fly to egg to maggot."

"By capturing flies in a jar?"

Again, the rude rolling of the eyes. "A living experiment. I purchased a slab of cagmag beef from the butcher and set it out on the porch yesterday, but someone—or something—absconded with it."

"I would bet on the something over the someone," I retorted. "There are a number of dogs wandering these streets; any one of them would be grateful for such a hearty meal."

"Mind you, this specimen was so scrappy the old Trinity cooks would not even feed it to the students. I had placed the beef in a wooden crate with lateral slats running half an inch apart. Nothing should have been able to reach inside. Nothing but flies. But this morning I found the beef gone yet the crate inviolate. I can only imagine how a dog got it out."

"You still haven't explained the need for a jar of flies," I said.

Delany gave the jar a little shake. "The beef was expensive, and I don't have the funds to replace it. Then I got to thinking: If enough flies died in a jar, would they lay eggs that would in turn become maggots in order to devour the bodies of the dead?"

I felt that slight pain behind my left temple that always seemed to surface when I got too wrapped up in a conversation with Willy. "So you wish to perpetuate insect cannibalism?"

Willy's face lit up like that of a child with his nose pressed to the window of a candy shop. "Yes! Fascinating, don't you think?"

"How long does it take for a fly to lay an egg which then can evolve into a maggot?"

Willy peered into the jar. One of the flies hung upside down from the lid, nervously jerking about in circles. "There may already be eggs. It takes about four days for an egg to hatch and go from the larva stage to an actual fly. I'm hoping to capture a complete cycle."

I thought about this for a moment. "I see a flaw in your plan. A fly in the ointment, as it were."

Willy frowned. "Flaw? Of course not; my plan is sound."

"Have you stopped to wonder what is killing all the flies?" I tapped on the lid of the jar. "You failed to punch holes in the lid for air. How can they devour their brethren when they cannot even breathe?"

Willy tilted his head, contemplating this revelation. "No, there is enough air. They're fine." His eyes began to track another fly on the windowsill, and he crossed the room. I took advantage of this development as an opportunity to take my leave before I lost another ten minutes of my life to his nonsense. I found our other flatmate, Herbert Wilson, sitting on the front porch. Herbert was a rather large boy—at least two inches taller than me, and I'm a rather tall fellow in my own right.

Herbert grabbed my shoulder and pulled me to the side. "Is he still filling that jar?"

"Very keenly so, yes," I told him.

Herbert let out a soft chuckle and pointed to a crate next to the stoop. "Last night, after he put a perfectly good slice of beef in that box, I took it out and hid it in the hanging corner cupboard. Tonight, I'm going to put it back in his box."

"Good-bye, Herbert," I said, pushing past him.

"Don't you want to see what happens?"

"Not particularly, no. I'm due at my parents' house."

Herbert said, "Maybe I'll put it under his bed! It will take days before he pinpoints the odor."

"Please don't." I shared a room with Willy, and any meat left to rot under concealment would surely become my problem as quickly as it would become his.

"Say hello to Matilda for me!" he called out from behind me.

I thrust a hand in the air, waving him off, and ran down the street at a fast clip.

MA AND PA had moved the family from the coast to Dublin proper in the summer of 1858, ten years ago now. Pa was getting older, and the long walk to Dublin Castle each day began to take a toll on his tired body. The house at 43 Harcourt Street was a stone's throw from his work.

The afternoon sun began to drop as I hurried along, descending in the distance behind the buildings and hills of Parliament House. The streets were a-bustle with activity as shopkeepers packed up their wares with the dying sun and toted them inside. As I turned the corner at the Royal College of Surgeons, I waved to Mr. Barrowcliff, feeding pigeons at St. Stephen's Green. One could set a watch by his regularity, for he stood there every day come rain or shine. He was so punctual, in fact, that if you were to arrive before him, you could witness the pigeons gathering in wait at the shore of the lake near the small falls.

I reached Harcourt Street and slowed my pace to a walk long enough to smooth out my hair before crossing the threshold of my parents' home.

I discovered Ma in the kitchen with my little sister, Margaret, preparing dinner. Margaret beamed at the sight of me. "Look who has come home to put food in his belly!"

Ma had turned fifty this year, and even though her dark tresses had conceded the battle to gray, I still saw the fiery woman who read to me as a child. Margaret, thirteen years younger than me but with the mind of a thirty-year-old, seemed to have grown taller every time I saw her.

Ma nodded at me, then pulled a golden brown apple pie from the oven and placed it on the table. "I bet you are surviving on stale bread and ale at that boardinghouse. You look like you dropped half a stone since you last brought your starving self home. Sometimes I wonder if you love me at all or just the cooking."

"It is strictly the cooking, Ma. My survival instincts draw me homeward." The scent of the pie engulfed me, my stomach gurgling loud enough for all to hear; we burst out laughing. "Where is everyone?"

"George and Richard are still at school. Thomas is in the parlor with your Pa, having a rather heated discussion about his continuing desire to run off to India and fight in the aftermath of someone else's war. Matilda is upstairs in her room."

I walked over to the pie and tried to slip my finger under the crust; Ma slapped at my hand. "Not until after dinner, Bram. It isn't going anywhere."

"It better not," I said, offering a wink to Margaret before heading into the parlor where I found Thomas leaning against the hearth while Pa sat in his favorite chair, pipe in hand. His face was flushed and locked in a scowl; neither of the two spoke as I stepped in. Pa waved a frustrated hand at my brother, then took another puff of his pipe.

"Ma says you are still set on lodging a bullet in your brain before your twentieth birthday," I said.

Thomas grew defensive. "You, too, Bram? Of everyone, I thought you would understand."

"And why would I understand?"

"You know precisely why."

Pa pulled the pipe from his mouth and blew a smoke ring before speaking, his voice subdued and somber. "He says I broke your spirit and saddled you with a desk job, that I am trying to do the same to him, and he will not have any of it."

"My situation is hardly the same," I replied, knowing it was only half true. "My position at the Office of Petty Sessions is a great opportunity, and it affords me the income I need to attend the theater, among other things."

"But you'd rather be *working* in the theater, wouldn't you, Bram?"

To this question, I said nothing. I didn't glance at Pa, but I felt his eyes on me.

Thomas continued, "If given the opportunity, I think you would leave the castle and become an actor at the drop of a hat! Imagine the life: traveling from city to city, country to country, all these far-off places and foreign people, all of them coming to behold the illustrious Bram Stoker alight upon their humble stage. They would shout your name and wait for a glimpse of you after the performance as you exit the theater, ask you to sign their playbills."

"Nonsense," I replied.

"It's the truth."

"What does any of this have to do with your gallivanting off to India?" Pa grumbled.

Thomas sighed. "If you had the opportunity to fight in the Coalition Wars, don't you think it would have made you a better man?"

"That is even before my time, my son. The only fighting I have done has been in the halls of our government, albeit just as bloody."

"In India, the challenge to rebuild British interests is enormous. The government, laws . . . it's a blank slate. I'll be fighting for what is right, no different than you. The only difference is the battleground."

"Hardly," Pa scoffed. "You will be a target for the locals."

"I'll be gone but two years; when I return, I will accept whatever post at the castle you wish. You can chain me to the desk alongside Bram. Or, better yet, I'll take his position when he finally runs off to the theater," Thomas said.

At this remark, I laughed. "Maybe I'll put the bullet in your brain and save us all the trouble."

"I've seen you shoot. I do not believe I have anything to worry about."

Pa chuckled. "I will grant him that, Bram. You are a horrible shot."

Ma poked her head around the corner. "Nobody is shooting anybody until after dinner. To the table with all of you."

Pa rose from his chair and patted Thomas on the back. "We will continue this conversation later."

Thomas said nothing, only pushed past him towards the dining room.

When he was gone, Pa turned to me. "He is going to go; there is little any of us can do to stop him. He has that same fire in his eye I had at that age. The service might actually do him good, give him a means to channel some of that grit burning within him. I will not sleep a wink, though, when he is gone; neither will your mother. I can see her now, running each day to fetch the post, waiting for a letter detailing her son's last day."

"You shouldn't think such things; I'm sure he'll be fine. Thomas can take care of himself. You taught him to handle firearms when he was a boy, same as the rest of us. And he's a fighter; I have yet to see someone get the better of him."

"I think I can take him."

The voice came from behind me, and I turned to find Matilda smiling at the two of us. "Matilda!" I scooped her up and spun her around, the hem of her skirt swirling out around us both.

"Put me down!"

I spun her twice more, then set her back on her feet. "How was Paris?"

"Let us not keep your mother waiting," Pa said, starting for the dining room.

Matilda leaned into me and in the lowest of whispered breaths said, "We need to talk."

8 AUGUST 1868, 6:48 p.m.—Dinner went as well as could be expected. Pa and Thomas glowered at each other for the duration. Their silence brought to mind a pair of deaf mutes, and Ma attempted to lighten the mood, reminding us that a few years ago she delivered a paper to the Statistical and Social Inquiry Society on the need for a state provision for the education of the deaf and dumb in Ireland. It was one of the many social issues she felt strongly about, and although membership of the society was strictly male and no lady had presented a paper before, Ma was never one to let something as trivial as a male-only club prevent her from communicating a message. She would have stood outside their halls and shouted had they not invited her in. Ma had since become an associate member, and presented more papers, most notably regarding the female emigration from workhouses.

I had attended her first speech, and the president of the society, Judge Longfield, pulled me aside to tell me how pleased he was by her delivery. I had learned later that twelve of the members refused to attend Ma's speech simply because she was a lady while others attended because she was. Ma had a serious manner about her that even the most hardened of gentlemen could not help but respect.

Matilda told us about her recent trip to Paris and her desire to return there as soon as possible. Father scoffed at this idea, no doubt concerned about the cost, but I had never seen her so happy, and a smile upon her face is worth any price. She spoke of the galleries and the food, the people bustling in the streets. "It's not like Dublin," she said. "Paris teems with people from dozens of countries. More people on holiday than actual residents, it seems."

"And you went with your entire art class?" I asked.

Matilda nodded. "Twenty-three of us. Twenty students and three teachers: Mrs. Rushmore, Sir Thomas Jones, and Miss Fisher."

Pa's eyes narrowed. "Thomas Jones? There were men on this trip?"

Matilda glanced at Ma, then back down at her plate. "There were a few gentlemen in attendance, yes, but they remained exactly that: gentlemen. Sir Thomas Jones saw to the men, and Miss Fisher was charged with the ladies. Mrs. Jones accompanied her husband as well. As head of the Dublin Art School's Figure Drawing Program, Mrs. Rushmore oversaw our itinerary. Both men and women were chaperoned and sequestered from each other; I scarcely realized the men were there."

"Uh-huh," Pa grumbled.

Ma placed her hand on Pa's. "Your daughter is a grown woman, Abraham, you cannot keep her locked away under your roof for her entire life."

"Of course I can."

Ma ignored him. "A trip like this is precisely where she will meet her future husband, of that I am certain."

"I adored the Louvre," Matilda chimed in. "To behold the *Mona Lisa* and *Venus de Milo* in person. There are no words to describe their beauty."

"May I be excused?" Thomas said.

Ma frowned. "And what do you need to do that is so pressing it cannot wait until we've all finished supping?"

"There is an unofficial rugby match at Trinity tonight."

"In the dark? Are you playing?" I asked. "I'll go with you."

Matilda kicked my ankle under the table and stared at me, her lips tight.

Thomas said, "No, just watching. My shoulder is still giving me some trouble after the last game; I'm sitting this one out."

"And you plan to go off to war?" Pa grumbled. "A sore joint will be the least of your worries."

"Enough of that, Abraham," Ma said. "Not at the dinner table." She turned back to Thomas. "Go ahead, enjoy yourself."

With that, Thomas pushed back his chair and stood. He glanced at me. "Coming?"

Matilda's eyes burned into me, and I shook my head. "Maybe later. Matilda wants to tell me all about Paris."

Thomas shrugged. "Suit yourself." He was out the door a minute later, a slice of apple pie perched precariously in his hand.

Matilda turned to Ma. "May Bram and I be excused from the table? I want to show him all my sketches from the trip."

Pa waved a hand at both of us, then reached into his jacket pocket to retrieve his pipe.

8 AUGUST 1868, 7:03 p.m.—In the room Matilda shared with Margaret, I watched as she took one last glance down the hallway before closing the door.

"This is about her, is it not?" I asked, sitting on her bed. "Why do you burden yourself with these thoughts? She is gone."

Matilda turned and leaned against the door. When she spoke, she did so in a voice barely above a whisper. "I saw her."

"In Paris?"

Matilda nodded vigorously. "On the Champs-Élysées. I was on the other side of the street, and there was a bit of a crowd, but I know it was her."

"Why would she be in Paris?"

"I do not know."

"And you're certain it was her?"

She nodded again. "As sure as I am standing here."

I pondered this for a moment. Neither of us had seen Nanna Ellen in nearly fourteen years, a lifetime ago. The way she left us, her trip to the castle, the bog, how she—

"There is something else," Matilda said, pursing her lips. She appeared unsure of what to say, then blurted out, "She appeared no older than the day she left. Younger, even. I daresay, she seemed younger than I."

I shook my head. "This must have been someone else, then, someone who reminded you of her."

"It was her. I swear my life on it."

"I have often thought I spotted her, too. Always in a crowd, always at a distance. When I got close, though, I realized I only saw another woman with similar features. I'm sure you simply took note of someone who resembled her and your mind associated this stranger with Ellen."

"It *was* her."

"So I am to believe our long-lost nanny is living in Paris and hasn't aged a day since she ran away fourteen years ago?"

"Yes."

I took Matilda's hand in mine. "You miss her. I do, too. But it wasn't her. It could not have been. At most, this was a trick of the light."

"Oh, hardly. I am absolutely positive what I saw."

"Did you go to her? Speak to her?"

Matilda let out a sigh. "I tried, but by the time I pushed my way through the crowd to the place where she stood, she was no longer there. I know what you're thinking, Bram, but I have no doubt; it was

Nanna Ellen and she was not a day older." Matilda picked up a small music box from her dresser and ran her fingers over the intricately carved wood. "You remember what she was like, particularly that last week. She looked like an old woman in those final days; before that, she appeared to be but a girl, a young woman, at the outside. Had you asked a passerby on the street to guess her age, you would have received a different answer from each. Not a single one would describe her in accurate detail any more than I am able to draw her."

"You must forget her."

"I cannot."

"No good can come from tormenting yourself like this, dwelling on the past in such a manner. We were children; we sought the mystical in everything. Remember the stories we told? The monsters and horrid things we would make up in order to frighten each other?"

Matilda's eyes remained riveted on the music box in her hands. She spoke not a word.

"At that age, the true and the fantastic blend together, becoming as one. Nanna Ellen told us tales of creatures, so in our minds she became one. Our imaginations fed on these stories, twisted them; we wanted to believe, so we did. But that doesn't make them fact."

Matilda placed the music box back on her dresser. "We saw her enter that bog and not come out."

"It wasn't real."

"The dirt under her bed. The crate in Artane Tower. That wretched hand. That god-awful, wretched hand."

"All imagined things, the ramblings of creative, overactive young minds, nothing more," I replied.

Matilda stormed across the room and pulled up my sleeve. "If all was imagined, then what is this?" She glared down at my wrist. "Why has this wound not healed after all these years?"

My eyes fell on the two red dots on my inner wrist above the vein, both freshly scabbed. I quickly pulled my sleeve back over them. "I pick at them, that's all. I'm sure if I left them alone long enough, they would fade away as with any other wound."

"Why don't we talk about that?" Matilda's face grew flushed, and I could tell she wanted to scream at me, but she kept her voice in check for fear of someone overhearing. "When was the last time you had even a hint of illness? When was the last time you got hurt?" she asked. "Hmm? Why don't we talk about that?"

"You know the answer. I've been very lucky. Not since Uncle Edward—"

"Uncle Edward did nothing!"

This time the words boomed out loud and sharp, and I thought Ma or Pa would come bounding through the door, but neither did. I held a finger to my lips.

Matilda went on. "You don't think they know? The whole lot of them know; they just don't speak of it. Hypocrites, all of them!"

"Hush."

"I will not!"

I stood and leaned over her. "Matilda, you are acting the child!"

Before I could react, she lashed out at the back of my left hand with a letter opener she must have picked up from the dresser, the metal blade leaving behind a thin red gash. I tried to cover the cut with my right hand, but she reached out and held me still. As we watched, the wound knit itself back together, first becoming a pink line, then that, too, faded, leaving nothing behind but a trickle of glistening blood, the injury otherwise gone within seconds. Matilda wiped the blood away, then peered up at me with sorrowful eyes. "What did she do to you, my poor Bram?"

I tugged my hand away and thrust it into my pocket.

"Removing it from sight does not make it less so," Matilda told me, the anger having evaporated from her voice. "Don't you want to understand?"

My mind raced. I felt the blood burning beneath my cheeks, my heart thumping in my chest.

I did not want to know.

I did not want to think about such things.

Not now. Not ever.

"If she were near," Matilda breathed, "would you know?"

Such thoughts had not dawned on me in years.

Nanna Ellen staring down at me from her ceiling perch, her eyes flaming red, burning so bright they nearly cast enough light to illuminate the room. And her falling, falling on me.

For the first time in ages, my arm itched.

NOW

———◆———

Bram looks up from the journal, the sound still echoing through his mind.

A wolf, no mistaking it, but the howl came not from behind the door. This howl came from outside.

Rising from his chair, Bram goes to the window and gazes out over the grounds. At first, he sees nothing; then he sees a large shadow inching through the thicket, parting the grass. The shadow moves slowly around the base of the tower, then raises its head and leers up at Bram.

Bram recognizes the wolf immediately. While he can't explain how he knows, this is the same wolf from his dream earlier in the night, the one that attacked him from behind the door. Only now, the fierce beast isn't trapped behind a door; the wolf isn't trapped at all. It roams free on the ground, and Bram is nothing more than the hunted trapped in a high tree.

The wolf glares up at him with the same red eyes as in his dream and lets out a savage howl. Surely such a howl will bring the townspeople running with guns in hand. Nobody comes, however, and the wolf paces back and forth until the weeds are flattened, until a path is worn in the earth.

Without abandoning the window, Bram reaches back and snatches up the rifle, already primed to fire. He balances the weapon on the level flat stones of the windowsill and follows the wolf with the barrel, slowly scanning back and forth as the wolf moves. When the wolf pauses, when it stops to stare up at him again, Bram squeezes the trigger.

The rifle kicks back into his shoulder as the shot leaps from the barrel.

He hears a yelp, but it does not come from below—it comes from behind the door, and is followed by the heavy thump of a body falling to the floor.

Bram goes to the door and presses his ear against the oak. He hears nothing.

After a minute, he returns to the window and peers below—the wolf is gone.

Had he really seen it? Perhaps he had imagined the wolf. But, no, the weeds are still pressed flat where the wolf had been. Yes, the wolf had been there, but maybe now it slunk off somewhere to die. Bram weighs going down to check, but he knows doing so would be the height of foolishness. He cannot leave this room.

A scratch at the door, followed by a soft whimper; the sound of an injured dog.

This has to be another trick.

He wants to open the door. He wants to see with his own eyes.

He finds himself back at the door, reaching for the lock, fumbling through his pocket in search of the key. He will open the door and—

No.

Bram pushes away from the door and scuttles across the floor.

Just another trick.

Then comes another howl, again from outside.

He returns to the window to discover two wolves—one black and one gray—standing in the grass beneath him, both staring up with fiery eyes. He spots a patch of red in the fur of the gray wolf—the one he had shot. The black wolf goes to the gray and licks the wound, then raises its head in a ferocious howl.

The creature behind the door answers with a howl all its own—a cry falling somewhere between that of a wolf and a human in dire pain.

At that, a third wolf comes into view down below. More follow. A pack of wolves, all with blazing red eyes.

THE JOURNAL of BRAM STOKER

———◆———

10 August 1868, 4:06 p.m. — My office within Dublin Castle was far from a lavish affair; it was cold, windowless, packed full with nine desks, nine chairs, and an assortment of cabinets and shelves brimming with old texts and papers belonging to those who came before me. Yet, the eight of us clerking in the Petty Sessions office were a jolly group. We often worked from 9:00 a.m. until 10:00 p.m., and since most of the castle staff, including our supervisor, Richard Wingfield, Esq., J.P. (Justice of the Peace), left at a more civilized hour, we felt free to make arrangements personally.

As I think about it, Mr. Wingfield rarely appeared in the office; when he did, he was known to come in late and leave early, leaving us to our own devices. On those long days, Thomas Taggart, a senior clerk, would cook dinner for us, a few snipe or teal one of us had shot, roasted with carrots or parsnips, but once during a holiday season, he roasted a turkey with all manner of vegetables, salad, plum pudding, and we each brought a beverage—punch, sherry, port, champagne, beer, claret, curaçao, and coffee. We covered a table with blotting paper gummed together and raised our glasses to each other and the Queen till the wee hours. That night, a very large armoire padded with old clothes served as a nest for a couple of the younger boys who could not keep pace.

More often than not, Mr. Wingfield wandered in just before lunchtime, when we were hard at work, and our office seemed normal. I would like to say normal meant tidy, but it was not so. Certainly, my desk was chaos, but I knew exactly where every pen, pencil, clip, or scrap of paper was to be found. And should someone attempt to organize my paltry possessions, they would do me a severe injustice.

As we tended towards diligence in the morning, the other clerks were subdued, and I had taken the opportunity to finish my review of *The Woman in White*, which I had seen the night before at the Theatre Royal in Dublin:

The tone of the novel is essentially gloomy, and Mr. W. C. doubtless wished to preserve its great characteristic, but he overlooked the fact that the action of a drama is so concentrated, the suspense so great, and the strain on the minds and feelings of the audience so intense, that occasional relief is necessary. Even *Hamlet* requires the gravedigger, and *Lear* the fool.

I was so wrapped up in my writings I did not hear Michael Murphy, the office messenger boy, approach my corner until he cleared his throat. I glanced up to find him staring at me, tapping an envelope on the corner of my desk.

"Telegram for me?"

He shook his head. "Only a note; I was asked to run it to you straightaway. The lady said you would provide a generous tip if I got here quickly."

"What lady?"

"Not my job to collect names, sir, only deliver." He held out his hand.

I dug into my pocket and pulled out a two-bob bit, depositing it in his palm.

He looked down at the coin, let out a little sigh, and held the envelope out to me. I took it and waved him off.

The envelope contained a single sheet of paper, cornered in fours. I unfolded it and held it up to the light of the lamp on my desk.

> Meet me at Marsh's. 6:00 p.m.
> —*Matilda*

10 AUGUST 1868, 6:00 p.m.—Marsh's Library was founded in the early eighteenth century by Archbishop Narcissus Marsh. It is a rather subdued structure located off St. Patrick's Close, nearly hidden behind the cathedral. When I was a student at Trinity, Marsh's Library was a frequent destination, but I found myself spending less and less time there as my studies progressed. At this hour, the library was well attended, not only by students but laymen in kind, finding themselves here after a day's work.

I took a deep breath and derived simple satisfaction in the scent of old leather-bound books, of which there were many. The library boasted a collection nearing twenty thousand volumes, with topics ranging from medicine and navigation to science, religion, and history. Much of the collection was original, procured by the archbishop himself, all painstakingly cared for. The walls of the library were lined with metal cages, referred to as "cells" by the students of Trinity. If you requested one of the rare texts, you would find yourself locked inside one of these cells with the treasured tome until you completed your reading of it. Only then would the keeper unlock the door of the cage, the book never leaving the protective custody of the library.

As my eyes adjusted to the dim light of Marsh's Library, I found Matilda ensconced in one of the cages near the back. Her door was open, which meant she had selected this cell intentionally but had not requested a rare text; if she had, she would have been locked in. I found her surrounded not by manuscripts but by newspapers. She was scribbling away furiously on a page in her sketchbook; it was not a drawing she was laboring over but writing, in her thin, neat script, nearly a pageful. She glanced up as I approached and closed the pad before my curious eyes could catch a glimpse of what she was writing.

With thoughts of our conversation from the day before in mind, I instinctively tugged at the sleeve of my shirt, ensuring the two tiny red marks were not in view. "Ah, my dear sister, that was a clever way to rid me of my hard-earned funds. Could you not have just stopped by my office?"

"Could that space accommodate one more body? I was under the assumption you discouraged visitors because you prefer not to have them standing on your shoulders."

I considered a retort, but I had plans to attend the theater and did not wish to be late on account of this unscheduled stop. "Care to share why I was summoned to your lair?"

Matilda gestured to the chair beside her, and I took a seat.

She said, "What do you remember of Patrick O'Cuiv?"

It took me a moment, then it came to me. "He nearly killed his entire family before turning the knife on himself. He also slew his employer's land manager that same night, or maybe it was earlier in the day. I really don't remember anything beyond that, though; I think Ma and Pa kept the stories from us. They probably felt we were too young to hear of such a thing."

Matilda pointed to a stack of newspapers to her left, all editions of the *Saunders's News-Letter*. "I gathered together every issue mentioning the case."

"What would prompt you to do that?"

She reached for the stack and dropped three of them in front of me, reading each headline aloud. "These are the three we saw: 'Family Murdered in Malahide,' 'Land Manager Killed in Altercation at Farm in Santry House,' and 'Mass Killing in Malahide Father Suspected of Santry Estate Murder.' The last one was dated 10 October 1854."

Matilda pulled a second stack forward and tapped them with her finger. "These four came later. Go ahead and read them; the stories are not very long."

"To what end?"

"Just read them, Bram."

I sighed and pulled the first paper towards me. As with the others, the O'Cuiv story dominated the front page:

CROWN AUTHORITIES PUTTING TOGETHER PIECES OF THESE LOCAL DEATHS SUSPECT THAT THEY ARE ALL CONNECTED

Patrick O'Cuiv of Malahide will be charged for the murder of Cornelius Healy, land manager of the Santry Estate. In addition, once thought of as a victim, Mr. O'Cuiv will also be charged with the willful murder of his wife and two children. The grisly account of the at-home murder will likely be corroborated by the one surviving daughter, Maggie O'Cuiv. The authorities have determined that in spite of her tender age, she is fit and capable and will be best served by having her testimony taken by deposition which shall be admissible as evidence.

I looked up at Matilda after reading the first story; she retrieved the next paper and placed it in front of me before I could say a word.

MURDER TRIAL

Crown authorities have issued a statement about the recent murders in Santry and Malahide.

Mr. Patrick O'Cuiv will be charged with unwillful murder of Santry land manager Cornelius Healy. Public defender Simon Stephens, acting as agent for the defense of Mr. O'Cuiv, has entered a motion to dismiss the case on the grounds of reasonable rationale for self-defense. Mr. Brian Callahan has further stated that the three murders of O'Cuiv's wife and family members were committed under duress of extreme hardship and drunkenness and will be tried as willful murders. Mr. Stephens claims that Mr. O'Cuiv was rendered hopeless by the prospect of being unable to provide food for his young, starving family. After being denied the purchase of grain at his place of work, he tried to steal an amount of grain. He was brutally punished by caning at the hands of Mr. Healy, which caused him to act irrationally and engage in fisticuffs with Mr. Healy. "Sadly," stated Stephens, "Mr. O'Cuiv felt justified in the slaying of his own family as a reasonable method to reduce their suffering." Stephens followed up by asking Judge Dermot McGillycuddy to dismiss charges on the basis that Mr. O'Cuiv was rendered insane by placing his family in such a sad predicament.

"My Lord, this is horrible," I muttered.

Matilda slid the third paper over to me.

O'CUIV CHARGED WITH
ASSAULT, NOT MURDER

The coroner has found that the death of Cornelius Healy was accidental, the result, according to witness accounts, of Mr. Healy's slipping during a fair fistfight and hitting his head on a rock. The judge took advantage of the finding to add that denying Mr. O'Cuiv the opportunity to purchase grain for his starving family while such grain was being shipped out of Ireland is not justification for killing a man but certainly may be grounds for driving a man to desperate lengths to provide for his family. Mr. O'Cuiv was sentenced to five years of penal servitude.

Matilda handed me the final newspaper. Patrick O'Cuiv was again the headline.

O'CUIV SUICIDE

While the Crown Solicitor was pondering on the first day of deliberations the case against Mr. O'Cuiv for the killing of his wife and two children, Mr. O'Cuiv managed to hang himself in his jail cell, thus putting an end to the debate about the solicitor's claim of insanity.

I set the paper down and turned to my sister. "So, as we suspected, he killed his employer over food and then killed his family rather than watch them starve to death."

"All but his daughter, Maggie, who escaped. She was six and a half at the time; she would be twenty-one today," Matilda explained.

"I wonder what became of her," I said.

Matilda ignored the comment and instead dropped another folder on the table in front of me. "I found the record of his death."

"Why would you—" I began a little louder than appropriate, and a number of library patrons glared at me through the bars of the cage. I offered an apologetic smile and lowered my voice. "Why would you extract his death records?"

She pulled a sheet of paper from the file, reading just loud enough for the two of us to hear. " 'Patrick O'Cuiv was found hanging in his cell on the morning of 9 October at twenty-six minutes past the six o'clock hour. Twisting his bedsheets into a makeshift rope, he looped it through the bars of the cell's single window, then twisted it repeatedly around his neck. Because the window was only five feet off the ground, and O'Cuiv stood at a height of five feet eleven inches, it appears he leaned back against the wall, then lifted his feet out from beneath him and held them extended out in front of him, the weight of his body forcing the noose to tighten and ultimately strangle the life out of him. As hangings go, this would have been a difficult one since he could have stopped it at any moment simply by lowering his feet. Instead, he committed fully to the task at hand and did not waiver until dead. Upon examination of the body, it was determined the cause of death to be strangulation and not dislocation of the cervical vertebrae. The wounds upon his arms had grown infected and were most likely very painful. I counted no less than six lacerations on the right arm, beginning at the wrist and continuing nearly to the elbow. The left arm had four cuts of similar size running the length of his forearm. Although he had been treated by Bartley Rupee with chloride, the skin had turned purple and yellow surrounding the wounds, and, even in death, the odor of infection was present. Because O'Cuiv died at his own hand, he will not be permitted burial at Saint John the Baptist but will instead be laid to rest in the suicide graves behind the main cemetery. May God have mercy on his soul.'"

I let out a sigh. "This is all quite fascinating, Matilda, but I still do not know why you are showing it to me. These events took place a long time ago."

Matilda pulled another paper from the stack at her side, this one a recent edition of the *Dublin Morning News* dated 9 August 1868. "This is yesterday's paper. Look—" She tapped at the headline.

VAGABOND FALLS FROM STEAMBOAT AND DROWNS IN RIVER LIFFEY

An unidentified man, thirty to forty years of age, stumbled while walking the deck of the *Roscommon* during the ship's final voyage last evening. He attempted to recover his step but instead tumbled over the rail and into the frigid waters. A gentleman passenger dove in after him and hauled his body to shore, but at that point life had deserted the victim. Other passengers aboard the *Roscommon* told this reporter that the man had begged his way aboard, receiving fare from no less than three other patrons, and upon departure from shore became extremely agitated. "The moment we left the dock, he began running up and down the length of the boat in sheer panic, believing the vessel was about to sink," one passenger said. "A number of times he went to the rail and peered over the side at the water, his face lined with fear."

The *Roscommon*, which was en route to Holyhead, has been held in port by the harbor police until the conclusion of their investigation. With permission of their office, we have included a photograph of the unidentified man. Anyone with information on his identity is asked to contact the coroner at Steevens' Hospital.

Matilda unfolded the paper so I could view the photograph. It was Patrick O'Cuiv.

I STARED DOWN at the page. "It cannot be him."

"But it is," Matilda replied. "Look at his arms."

The man wore no shirt, and his arms were clearly visible, each lined with long scars from wrist to forearm.

"Six cuts on the right, four on the left. The exact same as those listed in O'Cuiv's death records," she said.

"This is a coincidence; there can be no other explanation."

"The only explanation is the simplest one: this is Patrick O'Cuiv."

"Perhaps a son or close relative."

"The O'Cuivs were survived only by their daughter, Maggie. Patrick killed his only son."

"A cousin, then?" I lifted the newspaper and held the photograph to the lamplight. The image was grainy, decidedly so, but I recognized that face. As much as I wished to deny it were true, the man staring up at me with death in his vacant eyes was Patrick O'Cuiv. I reached for the folder containing O'Cuiv's death records and reread the documents. Then a thought occurred to me. "What if he faked his death?"

"The hanging?"

"Yes. Maybe he had help: someone, or a group of someones, who sympathized with him."

"Who would sympathize with a man who killed his wife and children?"

"Perhaps someone grateful for the death of Cornelius Healy?"

"The land manager?"

I nodded. "Perhaps he had friends at Santry House or others who also harbored hatred for Healy and were grateful for the man's death. If he wouldn't grant O'Cuiv grain, I imagine there were others. It's possible they faked his death and somehow snuck him from the jail."

Matilda was shaking her head. "There are records of his burial."

"The same people could have concealed that as well. A few shillings to the undertaker and he buries an empty coffin."

"That is a conspiracy of grand scale, too grand. But let us say for a minute you are correct and all of these people helped him fake his death, fake the records at the constable's office, then bribed the undertaker to fake his burial. If, after all of this, he finds a new life in Dublin and is killed again in a freak accident fourteen years later, how do you explain his appearance?" She reached into the stack of newspapers and pulled out the first one, which had a mention of him at the outset of the trial, and positioned it next to the paper from the previous day, pointing to both images of O'Cuiv. "He has not aged a day from this photograph to that. Fourteen years behind him, and these images seem to be taken a day apart."

Again, she was right. The man in the paper from the day before actually appeared a little younger than the older image. I did not want to hear her say the words, but I asked anyway; I had no choice. "How do you explain the likeness?"

"You know how."

"First, you tell me you saw our old nanny and she has not aged in fourteen years. Now you believe the same of this man. Who next? Old Mrs. Dunhy from the dairy? That drunkard Leahy, who used to wander the fields until all hours singing to the cows? People get older. They do not rise from the grave only to die again."

"Yet, here we are," she said, gesturing at the newspapers and paperwork littering the table. "And I'm certain that was Nanna Ellen I spied in Paris."

I took her hand in mine and lowered my voice. "Matilda, you are an intelligent, beautiful, talented woman. You should not waste your thoughts or your time on matters such as these. These are the fantasies of children. Things of fairy tales."

She squeezed my hand. "When we were children and you told me what you saw, I did not believe you. Even after witnessing Nanna Ellen walk into that bog and not come out, I did not believe you. When we found that disgusting dirt under her bed and it vanished a day later, I told myself we imagined it. When we climbed the steps of the castle tower and found the crate with . . . you know . . . and you told me Nanna Ellen had been in that room a short time earlier, I spent years convincing myself none of these things actually happened. But I cannot lie anymore, not to myself anyway. I cannot go to my grave without knowing what she did to you, what became of her. There is this burning need in me to find answers to all these things, and I fear I cannot move forward with my life until I do. I'm sure you feel the same as me."

I shook my head. "I rid myself of all this uncertainty as a child."

Matilda tilted her head. "Did you now?"

"I did."

"Then why don't you tell me what became of the ring? Just explain that, to my satisfaction, and we will pretend we did not meet today. Remember the ring, sweet brother? The one we found clenched in the dead hand?"

My chest tightened as my breath caught.

"This man, O'Cuiv, and Nanna Ellen are somehow connected. Of this I am sure, but if you tell me you do not know where the ring is, all of this goes away. I'll pretend I didn't see you take it that night. You can go back to your life, and I'll return to mine, neither of us the wiser," Matilda said. "Come now, Bram. End this."

I let out a deep sigh and reached for the silver chain around my neck. I tugged it out from beneath my shirt. The ring dangled from it. It had not left my neck in almost fourteen years.

Matilda flicked the ring with her finger. "Sometimes our deepest fears are the ones we keep closest to our hearts. You've never stopped believing, you only stopped admitting you believe."

I tucked the ring back under my shirt and fell silent for a long while. Finally, I gestured at the papers on the table. "I do not know what to make of all this, but I am willing to admit I am intrigued. If this truly is Patrick O'Cuiv, if you somehow saw Ellen, if there is a chance we can find her and ask her how she healed me, ask her what she did to me, I need to . . . I want to understand."

Matilda smiled and began stacking all the papers neatly. "That is the inquisitive brother I know and love."

She reached for her sketchbook and turned to a page near the center. "Do you remember these?"

I pulled the pad closer, my heart thudding. "The maps . . ."

"Yes, the maps." She flipped the page, one after the other. "All seven of them."

"I had forgotten these."

She tilted her head. "Did you? Somehow, I doubt that."

"The detail is astounding, how you drew so well as a child . . . such a talent will always amaze me."

She turned the sketchbook back around and tapped at the map, the one of Austria. "You know what amazes me? These marks. The marks that appear on each of these maps. I know exactly what they are, what they represent."

"What?"

"Cemeteries. Every one of them. And not just any cemetery, but the oldest of cemeteries. Each older than the last." She looked back down the map. "This is the Zentralfriedhof Simmering in Vienna. I was confused at first because most publications state the cemetery was founded only a few years ago, in 1863, but that isn't true. It officially became a cemetery that year, but the deceased have been buried at that location for nearly two hundred years prior." She turned the page. *Highgate—London* was written at the bottom. "This one here, Highgate. It, too, was *officially* founded recently. In 1839, the Church of England consecrated fifteen acres as burial grounds. They also set aside two acres for dissenters. Those grounds are the ones I found most interesting, because, like the cemetery in Vienna, the earliest records for this plot date back to the sixteen hundreds. Bodies buried, but not in consecrated ground."

I watched as Matilda turned the page again, the excitement mounting in her voice.

"The Cimitero Acattolico in Rome—officially founded in 1716 but built adjacent to the Pyramid of Cestius, a tomb that dates back to somewhere between 18 and 12 b.c. Bodies were routinely buried there for over a thousand years, long before the grounds were consecrated," she told me.

Her eyes met mine, and her voice took on a conspiratorial tone. "I must admit, brother, I did not visit Paris only to view art, I also walked the grounds of the Cimetière du Père Lachaise. Like the others, it was founded as a cemetery and officially consecrated in 1804, but the original site was that of a small chapel with burials dating back as early as 1682. The original thirteen graves were never blessed. The Church refused, not knowing who was buried there."

"Saint John the Baptist in Clontarf," I said softly. "The suicide graves we talked about as children, that ground is unconsecrated to this day."

Matilda nodded. "Every cemetery amongst her maps has such graves; burial plots never blessed by the Church."

"But why would this interest her?"

Matilda leaned back in her chair. "I remember the marks upon the maps distinctly. Each had a circle around the cemetery, and all but the location at Whitby had an X. I think she has visited each of these locations."

"For what reason?"

"Either in search of something or to place something, that would be my guess."

I thought about this for a moment. "How does this pertain to the information you found on O'Cuiv?"

Matilda let out a frustrated sigh. "That, I do not know, but I imagine it does; it *feels* like it does. All of this feels like the pieces of a puzzle fitting together, but the complete image is still unknown."

My sister turned the pages of her sketchbook, flipping past the many drawings she had made of Nanna Ellen when we were children, not one looking like the last. The same woman but different. She stopped when she reached new drawing, one of Patrick O'Cuiv, the scars on his arms highlighted in a harsh red. "Ellen, O'Cuiv, these maps," she said. "It's all connected somehow."

She closed the sketchbook then, her eyes meeting mine. "There is one person who probably knows something of all this."

I could only nod.

"You and I must speak to Thornley," I heard myself say.

THE DIARY of THORNLEY STOKER

(RECORDED IN SHORTHAND AND TRANSCRIBED HEREWITH.)

———◆———

10 August 1868, 8:00 p.m. — Emily finally found sleep, and for this mercy I was grateful. It took a substantial dose of laudanum in her evening's wine to make her do so. I found myself staring at my beautiful wife's face, so peaceful and content. Her skin glowed in the lamplight with the luster of fine china, her bosom rising and falling in a steady rhythm beneath the soft cotton sheets. I couldn't help but watch.

Who could turn away?

This state of being was such a far cry from only two hours earlier; I cringed at the memory of it. Her shouting at me from across the library as she hurled volume after volume into the consuming flames of the fireplace, loudly proclaiming, "The Devil breathes within these pages! The voice of Satan himself!" I tried to tell her she was wrong, for the book she held in her hand was nothing more than a medical journal, but when she opened it and read from the pages with eyes as wide as saucers, I knew there was no reaching her. "Bartholomew pressed his lips against Amelia's bosom and inhaled the stench of death as blood poured from her open mouth and ears!" Even as she read these words, her eyes flickering across some random page, I knew they were a fabrication of her own mind.

Again, this was a medical journal; I caught the page beneath her thumb, and the headline read OBSERVATIONS ON THE TREATMENT OF

ZYMOTIC DISEASES BY THE ADMINISTRATION OF SULPHATE. Yet, she continued to read imaginary words in a voice so loud I covered my ears. "It was her life he desired most, the very essence of her soul, and he held her until it was fully his before dropping her body in a heap at his feet, his eyes searching the night for another!"

As if to punctuate this last sentence, she slammed the cover of the book shut and heaved the text into the awaiting flames.

I raced over, tried to hold her, but she fought me. Oh, how she fought me! The strength possessed by her will was that of ten grown men! Of this I do not lie. She shook me off with a start and sent me falling backwards against the chaise. I was grateful for its soft cushions; another two feet to the left, and I would have crashed into the end table. With its surface populated with small china figurines, I might have been injured, and Emily's nurse, Florence Dugdale, had long been sent home for the night.

When I recovered, I found Emily staring at me, her mouth agape. A moment later, she turned away and seemed to forget all about me as she plucked another volume from the shelf. She had tossed so many books on the fire that she smothered the flames, and the room began to fill with thick gray smoke and the reek of smoldering leather. It was then that I grabbed the pitcher of water from the table and tossed it in her face. She gasped, and her body twitched at the cold shock of it. Her glazed stare focused in a blink of the eye, and her head pivoted this way and that in confusion. I recognized this look and went to her, quickly wrapping my arms around her. "There, there, my Emily. Everything is okay. I've got you now. Everything will be all right."

Her voice at my ear sounded like that of a frightened child, her words nearly lost behind thin breaths. "His red eyes again; they are just the same."

"Who, my dear? Of whom do you speak?"

"He will come for you, you know. If you injure me, he will come and inflict such wrath on the likes of you," she said.

"Emily, I don't know what you're talking about. You're rambling." I pulled her closer, feeling her heart pounding fiercely against my chest. "I would never hurt you, my love."

She let out a soft laugh, a tainted giggle. "He's watching you. Right this very instant, his eyes are upon you, and he is not happy."

I knew when she entered this state it was only a matter of time before she became violent once again. This momentary lapse was nothing but a respite, so I guided her gently to the chaise. "Wait here, my love. I will be right back."

I ran to the kitchen and quickly poured two glasses of wine, then retrieved the small bottle of laudanum from the pantry and added nearly double Emily's usual dose to hers. I stirred the drug into her wine and returned to the library only to find Emily sitting on the floor, the skirt of her dress bunched around her waist like a little girl at play. She glanced up at me with tear-filled eyes, red and puffy now. "Please make me better, Thornley. I don't want to feel this way any longer."

Clarity had returned to her, but for how long I did not know. I handed her the glass of wine and sat upon the floor beside her. "I will do everything within my power, my dear Emily. We will beat this illness and send it back to whatever hell from which it came. I promise you my word."

At this, she forced a weak smile.

I watched as she took a sip of the wine, followed by another after that. The anger and confusion that had lined her face began to fade, and soon her body began to swoon. When at last her eyelids drooped, I ran my hand through her flowing dark hair. "Finish the last of your wine, and I'll help you upstairs. You need your rest. It has been a very long night."

"It has indeed," she said. The words, no louder than a whisper, were garbled.

I helped her lift the glass to her lips and drink, then took it from her weak hand and set it on the table at my side. "Let us get you to your feet and upstairs, my love."

She nodded and said something I could not make out. I helped her stand, bearing most of her weight. At only five feet tall, she weighed next to nothing, even in this limp state. When we reached the door to the library, I scooped her up and cradled her in my arms, her head resting on my shoulder, then carried her up the stairs to the bed in which she now lay.

Her breathing was heavy, and her chest rose and fell in rhythm. I reached over to her nightstand and wound the small metronome, then released the pendulum, sending it swinging back and forth in a steady tick and tock, a sound she had always found soothing.

A sound that reminded me of a happier time.

It had been nearly a year since she had played the piano in the parlor; the keys were now out of tune and dusty, the candelabra resting atop the grand instrument gone months without being lit. The room seemed deserted and stale, and I rarely entered it anymore.

Oh, how I long for my Emily back!

Where is the woman with whom I fell so deeply and completely in love? And who is this being creeping into her body day after day?

The night before last, I found her standing over me in the dark. Her hands, taut, were stretched out before her, fingers quivering as they bent back at a painful angle. She stood looking down at me with one palm held over my forehead and the other over my belly, and from her lips came words I did not recognize. They were, in fact, words, though, of this I was sure, strung together in incoherent sentences. I saw only the whites of her eyes, the irises rolled up and hidden inside.

When she realized I had awoken, the entire episode ended in an instant. She simply dropped her arms, walked back to her side of the bed, and climbed beneath the sheets with her back to me. I could not help but wonder if I had imagined the entire episode, some sort of waking dream, but it felt too real to be a fictitious construct of the mind. The terror I experienced upon waking and discovering her looming over me did not fade, as most fearfulness incited by dreams did moments after waking; instead, it grew, and in that moment I realized I feared my wife. My dear, sweet, lovely Emily—I was afraid of her. For the remainder of that night, and each night passing hence, I slept with a scalpel beneath my pillow, my mind filled with dread of the hour I would be forced to employ it.

I pulled the note from my pocket, the paper now thin and cracking at the folds, dear Emily's beautiful handwriting worn by my fingers, tonight's tears rendering it barely legible:

> My love, my first and only true love, my heart will
> be with you today and always. My hand in yours as
> you begin this adventure.
>
> —*Em*

She had slipped the note in my shoe for me to find on my first day of teaching at Queen's College in Galway. Not a day passed without my reading it, the woman who wrote it slowly slipping from my grasp.

A LOUD KNOCK at the front door startled me out of my rumination, and I cursed whoever it was calling at such a late hour.

I quickly replaced the note, pulled the quilt from the foot of the bed up to my wife's chin, and tucked it in around her before hastening downstairs, closing the bedroom door at my back.

I found my brother and sister standing on my stoop when I opened the front door, both soaked to the bone by an icy night rain that must have started while I was upstairs.

"Do you have any idea of the time?" I asked them. "Aren't you supposed to be in Paris? When did you return?"

Matilda ignored my questions, pushed past me, and stood in the foyer, a puddle of water forming around her on the marble floor. "We need to talk" was all she said, and she shrugged off her coat and hung it on the rack.

Bram remained in the rain until I nodded at him and tilted my head towards the foyer; then he followed after his sister, stomping his wet boots on the flagstone outside before entering.

Beyond the door, the wind howled something fierce; the rain danced sideways for a moment before falling to earth. I closed the door and engaged the lock.

"Why is it so smoky in here?" Bram asked, starting for the library. "Is your flue closed?"

"Wait!" I shouted, my voice much louder than I hoped.

Bram stopped and looked back at me.

I did not wish for either of them to find whatever remained of the books in the fireplace, or the state of the library in general, for fear of having to explain.

Matilda saw through this immediately and stomped off into the library, Bram on her heels. We found her kneeling at the hearth, peering into the firebox. "I see my disdain for higher learning has found its way to you, brother. Burning your texts . . . I would not have suspected this is how you spent your free time. I am going to stop by unannounced more often, I think. You just became far more interesting."

"Emily and I had a fight—well, a disagreement. She felt the need to emphasize her point by destroying some of my books."

Bram snickered. "Can't she throw a plate or two, like a normal woman?"

I reached into the firebox and pulled three of the four volumes from the smoking tinders and placed them on the hearth. The fourth could not be saved, but there was hope for these three. "She is finally sleeping now, so please keep your voices low so as not to awaken her. She needs her rest."

I had not shared our troubles with anyone; I had forbidden staff to speak of such affairs beyond the confines of our home. I did not wish to burden anyone with our problems, particularly my family. I would find an antidote to what ailed her and I would do so without garnering attention. The last thing I needed was for the town gossips to learn of Emily's illness. Should word get out, my medical practice would be ended before it began.

I forced these thoughts from my mind, placed a fake smile on my face, and turned to my siblings. "What brings you to my home on this glorious evening?"

"Matilda thinks she spied Nanna Ellen in Paris," Bram blurted out. "And Patrick O'Cuiv has suddenly risen from the dead only to die again. What else could there possibly be?"

THE JOURNAL *of* BRAM STOKER

————◆————

10 August 1868, 8:15 p.m. —My brother's face was long and tired, and I instantly regretted intruding unannounced into his home. Even more, I regretted my outburst regarding Nanna Ellen and O'Cuiv, for the moment I said my piece, the color left his cheeks and I thought he might pass out. I quickly crossed the room and looped his arm over my shoulder. "Help me get him to the sofa," I told Matilda.

She, too, noticed his reaction, and I caught a sideways glance from her before she braced our brother from his opposite side and aided me in shuffling him across the room.

Thornley fell into the cushions like a drunk hitting the sidewalk and stared up at the two of us, his mouth slightly ajar but saying nothing for perhaps a minute. When he finally did speak, his next word was not a denial, as I expected, but—

"When?"

I frowned. "When what?"

"When to both," he said quietly. His voice had taken on a raspiness, more like Pa's brogue with every passing day. "When did you see Nanna Ellen last? And when did O'Cuiv die again?"

Matilda sat beside him on the sofa. "I saw Ellen in Paris only last week, from across the street. I believe she saw me as well, but I lost her in the crowd as I approached. I am certain it was her, though, as I've explained to Bram." She made this last revelation with slight trepidation; a part of her was prepared to argue the point, as she had with me, so she became confused when Thornley did not press her on the topic.

"And O'Cuiv?"

Matilda glanced up at me; I could offer nothing but a shrug of my shoulders. Reaching into her bag, she withdrew a copy of yesterday's newspaper. For a moment, I thought she had stolen copies of the *Saunders's News-Letter* from Marsh's Library and was relieved to see her bag held nothing else. She placed the paper on the table before Thornley and pointed to the story.

Thornley retrieved a pair of spectacles from his pocket, perched them on his nose, and leaned over the newspaper. He perused the story for a long while, long enough to read the article twice over. He leaned back in his seat and removed the spectacles, cleaning them with his shirttail before returning them to his pocket. "Bram, could you please pass me that glass of wine next to you?"

A full glass of claret stood beside an empty crystal decanter—I handed it to my brother and watched him drink the wine down without a single breath between gulps.

Thornley then placed the empty glass beside the newspaper on the table, studied us both, and sighed deeply. "He has been in my dreams of late, Patrick O'Cuiv. I suppose the stories of what he did, as horrific as they were, stuck with me over the years. Perhaps he is the reason I have not become a father as yet. The idea of murdering your entire family, your wife and children, for no reason other than an inability to put food in their mouths, this terrifies me."

"Only in your dreams? Did you see him?" Matilda asked.

Thornley fiddled with his empty wineglass. "Not him, no. Not at first anyway."

My heart thudded. "Not at first? But you saw . . ."

The theater performance I planned to attend now forgotten, I watched as my brother stood from the sofa and made his way across the room to the sideboard. He retrieved a bottle of whiskey and held it out to me. I shook my head. He shrugged and filled the wineglass about halfway, then resealed the bottle and gave the glass a wobbly shake, watching the amber liquid coat the sides, then run back down. Thornley returned to the sofa, took a sip, and let out another sigh.

"The first time I encountered her," he said, "a couple years had passed since she left us. I was walking down Castle Avenue after purchasing some cod for Ma down at the pier. The day was young; the sun's rays had yet to burn away the dew, and I remember how it made the toes of my shoes damp. But it felt good, too, to be away from the house, away from my chores, entrusted with the task at hand. Ma gave me two shillings for the cod and said I could keep any change for myself, so I was careful to find a fish that weighed just enough to meet her dinner needs while still depositing a few pence in my pocket.

"I stopped in Roderick's Confections and ordered a quarter bag of saltwater taffy, cherry-flavored, my favorite. I can still taste that taffy to this day. As I counted out six pence, I happened to glance out the window at the street and there she was, Nanna Ellen, standing on the other side of the glass, watching me as I watched her. She was standing very still, as if I might see past her. And I almost did, for something in my mind did not believe this was her. How could it be? But when I realized it *was* her on the other side of the glass, I dropped my change on the counter, forgot my taffy, and rushed out the door to greet her, the fish in Ma's canvas bag swinging from my arm. I expected to find Nanna Ellen standing there, waiting for me, arms wide and a smile across her lips. But when I found myself outside, she was nowhere to be seen. Only a second or so had passed, you understand, but she was gone, vanished. I searched up and down the street; I had a clear view in both directions, but there was no sign of her. She had no time to enter another store—frankly, she didn't have time to go anywhere—yet she'd gone *somewhere.* I told myself I imagined it, it was a trick of the light reflecting on the window glass of the storefront, nothing more. I repeated this explanation to myself over and over again as I walked home. Eventually, I realized I left my change and the taffy on the counter, but I didn't care. Seeing Ellen woke something inside me."

"Why did you say nothing of this before?" Matilda asked.

"To whom? Ma and Pa would not have believed me, and the three of us rarely spoke back then. I had no one to tell. By the time I arrived on our doorstep, I convinced myself it had all been in my imagination anyway," Thornley said.

I changed my mind about the whiskey and poured two fingers into a glass, held the bottle out to Matilda, who vehemently shook her head, then carried it back to the sofa and set it on the small table. "You said 'the first time' you saw her. It happened again?"

Thornley retrieved the bottle and refilled his own glass. "I was nineteen years old the second time I saw Nanna Ellen; I recall the event vividly as if only a week ago. It was a Saturday. I was in the Trinity Library at one of the small tables towards the back, with windows looking out on the Fellows' Garden. I had been awake for nearly two full days, preparing for an anatomy exam scheduled at Queen's that Monday. A thick rain fell for most of the day, and I remember thinking the square would surely flood unless there was a break in the weather. I overheard two instructors discussing the rain over lunch; this had been one of our dampest autumns, and they fully expected the dismal conditions to carry over into an equally harsh winter. Personally, I thought the rain could not have come at a better time because the bad weather kept me off the rugby field and firmly planted in my studies, exactly where I should have been. After I had devoted so many hours staring at texts, the lack of sleep began to take a toll on me—I needed to stand up and walk around in order to stay wake. I found myself drawn to one of the large windows, and I stood there for a good long while, my eyes transfixed on the heavy raindrops as they riddled the deep puddles. The entire ground danced with all this activity. Nobody was afoot, mind you, not in these conditions, the student body and faculty walled away behind closed classroom doors. When I spied a girl in the rain across the square, it gave me pause. She didn't rush through the storm from one door to the next, as one would expect; instead, she stood perfectly still, facing me, with her arms hanging slack at her sides. If I hadn't known better, I would have thought she was observing me as I looked out. And I found something vaguely familiar about her stance. And while she was too far away for me to clearly see her face, I believed I knew her.

"We both remained still for a long while, me peering out into the storm at her and her peering back at me, neither of us moving, just staring at each other from a great distance. I am not sure how I knew it was Nanna Ellen, but when the thought dawned on me, there was no shaking it—I was certain, as certain as I am now that I am talking to the two of you. When I embraced this realization, I stepped closer to the window and placed my open palms against the glass. The harsh iciness of the storm bit at my skin, and at that moment the glass seemed extraordinarily thin. Then she was right there—one moment she was across the square, the next she was inches from me, separated only by the window."

"And it was Ellen?" Matilda asked.

Thornley nodded. "There was no mistaking her; she stood as close as you and I, maybe closer. Her eyes were the deepest blue, and her skin appeared flawless. I think I noticed that first of all, watching the rain trickle down her perfect cheeks. I caught my own reflection in the glass and suddenly thought of myself as old, at least older than she. I think my mind grappled with this calculation simply because the last time I saw Nanna Ellen, I was but a boy; now I was on the edge of manhood, and I could see every one of those years between us upon my face. Not hers, though; she appeared as young as the day she left, as if not a single day had passed.

"She raised her own hand and pressed it to the glass opposite mine, and I swore the window grew colder. Her large blue eyes screamed with a sadness so profound I found myself bordering on tears, unable to turn away from her. Then she was gone. As simple as that. Perhaps I blinked, perhaps I did not, but, either way, she disappeared in that instant. I had full view of the square; as with the candy store all those years earlier, there was simply no place to go, yet somehow she had, leaving not a trace behind."

Thornley finished and studied his empty glass. I reached for the bottle of whiskey and poured another round for my brother.

I asked, "Was this the last time you saw her?"

Thornley shook his head. "The last time was no more than three days ago, but this final experience was more akin to the first. Emily and I attended the theater for the Friday-evening performance of *Caste*, and I thought I saw Ellen exit the mezzanine; only a glimpse, mind you, for we were in the balcony, but I am certain this was her. She wore a gorgeous flowing red gown and appeared to be in the company of a gentleman. I considered going to her, but I had no idea how I would explain such a thing to Emily, and I quickly realized how pointless it would be—she would no doubt vanish as I neared, as she had on the other occasions." Thornley took a long drink, then added, "I think the man who accompanied her may have been O'Cuiv. I recall thinking just that when I first saw him; but believing him to be dead, I dismissed the thought as preposterous. But, now . . ."

"How certain are you?" I asked of him.

"I cannot be sure; the light was dim, and we were far apart, but the man had a similar form and dressed his hair in the same way." He paused for a moment, then: "There was a child, too."

"A child?"

Thornley nodded. "Dressed in a beautiful little gown; she looked like a doll. She made me think of O'Cuiv's daughter, the one who lived."

"Maggie?" Matilda said.

"Ah yes, Maggie. That was it." He took another drink. "Of course, it could not have been her; she would be in her twenties by now. From what I recall, she was around six or seven at the time of the murders."

All of this information puzzled me. "Did Ellen know the O'Cuivs? I don't recall her ever mentioning them when we were children. Even on that one instance when the O'Cuiv family supped with us, they did not appear to be anything but newly acquainted."

Matilda said, "We were children. Would we have realized if they were familiar?"

"Ma would know," Thornley pointed out.

"We mustn't involve Ma in this," I said. "Pa, either."

Thornley finished his whiskey. "Involve them in what? I don't know what any of this means."

"It means Nanna Ellen never really left us. All of this means she has been nearby all these years," Matilda said. "Who or whatever she may be."

Thornley laughed gruffly. "And what do you mean by that? 'Whatever she may be'?"

Matilda looked to me, and I immediately understood what she contemplated. We never told Thornley what we discovered in the castle tower the night before Nanna Ellen left us. Nor had we told him what we found in her room, under her bed. We told only Ma and Pa and they both dismissed our story readily. When nothing was found there the following day, these mysteries were never spoken of again.

I gave Matilda a nod. "Tell him."

And so she did. Nearly an hour passed, and between Thornley and me the whiskey was almost depleted. When she finished, the three of us stared at the embers of the fire; I rebuilt it as Matilda recapped the events.

Thornley turned to me. "You have never seen her? You were always her favorite."

"No, not once."

Matilda shot me a glance, then looked back to our brother. "Bram may have been her favorite, but you had some kind of relationship with her, didn't you?"

He frowned at her. "What on earth do you mean?"

"I once saw you enter her room with a bag; something inside that bag was moving."

Thornley lifted his glass and took yet another hearty swig. He searched the amber liquid for an answer. When he found none, he finally spoke again. "Ellen sometimes asked me to bring chickens to her room. I didn't ask her why. I didn't want to know why. I went to the coop and got them for her and said no more of it."

A question burned in me then, and I asked it before the will abandoned me. "That day you showed me the chicken coop, all the dead fowl. Was it a fox that killed them? Or did they die at your hand?"

Thornley huffed. "I am not capable of such an act. I assumed it was a fox; I found the chickens that way, just as I showed them to you." His eyes were glossy with drink, but his speech was still sound. "I think I know why she came to me, why she still comes to me," he said. He dug deep into his pocket and pulled out a handkerchief folded over something. Setting the bundle on the table, he carefully unfolded the cloth. At the center sat a lock of blond hair tied together neatly with a leather band.

My eyes went wide. "Is that hers?"

Thornley nodded. "She gave this to me when I was a lad of no more than three, a year or so after you were born, Bram. I got lost in the forest the day prior—Pa had half the town out searching. They found me near one of the bogs with a makeshift fishing pole in hand, nothing more than a branch with string, and no bait. I told them I planned to catch supper. Ma had quite the fright; she cried for days at the sight of me and threatened to tie me to her leg if I wandered off again. As Ellen tucked me in bed that night, she gave me the lock of hair and told me to always keep it in my pocket; as long as I held it near, she would be able to find me and keep me safe. I know it's silly, but I kept this in my pocket for every day that has passed since."

"That may explain why she came to you, but why me?" Matilda asked. "Why would she be in Paris?"

"The maps," I replied. "The Cimetière du Père Lachaise."

"The cemetery?" Thornley asked. "What maps?"

I gave Matilda a nod, and she showed Thornley the maps she had sketched as a child, then explained how we came upon them.

"O'Cuiv may be the key," Thornley pondered aloud after all this discussion, tapping the newspaper with his empty glass. "Ellen hasn't been found in all these years simply because she doesn't want to be, but we know where to find O'Cuiv."

"Where?" I asked.

"His body would have been taken to the nearest hospital for autopsy, for verification as to cause of death."

"Swift's is closest," Matilda said. "Where you work."

Thornley shook his head. "Steevens' Hospital next door to Swift's is more likely. We work in tandem. The morgue is there."

A burning log crackled, causing the three of us to startle. I set my empty glass on the table; no more for me tonight. "What can we hope to find by viewing his body?"

Thornley waved his finger through the air. "Not 'we,' my little brother. If someone is to concoct a plan for a clandestine trip to the morgue, it will be me going it alone."

Matilda appeared ready to boil over. "We must do this together!"

"She's right, Thornley. We should all go."

"Under what guise? As a doctor on staff at the hospital, at least I have reason to be in the morgue. What calling would the two of you have to be there?"

Matilda frowned. "Do not fool yourself, brother. You work with the lunatics, not the corpses. You have no business down there, either. None of us can make an appearance there without drawing suspicion."

"And now you know the inner workings of the hospital?" Thornley shot back.

"Enough," I said. "All three of us go tonight. Staff will be scarce. Thornley can gain us admittance, and should anyone inquire, we'll say Matilda thought she recognized the man from his picture in the newspaper, and we thought it better to bring her in under the cloak of darkness to identify the body rather than go directly to the police and chance a scandal of a very public sort. We will say we didn't want our sister embroiled in a police matter unless we were absolutely certain she knew him. Any one of your coworkers would do the same for a sister, if access were granted."

Thornley mulled this argument over, then finally nodded. "I suppose if that doesn't work, we can blame whiskey for our lapse in judgment."

"You *do* reek of it." Matilda snickered.

Just then, a bell's ringing cut through the house, a silvery sound I had not heard since I was a child, when I rang such a bell to summon aid from the confines of my sickbed.

Thornley tensed and looked towards the stairs. "Emily is waking. The two of you must go. Meet me at the south entrance to the hospital in one hour. There is a bench there near the street overlooking the park. Nobody will question you for sitting there."

With that, my brother rushed us out of his home, and Matilda and I found ourselves in the chilly night.

10 August 1868, 11:30 p.m.—The bells of St. Patrick's rang promptly at thirty minutes past, a single strike to signify the bottom of the hour. I always found it odd how this tolling sounded so much louder in the still

hours of the night. During the day, the chimes provided muted background accompaniment to the city's bustle, but after dark they took on a sharper edge.

As the bell rang out, Matilda jerked back, then shifted on the park bench we were sharing. We had arrived at Dr. Steevens' Hospital ten minutes earlier and found our way to the bench at the south entrance that Thornley had mentioned. It looked out over a small pond, no doubt a view meant to comfort visitors. I, for one, harbored no desire to be near any hospital. The mere sight of such a place brought back all the suffering of my early childhood years—I could almost smell the various medicines and elixirs through its walls as easily as if I were sitting in the same room with them. When Ellen had cured my illness all those years ago, I swore to myself I would never return to such a sickly condition. I would do everything in my power to remain healthy. So I hoped visiting a hospital—regardless of the reason that brought us here tonight—wouldn't undermine my resolve.

"I feel like we should be feeding the pigeons," Matilda said. "Something to help us appear less conspicuous."

"The pigeons are sound asleep at this hour. Even they have more sense than the two of us."

Swift's Lunatic Hospital was clearly visible across a small field to my right. The tall stone walls stood dark and ominous. Unlike Dr. Steevens' Hospital, the grounds were not manicured and landscaped with colorful flowers; the lawns were brown with death and neglect, and the only color to be found on the building came from a hardy growth of ivy creeping up the walls. Most of the windows were dark; I counted only three with lights burning from somewhere within the gloom, but the place was far from sleeping—screams rang out at random intervals. Some from men, others from women, and some that sounded like they didn't come from people at all.

I considered how my brother spent so much time in such a place, surrounded by these atrocities. Should a patient arrive at Dr. Steevens' in a consumptive state or be harboring some other more traditional ill, such as heart failure, there were plans to follow, protocols in place, treatments to be administered. Such was not the case with mental illness. Thornley preferred illnesses of the mind over those of the body, perhaps thanks to his hunger to take on a challenge. How he dealt with the screams, though—

"There is someone standing over there," Matilda's hushed voice interrupted my thoughts. Her fingers wrapped around my arm. "There, under that ash tree."

I followed her gaze and saw the shadowy figure, too. A woman in a black cloak stood beneath the branches, her face hidden under a hood. This was not traditional attire for a lady who found herself on the streets of Dublin, whether her business was legitimate or nefarious. I did not get the impression she was a lady of the night, for they tended to remain in the trafficked quarters of the city. The hospital grounds were deserted; we had observed no other soul since arriving.

"Nanna Ellen?" said Matilda.

Even though the cloak obscured much of her face, I was certain this was not Nanna Ellen. I could see only the mouth and chin, a little bit of the nose—her eyes were lost in the gloom of the hood. Her skin seemed to feed on the moonlight, absorbing the rays and creating a soft glow over her otherwise masked features.

"It's not Ellen," I replied, standing away from the bench. "She's far too short."

Matilda had risen with me, her grip tightening on my arm. I peeled away her hand. "Wait here."

But she was shaking her head. "You mustn't."

"I'll only be a moment."

I started towards the ash tree, towards the woman. She remained steadfast, her arms at her sides. I found it curious I could barely see her, even as I closed the distance between us. My night vision had improved substantially in the years since Ellen healed me. I could make out every grain of gravel paving the path, I could read signs marking the River Liffey, yet I could not seem to lock my gaze on this woman. Or was it a girl? Even a child? As I neared, I got the distinct impression she was younger than I first thought. Each time I honed in on a particular feature, she appeared to slip farther into the night, even disappearing from view. She accomplished this feat without moving; in fact, she had not moved at all since we first spotted her. Instead, the shadows engulfed her.

"Who are you?" I finally found the courage to say. Though she was at least fifty feet away from me, I was certain she heard me. When her lips parted, her teeth caught the moonlight—the brightest of whites, nearly incandescent.

"Bram!"

The whisper came from behind me, and I spun on my heel to find Thornley standing at Matilda's side. When I turned back around, the person was gone. I frantically looked up and down the street and across the lawns, but there was no sign of her. I gave Thornley and Matilda a frustrated wave, then quickly circled the tree, thinking perhaps she had hidden on the other side of the trunk, but I found nothing. The air around the tree felt cold where she had stood, cold and thick like an icy fog rolling in off the harbor.

"Bram, we must hurry!" Thornley urged, doing his best to not raise his voice and attract unwanted attention.

I raced back to them.

Matilda asked, "Who was it?"

"I don't know. I lost sight of her."

"Who?" Thornley questioned.

I nodded back towards the ash. "There was a girl standing near that tree."

"At this hour?"

"She didn't say a word, just stood there, watching us."

"Perhaps a nurse from the hospital? Many of the staff walk the grounds to clear their heads," Thornley explained.

"This was no nurse," Matilda said.

"You cannot be certain of that."

"It was Ellen," Matilda insisted.

I shook my head. "It wasn't Ellen. She was too young."

Thornley eyed the building behind us. "We need to hurry," he repeated. "The staff changes shifts at midnight. Follow me—"

Thornley led us down a narrow gravel sidewalk to the south entrance of Dr. Steevens' Hospital. The gas lamp positioned to light the small alcove either had not been lit for the evening or had somehow been extinguished—I was inclined to lean towards the latter. Tall hedges surrounded this side of the building, blocking the view of Swift's Hospital for Lunatics, but they did not block the screams. They grew louder as we neared the door, as if the residents trapped in Swift's sensed our presence and called out to us across the dark field. If Thornley heard the outbursts, he did not acknowledge them. He went to the door while glancing back over his shoulder with a wary eye. He twisted the knob and, finding it locked, pulled a large ring of keys from his pocket. "We keep keys to the hospital in our administration office. In return, they retain a set of keys to Swift's Hospital for us. We have a fairly friendly relationship, sharing supplies and whatnot. In my early days at Swift's, I was cross-trained on rotation over here and I am familiar with most of the layout. Should I be discovered in the morgue or elsewhere in the hospital, it most likely wouldn't raise the alarm. But I'm not certain how they would react to the likes of you."

"If caught, we will just stick to our story," Matilda replied.

Thornley and I nodded in agreement.

I watched as he tried several keys from the ring before finding the one that fit. He inserted it in the lock.

. . .

10 AUGUST 1868, 11:36 p.m.—The south entrance door opened into a narrow hallway lit by a single lamp at the far end. Judging by the dust raised with our every step, the corridor witnessed scant traffic. We closed the door behind us and followed Thornley. His shadow seemed to stretch out a dozen feet or more, then grew shorter as we neared the other side. Thankfully, we left the screams outside, although they still rang in my head.

At the end of the hallway, we turned a sharp left, nearly running into a stout little man pulling a loaded cart covered with a brown tarp. I dared not think what was under that tarp, and the man's blank stare offered nothing by way of information. I fully expected him to stop and question our being here, but instead he nodded at Thornley and passed by Matilda and me as if we weren't there at all. We slowed our pace until he disappeared through double doors halfway down the corridor, then quickened again as Thornley led us in the direction from which the man had come. At first, I didn't notice the slight decline in the floor, but as we progressed farther down the hall, the angle became more pronounced; we, in fact, were descending. Of course, it made sense that the morgue would be located in the basement, that stairs would prove too difficult to facilitate the rolling in of corpses, so the floor had been angled at an accommodating pitch, with just a single switchback, thus allowing for ease of access to the lower level.

When we reached the door, Thornley motioned for us to stop. "Wait here. I want to check if anyone is inside." He pushed through the door, closing it behind him.

"It's cold down here," Matilda said.

I had to agree. The temperature dropped noticeably as we followed the hallway, so much so my breath was steaming visibly. "We won't be long." I could think of nothing else to say. We both should have been sound asleep in our beds at this hour, yet here we were in the basement of the hospital, preparing to identify the body of a man who had died not once but possibly twice, the first time being almost fourteen years prior.

Thornley returned moments later and beckoned us to follow him back inside. He held the door open as we passed.

I was immediately taken by the enormity of the room; I believe it occupied the entire footprint of the hospital. I found it unnervingly quiet, too, only the hiss of a gas lamp intruding on the silence. There was row upon row of tables. The room smelled sickly; a cloud of vinegar hung heavily in the clammy air, so much so that my eyes began to water. It was the underlying scent, though, that gave me pause: a sweet scent with a distinctly metallic edge.

"This way," Thornley said as he started towards the back of the room.

"Why so many beds?" Matilda asked.

"The morgue was originally upstairs on the second floor. The administrators moved the dead down here to the basement during the cholera epidemic years ago. At one point, this building overflowed with the dead, and not only down here; bodies lined the hallways, filled the courtyard, and even occupied the roof. Today, though, there is little use for all of them." He smacked one of the old beds as we walked past, and a large puff of dust rose through the air. "They store all these old beds here in case we are subjected to another epidemic. Emergency overflow is handled out here, with the morgue at the back. I once heard it said that 'Should the deathbeds of Steevens' fill, surely the Apocalypse will be upon us.'"

"Let us hope it never comes to that," I mumbled. I counted thirty beds in this one aisle alone before I finally stopped counting.

Thornley went on. "There is one more level beneath this one, housing the boilers and other workings of the hospital. Considering the structure is over one hundred years old, it is quite a marvel of modern technology. You won't find a more knowledgeable staff in all of Dublin, perhaps in all of Europe."

He led us past the beds, turning right at the last row. We came upon these movable walls—each section at least eight feet wide, and went from a wheeled base at the bottom to a height of nearly ten feet, brushing within inches of the ceiling supports. I saw no door to speak of; instead, an opening of about five feet stood between two of the movable walls. A small sign hung on the left side that simply read MORGUE— HOSPITAL STAFF ONLY.

An older gentleman was perched upon a stool near the entrance, a book in hand. His face was stamped with the years, and indeed he seemed frail, too frail to be posted on sentry duty, yet there he sat. He looked up warily as we approached, setting the book down on his lap. "Not much call for visitors at this late hour. What can I do for you three?"

Thornley smiled at him. "Ah, Mr. Appleyard, I didn't realize you were working here now. I trust you remember me from Swift's? My sister feels she may know the unidentified man from yesterday's paper. We hoped to view the body when few others are present, in case she is mistaken." He lowered his voice. "We need to be discreet about such things, you know. May I escort her inside?" He concluded by pulling a pound sterling note from his billfold and handed it to the man.

Appleyard hesitated, then took the bill and quickly tucked it in his pocket. "With circumstances as they are, I thank you for your kind generosity," he said, his eyes drifting over my sister, then me. They were milky gray in color, cloudy with developing cataracts, but he still seemed to see with more clarity than the glistening eyes of some children. He nodded towards the entrance, motioning for us to enter.

We passed through the opening and found ourselves standing amongst the land of the dead. The air was still in here, no movement at all, and any sound seemed to be swallowed by the walls, so silent that I heard the catch in Matilda's breathing.

I counted forty-eight beds in total, eighteen of which were occupied, each occupant carefully covered in a white linen sheet. A string protruded from under each sheet and was connected to a small bell on a hook at the top left post of the bed. I approached the nearest bed and ran my finger along the string.

"The string is tied to the hand of the deceased. In the event someone believed dead in truth is not, movement of the hand will sound the bell and alert the staff," said Thornley.

"How ghastly," Matilda said.

Thornley went on, "It happens more often than one would expect. I have witnessed patients with no hint of a breath or a heartbeat in them suddenly sit up in bed and scream hours after it was thought all life had abandoned them. When a body is brought here to the morgue, the bell must remain attached for twenty-four hours without sound before an autopsy may commence. My good friend Dr. Lawrence had just such a patient only two weeks ago. He believed she passed away due to failure of the heart, there was no sign of life. Her bell was mute for nearly thirty hours before he began the autopsy. As he applied his scalpel to her breast, he heard a small gasp. He requested a glass of water, then forced open her mouth and began to pour water down her gullet. When she choked it back out, one of the nurses, overcome by fright, fainted where she stood. In a minute, the patient's eyes opened and she looked out for the first time in days, unaware of where she was or how she had arrived." Thornley flicked his finger across the string of the nearest bell and the bell softly chimed. "Like life, there is much we do not understand about death."

Matilda's face was ghostly white. I watched her eyes as she glanced over the shrouded bodies.

"If her doctor believed her heart failed her, why the autopsy?" I asked.

"She was young, only twenty-three years of age, far too young for such an ailment to be expected. In such a case, an autopsy is always ordered. The same holds true with suspicious and accidental deaths, such as our friend Mr. O'Cuiv." Thornley nodded towards the clock mounted on the far wall; it read quarter to midnight. "The third shift arrives in about fifteen minutes. Start checking the cards; we are searching for a male without a name noted."

The three of us spread out amongst the bodies and systematically began reading the cards posted at the foot of each bed. I had never beheld a dead body before, and knowing that so many were close at hand was unnerving. My memory brought back the hand Matilda and I discovered in the castle tower all those years ago, the fingers groping at the air and flexing. A hand that should have been dead but was not. A cursed hand.

I shuddered and focused my attention on the cards, doing my best to not look at the sheets or consider what lay beneath them.

"Here—" Matilda said.

She was hovering over a body at the far corner, on a table with a large drain at one end; the sheet had been folded from the bottom up and covered only the face. I wasn't sure if Matilda moved the linen or found the body that way. I quickly crossed the room to her with Thornley a pace at my back.

Matilda covered her mouth and nose and simply pointed at the body in front of her. As I followed her finger, I shuddered.

The deceased lay before us with his legs and arms spread wide; there was no modesty to speak of, for he was utterly naked as the day he was born. His chest was open, a long cut initiated below the navel and intersected at the lower part of the sternum with two incisions extending to each shoulder joint, forming a large Y. The rib cage was split down the center, cut with some kind of saw. A pair of wooden braces held them apart.

"His organs have been removed," I said, staring at the empty cavity.

"Over here." Matilda pointed at a series of bowls on a table at her side.

Thornley ignored her; he was busy examining the body. "This is fresh; perhaps an hour or less."

"Look at the arms," I said quietly. The cuts were there; six scars on the right arm and four on the left, just as detailed in the documentation found in O'Cuiv's file that Matilda had shown to me back at Marsh's Library. It was clear these were old wounds, long ago healed. The flesh was rough and dark in color, which contrasted with the pale white of the surrounding skin. His fingernails were long and filed to points. I found this noteworthy, for surely I would have remembered such a detail had I observed it as a child. I could think of no practical reason for keeping one's nails in such a condition.

Thornley reached for the sheet covering the man's face. I felt Matilda's hand wrap around my arm and squeeze; she then gasped as the sheet was slipped away.

There was no mistaking the man's face; this was Patrick O'Cuiv. He appeared no different than he had on the day he came to supper at our house all those years earlier. He could have stepped from our table to this room only yesterday.

"He has not aged a day," Matilda breathed.

Thornley slowly shook his head. "This cannot be. This man is a relative of some kind, of that I am certain, but he cannot possibly be the Patrick O'Cuiv we knew as children."

"You still believe this to be some kind of trick?" Matilda asked.

"I'm not sure what to believe." An idea came to me, and I began to explore the table.

"What are you searching for?" Thornley asked.

"His clothing and personal items. Perhaps there is something there that may help identify him."

Matilda frowned. "I'm most certain the police searched his body thoroughly and any belongings found on his person. They found no identification."

"Nothing to identify him by name, but there might be something familiar to us, something we might recognize."

Thornley pulled a sack out from under the table. It was labeled with number 28773; this same number was inscribed on the body's identification card. He removed the string at the top of the bag and dumped the contents on the floor.

Nothing but damp clothing. We searched the pockets but found them all empty.

Matilda screamed. Shrill and sharp, her voice cut through the morgue with the precision of a scalpel.

I turned from the bag's contents to find her hovering over the jars containing O'Cuiv's organs, pointing at one of the containers. I crossed over and placed my hands on her shoulders. "What is it?"

She shook her finger, pointing at the jar holding his heart.

"It just beat."

NOW

Five wolves pace beneath the window, staring up at Bram, hunger in their eyes.

Bram pauses every few minutes in his writing to stand up from the chair, cross the chamber, and glance out the window. By this point, he has shot each of the wolves in turn, but little good it did. While the bullets pierce their thick coats and draw blood, they don't injure the vile creatures in any way. Within minutes, the wounds heal, leaving behind no trace but for dried red patches of blood on the fur. He begins to suspect they actually wish to draw his fire—a distraction, possibly an attempt to get him to expend his ammunition.

The wolves watch him as he watches them.

The gray one is the leader, of that Bram is sure. Always the first to move, with the others responding to its cues—to what end, he is not certain.

My pets adore you, you know.

Ellen's voice, muffled, behind the door. Bram glances back but says nothing.

Why not go down and introduce yourself? Or would you rather they come to you? They so like to play.

Bram believes these animals cannot traverse the path to this room, but there is no way to be sure. These wolves are not natural beings, and there is no knowing their true capabilities. As he thinks this, one of the black ones comes to the wall and stands on its hind legs, thick forelegs stretched upwards, reaching for Bram. The wolf's ears are drawn back, and a long tongue laps at its nose. It whimpers as it glares up at him.

A sudden chill fills the air, and Bram closes his coat.

He hears a giggle—not that of a woman but a girl's.

Wolves prefer the cold. Their fur shields them from the elements, whether hot or cold. In the heat, they sweat only through the pads of their paws, and their fur provides cooling insulation. In the cold, though, they thrive. Their fur becomes heavy in the winter months as the undercoat grows in.

The temperature in the room drops further still, and Bram can see his breath. The rifle feels like a block of ice in his grip, and he sets it down, shoving his hands into his pockets.

When it gets really cold, wolves tend to return to their den and huddle together. In most cases, they hunt first and then bring the kill back to the den to feed one another and their young.

Bram turns back to the window; the wolves now seem fueled by a restless fire, their whimpers mixed with howls.

My pets are hungry, Bram. They long for a taste of fresh meat. If you went down there, they would feed for days.

That giggle again, louder than the first.

Bram shivers.

Their den is so warm, Bram. Imagine going back there with them. The heat of their bodies pressed against you, surrounding you, all that warmth. Your death would be painless, I can promise you that. They can make it quick . . . if I ask them to.

The temperature drops yet further, and Bram retrieves the last vial of holy water from his bag and holds it up to the lamplight. The water is nearly frozen, the bottle filled with flecks of ice. His hand shakes, and he finds it hard to hold, his fingers aching. He fumbles with the cap and after three tries finally removes it, before returning to the window.

The five wolves huddle in a small group, all perfectly still, looking up at him in the window.

Bram throws the vial in the wolves' direction, aiming for a rock next to them. The bottle strikes the rock and explodes in a mist of glass, ice, and water. The wolves scatter, their cries cutting through the night.

You've only agitated them, my dear Bram.

Bram has accomplished more than that, though, for the temperature begins to rise, the spell broken. He works his fingers, opening and closing them in a fist, the feeling slowly returning. If the wolves are still near, he cannot see them.

The voice changes, becomes deeper, a male voice that Bram doesn't know.

He is coming, Bram. He'll be here very soon.

LETTER FROM MATILDA
to ELLEN CRONE,
DATED 11 AUGUST 1868

My dearest Ellen,

I write to you at the latest of hours, for sleep is the furthest thing from my mind.

I am sure of what I saw! What is that, you ask? Well, I shall tell you. I saw the beating heart of Patrick O'Cuiv not only fourteen years after his "death" but while the organ rested in a jar at his side rather than within his chest!

My less than insightful brothers are both convinced my imagination simply got caught up in the moment, lost in the macabre atmosphere of the morgue, the scents and sounds overwhelming me to the point of delusional visions, but I can attest with complete certainty that such is not the case. I was looking directly at O'Cuiv's heart, and I witnessed as it first contracted, then expanded, with one quick beat. I even saw the heart expel blood from one of the arteries severed at its top with enough force to propel a crimson stream down the inside of the jar, where it puddled at the bottom. The blood was nearly black and thick as molasses. I imagine it smelled of canker and decay, beef gone bad.

His heart beat only once. I did not tear my eyes away even as the morgue's guard entered and demanded we take our leave. As Bram and Thornley pulled me away, my eyes did not break away, not even for an instant, but the heart did not beat again. I was certain it would, though; I still am certain. I believe his severed heart is beating even now, perhaps slower than a normal heart would but beating nonetheless, for whatever evil kept O'Cuiv alive all these years lives on in his heart. Just because nobody is there to witness such things doesn't make them less true.

With my scream, the guard hurried us out of the morgue, and Thornley led us out of the hospital, until we found ourselves standing outside the south entrance again, the past hour feeling more dream-like than real.

Was that you under the ash tree earlier? Were you watching us?

I thought it was you, but Bram claimed the woman we spotted was someone else. He believed it to be a girl, perhaps a streetwalker. Apparently, none of my opinions hold much weight this evening.

After leaving the hospital, the three of us found ourselves under that same tree arguing about what we saw. I have no doubt this was the body of Patrick O'Cuiv. I cannot explain how or why I know this, but I am sure of it. Bram and Thornley feel differently; they both believe the man to be a distant relative of O'Cuiv, or possibly a son unknown to us during our childhood, but I think such speculations are rubbish.

It clearly was him!

I am absolutely certain.

I will find proof.

After much debate, I convinced my two brothers of the only course of action open to us. We must travel to Clontarf and further investigate O'Cuiv.

How did his heart beat? Do you know the truth behind this?

I imagine you do.

If your heart were sliced from your breast and placed on a tray within sight, would it continue to beat?

I realize such thoughts are morbid and not those of a lady, but they speak to me from the back of my mind whether I want them to or not, begging to be answered, and there is no other acceptable option but for me to go with them to Clontarf. There, I said it. Even though they forbid me from taking this trip, I will go.

I cannot trust them, really. That is my primary reason for going. I do not doubt they will go to Clontarf, but to what extent will they really search for truth? Enough to find answers or just enough to appease me? The only way to be certain of conducting a proper investigation is to undertake the journey myself. Even though the town is relatively close by (Pa used to walk the distance when we lived there and he was employed at Dublin Castle), a lady should not go alone; therefore, I require the company of my brothers. I also worry that should I go alone, I may find it difficult to obtain answers to some of my questions, particularly when asking men those questions. Men can be so pigheaded sometimes. No, I cannot, and will not, go alone; nor shall they. I will be in their company, regardless of their wishes.

What is your connection to Patrick O'Cuiv?

Was he a lover?

Dare I foster the thought?

But all those nights you snuck away under the cover of darkness, where else would a young woman flee but into the arms of her lover?

If such is the case, how scandalous! I am blushing at the very idea of it. A married man, nonetheless. A married man with children. I think you better than that; therefore, I do not believe this to be so. I do not wish it to be so.

Then what?

If not your lover, what was he to you? Who is he to you? Now that he is dead, do you mourn him? What if the opposite is true? What if you hate him so much you wanted him to tumble off that boat into the sea and drown?

Perhaps you even pushed him.

What is your connection to this man?

You possess so many secrets, my dear Nanna Ellen. And, I daresay, I will uncover them all.

We leave tonight, the moment Bram concludes work at the castle. I will accompany them, even if I must stow away in the coach.

Affectionately yours,
Matilda

THE DIARY *of* THORNLEY STOKER

———◆———

11 August 1868, 9:21 p.m. — Oh, to put down on paper what has happened! Even now, only minutes later, all of the evening's happenings seem more dream-like than actual events, the makings of a terrible tale told to frighten a child. It is only now, from the safety of my own home, that I even consider pausing to document what has transpired. I feel to do so is necessary—nay, may I say it is required of me? To fail to write down these events would be irresponsible, for others must be made to know.

I arrived home from the asylum at slightly past six in the evening, no later than usual, only to find Emily standing statuesquely in the foyer. Her eyes were fixed forward, locked on the door, and in her hand she held the silver cross from our bedroom wall in a grasp so tight that blood was trickling out between her fingers.

Emily's nurse, Miss Dugdale, approached me when I crossed the threshold, her face etched with worry. "She has not moved from this place since early this morning. She will not speak. I tried twice to escort her to the parlor, but the moment I laid hands on her she screamed; I dared not try a third time."

I offered Miss Dugdale a compassionate glance and thanked her for her efforts; this was not the first time I discovered my spouse in this condition, and when last it occurred, only time broke the spell. I asked

Miss Dugdale to leave us, and when she had departed I went to my wife, circling around her slowly.

If she had been silent earlier, that wasn't the case now. As I leaned in close, whispers escaped from her lips, the words so soft I could not make them out. I thought it might be the Lord's Prayer, but I wasn't certain. I tentatively reached for her hand, the one holding the cross, and gently took her into my own grasp. She did not cry out as she had for Miss Dugdale; instead, the whispers stopped, and she gasped.

I leaned into her. "You should go to bed, my love. You've had a long day. You'll feel better by the light of morning."

With this, I tried to walk her towards the stairs, but she would not move—her feet held to the marble as if they were part of the stone. "What is it? What bothers you so?"

I knew she heard the words; I saw this in her eyes, but she did not answer. Beneath my grasp, her fingers clutched the cross tighter still, causing it to slice into a finger. The warmth of her blood rolled over the back of my hand. When I tried to pry her fingers from the silver, the start of a scream welled within her throat. I dared not continue; I would get it from her after she calmed.

"He is putting the man back together again," she said softly. Emily followed this with a short laugh. "Humpty Dumpty sat on a wall, Humpty Dumpty had a great fall, but the man in black can put him back together again. The man in black can make him good as new." Her face twisted into an expression of horror, and she turned to me, her eyes wide, her mouth opened slightly. "You must stop him."

"Stop who? I do not understand."

"You cannot let him put the man back together again."

"Who?"

At this juncture, she began to hum. Not a tune, mind you, but a sin-gle note held for an ungodly length of time, as if breathing were not a necessity. I knew of no other course of action, so I took her shoulders in hand and shook her violently in hopes of breaking this stuporous spell. "Who do you mean, Emily?"

"The man in pieces who fell off the wall, the man who had a great fall."

It was then that it struck me. "Do you mean Patrick O'Cuiv?"

She raised the silver cross to her lips and kissed it. "God has turned His back on him. The man in black has made it so."

My eyes grew wide. "How do you know of Patrick O'Cuiv?"

I know I never mentioned the man to her, not in the past years or the past day. Maybe she heard us speak of him last night when I thought she was asleep? I supposed that was possible, but our bedroom was located a great distance from the library, and with all doors closed, it seemed very unlikely. Maybe she snuck down the stairs and we did not hear her. But I administered her so much laudanum, I cannot imagine her waking, let alone coming downstairs.

At this point, her arms went limp, and she began to shuffle towards the stairs. I took the opportunity to help her; there was no telling when she would be willing to move again, and I didn't wish to ply her with a drug for yet another night. I assisted her up the steps and went about the business of unfastening her dress. When my fingers worked the buttons at her collar, they came away moist and sticky. I held them to the lamplight. They were damp with blood.

I sat Emily upon the bed and held the lamp closer; there were two tiny pinpricks at the point where her shoulder met her neck. They didn't appear fresh, perhaps a day or two old. Most likely, her clothing aggravated the injury and reopened the wound.

"What did you do to yourself, my dear Emily?"

Her free hand went to this spot, massaged it, then fell back to her lap, but she didn't utter a sound.

I removed the rest of her clothing with some difficulty, for she wouldn't release the crucifix, and I had to work her sleeves around it;

then I laid her down on the bed. She clutched the cross to her chest and closed her eyes. As I started for the door, she spoke one final sentence in her calm voice. "Death is coming to us all; it will be marvelous." My wife then drifted off into the quietest of sleeps.

A MOMENT LATER, a knock came at the front door, and, knowing it to be my brother come to fetch me for our trip to Clontarf, I felt a profound déjà vu wash over me. I hurried down the steps to let him in before he knocked a second time. The sight of Matilda at his side startled me.

"Why are you here?"

She let herself in with Bram on her heels. "I told you I was going, and I will speak no more of it."

I turned to Bram, prepared to argue, then held my tongue when he shrugged his shoulders. "Apparently, she doesn't trust us to see this matter through properly."

"Perhaps this is for the best; I cannot go."

Bram frowned. "Why not?"

"Emily has taken ill of late; I'm afraid she cannot be left alone."

Matilda glanced around the foyer. "Surely your staff can watch over her."

Until now, I had no desire to share the extent of my wife's condition, but in light of what she said I thought it necessary to inform them. When I finished my account, the three of us fell silent.

Matilda spoke first. "But who is the man in black? What did she mean by 'put him back together again'?"

"I have no idea."

"Did we miss something?" Bram asked. "Something on the body?"

"You're assuming her words are actually meaningful, she spoke in a delirium. Most likely, she overheard part of our conversation last night and her subconscious twisted it into some kind of false memory, nothing more."

I knew by the expressions on my brother's and sister's faces they did not believe this; they thought her words to be more. And though I wasn't sure what do about it, I agreed with them. When she spoke, I got the distinct impression her words rang true. Although cryptic, they weren't of the garbled nature she usually spoke when her illness came upon her. There was a conviction behind them, one that carried hints of the strong woman I married, the woman I hoped still lived somewhere within that mind.

I knew then what must be done.

"Both of you, go to Clontarf. I will arrange for Miss Dugdale's return to care for Emily, then I'll go back to the hospital and revisit the body."

"Will the guard allow you back in?"

"Money opens many doors, dear sister." I turned to Bram. "How do you plan to get to Clontarf?"

"We'll walk," he replied. "It's but a few miles."

"Nonsense; take my carriage and driver."

They attempted to protest, but I told them this was a time for haste, and walking these streets in the dead of night was not the safest course of action. After rousing my driver (who preferred to sleep in the stables with the horses), they were soon on their way. I donned my overcoat and started for the hospital, stopping only at Miss Dugdale's small home long enough to tell her I had an emergency that required attending, and ask her to stay with Emily until I returned. She wiped the sleep from her eyes and agreed.

UPON RETRIEVING THE KEYS for Dr. Steevens' Hospital from Swift's Hospital for Lunatics, I crossed the open field to the south entrance and, like the previous night, let myself in. I then quickly made my way back to the morgue without spying a single soul in the hospital corridors. I found the guard post vacant. A book sat opened on top of the stool where we had found Appleyard the night before, but there was no sign of him now. Most likely, he had left to attend to his personal needs and would be back momentarily. I considered waiting for him before entering, then decided it would be best to hurry.

I entered the morgue and rushed to the back corner where we had found the body thought to be Patrick O'Cuiv's. The steel table was empty. The jars that held his organs were empty, too. There was something peculiar about the condition of the room, though. Blood and filth covered the autopsy table, and the workspace reeked of rancid meat, as if the mess had festered for a week rather than just for one day. Upon completion of an autopsy, it was standard practice to clean and sterilize the space in order to prepare for the next procedure. Leaving the table and accoutrements in such a state would surely land someone in trouble. As I circled the table, my shoes made a sick sucking noise with each step. At first, I dared not glance down, but I knew I must, so I forced my eyes to the floor—bloody footprints littered the marble, a number of them from bare feet. They seemed to encircle the table, then beat a path between the beds off to the right, fading as they went, until terminating at the third bed in. That bed bore a card numbered 28773—O'Cuiv's— the same number that appeared on the bag containing O'Cuiv's personal effects, a bag I now noted as missing.

There was a body on the bed, covered by a white sheet.

My heart tightened within my chest.

You cannot let him put the man back together again.

My wife's words echoed through my mind, and I shook them away.

Certainly O'Cuiv's organs were returned to his chest cavity, and his body placed back in his bed, following the autopsy; that would be standard procedure. The bloody footprints were probably nothing more than a mess left by a careless doctor.

Bloody, bare footprints, my wife's voice whispered at my ear.

He walked from the table and returned to his bed—the moment his heart was returned, he was whole again—with the heart came blood, with blood there is life. The blood is the life.

SURELY THIS WAS NOT what she meant. It could not be what she meant.

It was then the sheet moved.

Not a sudden move, not even a major move, just a slight shift in the sheet; a bulge towards the center that came and went in an instant, as if the body beneath considered turning on its side, then thought better of it.

Nonsense!

A trick of the light, or perhaps a stray breeze had found its way to the basement from up above.

The sheet moved again, this time accompanied by a soft moan.

I took a step closer.

I did not want to approach it—that was the furthest thought from my mind—but my feet shuffled closer anyway. First one step, then another, then another after that, following the bloody footprints from the autopsy table to the bed, towards whatever stirred beneath.

In my mind's eye, I saw O'Cuiv's organs in the bowls, the heart somehow beating with life, beating so ferociously that its bowl vibrated on the table with each thumpity-thump, that steady double patter I heard so often through the stethoscope. Following each contraction came the expulsion of blood, thick and black, unhealthy blood, riddled with clots. The clumps reached the rim of the bowl, then somehow tried to climb out under their own volition, escaping the evil heart and oozing away, oozing towards me. In the bowl beside the heart, the lungs inflated like yellow mucus-filled sacs, sucking in the surrounding air, then exhaling it with a watery gasp.

I forced my eyes shut and shook my head, driving these thoughts from my mind. I knew they were not real. I knew they existed only within my imagination, but they held fast.

When I opened my eyes, the organs were gone, the bloody bowls were empty again, and I breathed a sigh.

The sheet moved, I was certain of this. A small red dot appeared near the center.

My feet took another step towards the bed, forcing me to follow.

I heard the lungs again, the rough thump of the heart, only this time the sounds didn't come from phantom organs in the bowls at my back; they came from under the sheet on the bed in front of me, only inches from me now as I somehow drew closer. I reached for the sheet and took it by the corner, pulling it away in one quick, fluid motion.

I stifled a scream.

On the bed lay Mr. Appleyard, his uniform shirt soaked in blood and his face whiter than any I had ever seen, nearly alabaster. Frothy blood dripped from the corners of his mouth when he tried to speak. His eyes were glossy, like fluid-filled marbles, but they still held life. They focused on me for a moment before rolling back up into his head. A gash in the man's neck was spurting blood, the flesh hanging in a loose flap. When he drew a breath, I found the source of the sound. It wasn't the lungs in the bowl; it was the air seeping through the gash. Red spittle was draining from it and seeping into the blood-soaked mattress beneath him.

As a doctor, I would like to say I immediately began treatment to help this man, to save what little life still flowed through his ravaged body, but I did not. Instead, I froze, my eyes locked on him, my limbs unwilling to move. I stood motionless as his final breath escaped from that gaping hole in his neck and he finally found peace.

The room fell quiet then, so quiet I thought I heard the mice as they scurried through the walls and my own heart as it continued to work at a fevered pitch. I stood there, one hand clutching the sheet, the other limp at my side, unable to look away from the wound at this man's neck. It appeared to be an animal attack, but that was not plausible, not here, not in the basement of this hospital. Then what? Surely not a man, for what instrument would yield such a ghastly tear? It certainly wasn't a knife, but the alternatives were unthinkable.

A man it must be, though, for Appleyard hadn't climbed up on the bed by himself and hidden under the sheet on his own.

At that moment, another thought entered my mind, one that I wished I could quickly expel, one that gripped me with an entirely new fear.

Where was the man who had done this? The wounds were surely fresh, inflicted no more than minutes before I arrived. The perpetrator couldn't be far; had he left, I would have passed him in the corridor leading to the basement. Yet I had seen no one.

Could he be here now, watching me?

This thought was enough to force my eyes from the body of the security guard to my surroundings, to the dozens of beds around me. I realized I wasn't alone, not truly. There were bodies on many of those beds—twenty, if not more—each lying in perfect silence.

Could the killer be amongst them? Waiting for the right moment to strike me down?

The ring of a little bell came from my left, and I spun to meet the sound. I was faced with nine occupied beds. My eyes quickly followed the strings tied to the hand of each body to the little bell hanging above each bed, but none betrayed the stillness. Another bell sounded, this one behind me, and I spun yet again only to find more motionless beds, more bodies lying in wait. Another bell rang out at my right, then two more on my left, more yet behind me. Within moments, the room came alive with dozens of chimes, all ringing out louder and louder. I threw my hands upon my ears and spun in circles, for the sound grew horribly loud; bells, bells, all around.

In the bed to my left I spied movement. Subtle at first, a small shuffle of the sheet over the body, but enough to catch my eye. The arm twitched slightly, which tugged at the string and rang the attached bell, a high ping that joined in the chorus of others.

Could this be the killer?

My eyes searched the room for a weapon and found a bone saw on the shelf behind the autopsy table—bloody, unclean, like the table itself. I crossed the room in haste and scooped up the tool, then made my way back to the bed where I had seen the sheet move. I held the saw in a firm grip, raised it above my head, and yanked away the sheet.

An enormous black rat peered up from the hole it had gnawed in the body's thigh, a thin strip of flesh hanging from sharp little teeth. It glared at me without fear before returning to its meal of fresh corpse. I fought the urge to vomit as the foul rodent tore away another piece of meat with enough force to send the bell tied to the arm jingling wildly.

All around me, dozens of other bells rang, and I watched in horror as rats poured out from under the various sheets with mouths full of carrion, only to disappear under the beds and into the shadows bathing the walls. These vanishing predators were replaced by reinforcements darting out from the same hiding places and quickly scurrying up the sides of the beds and disappearing under the sheets in an endless cycle of dreadful defilement. With each stolen meal of flesh from the dead came the ringing of a bell, and with all the bells ringing so, I could only imagine the carnage taking place beneath the white linens.

I ran. I ran as quickly as I could from the morgue, from the basement, into the dark cavern of night, leaving Dr. Steevens' Hospital in my wake. I finally paused to catch my breath when I reached the Grand Canal.

I considered going back, if only to warn the staff of the unimaginable horrors taking place, but then I remembered the missing body of O'Cuiv and the mutilated body of Appleyard. If I were to return, blame may be cast upon me. After all, I was not authorized to be in the morgue. For that matter, I had no business in the hospital. It would not be a stretch for the police to suspect me of committing the guard's murder. The fact that I had no motive would hold little weight against my trespassing. I had seen men hang for less.

Until that very moment, I did not realize I was still holding the bone saw. The bloody blade shimmered in the moonlight, black streaks upon the silvery metal. Without so much as another thought, I tossed it into the canal and watched it sink beneath the surface.

This was such a careless act, for I didn't consider whether or not I was alone until after I lost sight of the blade; it was only then that I looked up and down James Street in search of prying eyes. Although I found none, I felt the eyes of a stranger upon me. I pulled the collar of my coat up tight around my neck and began walking with haste in the direction of my home. I headed towards St. Stephen's Green, hoping to draw out anyone on my tail. When five minutes passed and I spotted no one, I hoped the anxiousness would leave me, but it did not. Instead, an intense malaise crept over me, and the hairs on the back of my neck pricked up. When I reached the corner of Thomas and Francis streets, I stopped suddenly, whirling around in hopes of catching sight of whoever followed at my back. My eyes landed on the silhouette of a very tall man dressed all in black with a cane and top hat. He stopped as I did and stood motionless about thirty feet behind me. Although gas lamps burned all around, this man was nearly lost within the shadows, so much so I could not make out any details of his face. His hair, too, was long and black, framing the near white of his pale skin, what little was visible.

"I see you, sir!" I said in the most authoritative voice I could muster. "Why are you following me?"

No reply came, only the slight tilt of his head.

"Should you continue, I will summon a constable!"

Had he seen me throw the bone saw?

Had he seen me flee the hospital?

I could not be sure.

I turned back around and continued down Francis Street, my ears keen to the sounds behind me. I heard the click of the man's cane but not his shoes; they made not a single sound on the cobblestones. Now I wished I had kept the saw; I had no weapon on my person, and while I could hold my own in a fight, this man was half a head taller than me and broad in the shoulders. At such a distance, and under these brooding conditions, discerning his age proved impossible. But he stood tall and firm, lacking the telltale slouch of an older man, so I imagined him to be no older than I, and a formidable opponent.

I hastened my pace, not to the degree that I would appear to be fleeing but just enough to increase the distance between us. He moved slower than I; I could tell from the steady click of the cane. At this point, I suppose I moved at a speed nearly twice his, yet there was something abnormal about his gait—at such a clip, I should have noticed a diminishment in the sound of the cane clicking behind me as the distance between us increased, but instead the click of his cane grew louder, as if he were gaining ground on me despite only taking half the number of steps.

As I neared St. Patrick's Cathedral, I stopped and turned around again and found my fear confirmed. When I first spotted him, he had been maybe thirty feet behind me, yet somehow he managed to close that gap by more than half. He stopped moving when I did and again stood stock-still, aside from the slight tilting of his head a moment after my eyes fell on him. He was close enough now that I could make out his face and it caused a chill to rush over me. His skin was nearly translucent, lined with tiny red veins that seemed to absorb the light from the streetlamp and glimmer with the dancing flame of the gas. His nose was best described as aquiline, with a prominent bridge and slight curve at the base, yet perfectly in proportion with his other features. His eyebrows were of the thickest black, and his long hair flowed out from his top hat to nearly his shoulders. He had a light beard, not thick enough to be considered unruly but enough to aid in the concealment of his face, for it seemed to grasp at the shadows around his head and pull them in a little bit closer. Those eyes, though! My God, those eyes. His sloe-black eyes were death's own and yet they teemed with life. As his head tilted, I swear on my soul they flickered bright red before returning to bottomless black pools. His lips were a ruby red, enhanced by the dark hair and pale skin, and they were parted ever so slightly, as if he were sucking in a breath, yet he made no such sound.

I daresay his teeth frightened me most, for when his lips opened, I saw them protruding; they were profoundly white and appeared to be filed to points, resembling the teeth of a canine more so than those of a man.

"I have money, if that is what you want." The words escaped my lips before I realized I uttered them. I felt so completely alone, vulnerable in the open street, for there was not another living soul in attendance. What I would not give for a knife or a gun, anything I could use to defend myself.

"I do not want your money," the man said. Oh, and that voice! His voice was rich with bass, thick, each word pronounced with deliberate care. There was also an accent I couldn't quite place other than being Eastern European in origin, the accent of one well traveled over many years.

"Then be on your way. I have had a very long day and wish for nothing but the comfort of my own bed and a cup of hot tea," I replied.

"And I am only out for a late-night stroll. Imagine my surprise at finding another out at this hour, particularly someone leaving the hospital with such haste. I could not help but find such a man intriguing." His fingers flexed around the knob at the top of the cane that served as its handle. Long fingers, the carefully manicured hands of a musician. I thought of O'Cuiv's cold, dead hands with the nails fashioned in long points. "I, too, recently left the hospital; I was visiting an old friend."

I found myself lost in his eyes, simply gazing into them. They were mesmerizing; I felt as if I were staring into a hole in the earth that had no bottom, a pit so deep it passed through the realms of Hell and continued out the other side. They were made up of the roiling sea, hard, raw waves crashing into one another on a moonless night. A fascination, a wonder. I'm not sure how long I stood there in such a state before getting my wits about me.

"I wish you and your friend nothing but the best," I told him, glancing down at my shoes. "Now I must be on my way." At this, I turned and continued down Camden Row towards my home, all the while feeling those eyes on my back, listening for the click of his cane.

"Perhaps you know my friend as well?"

I walked a solid ten paces before he spoke these words, but when I stopped and turned back towards him I found him to be only a few feet behind me, even closer than before. There had been no clicks of the cane, no shuffling steps on the cobblestones; he was simply there at arm's length. Although he was otherwise motionless, the red silk lining of his black cape danced along behind him, fluttering in little waves as if alive. There was no wind to speak of, not so much as a breeze, only the cool evening air, which seemed to become cooler still in his presence. The flickers of the cloak were the only evidence that he had moved at all.

The man grinned slightly, and I saw those teeth again, those godawful teeth.

I pictured the torn neck of Appleyard as he was lying upon O'Cuiv's bed, a wound that might have easily been inflicted by these teeth. In an instant, I pictured the man leaning over the body, his mouth tearing into flesh with the appetite of a savage beast. I shook this ugly image from my mind and returned my gaze to him, hoping the anxiety in my bones was not evident. "What is your friend's name?" I asked the question, knowing the moment this man uttered the name *Patrick O'Cuiv* I would bolt off down the street at my fastest. I could see my house from here, the tall gables visible over the other rooftops, but that sanctuary seemed a desert away.

His smile widened and his head tilted again as if I asked the most profound of questions. When he finally spoke, the name that escaped his lips was not the one I expected. "Why, Ellen Crone, of course."

My heart thudded, and although I attempted to conceal it, I have no doubt he registered my surprise at hearing this. Again, his eyes caught mine, and I found it difficult to turn away. The grip he had on me! As if he could reach into my thoughts with those eyes and extract whatever facts he wished, holding me there until finished. I was reminded of a snake charmer I once witnessed as a child. The man mesmerized a king cobra with nothing but his eyes and the movement of his head and body. He put the snake into a hypnotic state so strong he was able to pick it up and place the killer serpent inches from his face without fear of a bite. All the while, his eyes remained locked on the creature. I couldn't help but wonder, if he looked away, even for a brief instant, would the spell have broken? Would the snake strike?

I wanted to look away.

I wanted to look away with all my heart and soul, but I simply could not. I stood perfectly immobile, as if this man gripped my head with both of his long, bony hands and held me at arm's length, eye to eye.

"When did you last see Miss Crone?" he asked in that thick, smooth voice.

"Not since childhood," I replied softly. The instant before the words left my lips, I told myself I would say I knew no such person. I intended to tell this man, this stranger to me, this hypnotic snake charmer, nothing. "She left when I was scarcely more than a boy." The words flowed from my mouth as if I were in a dream state, an outside observer. I said this knowing I could say nothing else even if I wanted to. And I did want to. But I was no longer in control.

Oh, those eyes! Those horrid, godless eyes. They bore through me, piercing every inch of my soul with a blackness blacker than the blackest pitch. An itch erupted so deep within my skin it was as if ants were crawling over my bones. I wanted to run. I wanted to run so badly, yet my will held no power over my body; there was only this man somehow holding me inert and compelling me to speak against my every wish.

"If you had, you would tell me, correct?"

I heard these words not with my ears but my mind. I told him about the time I saw her at the sweets shop as a child, then again while at college, and finally I told him how I thought she was at the theater only days ago. When I finished, his lips twisted into the most fiendish grin, and the force with which he held me fell away. My body slackened and drooped, my muscles aching with exhaustion.

His hand went to my shoulder and squeezed it, almost a caring gesture but with enough pressure to induce pain. "I have not seen her in many years; a visit is overdue. Should you run into her again, you will give her my best, will you not?"

"But your name," I heard myself say. "I do not know your name."

At that, he released my shoulder and the grin returned. I could not help but look at those teeth, those savage teeth, glistening white, accentuated by dark red lips and his pale, vein-stenciled flesh. "You should hurry home; your wife needs you."

He was gone then. I do not know if I lost time or he simply vanished, for after such an encounter even that crazy notion did not seem so farfetched. One second he was standing there, mere inches from me, and the next there was no sign of him. I looked up and down the street to no avail. My house beckoned to me in the distance, and I welcomed the sight.

Again I ran.

I ran as fast as my tired legs would take me, and all the while I felt eyes on my back. I pushed through the door and closed it quickly behind me. The instant it shut, a heavy force thudded against the other side with enough strength to jostle the light fixtures in the room. I pulled the curtain aside from the window next to the door and witnessed a black dog, the largest dog I had ever seen. It crossed my yard and disappeared among the trees. The creature glared back at me only once before disappearing, its eyes a glowing red.

Upstairs, Emily cried out.

THE JOURNAL of BRAM STOKER

11 August 1868, 9:30 p.m. —I ran my hand over the soft velvet seat of my brother's coach. "Thornley has done well for himself."

Matilda studied the interior, too, her eyes drifting over the meticulously carved and polished mahogany, stained a beautiful chestnut brown.

As promised, Thornley had ordered the coach prepared quickly, and we were off to Clontarf with little delay. His driver had hitched a team of four horses for the trip, insisting it was no bother and would only improve our time. I also had observed him loading a shovel into the back of the coach; no doubt it was Thornley who had made the request for such a directive did not originate with Matilda or me. The shovel reminded me of the gruesomeness of the task at hand and I tried to shake the implication away, but it lingered. If Matilda harbored any concerns, she made no indication, appearing perfectly calm, devoting her time to writing, with the occasional glance out the window. There was little to view at this hour; most people were safely tucked away with their families behind closed doors. The coach rocked on thick springs and swayed from side to side like a boat. I found the motion to be rather comforting, although sleep escaped me. The anxiety burned deep within me, and it was all I could do to keep from jumping out of the coach and running alongside to burn off some of this energy.

As we passed the road to Artane Lodge, then Marino Crescent—the dignified Georgian row of houses—and number 15, where I was born, an overwhelming nostalgia washed over me. Although we still lived relatively close by, I rarely returned, for this place only generated memories of my illness, years in bed wondering if I would live to see the following day. Matilda, on the other hand, looked out with a fondness I simply did not share. Was this wrong of me? Perhaps. This was, after all, just a place. Did places harbor memories? I often thought they did, recollections both good and bad somehow absorbed by the walls. I couldn't help but wonder who lived there now. Did another little boy dwell in my little attic room and look out the very window I had looked out of so many times? Maybe he watched us now as we rolled past the park into the white mist.

In the distance, I spied the steeple of St. John the Baptist Church, and I felt the muscles in my body tense, knowing we were close.

Matilda must have sensed something, too; she placed her pad aside and again took to the window. "He was buried amongst the suicide graves just outside the main cemetery," she said. "I never told you this, but I visited his grave as a child, shortly after Ellen left us. I don't know why, but I was drawn towards it. I suppose after reading the articles, I wanted to see for myself."

"Is the grave marked?"

She nodded. "A crude stone bearing his name."

The driver maneuvered the coach into the lane off Castle Avenue, which took us to the outskirts of the cemetery. The stone wall topped by black iron seemed endless, foreboding, not a place we should find ourselves at this godforsaken hour, and although I had not detected another living soul in some time, the fear of getting caught was palpable.

We came to a stop amongst a group of poplar trees, just out of view from the road. The driver tapped twice on the roof.

"Are you sure we should do this?" I asked.

Matilda was already halfway out of the coach, the driver's large gloved hand reaching to help her down the step.

As I exited, the driver handed me the shovel and glanced nervously up and down Kincora Lane. "I cannot leave the coach here, so I am going to circle the block. Should I come across anyone, I will do my level best to distract them. When you are ready to leave this place, meet me back here." He glanced at the shovel. "I would offer to help, but I think if I leave the coach here it will just draw unwanted attention."

"I understand."

"Bram! Let's go!" Matilda said in a loud whisper. She pulled herself halfway up the wall and peered over the other side, the cloth of her petticoat waving beneath her.

"She is a feisty one," the driver said.

"That she is." I glanced down the empty road. "Head back to Clontarf Road and drive around for thirty minutes. That should give us enough time. We'll listen for the coach coming back up Castle Avenue. You're less likely to attract attention if you stick to the market district and the harbor; these areas are fairly lively, even at night."

"Yes, sir." The driver tipped his hat and climbed back into the seat. With dispatch, he was gone, the steady clip-clop of the horses' hooves dwindling to nothing.

"Bram!"

I turned just in time to watch Matilda slip over the top of the wall and drop to the other side with a thud. "My God, are you all right?"

I went to the wall and peered through a small crack. Matilda stood on the other side, brushing dirt from her dress. "I'm fine," she said in a hushed tone. "Toss me the shovel."

I lobbed the shovel over the wall a little to the right of her, then, first checking up and down the road, I jumped straight up and grabbed the iron spikes at the top of the wall. I pulled myself up, careful not to catch my clothes on the ironwork, and launched over the top. With a quick push off the wall, I jumped to the ground, landing on my feet.

"I half expected you to jump straight over the wall," Matilda snickered.

"Perhaps next time." I took in the graveyard, its rolling hills of somber grass and mysterious mist. "Where is it?"

She pointed southward. "The traditional graveyard ends at that walkway; the suicide graves are on the other side of the old church wall." My sister started off in the direction of the ruins.

"Careful!"

I retrieved the shovel and raced after her. The air felt very still—not even the slightest breeze worked through the willow trees—the branches slept soundly, each one casting a thick dark shadow upon the ground. The only light came from the moon as the gas lamps were extinguished when the cemetery closed to the public at eight in the evening. Wood mice scurried about, angry at the intrusion, their eyes on us and following at a safe distance.

"Is there a guard?"

Matilda thought about this for a moment. "I imagine there is."

My eyes drifted to the church at our left, now inky and silent. If anyone was inside, I detected no sign. I could see the gate from here, too, but no movement beyond it. "He is probably walking the grounds."

When Thornley first enrolled in medical school, he told me many of the students retrieved corpses from the graveyard for the purpose of dissection. I found this appalling, but he said they were left with little choice. The schools and hospitals supplied only a few bodies and those went to students hailing from wealthy families with the means to make such a purchase. While our family seemed well-off compared to most, there wasn't enough money in the coffer to secure a body. Although Thornley never outright admitted to participating in such a gruesome endeavor, he didn't deny taking part, either. I imagined him strolling through a graveyard much like this one with shovel in hand, hoping to retrieve a fresh specimen in the name of science. Perhaps with this same shovel.

"Grave robbers tend to come out when there is little or no moon, and there's too much light evident tonight. It would be too easy to get apprehended. This is the kind of night security finds rest. The guard is probably passed out behind one of the graves with a bottle of rum in one hand and questionable reading material in the other," Matilda said.

"I hope you're right."

"Or he could be right behind us, loaded and ready to deliver a round of buckshot in your tail end."

"What makes you think he would shoot me?"

"Because," Matilda replied, "a righteous man would never shoot a lady. Clearly, you would be his first choice."

"Clearly," I agreed, "providing he is a righteous man."

We approached the ruins of the original church with caution. The stone structure stood at the back of the traditional cemetery and still had four walls despite years of neglect; the roof, most likely thatch, had long since rotted away. The western wall stood tall—by far the most impressive, extending high into the sky, once having housed the bell tower. The north and south walls each housed four large windows, which were rounded at the apex and flat at the sill, along with a smaller window towards the front of the church. The back, east-facing wall rose tall and pointed, with an entrance that once boasted a pair of grand wooden doors, but since the church had fallen from grace the doors had been replaced by a single door consisting of black iron bars. My mother and father surely would have shed tears had they seen the building in such a state, for the Holy Baptism of each of their children was recorded here. But it had been deemed unsafe a number of years back, and a re-placement had been commissioned. Construction on the new chapel had finished two years ago, at which point this building was officially abandoned.

I peered through the iron bars of the door at the nave inside. The stone floor and much of the walls were crumbling, host to weeds and vines that eagerly climbed the surface for better exposure to the sun, and only two of the original pews remained. A third had collapsed to the ground and had been reduced to rot by the relentless elements. I tugged at the door—locked. I wanted to get inside, to view the space from the interior, but tonight was not the night for such access. I would have to return during daylight hours.

"Come on, his grave is just beyond this wall," Matilda said.

I snapped to and followed after her, taking one last look at the main section of the cemetery before rounding the corner.

Beyond the walls of the ruin we found more graves, some with the largest stones I had seen so far. Matilda pointed out that this section was still part of the original cemetery, and because this was holy ground the church pastors were typically buried here. We walked past these graves and through thick weeds and came upon the remains of a much smaller wall, this one constructed of stone. At some point, someone had knocked most of it down, the remainder standing about four feet tall.

"This is the original wall of the church. The suicide graves are on the other side." She stepped over the wall and leaned on a blackened tree stump. "When they buried O'Cuiv, the ground on this side was not part of the church proper. This place was never blessed, and those buried here were considered lost souls not only to the Church but to their families."

"I remember the stories."

"When they completed the new church two years ago, they extended the new wall all the way around this property, enclosing this area with the rest. I don't believe the grounds were ever blessed, though. I found no records; for many, this place was forgotten. Without the blessing, the new wall is meaningless; the sacred ground ends right here." She indicated the remains of the stone wall, now nothing more than a pile of stepping-stones. "O'Cuiv's grave is over there."

I followed my sister's finger to a small stone about ten feet away, near the back wall. Weeds grew all around, some waist-high—clover, dandelions, shepherd's purse. I crossed to the grave, mindful of the other stones haphazardly around. How many burials here were unmarked? Was I treading on one now? Not only criminals and those damned by suicide, but also children. It was commonplace to bury the unbaptized dead here, stillborn babies and the like. When I reached the headstone, I knelt. I found it not to be a traditional grave marker but an actual stone about one foot in diameter. At one time, its surface may have been polished, but not any longer. If not for the name *O'Cuiv* chiseled into it, I would have mistaken it for everyday rock. The letters of the name were uneven, partially obscured by a thin blanket of moss and worn with time. No dates marked his birth or death, only the crude inscription of his surname. Nobody deserved to be disposed of like this, not even the criminals of the world. I carefully shoveled away the green grass covering the grave and turned to Matilda. "Nobody has been here in years. Are you certain we should do this?"

"If you don't dig it up, I will."

There was no arguing with her; she had made up her mind long before we left Dublin. I rolled up my sleeves and again took hold of the shovel. "Keep an eye out for the guard."

And I began to dig.

The work went slowly. In order to discourage grave robbers, the grave diggers mixed straw in with the dirt, and each bite of the shovel's blade seemed to uncover more and more of it. It was like digging into a rug, and I found it impossible to dig deeper without first removing the shafts of straw. Before long, Matilda joined in, plucking up the straw and piling it at her side. I told her more than once that I would rather she continued watching for the guard, but she would have none of it, insisting we would be here until morning light if we both did not help. So we continued, both stealing the occasional glance around the corner of the church ruins whenever we stopped to rest. More than an hour passed before I felt the blade of the shovel impact the lid of O'Cuiv's coffin, and I thought of our driver—he easily had circled twice by now; this retrieval was taking much longer than expected.

The wood was rotten. The box was constructed of cheap knotted pine, and the earth had gone to work on the wood the moment the townsfolk lowered it into the ground. I had to forgo the shovel for fear of breaking through the lid of the coffin. Instead, I scooped away the dirt by hand and tossed it out of the hole, which had grown to nearly five feet deep.

When at last the coffin was uncovered, I ran my fingers along the edges in search of some kind of handle; I found none. The lid had been nailed shut from the top, six nails in all, one for each of the four corners and two midway down the side. The pine was swollen and brittle, so much so that I dared not stand upon it; instead, I placed one foot on either side and slid the blade of the shovel under the lid. I turned to my sister, silently offering a final opportunity for her to walk away from this terrible task and forget all about it, but she remained steadfast and granted me only a resolute nod.

I pressed down on the shovel's wooden handle until the metal blade dug into the wood. Then I gave the handle a slight wiggle to force the blade deeper before pressing down again. This time the lid buckled slightly and the nails near the shovel's blade groaned, pulling out enough for me to able to get my fingers beneath the wood. I set the shovel aside and gripped the lid. With all my strength, I pulled up and to the side, and the lid tore away with a ghastly squeal, each nail screeching in protest.

As the lid separated from the coffin, cockroaches poured out. Thousands of them. Moving so fast, their plump bodies scuttling up and over the sides. They ran over one another, each faster than the last, tiny black legs shuffling, sounding like sheets of paper rubbing together. The roaches covered my legs, my chest, my arms. I heard Matilda scream; then she began stomping on the bugs as they crawled from the grave and scattered amongst the leaves.

I climbed from the hole with haste and brushed them off. There were so many, I could feel them scurrying over every inch of my body. I dared not open my mouth to scream for fear one of the creatures might seize the opportunity to slip between my lips. Just the thought of one in my throat, my stomach, writhing about . . .

When at last the mass exodus of the cockroaches concluded, I realized I had shuffled nearly ten feet from the open grave. Matilda stood even farther away, near the front of the church ruins, stomping the ground with undeterred resolve until the last of the roaches were finally either dead or gone. I ran my hand through my hair, then turned my back to her. She brushed one more off my shoulder, crushing it with the toe of her shoe, before proclaiming me roach-free. I found none on her.

Together, we cautiously made our way back to the grave. The smell was horrible. I covered my mouth and nose with the collar of my coat and peered into the hole.

The corpse was wrapped in an orange shroud. At least the shroud appeared orange, most likely having earned that color after years of absorbing the remains it shrouded. Dirt covered the bottom of the coffin. Whether it had been placed there deliberately or found its way in through one of the rotten boards, I could not be certain. I could not help but recall the earth we found beneath Nanna Ellen's bed, smelling so much of death yet teeming with life.

Around the body were various personal items—a book, a mirror, a brush, some clothing . . . a very bizarre assortment indeed.

"Would he have been buried with such things?" Matilda asked.

"It would appear so."

"How did the roaches breathe down there, buried in that box?"

To this question, I had no answer. Did roaches, in fact, breathe? I imagine so, but I have never studied their physiology. Most likely, they were perfectly capable of sustaining themselves underground, or, possibly, they burrowed back and forth. Or perhaps they were just like flies in a jar.

"We need to get closer."

"You stay here, I will—"

But she was already gone, slipping down the grave's wall and landing with a soft crunch on the earth below as her shoes crushed a few of the remaining roaches.

I cursed under my breath and slid down next to her, careful not to catch on one of the thick roots I had cut with the shovel but which now stuck out from the grave walls like angry fingers attempting to grab at anything moving past.

"I must see his face," Matilda said from my side, barely visible in this deep hole. "Please, Bram."

My attention was elsewhere. Something was not right; there was something off about this body. The shape, the length of the arms and legs, the proportions were all wrong. I reached near the head for the orange shroud, cringing as my fingers wrapped around it. The shroud felt moist, as if were covered with some kind of bile or slime; it was akin to reaching inside the carcass of some dead thing and taking holding of the stomach.

I tugged the cloth out from under the head and peeled it back to the sound of Matilda exhaling beside me as the head became visible. At the sight of it, I gave the shroud a swift tug and tore it from the box, tossing it to the ground beside us.

"Rocks, nothing but rocks," my sister said.

Where a body should have lain were rocks instead, arranged so as to form the shape of a body. Wrapped in the shroud, they presented the illusion of form. And with the lid of the coffin closed, certainly the weight, too.

"Was his body stolen and replaced with rocks?"

"If grave robbers stole the corpse, there would be no need to go to all the trouble. They would simply replace the lid and bury the coffin as is, if they bothered to rebury it at all," Matilda said. "This coffin never contained a body; someone placed the rocks there to fool whoever was tasked with burying O'Cuiv."

"Possibly."

"What do you make of this?" Matilda picked up the mirror lying in the open coffin. Ma had a similar one, which she called her looking glass. This mirror appeared to be made of silver and gold; the remarkable craftsmanship was evident despite heavy tarnish.

"Something is written on the back, just above the handle. Can you read it?"

She flipped the mirror over and raised it to what little light was seeping in from above.

"*Um meine Liebe, die Gräfin Dolingen von Gratz.*"

"That is German. 'To my love, the Countess Dolingen von Gratz,'" I translated.

"Who is that?"

"I have no idea."

She picked up the brush. "The same inscription appears here."

I took it from her and ran my fingertips over the writing.

"Maybe some kind of family heirloom?" Matilda suggested.

"These belong to a woman. I don't understand why they would be buried with Patrick O'Cuiv. Maybe they belonged to his wife and someone placed them in here so he would not forget what he had done? Or maybe—"

"Bram," Matilda interrupted.

"What?"

She held up a black cloak. It had been bunched up near the bottom of the coffin, by the false feet. "This is Ma's cloak. The one Nanna Ellen wore that night we followed her out to the bog."

Before I could argue, she pushed her finger through the small hole on the right sleeve. The same hole I identified it by all those years earlier. The material was matted and worn but familiar nonetheless.

"How can that be?" I heard myself say. "Wasn't he buried before we saw her that night?"

"I'll have to confirm the dates, but I think so, yes."

We both stared at the cloak for some time, neither sure of what to say next. None of this made sense. Matilda worked the material nervously with her fingers. "There's something in the pocket."

She reached inside and withdrew the most stunning necklace, a gold chain with a heart of shimmering diamonds surrounding a red ruby of an unimaginably large size.

"That is extraordinary. May I?"

Matilda handed the necklace to me. The jewels had heft in my hands, more so than I expected. And they sparkled so! I daresay, I could barely drag my eyes away. The jewels were of exquisite quality and had been mounted by a skilled hand, for I couldn't determine what held them all together in place. The ruby was a deep red, and as I stared at it in the palm of my hand I couldn't help but think of a drop of blood afloat on a sea of light. I couldn't begin to imagine what such a piece would cost.

I returned the necklace to Matilda. She placed it carefully back into the coffin atop the cloak. "What of the book?"

Although I had been taken by the jewels, her thoughts were still clearly fixed on Ma's cloak, her fingers continuing to work the material nervously. She let go with some trepidation and reached for the small book—old as well, I could see that much from where I sat, the pages yellowed. Matilda opened to the first page, her eyes scanning the text, first going wide, then narrowing as she flipped to the next page and the next after that.

"What is it?"

"It's in Nanna Ellen's hand, but I don't recognize the language," Matilda said.

"May I?"

She handed me the book and I studied the text. I, too, recognized the handwriting as Nanna Ellen's, there was no mistaking her carefully executed swirling script. I had seen it as a child on many notes and letters, but the language of origin escaped me as well.

I thumbed through the pages, finding that nearly half the book was filled. Turning back to the first page, I paused and took in the very first line, for even in an unknown language I could figure out what it meant. It was a date:

12 Október 1654.

LETTER FROM MATILDA
to ELLEN CRONE,
DATED 11 AUGUST 1868

My dearest Ellen,

Oh my, where to begin!

Tonight, Bram and I did what I would have considered unthinkable only a few weeks ago. We dug up the grave of Patrick O'Cuiv! Not only did we accomplish such a ghastly task, we did it under the cloak of darkness long after the cemetery closed. We were in a state of acute apprehension for fear of being discovered by the guard, who, I must admit, executes his office most poorly, for we saw neither hide nor hair of him, not even once. I found all the stealth quite exhilarating.

Dare I say it, we found the most irregular assortment of items within the confines of that pine box. I will touch on these in a moment, but first I would like to point out what we did not find in the coffin—the body of one Patrick O'Cuiv. As I suspected, Mr. O'Cuiv was quite obviously missing from his own burial plot! Someone took the time to place rocks in the coffin as a crude substitute for the body and wrap them in a shroud, but that is all it was. Anyone with half a mind could plainly see this was not a man. The only reason to insert rocks in a coffin in such a manner would be to fool those burying it initially—the men shouldering the coffin to the grave and lowering it in the ground to its eternal repose—so that is what must have transpired.

I have no doubt that the man who recently died in Dublin was the same Patrick O'Cuiv who belonged in this grave. How he lived, I have yet to determine. Nor do I know how he faked his own death or how he failed to age in all these years after. I imagine you will have something to say about that. We will discuss it in great length when we find you, of that you can be assured.

Let us now devote a moment to discussing what we *did* find within Mr. O'Cuiv's not-so-final resting place. Ma's cloak, for a start. How did a cloak you clearly stole from our mother wind up in this grave? How did you get it there? And why? And what of the looking glass and hairbrush? Are they both your possessions as well? If so, did you steal them from this Countess Dolingen von Gratz? Who is she? The moment we return to Dublin, I plan to visit Marsh's Library to determine exactly that.

I imagine she wants that necklace back. So exquisite!

We are closing on you, my dear Nanna Ellen. We are drawing closer by the minute.

The book was perhaps the most puzzling thing of all. Written in your hand but dated centuries in the past. Had I seen it a year ago, I would consider it to be nothing more than a ruse, but after the things I have seen of late . . .

Is it dear to you? Are all of these things of some personal value to you?

I want you to know we took them. The cloak, the looking glass, the brush, the necklace, and the book—we took all of it. Much to Bram's dismay, I wrapped your mementos in Ma's cloak and brought them with me.

We did not leave the rocks to rest alone, though—I left each of the letters I wrote you in the grave. If you return at some point for your possessions, you will find my words waiting in their stead.

Bram and I refilled the hole with much haste, then quickly returned to the place where we had arranged to meet Thornley's driver. Upon scaling the wall, we found the coach in the grove of poplar trees, but there was no sign of the driver. The horses appeared impatient; their stamping hooves indicated they had been there for some time.

Bram instructed me to stay with the carriage as he searched the surrounding grounds for the driver. I observed him walking out to the road and following it around to the far side of the cemetery, where he disappeared from sight. I checked the cab for any note from the driver but found none. I then climbed up to the driver's box in case he had left a message for us there. I found the horse's reins not tied off, as one would expect, but lying on the floorboards as if dropped in panic. At this point, I discovered the blood. Only a few drops on the seat, mind you, and a couple more along the footrail, but enough to cause concern. These drops were fresh, shed within the hour.

I immediately considered the possibilities: either the driver injured himself and went in search of help or he was injured in some type of struggle and taken. Aside from the blood, I had no reason to believe there had been a confrontation, but my mind grasped on to that possibility and held firm.

I jumped from the coach, ready to go off in search of Bram. That is when I spotted her.

This girl of no more than six or seven years of age, with brown hair and the most radiant green eyes. She stood perfectly rigid at the center of the road, gazing at me. I did not hear her approach, nor did she make a sound once I spotted her; she just stood there in utter silence. She wore a somber brown cloak with the hood pulled up over her head, but not so much so that her face was lost in gloom. On the contrary, her face gleamed, as if her skin captured the light of the moon and was aglow with it. Her eyes, bright as stars, remained fixed upon me without fail.

I knew at once this was the girl we had spotted under the ash tree back at Dr. Steevens' Hospital.

"Who are you?" I inquired, hoping my voice did not betray the unsettling feeling that had crept over me. Her gaze triggered some deep instinct within me, one that told me to run. As I think back on this encounter now, it makes me think of a cat watching a mouse, a beast studying its prey.

"Why did you disturb my father's grave?" Her words carried across the street, her voice melodic.

"Your father?" I made the connection then, my mind returning to those newspaper articles of so long ago. "You are Maggie O'Cuiv?"

The girl said nothing, her dark eyes locked on me. I ventured a step towards her, but as I neared she withdrew an equal distance away. It was not her feet that carried her, though; I did not see them move at all. She simply drifted back, as if riding a carpet of air. I could not help but gasp at the spectacle, and this girl found humor in my reaction, her lips curling upwards in a grin. Her now exposed teeth were quite white, unnaturally so. Her skin struck me as odd, too—deathly pale and stamped with tiny veins. Her cheeks, flushed with color when first I spied her, now appeared to be fading.

My thoughts returned to the missing driver. Could this girl somehow be responsible? Nonsense, of course. He probably outweighed even Bram, and she was a slight little thing, but there was something about her, something that made the hair on the back of my neck stand up.

"Your father is not in his grave, Maggie. Do you know why?"

At this, her grin grew wider. "Perhaps he is standing behind you?"

To say such a devilish thing, I know she only wanted to get a rise out of me. I refused to turn and look behind me; I would not give her that satisfaction.

"Perhaps he is standing directly behind you ready to drain the lifeblood from your pretty little body." As she had floated away from me a moment earlier, she now floated nearer, drawing within a few feet of me. Only the slight ruffle of her cloak betrayed any motion, her person remaining perfectly still. The air around us grew silent. I could not hear the sounds of the city nor the creatures of the night, not even a single cricket.

At this distance, I found her eyes, so sharp and hungry, to be haunting. I wanted to turn away from her but discovered I could not. I could do nothing but stare back.

"My father would like you," she said, her voice but a whisper. "He has always liked girls like you."

"Where is Ellen Crone?" I forced the words out, unwilling to let my voice betray my fear. If she recognized your name, her face did not indicate so; she remained perfectly still. I tried not to think about the things I took from Patrick O'Cuiv's grave. Something told me that if I did think of them, this girl would know. She would pluck the thoughts right out of my head and take these items from the coach, and I would be unable to stop her. So when thoughts of these items tried to enter my mind, I pushed them aside and instead focused on Bram, my brother, my loving brother. I shouted his name then. My voice echoing off the black walls of night. I shouted it so loud a murder of crows flew from the trees around us and batted off into the darkness.

This girl, this thing that was Maggie O'Cuiv, drifted back again, but only a bit, still floating out of reach. At the sight of this, my hand went to my chest and pressed against the silver cross I wore around my neck. The icy metal stung my chest, and I welcomed the cooling embrace, finding it comforting. My subconscious told me to run, to bound back over the fence and race through the door of the church and stay there until daylight won the battle for the sky, but instead I did not move, my feet remaining firm.

At this point, I spotted Bram. He rounded the corner of the street and was running back towards me. I took my eyes off Maggie O'Cuiv for only an instant, but when I turned back she was gone; no sign of her remained.

"I couldn't find him," Bram said. "Wherever he went, he left no trace."

I walked to the spot where Maggie O'Cuiv had stood and pivoted in a leisurely circle, peering into the trees and surrounding flora. "Did you see her?"

Bram had not seen her, and for a moment I thought I had imagined the entire encounter. I told him about it anyway, careful not to leave out a single detail.

"Was she watching us the entire time?"

I shook my head. "I don't know. I don't think so."

"And she was still a girl? A child?"

I nodded.

I then showed him the blood on the coach, the drops beginning to dry now, grim speckles on the black leather. Bram covered them with a blanket. "We cannot leave without the driver. I think we should take a room at Carolan's Inn and report him as missing in the morning if he has not turned up."

I welcomed this suggestion. I harbored no desire to travel back to Dublin tonight. I wanted to be someplace surrounded by people, as far from this isolated place as possible. Carolan's Inn stood on Howth Road, not far from the graveyard. The inn had a good-sized stable block attached, with all provisions for the horses. If the driver had simply wandered off, he would spot the coach easily enough there.

These events took place two hours ago, and now I find myself sitting at a small table in the corner of our shared room, for I was too unnerved to consider renting a room of my own, writing you this letter while Bram snores loudly in the bed. The poor thing was exhausted from tonight's activities. Sleep, however, is the furthest thing from my mind.

Instead, I am writing you. I am writing you while the things we took from O'Cuiv's grave lie on the table before me, each one generating more questions than answers.

If you want these things back, you know where to find us.

Until then, I will find some way to rest. Tomorrow I plan to learn who this Countess Dolingen von Gratz might really be. Then I will find someone who can read and translate your book.

I hope you find my other letters, now seven feet deep in the earth. I hope you read them and come to me. I believe you are near. I can feel it.

Or is that the O'Cuiv girl?

Affectionately yours,
Matilda

THE JOURNAL *of* BRAM STOKER

---

12 August 1868, 2:23 a.m. — I awoke to the rumble of thunder.

A bold clap reached deep down into my dream and pulled me back with a jolt. At first, I didn't understand where I was; the strange room, the unfamiliar bed. Not until my eyes adjusted to the gloom and the sleep dissipated did I recall our decision to spend the night at the inn.

Clontarf.

I was in Clontarf.

My throat ached, as if a cold were coming on. My imagination at play, for I never got sick anymore.

I sat up as the rain began to patter against the windowpane, only a few drops to begin with, then many more. Within minutes, the deluge was coming down in thick sheets. When flashes of lightning flooded the chamber, I caught a glimpse of Matilda asleep at the little desk near the door. The single candle she had lit earlier had long ago sputtered and gone out, now just a puddle of dry wax upon the plate.

Sleep had at first eluded me, and I must admit I took more than one nip of brandy before finally being able to rest. The events of the night seemed like nothing more than a bad dream, but I knew better. At first light, we would have to go in search of Thornley's driver. I do not believe the man would have wandered off, and Matilda's discovery of blood on his seat proved very disturbing. This coupled with O'Cuiv's grave and the findings inside, worse still.

I stood from the bed and went to Matilda. Her breath flowed steadily. Although she found the wherewithal to seal her envelope before drifting off, she still clasped her pen in hand. I carefully extracted it from her fingers and lifted her from the chair. She stirred slightly but did not awaken. I carried her to the bed and gently set her down, covering her with the thick quilt. I had forgotten how nippy Clontarf could be at this time of year, particularly this near the water.

I found myself at the window, peering through the rain towards the harbor. My arm began to itch, slight to begin with, then growing so persistent that I had no choice but to scratch. And although irksome nearly to my elbow, it was more acute at the wrist, the site of those two little lewd marks.

Bram. Come to me, Bram.

When I first heard the voice, I spun around expecting to find her in the room with us, but there was only Matilda, still slumbering soundly a few feet away.

It was her voice, though, no mistaking it.

"Nanna Ellen?"

I said her name aloud, and at hearing my own voice, I realized her voice somehow came to me in my mind, and while my voice sounded thin in the little room, hers seemed to come from all directions at once yet from no particular direction at all.

"Where are you?"

I eyed the door and it was locked; there was no place in the room for one to hide.

My head shot back, and I stared at the ceiling as that horrible vision from my childhood came to me. I found nothing but cracked plaster and spiderwebs.

I am out here, Bram. The window.

I spun back around to face the window and there she was, her face inches from the glass. The rain dripped from her hair, cascaded over her skin. She was so pale, more so than I recalled ever seeing her. She had not aged, just as Matilda and Thornley had said, appearing no older than the day she left.

Her being there was impossible, though; our room was on the second floor of the inn, with no balcony or patio on which to stand. The front of the inn boasted no walkways or ledges, nothing but a rough brick façade.

She raised her hands to the window, pressing her palms against the glass, her fingers moving slowly as if scratching at it. I tried to take a step closer, but fear held me inert. I could only look at her, watch her.

When a second face appeared in the window next to her, I gasped. It was a young girl with long dark hair. I recognized her immediately from outside the hospital. From what Matilda told me, I had no doubt this was Maggie O'Cuiv.

You must come outside, Bram. I need to talk to you. It has been so long.

My arm itched horribly.

Ellen pulled at me, the same tugging I once felt as a child that drew me through fields and forest to find her. I backed up towards the door, one cautious step after another, until I was in the hallway, until I was downstairs. I moved silently through the inn until I found myself step-ping outside into the icy rain.

Ellen and the girl were no longer at the window; I found them stand-ing across the street, holding hands. Both wore cloaks that had been dismally soaked by the storm. I realized I was wearing no jacket at all; I was standing in the rain in my nightshirt, my feet bare upon the cobble-stones.

There's my Bram! Come to us now, let me help you.

Her voice sounded so sweet, nectar to my ears, and I desired to hear it again.

Help me? Help me how? I questioned this for the briefest of seconds before finding myself crossing the street, drawn to them as if by that taut cord from my distant childhood memories.

I could think of no place I would rather be than cradled in their arms.

NOW

————◆————

Alone.

The wolves do not return—or if they do, Bram doesn't see them. He stands guard at the window, writing feverishly in his journal in hopes of documenting all while still able.

He can still hear them, though. Their brooding howls break through the night from all around, and occasionally the creature behind the door answers them, sometimes with a howl of its own, other times with nothing more than a frustrated-sounding grunt or the shuffle of agitated feet. At one point, it sniffed at the doorframe again, first at the bottom, then somehow going up the side and over the top—high above Bram's head. Bram has no idea how it could do such a thing and he tries not to even think about it.

Now the creature scratches at the wood. Not the sound of a dog pawing at a surface, but that of a person with long fingernails dragging them from the top of the door to the bottom and back up again. Bram cringes at the thought of splinters digging beneath those nails, yet the creature only presses harder, oblivious to the pain. This repeats over and over again. When the scratching does stop, the room falls into silence.

It is then Bram catches sight of him.

A lone man standing atop the very rock on which he broke the holy water. The man is tall and dressed all in black. Long, dark hair frames a pale face beneath a black top hat. He wears a cloak the full length of his body. It wavers in the night air, fluttering at his feet. Bram can't see his face. The man looks to the earth, and shadows blot out his features. As he turns his head, those same shadows seem to follow the contours of his face, keeping him in constant darkness.

Bram reaches back and takes the rifle in hand. Simply touching the cold steel brings comfort, although he knows the weapon will be of little good. Whoever or whatever this man is, he does not fear bullets.

He's come for us, Bram. He wants me, but he wants you most of all. We are not that different, you and I, the blood of others thriving within our veins.

The voice is male this time, unfamiliar.

If you release me, perhaps he will spare you.

Bram plans to do no such thing.

He sets down the rifle and pulls the last two roses from the basket, blesses them, and places one on each windowsill.

Drawn either by the movement or the act itself, the man looks up. A smirk plays across his thin red lips. Bram catches the faintest hint of white teeth beneath those lips and is reminded of the wolves, their hungry fangs dripping with thick saliva.

Behind the door comes the little girl's giggle again.

The man stares up at him for the longest time, still as a statue, his eyes glinting in the moonlight. Then he raises his hand and points— long fingers outstretched, reaching across the distance, reaching for Bram.

Bram's arm begins to itch furiously. First at the two small bite marks, then up his forearm and all the way to his shoulder. No one other than Nanna Ellen had ever brought this condition on before, this itching. He closes his eyes and attempts to reach out to her, to Ellen, but finds nothing of her presence; there is only *him*, this strange man staring up at Bram.

The floor shudders under Bram's feet, and he nearly loses his balance.

The man's fingers are pointing directly at Bram, and with a small twitch of his fingertips he causes the room to vibrate again. The crosses jump against the wall, two tumbling to the floor, and the mirrors rattle. When the man points yet again, one of the mirrors slips off its nail and crashes to the stone at Bram's feet. Dust cascades from the ceiling as the room rocks, and Bram watches nervously as the paste he had affixed around the door continues to crumble and fall.

"Come down and you will be spared," the man says. He is speaking in a low voice, yet Bram somehow hears him perfectly. Much like the voice behind the door, the man's voice penetrates Bram's mind directly somehow.

Bram closes his eyes and pushes back. He imagines an invisible bubble, first around himself, then around the entire room, a bubble so strong not even the bullet of a rifle will pierce it. He pushes back until the room falls still. He pushes back until the man's voice is gone. He pushes back until he feels nothing of the creature behind the door.

It is then Bram hears a snake hiss.

POST OFFICE TELEGRAM

FROM: M. STOKER
CAROLAN'S INN
107 HOWTH ROAD
CLONTARF

TO: THORNLEY STOKER, M.D.
43 HARCOURT ST.
DUBLIN
12 AUGUST 1868, 3:12 A.M.

MY DEAREST BROTHER—
SOMETHING HORRIBLE HAS HAPPENED.
GRAVE AS SUSPECTED.
BRAM INJURED.
DRIVER MISSING.
SOMEONE POSSIBLY IN PURSUIT.
IF YOU RECEIVE THIS MESSAGE BEFORE WE
RETURN, SEND HELP.
—M

THE DIARY *of* THORNLEY STOKER

———◆———

13 August 1868, 6:43 p.m.——I feel the need to continue to document all that has happened. So much has occurred in the past days that I find it difficult to know where to begin, so I will begin with the events of today.

I woke yet again to a pounding at my front door. At some point during the night, I drifted off to sleep in a chair at the front door with my rifle cradled in my arms. The large dog returned multiple times throughout the lonely hours, each time circling my home just a little closer than before. Although safely inside, my entire body quivered when the dog stopped on the walkway in front of the house and stared at me with its large red eyes. I heard its hungry growls, such a deep rumble, but only once did I glance out the window. Although I had a powerful weapon in my hands, that beast would prove to be faster than I could ever hope to be on the draw.

But, as I said, I woke here. Daylight came and the dog had gone, light washing away all that is dark, and there was a fierce pounding at my front door.

I opened it to find Matilda and Bram standing there yet again, but I saw in their eyes the fear I had felt only hours earlier, so I rushed them inside. Together, they recounted their trip to Clontarf and their findings at O'Cuiv's grave. The items they had found were laid out before us on my table. My lost driver, missing still. What happened to Bram—

. . .

"TELL ME AGAIN," I said.

Matilda took a deep breath. "I woke to find the door to our room open and Bram missing. A storm raged outside, so I went to the window and saw him . . ."

"Please, Matilda, do go on."

Matilda glanced at Bram, who nodded. She continued. "The O'Cuiv girl held him while Ellen sucked at his wrist. And Bram . . ."

Her eyes welled with tears, and she tried to shake them off, unwilling to bow to her emotions. ". . . Bram had Ellen's wrist pressed to his lips. He was . . . he was drinking from her as she was drinking from him."

With the utmost of restraint, I forced myself to look at my brother. Not that I wanted to. The emotions flowing through me at just the notion of him committing such an act were overwhelming. Yet, this was the third time I made her narrate the story, and not a word has changed, as much as I hoped it would.

"And you do not recall any of this?" I said.

Bram shook his head. "I remember waking and carrying Matilda to the bed, and I remember the start of the rain, but all after that moment is lost. I remember nothing else until hearing Matilda screaming my name."

"I ran across the street," she said. "I nearly slipped on the wet stones and took my gaze from him for only a second. When I turned back, he was on the ground, unconscious, alone. I found no sign of Ellen or Maggie O'Cuiv."

"And Bram?"

"Like I told you. Blood covered his lips and wrist, but the rain made quick work of the mess, washing it away. I couldn't revive him; I tried for ten minutes. Two men on their way to the harbor were kind enough to help me get him to our room; I told them he spent too much of the night in the pub. While he slept, I arranged for another driver with the aid of the innkeeper, and we left at first light. By that point, Bram had awoken but was groggy. It took some time to coax him to the coach. Once in the light and fresh air, he began to get his wits back about him."

I turned to Bram and held out my hand. "Let me see your wrist."

Bram hesitated for a moment, then held out his arm, turning it over.

The two small puncture wounds at the wrist were clearly visible at the vein, but neither appeared fresh. Had I seen them without the benefit of Matilda's recap, I would have thought them to be an old injury, far on their way to healing. I touched one tentatively. "Does it hurt?"

"No," Bram replied. "They itch. They have always itched."

His response gave me pause. "This has happened before?"

My sister and Bram both glanced at each other. My brother nodded. "They first appeared the night I was healed as a child. They have been with me ever since."

"Why have you not spoken of this?"

"I knew . . ." Matilda said hesitantly. "Ever since we were children."

This was of no surprise to me. Bram and I were not close as children, nor was I close to Matilda.

"There's more." Matilda plucked a letter opener from my desk and handed it to our brother. "Show him, Bram."

Bram took the instrument and without hesitation cut a three-inch gash in his arm.

"What are you doing?" I cried, pulling my handkerchief from my breast pocket and wrapping it around the wound.

Bram calmly placed the letter opener down on the side table. "There is no need for that." He peeled away the handkerchief, now damp with his blood, and used it to wipe away at the cut.

I stared in awe. The gash was gone! There was no sign of the injury aside from a thin pink line. And, within a moment, that, too, had vanished.

"How can this be?"

Bram perched on the edge of the sofa. "It has always been this way, at least since Ellen cured me as a child."

"He hasn't been sick, not a single day," Matilda pointed out. "Not since that night."

I frowned. "And last night was, what, some kind of treatment? An exchange of blood?"

Nobody answered this query; there was no need to. We all understood it was true. I took a deep breath, then resigned myself to reveal a secret of my own. "There is something I must show you both."

I led them through the house and up the grand staircase to the master bedroom, where Emily slept soundlessly atop the covers. Matilda and Bram both hesitated at the door, and I motioned for them to enter and gather around the bed. We kept an oil lamp on the night table; I lit the wick and held the flame close to my wife's neck. The two tiny pinpricks were scabbed with dry blood. "I first saw these Tuesday night. They appeared to be healing, but last night something reopened the wound and left fresh marks. I heard her scream when I was coming home and found her in a swoon next to the bed, bleeding."

Bram leaned in closer. "They're like mine, only more ragged, as if healing slower. Has she demonstrated anything like I showed you downstairs?"

I shook my head. "Not at all. The opposite, in fact. See this little cut on her cheek? She did that yesterday when she fell; I think she hit the bedpost. It has barely healed at all; I had the hardest time getting the bleeding to stop—nothing like what you showed me. Today she hasn't moved from this bed. She seems to be lost in a deep sleep. I tried to wake her earlier to no avail. She has no fever or other outward sign of illness, but her breathing at times seems labored, and she has complained of a headache nearly the entire week. Even now, she doesn't stir. She talked in her sleep a few hours ago, but the words made no sense; she seemed very agitated and anxious. Her feet and hands flailed and kicked with such strength I couldn't hold her down; I called in two of the servants to help. When she finally calmed, the deep sleep came again, and her mind seemed to drift even further away. Whatever is happening to her is worsening, I'm afraid."

Matilda bent over Emily, inspecting the wound. "I doubt Ellen did this, she wouldn't have had time, not if she followed us to Clontarf."

"I don't believe Ellen is responsible," I told her. "I had the misfortune of meeting Emily's 'man in black' that night as well. Come, let us return to the library and I shall tell you more."

An hour later, surrounded by the volumes from my collection—that is, those spared Emily's fury—I shared all that had happened that night, including the death of the security guard and my encounter with the man in black.

"So this man now has Patrick O'Cuiv's body?" Matilda asked.

"I would presume so. Either that or someone else got to him first."

"For what purpose?"

I shrugged.

Bram poked at the fire, adding a new log. The fresh wood let out a loud pop and settled upon the flames of the old. "What would this man want with Ellen? How would he even know you are acquainted with her?"

Again, I had no answer.

"All of this is connected somehow," Matilda said. "O'Cuiv, this man, Ellen, whatever she did to Bram."

"Whatever one of them did to my Emily," I added.

"Yes, Emily, too."

I watched as Matilda crossed the room and retrieved the black cloak they recovered from O'Cuiv's grave. She draped the garment over the round tea table next to my chair and carefully unfolded it, revealing the contents: a looking glass, a brush, a necklace, and a book. She handed the volume to me. "Do you recognize the language?"

I opened the book and began flipping through the pages. "Ellen wrote this?"

"We think so," Bram said. "The handwriting is very similar to hers, if not an exact match."

"But these dates?"

"It makes no more sense than the rest of this," Bram said, spreading his hands wide.

"Do you recognize the language?" Matilda pressed.

The language did seem familiar to me, not something I have studied, but most definitely a language I had encountered before. "I think it may be Hungarian. I own a medical text—" I stood and made my way to the bookshelves lining the east wall. From high atop the third from the right, I plucked out a volume. Returning to the table, I laid the text out beside the handwritten book found in the grave. "This is a copy of the *Orvosi Hetilap*; I acquired it a few years back while studying abroad." Running my fingers over both texts, I began to identify words. "Many words are similar. Yes, I am convinced this is Hungarian."

"But can you read it?" Bram asked.

"No," I told them. "But I know someone who can, and he may be able to shed some light on everything else."

"Who?"

I closed the covers of both books. "Have you ever heard of the Hellfire Club?"

13 AUGUST 1868, 9:51 p.m.—I was surprised to learn that Bram knew of the Hellfire Club by name, though not by location. The organization familiar to him was a group of rowdy gentlemen who frequented the Eagle Tavern near Dublin Castle in the heart of the city. These bucks were known to undertake the night's festivities drinking scaltheen, a concoction of whiskey and butter, until good and liquored up, then they

would wander around Dublin in quest of mischief. The police feared them due to their numbers and a tendency towards things violent, but they were hardly the club I planned to introduce Bram and my sister to this particular evening. The men he knew as the Hellfire Club were nothing more than a smokescreen devised by the actual members meant to divert attention should the name ever be spoken in public.

The true Hellfire Club was an old stone hunting lodge that stood high atop the summit of Montpelier Hill, built nearly one hundred years ago by William Conolly, the onetime Speaker of the Irish House of Commons. The location was unique, for you could clearly see the city from the building, but the structure was hidden from below—and the road that led to it was concealed and guarded.

As a doctor, I was welcomed into this fold by my colleague Dr. Charles Croker when I first joined the staff of Swift's Hospital for Lunatics. He saw in me a curiosity and desire that reached beyond the teachings of modern medicine I had received at Queen's College, and believed I would benefit from the higher conversation often found at the Hellfire Club during late-night debates and discussions, particularly in the upper halls, which could be accessed only by an additional invitation. These conversations would often turn to the supernatural, the occult, and discussions of medical theory so extreme Mary Shelley's vision seemed as tame as a commonplace medical text.

I did not attend these discussions often, for I found the subject matter so disturbing that sleep would elude me for days after taking part in even a single session. It was during one of these roundtables that I met the man I hoped to find there tonight, a Hungarian professor named Arminius Vambéry.

"You believe this Vambéry will assist us?" Matilda asked, piercing the cloud of silence that had smothered the coach. My driver remained missing, and his son drove in his stead. I gestured for Matilda to keep her voice low, for I did not know the boy as well as his father and I figured it would be best if he overheard little of our plans.

I tapped the cover of the book Matilda and Bram had retrieved from O'Cuiv's coffin. "I am certain this is written in Hungarian, and Vambéry will make the translation with ease. He is also quite knowledgeable in matters of the dark arts."

"And you trust him?" Matilda asked. "With something like this?"

I nodded. "I have known him since medical school. He has shared some horrific tales with me over the years, and I have shared a number of secrets with him. Not once did any of those secrets pass from his lips. I would trust this man with my life."

"Why is it you never spoke of him before?" Bram asked.

"Matters discussed at the Hellfire Club never leave the walls; that is the golden rule. To speak of something learned at the Hellfire will get you barred from admittance for life, sometimes worse."

"Worse?"

I lowered my voice. "There are stories of men disappearing simply for mentioning the names of other members, let alone discussing a topic learned at the club. You might find high members of society freely speaking to the working class; sometimes even royalty can be found in attendance. They will share an ale and talk about things unmentionable in other circles, but should you run into these men the following morning on the street, they will not so much as nod a hello to you. Nothing leaves the club, not ever."

Matilda's brow creased with concern. "If this 'club' is so secretive, how do you plan to spirit Bram and me inside?"

"As long as you are with me, I can gain your admittance. Don't you worry about that."

Matilda snickered. "Our brother, the aristocrat. Who would have thought such a thing when you were mucking out stalls back in Clontarf?"

The coach slowed as it rounded the bend at the top of the hill, then stopped altogether when it arrived at the first checkpoint. There were two quick knocks on the door of the coach, which I followed by knocking five times in succession. My response was in turn followed by a single knock, to which I knocked thrice more. A moment later, the coach began to roll forward again. Bram and Matilda were both staring at me, Matilda grinning like the cat who had swallowed the proverbial canary. Five minutes later, at a second checkpoint, we halted once again. This time a voice simply inquired through the door, "Password?"

I leaned forward and supplied the secret word: "Mitten."

The coach again continued on its journey up the path.

Matilda said, "Do they not open the door? How do they know who is inside?"

"That is precisely the point; nobody is to know who is riding in any given carriage. This precaution is taken to ensure anonymity; nobody will actually see your face until you are safely within the confines of the club. The same secrecy holds true when you leave. Many visitors rent hansom cabs rather than take their own coaches to ensure they are not identified through association with specific vehicles."

Matilda furrowed her brow. "Are these men hiding in the bushes or are there little guard posts along the way?"

I shrugged. "I've been told it's forbidden to look, so I don't look."

"Boys play the most peculiar games," Matilda said, peeking out from behind the curtain covering the window.

As the coach achieved the summit, I felt us round the building and come to rest at the side entrance. I reached for the door handle. "Come, now."

Stepping down from the carriage, I offered my hand to Matilda to guide her down the steps.

Bram glanced around the small enclosure. "The secrecy continues."

He was right, of course. The side entrance of the Hellfire Club was outfitted with walls and a roof which butted up directly against the coach with heavy curtains sealing out the outside world and defining a path from coach to the interior of the club, which curious eyes could not see in or out.

"The location of the club is a closely guarded secret, and this side entrance allows members to ferry guests in without revealing its address. Come, this way."

Once inside, I led them through a short tunnel illuminated by gas lamps set in the stone walls on either side. Ahead, voices filled the air, a dozen or more. I always found it difficult to tell how many I was hearing due to the way sound bounced off the walls.

As we entered the main hall on the first floor, eyes fell upon us, mostly on Matilda and Bram, for I was recognized by a number of familiar faces. No verbal greetings were exchanged, for that was not the members' custom. At most, there was a slight nod of one's head.

"Is that . . ." Matilda said softly.

I followed her gaze to a rather attractive man standing amongst a group of four others engaged in what appeared to be a heated discussion. I could not make out his words, but judging by the redness of his face, the topic was not a pleasant one. "Yes, that is Arthur Guinness. The man he is addressing is William Wilde, Willie and Oscar's father. This will be interesting."

"Oh, blast," Bram muttered behind me.

I turned to him. "What is it?"

"The man over in the corner there, with the cigar, that is Sheridan Le Fanu."

"The owner of the *Evening Mail*?"

Bram nodded. "He is also its editor. Probably best that he does not see me here. I still owe him a review."

I took Bram and Matilda by the arms and led them through the crowd, granting wide berth to Le Fanu as we passed on our way to the staircase at the back of the room. A hefty man in a black bowler hat stood at the foot of the stair, blocking our path to the second floor. He eyed all three of us curiously, his gaze lingering just a bit too long on my sister. Like his eyebrows, his mustache was thick, black, and bushy. His attempts to tame it with wax caused the hairs to jut out randomly in protest. His hand kept attending to it, endeavoring to smooth out the wild mess, but his efforts made matters worse. "Only select members are permitted upstairs," he finally intoned in a rich Irish brogue.

"We're here to speak with Arminius Vambéry," I told him. "He's expecting us."

The man considered this request for a moment. "Wait here."

He climbed the stairs, favoring his right leg with a pronounced limp.

"Did you get word to Vambéry? How is he possibly expecting us?" Matilda asked.

"Getting word to Vambéry is akin to sending up a smoke signal and instructing it to turn at the top of the hill and proceed west. He has no permanent address or mail drop for receiving letters, telegrams, or messages. Nobody knows where he rests his weary head at night; he once informed me that he never sleeps in the same place twice. I'm not certain Vambéry is even his real name. Most believe he is some kind of spy working for the government, but of course there is no evidence to prove or disprove this theory. He always seems to know the most obscure facts, and in that regard has served as an instructor at a number of institutions of higher learning; speaking to him, in fact, is a bit like conversing with a library in human form. I have yet to find a topic on which he cannot speak with confidence."

The man in the bowler returned, carefully navigating the steps to accommodate his bad leg. "Mr. Vambéry is in the Green Room."

He ushered us past, and we climbed the stairs.

. . .

THE DOOR TO THE GREEN ROOM was at the end of the hall, the chamber being Vambéry's preferred space while in attendance at the Hellfire Club. We found him inside, sitting at the head of a grand table, with two other gentlemen in attendance I did not recognize. As we stepped into the room, both men stood and simply left; there were no hellos, no good-byes. They passed us and walked down the hall towards the stairs leading back to the main floor.

"Come in, my friend!" Vambéry said. "It is most excellent to see you again."

Vambéry was about my height and appeared ten or so years older. His dark hair was closely cropped, as were his beard and mustache. I had once heard that both beard and mustache were false and attached with glue, offering him the ability to quickly alter his appearance. In all my time around the man, I never once saw anything to indicate that either were anything but authentic.

"Please, close the door behind you," he said.

Bram did so, the lock automatically engaged with an audible click.

Vambéry reached out and took Matilda's hand, raising it gently to his lips. "Who is this beautiful young woman?"

Matilda's cheeks flushed. "I thought names went unspoken in this little clubhouse?"

Vambéry shrugged his shoulders. "The old, stuffy members would like us all to adhere to that little rule, but I, for one, prefer to know who I am speaking to at all times, particularly when that company is one as glowing as yourself."

"That is my sister, Matilda," I told him. "And this is Bram."

He encased Matilda's hand with his own. "A pleasure." He then turned to Bram. "And how are you enjoying your post at Dublin Castle?"

Bram tilted his head. "How do you know where I'm employed?"

"I make it my business to know everyone with a position in the government, from the very top down to the clerk's office. I have heard good things about you, Bram. Sounds like you might be the one to finally bring some organization to the Petty Sessions office. I look forward to seeing what you do there. I am also very fond of your father. He is a man I deeply respect. And your brother as well; there is not a finer physician in Dublin."

A servant entered through a door at the back of the room and set a tray with an assortment of meats and cheeses on the table. There were also three cups and saucers and a black kettle with steam rising from its spout. "Please, join me for tea," Vambéry said. "I grew fond of this particular spiced tea while traveling in the Balkans. I made sure no matter how spartan my kit, a small kettle and cups and saucers were always with me. Try it, please. If it is not to your liking, I will have some coffee brewed instead."

I found the tea to be quite enjoyable and told him so; both Matilda and Bram concurred.

He gestured at the table. "Please, take a seat. Tell me how I may help you."

A benign question, but with matters such as this, where does one begin? I turned to Matilda and Bram, and both glanced back at me, none of the three of us certain where to begin. We took places around the table.

After nearly a minute, Vambéry broke the silence. "During my years on this planet, I have killed seven men, five in self-defense, the other two under, well, different circumstances."

I stole a look to my right—Bram's eyes flicked over to meet mine for a moment. Matilda's mouth had dropped open. She quickly pulled it shut. If Vambéry noticed, he gave no indication, not missing a beat before going on.

"I witnessed crimes far too gruesome to detail in the company of a lady, and I encountered creatures previously thought to exist only in the nightmares of children. I met kings with the brain capacity of a pea, and politicians with more skeletons in their closets than an undertaker's wife. I have spied on governments and men for other governments and men, and I have been compensated well for doing so. I have seen many things in this world and yet I know there are far more things to see than I ever will see; I embrace each day knowing this and hope to glean something new every day." He leaned in closer, taking a sip of his tea. "I tell you all this not to impress you but to comfort you. There are no secrets here, nothing you should feel you cannot tell me, for I have full confidence that anything we share will remain between these walls and venture to no one else." He placed his teacup on the table and leaned back in his chair. "I confessed to murder here in the presence of the three of you. Now each of you must confess a secret here in turn, something you would normally never disclose to another living soul, something that can be held by the rest of us as a key, of sorts, a key to a lock that binds us together from now until the end of our days, for to reveal one of these secrets to another party would open the door to revealing all our secrets."

Such pacts were common in the Hellfire Club, and I had heard Vambéry's speech before. Although, I must admit, the last time he confessed to only six murders in total.

I turned to Bram and Matilda. "When I was attending medical school, three other students and I dug up the recently deceased remains of one Herman Hortwhither and transported his body to an abandoned warehouse on the outskirts of Dublin for study. There we spent three days dissecting the poor man, first in an effort to ascertain how he had died, then to study his internal workings. We attempted to do so with the utmost respect and skill, but since this was our first dissection, we failed miserably at both. Frankly, we made an undignified mess of Mr.

Hortwhither. Upon completion of our ill-conceived task, his death remained a mystery to us, and although the study of his organs proved insightful, it only left us with more questions. The following weekend, we returned to the cemetery and disinterred the body of one Lily Butler, a local prostitute who died at the age of sixteen from causes unknown. We brought her back to the same warehouse and went about dissecting her as well, this time with steadier hands than our first venture. Sad to say, these forays were conducted for the better part of a year. But we had little choice; the Royal College of Surgeons made few cadavers available, supplying only one for every thirty or so students, and without these additional opportunities for study, learning my craft would have been impossible. I return to the cemetery each year and place a rose upon each grave I desecrated and pray for each soul I violated, hoping they somehow understand that the knowledge I derived from each of them gave me the skills to save lives."

When I finished, I could not look at my brother or sister; instead, I stared down into the bottom of my empty teacup and tried to block the horrible memories these images visited on me year after year, thoughts I longed to forget.

Matilda spoke next, and when she spoke her voice reminded me of her voice as a child, not like the woman she was now. "When I was seventeen, I attended a Royal Dublin Society Ball at Leinster House. Ma and Pa had no idea I was going; I told them I was visiting my friend Philippa Ferguson, and she told her parents she was staying overnight with our family, as we intended to be out until dawn. I wasn't fond of lying to Ma and Pa, and I rarely did so, but they could be so protective of me, this was the only way I could win any freedom from their control.

"Philippa and I dressed in gowns borrowed from her older sister, Amelia. We styled each other's hair, and pinched our cheeks until they glowed. By the time we were done, we both appeared several years older than our actual age—or so we believed. We left for Leinster House in a hansom cab. Philippa was always beautiful, but on this particular night she was positively radiant. I suppose I was a bit radiant, too, for it didn't take long before we had a line of suitors asking us to dance. At this juncture, we had little time for attending each other, and before long I had lost track of her amongst the crowd, but since I was enjoying such a delightful time, I thought little of it. Philippa could not have ventured far, and I assumed she was off dancing somewhere else out of my sight. Nearly three hours elapsed, then four. At this point, I began to worry. The hour was late, the number of revelers had thinned, yet I spied no sign of my friend. When I made inquiry of the gentlemen she had danced with earlier in the evening, each told me they had not seen her in a long while. When the clock struck midnight, indicating the conclusion of the ball, I still had not found her. I considered taking another hansom back to her home, but I knew she would not have left without me, so instead I strolled the vast gardens. It was near the gardens' rear wall that I heard her crying. At first, I couldn't tell where her sobs came from and thought I imagined them, but then I spotted her huddled in a gazebo next to the rose garden. I went to her quickly and wrapped my arms around her, so glad to have found her, and at my touch she pulled away, her eyes gleaming with terror. When she realized it was me, her face softened, and tears flowed freely again as she held me, her entire body quivering with each sob. We remained embraced like this for some time, and when she was finally able to speak, she told me a most horrific tale. One of her suitors, a man who had claimed to be Thomas Hall, had taken her on a stroll in the garden. Initially, she said it was lovely, walking hand in hand amongst the blossoms, hearing him speak of his travels, throughout Ireland and the United Kingdom, and to America, where he had traveled on three different occasions and would love to take her the next time he went. In the short time they spent together, he made her feel as if they had been friends for many years. When they reached the gazebo, he took her in his arms and kissed her, a deep, passionate kiss, the kind of kiss every girl dreams of, and Philippa thought she found her true love. When that first kiss concluded, he kissed her again, and again after that, before long his lips meandering over her neck and breasts. Although she was greatly attracted to him, she knew they must desist, and she told him so, but he did not, would not; instead, his grip on her arms tightening as he forced yet another kiss upon her.

"I saw then that her dress was torn, the material at her bosom held up only by her hand, and she told me of the terrible things he did to her, all while her begging him to stop. She pleaded with him again and again, and he ignored her again and again, until finally he slapped her across the face and told her not to utter another sound or he would kill her where she now lay, upon the floor of this gazebo. This went on for nearly twenty more minutes, and my friend Philippa remained mute throughout it all. When it was finally over, he told her to stay there until the band stopped playing. And she was never to speak of what happened; if she dared do so, he said he would seek her out and choke the very life from her body. With that threat delivered, he left. He left her there, in the gazebo, and disappeared in the night. Philippa did as she was told, remaining in the gazebo, until I arrived."

Matilda's eyes had grown red and were filled with tears of her own, yet she fought back the sobs to continue her story. "Had I stayed with her, had I watched over her as we had promised each other we would do, this would have never happened. I knew this was my fault even as Philippa assured me it was not. We stayed at an inn that night and returned to her house in the morning. When we got there, she washed her face, combed her hair, burned the dress in the fireplace, then crawled into her own bed, before asking me to take my leave. I called on her twice during the next week, but she refused to receive me. Although she said she didn't blame me, I knew that she did, for I so readily blamed myself. A month later, she left for London to stay with her father's sister. I never saw her again, but thoughts of her are always in my heart."

Bram placed a hand over Matilda's and squeezed it. "It wasn't your fault. You could not have known. I'm only glad it did not happen to you."

"I wish it had happened to me," Matilda said. "It would be easier to live with than this guilt. A true friend never deserts another. I will take this guilt to my grave."

"There is no judgment here, only confessions," Vambéry said. "You are strong to be able to share such a tale, and I am honored to have you in my life."

Vambéry turned to my brother. "And you? As the brother of Thornley Stoker, I can only imagine your life is chockful of things to confess."

Bram gazed at one of the gas lamps for a moment, then each of us in turn. "When I was a little boy, I was very ill. I often thought I was just this side of death's door. My parents brought in numerous physicians, and none could diagnose my sickness. Illness confined me to my room, to my bed. At the age of seven, on the eve of what might have been my final hours, I found myself alone in my room with my . . ." He paused for a second and glanced at both Matilda and me. "With *our* nanny. She asked me for my trust, and I granted it. In a fevered state, I granted it. She then bit my wrist and drew blood from my veins between her lips. She drew so much blood I thought I would perish from the loss. Then, just when a black veil began to cloak my vision, she raised her own wrist to my mouth. She had cut the flesh so her blood flowed freely, and, God forgive me, I drank of her. I drank until I could drink no more. When I woke the next morning, my illness was cured. I was healthier than I had ever been. Our nanny left us shortly thereafter. I have never been sick again. If I feel the hint of illness, it leaves me shortly thereafter."

Matilda reached for his hand and squeezed it, but Bram shook her off. "There is more, something I never shared with anyone. Something I wanted to tell you but could never find the courage to do so. But I fear if I do not tell you now, I never will."

"What is it?" Matilda asked.

"She has come to me many times since that night." Tears welled up in his eyes. "My dear, sweet sister, when you saw us in the rain the other night, when you saw her drinking my blood and I drinking hers . . . this was but one time of many. Over the years she has visited me more times than I can count. It is her blood that holds my illness at bay. If not for her, I would be dead now. Of that I am certain."

All of us fell silent at this confession, Matilda's face had gone ashen, for she and Bram were extremely close and shared all. To learn of something this grave, in this way; to realize he had not been willing to confide in her until now—she stood from the table and turned her back to us, her eyes fixed on the door.

Vambéry reached for Bram's hand. "May I?"

Bram nodded and turned his wrist over, pulling his shirtsleeve back to reveal the punctures.

Vambéry took hold of a lamp and brought the light close. "How often would you say she comes to you?"

Bram shrugged. "It is difficult to say. She only comes at night when I sleep. I am often unsure whether her visits are real or the stuff of dreams. For many years, I thought them all to be dreams. But as I got older, as I realized this wound never quite healed, I came to the truth, the reality of her visits and their role in maintaining my health."

"And did you speak to her?" Matilda asked. "Have you been speaking to her for all these years and not telling me? How much more have you hidden from me?"

Bram shook his head. "There have never been words adequate enough. I have only faint memories of her visits. They're dream-like. I would wake and wonder if it had happened at all. I wanted so to tell you, you must believe that."

"How often, if you had to guess? Once a week? Once a month?" Vambéry pressed.

"Probably five to six times in a given year."

"And yet you said nothing," Matilda whispered. "When I told you she came to me, you stared at me as if I were a crazy person. The other night, when Thornley confessed to seeing her, you again said nothing. Why didn't you trust us?"

"I am truly sorry. I suppose I convinced myself that it wasn't real. I couldn't tell you for fear of admitting the truth to myself."

Vambéry said, "We all confessed secrets tonight, secrets that now bind us together and make us one, secrets we will all take to our graves. I am honored to know the three of you, to trust you, and to welcome you into my life." He gestured to Matilda. "Please return to the table, join us. I suspect we have much more to discuss."

Matilda did so with reluctance, and she seemed to find it hard to look at Bram and he to look at her. One of the servants returned and refilled our teacups. I believe we all welcomed the interruption; the silence gave us pause to organize our thoughts.

When the servant left the room, Vambéry turned back to me. "How can I help you, my old friend?"

For the next hour, we told him all we knew. I began with my sightings of Nanna Ellen, as experienced throughout my life. Then Bram and Matilda told him all they recalled from their childhood, and the horrors discovered in the tower of Artane Castle; they also told him about the maps found in her room they transcribed. We then told him of O'Cuiv, my missing coachman, and the items Bram and Matilda recovered from the grave. I concluded with the events at the hospital, the strange man I met in the street, and the black dog that followed me home. Vambéry took all of this in while asking the occasional question. I had never once witnessed him writing anything down, and he did not take notes now, either; instead, he memorized everything. I saw his mind churning, organizing the facts and conjectures into a coherent narrative.

When we finally finished, Vambéry sat back in his chair and laced his fingers behind his head. "This girl, O'Cuiv's daughter, you think she is somehow responsible for your coachman's disappearance?"

"We saw no one else that night, only her," Matilda said.

"You believe her to be one of them, though? Like your Ellen? Like O'Cuiv? But a child?"

"Her movements were not natural," Matilda explained. "I felt I was in the presence of a predator. Had Bram not returned when he did, I think she may have hurt me as well."

"Yet she only held Bram while Ellen drank, is that not so? Why would she abstain with the opportunity at hand?"

"I did not witness her drink; that doesn't mean she did not," Matilda countered.

"The only mark on my person is the one at the wrist; if she drank, wouldn't there be another?" Bram said.

"Perhaps she got her fill with my unfortunate coachman?" I pointed out.

Vambéry nodded at this. "As always, Thornley, your logic prevails."

"You know what is happening here, don't you?" Matilda asked of him. "You have seen this before?"

Vambéry leaned over the table, his voice hushed. "In my travels, I have seen and heard many things, some treading far beyond what one would consider to be rational. Your tale reminds me of those told to me in Eastern Europe of Ottomans, Romanians, Slavs, and the like. I will share those tales with you eventually, when I deem it appropriate, but for now I would prefer to hear more from you, to ensure my deductions are correct." His gaze again fell upon my sister. "May I examine the items you retrieved from the O'Cuiv grave?"

Matilda had stored these things in a small leather satchel. She retrieved it from the floor at her feet and placed it on the table, then extracted each item, lining them up on the table between us.

Vambéry's eyes grew wide at the sight of the necklace, and he reached for it. "This is exquisite, and quite valuable. Clearly crafted in Romania, I can tell by the setting—handmade by a very talented craftsman. This ruby is one of the largest I have ever seen. Please put this necklace back in your bag; I fear what might befall you should a thief realize you are harboring this treasure. The Hellfire Club is safe, but, still, there are prying eyes everywhere."

I watched as Matilda collected the necklace and carefully placed it back into the small leather satchel. Vambéry then inspected the mirror. "I find this a little odd."

"How so?" Bram asked.

"The fact that you found a looking glass is quite peculiar, but for it to be made of silver and gold, that is odder still." His finger ran over the engraving. "This inscription will no doubt prove useful; we must devote some time to ascertaining who this Countess Dolingen von Gratz was. Like the necklace, this mirror is very old. The same is true of the hairbrush. Such craftsmanship is typically reserved for the wealthy. Possessions such as these would not belong to a nanny, nor this O'Cuiv family as you described them."

Matilda handed him the cloak and told him it belonged to our mother, yet it was found in O'Cuiv's grave.

"You are certain?"

"There is no mistaking it. See the hole in the sleeve there?"

"And the last time you saw it, the cloak was worn by your Ellen?"

"On the night before she took leave," Matilda said.

"So we have all these things that presumably belong to your former nanny hidden within the grave of your former neighbor. A grave lacking a body, mind you."

Matilda produced her sketchbook and turned to the map of Ireland indicating the position of St. John the Baptist Church. "I believe the location of the grave is marked here."

Vambéry's eyes went wide. "You drew this? From memory?"

"I did."

"Remarkable." He studied the image. "And you said the grave was amongst the suicides?"

Matilda nodded, then turned the pages of her sketchpad, flipping through the other maps. "All of these marks indicate cemeteries containing either suicide graves or unconsecrated ground."

Vambéry retrieved a small magnifying glass from his breast pocket and leaned over the map. After a few minutes' study, he proceeded on to the next, then the next after that. "I have been to some of these locations, but not all. Did Ellen ever speak of these places?"

The three of us shook our heads.

"But clearly they were important to her." He closed the sketchpad and handed it back to Matilda. "The purpose of these maps will present itself in time, as is always the case. Of that I am confident. Until then, keep them safe."

Vambéry turned to Thornley. "You mentioned a book? Our reason for gathering?"

Bram retrieved the book they had found in Patrick O'Cuiv's bodiless coffin, placed it in front of Vambéry, and turned to the first page. "Look at this date. The entire book is written in Ellen's hand."

"The twelfth of October 1654." He raised the book to his nose and sniffed the pages, then inspected the binding. "The construction is correct for that period, so the book is at least that old, but there is no way to determine when she actually wrote in it."

"Can you read it?" Matilda asked.

"Of course; this is written in my native Hungarian. Was your nanny from Hungary?"

"I always assumed she was Irish," I replied, and as I looked to my brother and sister, it was clear they knew as little about Ellen's history as I did.

Our blank stares gave Vambéry his answer. "If she was not from Hungary, it is an unusual choice of language for one's diary. Most would default to German or a tongue closer to their own. Unless, of course, she wanted to keep these writings hidden from someone. Then employing such a language makes perfect sense."

"Is that what this is?" Matilda asked. "A diary?"

Vambéry pulled a pair of spectacles from his right breast pocket, secured them to the bridge of his nose, and returned his attention to the pages in front of him, reading silently for nearly three minutes before speaking again; when he did speak, he placed his palm upon the book. "This is far more than a diary, my friends—I must read it to you."

AT THIS POINT, the servant returned again and replaced our empty tea-kettle with a fresh one, then topped off our cups before leaving us. Although the visit probably lasted no more than a minute, it felt as if an hour passed. When we were finally alone, Vambéry turned back to the first page and drew one of the lamps close to the text. "I will do my level best with the translation. If something is unclear to you, please stop me so we can review in more depth."

Not a breath could be heard as he began to read aloud.

"*She lived many years ago in southern Ireland near Waterford. A legendary beauty, with the reddest lips and pale blond hair. Her true name has long since been lost, but at the time her beauty was known far and wide. Men traveled great distances, not only for the chance to gaze upon her but in hope of winning her hand in marriage. It is said her outward beauty was no match for the beauty she held within. She was the brightest of spirits. She lived alone with her father, her mother having passed in childbirth.*

"*This beautiful, well-natured girl fell in love with a local peasant. His name,* too, has been forgotten, but he was a true match for her in all things; he was handsome, kindhearted, a gentleman by any measure, but he lacked the one feature this beautiful girl's father cared about above all others—money. As it does today, money dictated one's place in society, and her father knew the only way to elevate the family name was to marry his daughter into a family of wealth. Because the peasant boy would never be rich and therefore could not bring the family the standing her father wished, she was forbidden to marry him.

"The beautiful girl's father instead arranged for her to marry a far older man, a man who promised the father great riches in exchange for the daughter's hand. This suitor was known throughout the land for his cruelty and his wicked ways, but these deficits were of no concern to the father; he was blinded by the promise of wealth and the position he could attain amongst the local families. He soon forgot about his poor daughter, and most of the other villagers did, too. Her husband locked her away in his castle, barring contact with the outside world. He thrived on the knowledge that he possessed a treasure so sought after and reveled in keeping it locked away from all. She suffered tremendous abuse, mental and physical, at his relentless hand; he would hurt her for the sheer amusement of it, finding enjoyment in her cries of pain and lamentations of sorrow.

"And even though she was locked away, word of his tortures leaked out on the lips of his servants and visitors. It was said he was fond of bleeding her, inflicting tiny cuts along her perfect alabaster skin. When he finally tired of her, he would lock her away in a tower of his castle where no one would hear her sobs as she cried late into the night, waiting for her only true love, the peasant boy, to come and save her.

"As the days turned into weeks and then into months, her hope began to leave her. She would stand at the small slit in the wall, her only window, and watch the countryside for a sign of her beloved. But he never came. In her eleventh month, she refused to eat, throwing the rancid scraps of meat back at the servants who brought it to her, the stale bread, too. She vowed not to allow a single morsel to pass her lips, and she began to fade away to nothing but skin and bones. Two weeks later, she refused water as well, and soon she began to seethe and rage like a lunatic as dehydration worked through what remained of her failing body.

"On the first anniversary of her marriage to the evil tyrant, she pulled the stool from the corner of her room to the window and stood upon it, gazing out over the land, one last hope of seeing her love. When she found no sign, she climbed up onto the ledge. She was so thin now, so like a twig from a tree, she had no trouble fitting into the narrow space. She filled her mind with thoughts of her true love, a recollection of his smile as he gazed upon her, his hand upon hers, then cast herself from the tall tower window to the unforgiving rocks below. Three days would pass before anyone discovered her sorry shattered remains.

"I often wondered where her true love had been. Why had he not come for her? Why had he not rescued her? I later learned the girl's husband, the evil tyrant, told the boy long before that if he were to step foot near the castle, she would be killed immediately. He dared not approach for fear of causing her death.

"The peasant boy spent all his waking hours, and nearly as many sleepless nights, trying to find a way to get to his beloved without endangering her, but the castle was secluded, perched high above the village on the edge of a great forest and surrounded by open fields and bogs. There was no way to approach without being seen. He wrote letters to her daily, hundreds of them, and put them in a box, hoping to find someone who might deliver them to her. But that day never came; she died a broken soul before he even made the attempt.

"It is said she renounced God as she plunged to her death, blaming Him for cursing her with an unloving father and an evil husband. She vowed a terrible vengeance upon all those who wronged her. Because she committed suicide, her soul was guaranteed never to know rest; she was doomed to spend eternity in torment."

. . .

"Like those in the suicide graves," Matilda said.

"Exactly like those in the suicide graves," said Bram.

"According to this account, she was buried in a suicide grave of sorts," Vambéry said, before continuing on.

"When her true love learned of her death, he alone went to the base of the tower to retrieve her body and bring her to a final resting place within the village, but they would not permit him to bury her in the cemetery, in holy ground. He was forced to bury her behind the cemetery in a lonely plot of land. Although it was customary to pile rocks high upon the graves of the recently deceased, he could not bring himself to do so. His heart was broken, and he wanted to climb into that grave with her, not distance her further with stones and dirt. Instead, he buried her in the best dress he could procure and placed a single white rose upon her grave, vowing to visit her daily, a promise he could not make to her in life.

"Even in death, her evil husband would not end his torment. He, too, went to her grave, and seeing the rose, tore the petals from the stem. He cut himself on the thorns and cursed her further still as blood dripped from his fingertips to the soil of his wife's grave. Then he tossed the remains of the flower aside, swearing he would do the same for any gifts he found at her gravesite. He wished her to be as lonely in death as she was in that final year of her life.

"That very night, not long after her husband left, she rose from her grave. Her fingers clawed through the earth and cast it aside, and she pulled herself out and stood there, free for the first time since her father married her away. It is said that the thoughts that had plagued her in her final moments, those twisted thoughts, clouded her mind and obscured the goodness she had always exhibited. Vengeance and hate flowed through her veins. Her beauty remained, though; in fact, when she rose that night, she was physically more beautiful

than she had been in life, but with the heart of a monster. By the light of the rising moon, she made her way to her husband's castle high atop the hill.

"A guard was posted at the lair's gate, but as she approached the hapless sentry was mesmerized by her beauty, unable to speak at the sight of her. If he tried to stop her from passing, there was scant evidence, for no one heard him raise the alarm as he should have done. She just came upon the guard and offered a smile so radiant that he could not turn away; he could do nothing but stand there as she leaned in close and sank her teeth into the fleshy pulp of his neck and drank the life from his body. Eight others died as she made her way through the castle, not only guards but her husband's cook and two of his servant girls as well, both of whom had observed her suffering over the course of that year without ever uttering a word of protest. She moved from chamber to chamber, taking each life she came upon, until she finally found herself at her husband's apartments.

"Through all this, he slept. She had brought about all this death without allowing a single warning cry to escape from one of her victims. She crossed his bedchamber to the foot of his bed and glared down upon him, upon the sleeping form of the man who took her life, stripped her of all happiness, the man who drove her to death and brought her back black-hearted. She leaned into him, her breath icy, and whispered at his ear, 'I missed you, my dearest.' When he awoke, she smiled. Her once-beautiful dress was now covered in blood, drops of which fell upon him.

"While she had killed all her previous victims quickly, she wished for her husband to suffer as she had. Instead of giving him a swift bite to the neck, she bit him repeatedly, hundreds of bites all over his body until blood poured from him, drenching the sheets and mattress. When he was discovered shortly after dawn, he lived long enough to tell of what happened, then collapsed upon his mattress, his skin gray under the gleaming trails of blood. There was no sign of her, though; she had fled before the rise of the sun.

"The following night, she paid a visit to her father. He had been out at a pub

and was quite drunk when he stumbled into his house—a very large house he purchased with the money he received from his daughter's tyrant of a husband. He shuffled inside, forgetting to close the front door, and fell into a chair in front of the dwindling remains of a fire with a tall glass of aqua vitae in his hand.

"When his daughter appeared at the front door, he stared at her for a long while, so drunk he wasn't sure what he saw was even real. He didn't say anything to her, nor was he frightened. He only stared, his drink never far from his lips. When at last someone spoke, it was she: 'I missed you, Father. I couldn't bear another day without the sight of you, so I had to come back.'

"The sound of her sweet words startled him. Until that moment, he had thought of her as a mirage, but the voice made her real to him. He tried to stand up, nearly fell to the floor in the attempt, then collapsed back into the soft leather of the armchair with a grunt-filled laugh. 'My daughter! My beautiful daughter! You have come home to see me!'

"His words were slurred, but she understood him well enough, and a smile graced her ruby lips.

"The blood from the previous night's kills had vanished, her dress again the purest white, unblemished by death. She was truly a vision. Her flowing blond hair waved in the breeze, the moonlight shone brilliantly on her otherwise waxy skin. Her teeth were as white as her gown. And her eyes glowed. When she spoke again, her father looked up, his eyes bloodshot. 'Father, it has been so long. And it is so cold and lonely out here. May I come in and warm myself by your fire?'

"Her father must have sensed something was amiss for even in his drunken state her request gave him pause. Studying her as she stood at the threshold of his ill-gotten house, he took another drink of aqua vitae, then replied, 'Why can you not come in, then? Who is stopping you?'

"She remained at the door, looking in, but did not venture closer. It was then that he noticed something bizarre; even though her dress and hair moved with the breeze, the branches of the tree a few feet behind her did not. It was as if the air found purchase with her and nothing else. He again raised his glass to his lips, but this time he did not drink. Fear began to grow within his breast, and the haze brought on by the alcohol was little match for it. 'My daughter is dead,' he spat. 'She cast herself down upon the rocks rather than service her husband as any good wife should. She is a disgrace upon this family. You are a disgrace upon this family. And you are not welcome here, whatever you may be.'

"His daughter stood there, unable to enter, the look of love upon her face transforming to one of hate, her eyes taking on the red of flaming embers. 'If you will not welcome me in, I will wait out here for you. I have nothing but time.'

"'I am a patient man, my daughter, with no reason to leave.'

"And he did not leave. He remained in that house; food was brought to him. And he dared not venture out even when he realized she only came during the hours of night. When daylight came, and she was nowhere to be seen, he supposed it was a trick to lure him outside.

"They continued this game for a full month. Each night he would open his front door and sit himself in front of the fire and wait for her, but he would never invite her in. They would speak only through the open door as he drank and cursed her in death with as much contempt as he had held for her in life. On the thirty-first night, something changed, and she did not appear. He opened the door as he always did and stared out into the night, but she never came. In the morning, he learned why: She had killed the boy who had been delivering food to him. His body was discovered in the middle of the street, drained of all blood.

"Still unwilling to leave the house even in daylight hours, her father shouted from his doorstep, 'A gold piece to anyone who brings me food!' A local farmer heard him in passing and agreed to the proposition. He went to the market, retrieved a bushel of fruit and vegetables, and returned with it not an hour later. The father promptly paid the farmer and instructed him to return every two days with the same produce, and the farmer happily agreed. He did not return, though; that night, the daughter killed the farmer, his wife, both their children, and the cattle that grazed on his land, leaving them all as bloodless husks. Upon the side of her father's house, she wrote the words HE STARVES in blood.

Word quickly spread. Anyone who aids this man would be brutally murdered by the ghost of his dead daughter, the Dearg-Due.

"As before, she returned to his open door each night and waited for him at the threshold, vowing to end his suffering if he invited her inside, but he would not. The townspeople gathered, too, standing at a distance, watching this phantom watching her father until she began to take them as well, one at a time, one each night, blaming everyone for abandoning her in that castle. Three more weeks went by, more than two dozen dead, and her father wasted away from the portly fellow he had become with his newfound wealth to nothing but skin and bones, yet he didn't come out. Nor would he invite her in.

"The town slowly died around him. Few people were willing to venture out even during the daylight hours, for though she was seen at her father's house only during the lonely hours of the night, some swore they spotted her during the daylight hours, too, pacing atop the high battlements of the castle, and no one was willing to risk an encounter.

"On the fifty-eighth night, she was spotted crossing the threshold of her father's house and stepping inside. A moment later, the most horrendous scream came from inside as she stared down at the dead body of her father. He had succumbed to starvation and passed. At his feet, she found a note scrawled in the shaking hand of a dying man. It read I SHOULD HAVE DROWNED YOU AT BIRTH, RIGHT AFTER YOU KILLED YOUR MOTHER.

"It was then she realized why her father hated her so—he blamed her for the death of his wife. He carried that hatred with him his entire life. It only grew as she got older and came into her beauty, a beauty matched only by her mother's all those years earlier, a beauty that reminded him daily of the woman he lost at childbirth.

"When the Dearg-Due realized this truth, the anger which had burned within her so strong, the anger which snuffed out the beautiful light within her, began to fade as guilt took its place. Both her parents were dead at her hand, along with dozens of others victims, and none of this revenge filled the hole she felt in her heart. For the first time since rising from the dead, she thought of the peasant *boy, she thought of her true love, and longed to be at his side. She wished for nothing more than to be held in his arms and whisked away from all this death. She left her father's house, crossed the town square, and started across the fields to the peasant boy's little hovel in the woods as the few remaining townsfolk watched her through the slits of closed shutters and from behind doors.*

"She arrived at his cabin shortly after midnight. The moon was high and full in the night sky, casting a pale yellow light over the little clearing in which he lived. She found him sitting on the porch of his small home wrapped in a blanket to fend off the cool night air. Because she had killed just the previous night, drinking the blood of her victim, her cheeks were flushed and her skin warm. Her hair fluttered behind her, draped over her shoulders, over the flowing white gown he had dressed her in before burying her broken body. She was breathtaking, more stunning even than he remembered her in life. He watched as she approached, then motioned for her to sit on the bench at his side. 'I knew you would come; it was only a matter of time before you came for me, too. I do not fear death, not if it will bring me closer to you.'

"'I am not here to kill you,' she replied.

"Her voice seemed to come from all around him as well as from inside his own head, the sweet voice of his beloved, a voice he thought he would never hear again. 'But I failed you,' he told her. 'I could not rescue you from that place, from that man. I am no better than the rest; you might as well have died at my own hand.'

"She placed her hand upon his, expecting him to pull away at her cool touch, but he did not; instead, he wrapped his fingers around hers. His warm fingers—she could feel the blood pulsing through them, and it aroused something within her. 'I missed you so,' she said. He smiled at her. 'And I missed you, too, more than you could possibly know. I thought more than once about climbing to the top of that castle and joining you on the rocks below. Had I known it would place me by your side once again, I would have surely jumped, but there was no way to be certain. I am weak, and I hesitated, and I have done nothing since but spend my nights on this porch waiting for you to find me.'

"For the longest time, she did nothing but watch him, their hands intertwined. A tear slipped from her eye, a drop of crimson. He wiped it away and fought back tears of his own. She was so happy to be back in his arms that she did not see him pick up the metal blade from beside the bench, nor did she notice the hammer he had placed there beside it months earlier. With one quick motion, he pressed the sharp blade deep into her breast. She fell back in awe as he raised the hammer above his head and brought it down with all his strength, sending the steel through her heart with such force it embedded in the frame of the bench. A moment later, it was over, her body was still, and he wept until the morning light crept over the forest.

"He buried her for the second time on a little plot of land to the south of his cabin under an old willow tree. This time he took care to stack rocks high upon her grave—rocks he topped with a fresh white rose each night for the year that followed, hoping they would be together one day, but taking solace in the fact that she finally slumbered in peace."

WHEN VAMBÉRY looked up from the book, the four of us were silent. It was Matilda who spoke first. "That is the saddest story I have ever heard."

Vambéry turned to the last page. "There is a bit more."

His gaze remained fixed on the final words, and at first, he said nothing. I know now he hesitated because he was unsure of whether he should tell us, knowing it would lead to more questions. When finally he spoke, he did so with reservation. "It says—

"She awoke from death for a second time three years later, her tired eyes peering into the gloom of what could only be the inner walls of a castle, a room so similar to the one her evil husband had locked her in that for a moment she thought all of this had been nothing but a dream and she was back in that dreadful

place. Then she saw him; she saw this man bending over her. He held a rabbit by the leg over her, the neck sliced open and blood flowing freely from the wound to her mouth. She tasted every sweet morsel of it; she could feel it racing through her body, awakening limbs and muscle and tissue.

"'How can this be?' she said in a hoarse voice.

"The man said nothing at first, just gripped the rabbit, his free hand squeezing the carcass to release every last drop of blood. When he did speak, she found his voice to be deep and rich, but thick with an accent she could not quite place. 'I have woken you from a deep sleep. I have brought you back to life.'

"I have recorded these words as I remember them to be.

"Countess Dolingen von Gratz, 12 October 1654."

WHEN HE FINISHED READING, Vambéry slid the book to the center of the table, still open to that last page. Nanna Ellen's handwriting stared back at us from the yellowed paper.

He rang the bell for the servant and this time ordered a bottle of brandy. Matilda refused to drink, but Bram, Vambéry, and I harbored no such qualms. The three of us each enjoyed a glass, then another. The warmth of the alcohol did little to banish the chill from my bones. But, then, I doubted anything could.

"Who is this Countess Dolingen von Gratz?" Bram asked aloud.

"She is clearly Ellen. Or Ellen is she," Matilda said.

I cleared my throat and rolled the stem of the brandy snifter between my fingers. "Are we to believe Ellen wrote this more than two hundred years ago? Is that what you are implying?"

"If Ellen did write it, is it fictional or an account of the events she actually experienced?" Bram said.

Vambéry tapped the book. "I have heard the tale of the Dearg-Due, but never in such detail; only in whispers while amongst the Pavees."

"Pavees?"

"Minkiers . . . *Lucht Siúil* . . . knackers . . . They go by many names. They are Irish travelers, gypsies."

I turned to Vambéry, my friend, and asked him the question on all our minds. "Are we to believe our Nanna Ellen is this Dearg-Due?"

He shook his head. "I do not know what to believe."

"Isn't it just the stuff of superstition?" Bram said. "A tale meant to frighten children late at night?"

"Maybe, maybe not," Vambéry replied. "The Pavees believe it to be true, and . . ." He paused here, closing his eyes. Then he spoke slowly, saying the words aloud as his mind worked, slowly, deliberately. "The box you found as children, you said you found it in the ruins of a castle tower, did you not?"

Bram nodded. "In what remained of Artane Castle."

"Many believe the Dearg-Due was held captive in a castle outside of Dublin, near the coast. It is very possible that castle and the one in Artane are one and the same," Vambéry said. "It was built by the Hollywood family in the fourteenth century, but who is to say who occupied it in 1654 or the years prior when this story originated?"

"Or actually took place," Matilda pointed out, "if the story is true."

"Matilda, remember the lock?" Bram asked. "The lock on the tower room was on the outside of the door, meant to keep something in."

"We must go there at once," said Vambéry.

THE JOURNAL of BRAM STOKER

14 August 1868, 12:21 a.m. ──I only wish to make note of our departure, late into the night.

Vambéry summoned his coach, and we left the Hellfire Club in much the same way as we arrived: through a dark passage, never once gazing upon the exterior. Thornley elected to return to his home rather than ride with us; he feared he had already left Emily alone with his servants far too long and could do so no longer. We rode in relative silence, each of us lost within our own thoughts.

Matilda ignored me for much of the journey. I attempted to apologize for deceiving her, but she only mumbled in return and continued to stare out the window. Vambéry did not seem to notice this, though, instead focusing his attention on his notes, filling page after page without pausing. I couldn't help but envy the ease with which he wrote, for I sometimes found myself at a loss for words while attempting to recount these events in my own journal. He had not taken down a single word as we spoke at the Hellfire Club; I could only imagine he was documenting all of it now, for the hearty speed at which he wrote could only be fed by such a fire.

FROM THE NOTES
of ARMINIUS VAMBÉRY

(RECORDED IN CIPHER AND TRANSCRIBED HEREWITH.)

───── ◆ ─────

14 August 1868, 12:21 a.m. — I write in my own version of shorthand to ensure my words cannot be read by another. I do so with great hesitance, for if these words were to fall into the wrong hands, I have no doubt they could break my code, given enough time. That in mind, my shorthand is nothing more than a means to slow down others. I feel the risk of not documenting far outweighs my fear of discovery.

Thornley's brother sits across from me now, and I dare not take my eyes off him, for he has drunk of the blood of the undead, of this I am certain. He told me so in his very own words. He bears the mark from where they, too, drank from him in some twisted exchange I have yet to understand.

The story they shared is extraordinary, to say the least, and while most persons would not believe a word of such a tale, I have seen and heard enough in my lifetime to know the only thing we know for certain is that there is much more we do not know for certain.

With the blood of the undead flowing through his veins, I am curious to see what will become of him when the morning light breaks. Does he even understand what he has become? What he may become if this perversion is allowed to continue? I think not. It is clear he was meant to die as a child, yet his alliance with this unholy creature has garnered him more years; a deal with the Devil, possibly worse, if such a thing is imaginable. The good person he once was has been driven from him, and with that innocence all comprehension of right and wrong. It is for his sister I fear the most; she is but an innocent in all of this, yet somehow she leads the way. Her desire for information blinds her, and it is a lack of self-preservation that will be the death of her if I am unable to protect her. When the time comes to rid her brother of this evil and save his immortal soul, will she stand by my side or in my way? I would like to believe clear thinking will prevail, but such is rarely true when love or family is involved.

I wish I had had the foresight to bring a more formidable weapon. All I have on my person is the sword hidden within my cane, and while the blade is plated in silver, I know it will not bring an end to creatures such as this; it will only buy time.

THE DIARY of THORNLEY STOKER

(RECORDED IN SHORTHAND AND TRANSCRIBED HEREWITH.)

14 August 1868, 12:21 a.m. — My coach dropped me at my front door before proceeding to the stables. I considered going with the others back to Artane Tower. Foolish, I know, but I did not wish to go back inside my own house for fear of what I might find there. I had no reason to believe anything was amiss, nothing but this lingering anxiety dwelling beneath my flesh. I told myself repeatedly there was no truth to this apprehension, yet there it was, clawing to get out.

As we neared my home, I found myself scanning the bushes and trees for signs of the dog from the night before. There were none, of course, and I began to wonder if I had seen this creature at all. With all the happenings of late, my mind screamed. That, combined with the lack of sleep, could no doubt create any number of imaginings. Many of my own patients presented worse under far less stressful circumstance.

I stood at the front door and watched the coach disappear into the stables. I stood at the front door and listened to the sounds of night. I stood at the front door for another minute before finally finding the courage to twist the knob and step inside.

The house was silent. The servants had long ago left for home.

"Emily?"

I do not know why I spoke her name, only that I did, and I thought myself silly for doing so. I found no sign of her in any of the downstairs rooms. I checked each, moving slowly through the house, space by space. Strange how different a place seemed in the dark of night—the utter lack of life made the walls seem a little closer together, every sound amplified.

I did not find her on the ground floor, so I ascended the staircase and went into the master bedroom. I found this room empty, too. The bed-clothes were all rumpled and bunched up at the foot of the bed, as if recently discarded. A full pitcher of water sat on the bedside table, along with an empty glass. I picked up the glass and held it up to the moonlight—bone dry, unused. The servants had prepared a bowl of stew for Emily; it sat upon a tray beside the water glass, long since grown cold, untouched.

The window stood wide open, and a breeze drifting into the room was sending the curtains a-flutter. It also wrapped around me in an embrace that caused me to jitter. When it left, I felt alone. How easily a breeze can capture you in its grip, then abandon you, I thought.

"Where are you, my Emily?"

Even to my own ears, my voice sounded thin and distant. Not the authoritative voice I wished to employ but a much lighter one, the voice of a child calling for his mother after a bad dream.

I left the bedroom and proceeded to check the remainder of the second floor. With each room, my heart grew heavier. If Emily was not in this house, where might she have gone? I must speak to Miss Dugdale and the others, I told myself; Emily was not to be left alone, not anymore, not until a cure for her affliction could be found. They would work in shifts if I was to be away from home for even the shortest while.

The thump from downstairs startled me, and I walked back out to the hallway, to the landing at the top of the stairs. There I listened, but the sound did not repeat a second time. But the first thump had come from downstairs, of that I was certain.

Returning to my bedroom, I retrieved my Webley revolver from the night table and checked the cylinder. I do not know why I felt the need for having a weapon in my own home, but I found comfort in its heft.

I descended the stairs.

When finally there was another thump, not as loud as before, I determined it came from the cellar off the kitchen. I found its door standing open, squeaking on tired hinges. When the residence was outfitted with gas lamps, we had limited the work to only the top two floors. There was little need for such extravagance at the lower level. I reached for the candle we kept at the top of the stairs and lit its wick on the lamp in the kitchen, then returned to the open mouth of the cellar door.

Again, I called my wife's name. My words echoed off the stone walls and were swallowed by the musty air below.

Why she would go downstairs, I did not know. Nor did I understand why she would go down there in total darkness. If she had brought a light, I would see the glow from where I stood, but there was none. There was nothing beyond the glow of my candle.

For some reason, I thought of the dog again. The beast from the night before that I wanted to believe had not been outside my home, although I knew it had. I pictured the dog down below, waiting at the foot of the stairs. This was silly, and no doubt my mind's way of offering caution, but the image lingered nonetheless.

I descended the stairs into the cellar, one hand holding the candle while the other batted away the cobwebs that clung to the walls and ceiling. When the flame of the candle caught one of the webs on fire, a quick sizzle was followed by the scent of burnt hair mixing with the coal, wintered-over potatoes, and other unrecognizable odors emanating from this dark, dank place.

"Emily, my dear, are you down here?"

At this, I heard a shuffle off to my left.

I turned, the glow of my candle washing over the walls, the low ceiling, the dirt floor. When the light found my wife, I nearly did not see her. My eyes washed right over her, for she was crouching down, her thin frame rigid and unwavering as a statue. She was huddled in the corner, with her back to me. Her feet were bare, her body draped in a thin, white nightgown.

"What are you doing?" I heard myself ask.

At the sound of my voice, her body twitched, then went still again.

Again, I imagined the dog, saw the black, muscled beast huddled in the corner in my wife's stead. I shook the image from my mind's eye and crossed the room to her.

A growl. I found it disturbing that such a warning would come from my lovely Emily, but I was certain it had. A feral sound.

When I placed my hand upon her shoulder, her head snapped back in a motion so quick it was as if she had not moved at all. I saw the red around her lips, on her cheeks and chin. In her hand, she held the remains of a mouse. The head was ripped off, yet the tiny body still twitched in her fingers, blood dripping from the ravaged remains. Piled at her feet, against the wall, were at least six other little corpses, one with nothing left but a tail and a bit of meat. I watched as her tongue lapped at the bloody carcass, then licked her crimson lips, before she swallowed it whole, finishing off the nest.

NOW

The hiss comes from the right, from the corner of the room.

Bram pulls his bowie knife from the sheath attached to his belt.

The man is still staring up at him from his perch on the rock below, his hand still outstretched. He says nothing, but the look stamped on his face tells Bram enough. The man closes his eyes and straightens his finger, and the hiss punctuates the silence again.

Bram tightens his grip on the knife's handle and picks up the oil lamp, cautiously inching towards the corner. He does not see the snake until he is nearly upon it. It raises its menacing head and lunges at him in a lightning-swift arc. Bram stumbles backwards and almost falls.

The snake hisses again.

Bram holds up the lamp.

At least two feet long and coiled, the snake at first appears black, but Bram realizes it is actually a dark brown. A zigzag pattern crosses over the slender body with an inverted *V* at the base of the neck, the eyes black as coal. In those dark pools, Bram's own face stares back at him. The snake's head moves back and forth like a pendulum, ready to strike.

Bram knows little of snakes, as Ireland is free of them, but he recognizes this one as an adder from books he has seen.

Adders are venomous, he is aware, but he is not sure if they are deadly.

Another hiss, this one from behind.

Bram turns to find a smooth snake on the floor in the middle of the room. Smooth snakes do not carry poison, he knows, and with one swift motion he severs its head.

Bram removes his coat and wraps it around his left arm, lunging at the adder. The snake jumps out and sinks its fangs into the makeshift shield, and Bram brings down the knife on the back of its neck, killing it instantly. He scoops up both snakes and throws them from the window, watching the pieces land at the feet of the man below.

THE JOURNAL *of* BRAM STOKER

———◆———

14 August 1868, 12:58 a.m.——As the coach drove through Clontarf and on to Artane Parish, I had to wake Matilda. She had dozed off shortly after leaving the Hellfire Club. I could not blame her; neither of us had rested fully in days, and we only made stabs at it when not plagued with wild thoughts. She looked so peaceful in the moments before I woke her that I almost regretted doing it.

Vambéry said little. When he finished with his notes, he turned to the window and watched the city roll away outside and make way for the countryside. I had forgotten how quiet it was out here, even more peaceful than Clontarf and the coast.

The way to Artane Castle was well known, and the driver made good time with four horses traveling at a daring pace. When we came to a stop, the horses snorted and blew the night air. The leaders lunged forward; the wheelers held them steady, yet the carriage rocked. All four horses had seemed to enjoy what was surely a tiring gallop in contrast to their confined work in the city.

The coach door opened, and the three of us stepped out.

Artane Castle was gone.

I stared at the place where the ruin had once stood and tried to summon words to describe what I felt, but nothing came. The tower was gone; only a bit of the original church remained, surrounded by a small number of tombstones standing cracked and tilted.

In place of the castle stood a formidable structure still under construction. The building appeared to have four floors at the center, while the wings on either side had three. A fence encircled the entire site. A sign affixed to the gated entrance read:

FUTURE SITE OF THE ARTANE INDUSTRIAL
SCHOOL FOR ROMAN CATHOLIC BOYS

"It's gone," I heard Matilda say at my side. "Did you know of pending construction here?"

"No," I said. "With work and my reviews, there has been little time for much else."

Vambéry drew closer and pecked at the dirt with the tip of his cane. "I spent time in a place like this. I was injured as a toddler, and my leg was paralyzed. My father died when I was six. Soon after, my mother remarried and turned her attention to my stepfather and the children she bore for him. My mother relinquished me—I was orphaned, for all intents and purposes. There were hundreds of boys, many of whom were criminals by the age of ten. And me—a cripple with a cane—you can imagine my life was hell. Thankfully, I was quite clever and a good student, and was chosen to be a tutor for other boys. Still, I loathe my memories of that place. I knew I would be better off in the streets than incarcerated in that cesspool of abuse. I escaped at age twelve and never looked back."

I faced the remains of the church, the only remnant of the original structure. "The tower where we found the box stood right there."

"You said yourself everything you found had been removed the very next day. Had the castle still stood today, perhaps we would have found nothing of value inside," Vambéry said.

I turned to him, puzzled. "Then why are we here?"

He turned towards the forest on our left and pointed at the trees with his cane. "You must take me to the bog you found as children. The castle may be gone, but the woods remain untouched."

At the mere mention of this, my thoughts went to the image of the hand reaching out from the water and snatching a dragonfly mid-flight. I saw Nanna Ellen walk from the shore into the murky water and disappear beneath. I saw all these things I had refused to see for so many years.

"Do you recall where it was?"

When last I stood here, I had been drawn to Nanna Ellen, pulled along behind her with Matilda following behind me. I had sensed her nearby. On this night, there was no tug at my mind, no invisible cord tethering me to her. No trail to follow.

Regardless, I started towards the woods. I knew the location as well as my own hand. "This way."

Matilda gave me a knowing glance. When we had made this journey as children, I could see in the dark as if it were daylight. I think she wondered if the same held true now. The look I gave her told all, yet I dared not speak of it aloud; I could only imagine what Vambéry thought of me as it was.

Although years had passed, I recalled each footfall, each twist through the brush. The ash trees had grown taller and wider, yet each one was familiar. I recognized the swirl of their bark, the roots protruding from the moist ground. Night creatures studied us from the brush, and I wondered if these were the same animals I spotted all those years ago, or their descendants now plodding away on the same grounds as their ancestors. Vambéry and Matilda swatted at mosquitoes and other irritating insects, none of which bothered me, not a single one.

When the bog came into view, I saw the gloomy waters through the eyes of my seven-year-old self. This time Nanna Ellen was not standing upon the shore. This time we were alone.

"Is this it?" Vambéry asked.

I nodded.

"You are certain?"

"Yes."

He walked to the water's edge and poked at the moss upon the surface with his finger. The oily black water beneath revealed itself for a moment.

"Where did you see the hand?"

"Over there, to the right of that large root."

Vambéry followed my gaze, then circled around to the side of the bog, getting as close to the edge as possible. He dipped his cane into the water up to the handle without striking bottom. "It is very deep."

"When Ellen walked in, she disappeared beneath the surface only a few feet from shore."

Vambéry acknowledged this fact with a slight nod, then plucked a long, dead branch from the tree next to him. Like with the cane, he submerged it until his fingers brushed the water. "Still no bottom. This branch is my height; that gauges the depth at greater than six feet."

I pictured the hand reaching out from the depths and pulling the branch into the waters, then coming up again and taking Vambéry down, too. It would be over in an instant, nothing but a slight ripple on the surface of the water, then stillness. I shook off the morbid thought.

Vambéry released the branch and it disappeared under the water. "Can you feel her, Bram?"

"What?"

"You said as a child you could feel her. Is she near us now? Is she in these waters somewhere?"

"If she is nearby, I cannot tell."

"It is possible she can block the bond binding you to her. I have witnessed such things before, particularly with the more experienced. A wall, of sorts, severing the tie."

A single dragonfly buzzed past Matilda and she let out a startled gasp. My eyes immediately jumped to the other side of the bog, but I saw no other dragonflies, not like the last time.

Vambéry saw, too, and followed my gaze. "Some of them have the ability to command nature. Not only small animals and insects, but larger mammals as well. I have heard of them even controlling the weather."

"How is that possible?" Matilda asked.

"I am not going to pretend to understand; I can only tell you what I know. They enlist the weaker minds and deploy them for protection. How they influence the weather is anyone's conjecture."

Then a thought flooded my mind. "What was she protecting? The person I saw in the water?"

"You did not see a person; you saw a hand, correct?"

"Yes, but—"

"You saw a hand snatch a dragonfly from the air and disappear beneath the surface," Vambéry said.

"A hand cannot act alone."

Vambéry dismissed this with a wave. "In our world, perhaps that holds true. Tell me, Bram, was the hand you saw the same hand you saw in the box in the tower? Think hard on this; it is crucial. Was it a right hand emerging from the watery abyss or a left? And what of the appendage discovered in the tower? Right or left?"

"The hand in the tower was left," Matilda said.

"Good," Vambéry replied. "And the other?"

I squeezed my eyes shut and strained to remember. I pictured the fingers breaking the surface of the water, the green peat sliming away as the hand came into view and snatched—

"Right," I said. "It was a right hand."

"I see," Vambéry said, turning back to the water. "Would you be willing to indulge in a little experiment?"

"If it will help."

"I want you to stick your own hand into the water."

I thought about the creatures living in that water—eels, frogs, toads, newts—the surface clogged with sodden peat, immune to the moonlight's attempts to penetrate the surface and illuminate what lurked beneath. The bog was deep, deeper than we could measure with a cane or a tree branch. I thought about the hand reaching up, grasping at the dragonfly, and pulling it below. Would that be my fate if I touched the water?

"You only need to touch the surface."

"Why? What will that prove?"

Vambéry walked over to me, carefully planting his feet on the firmer ground and avoiding the puddles of moss. "This link you have with Ellen Crone, have you ever tried to control it? Or to strengthen it?"

"No, I—"

"Water is a conductor of electricity, much like our very own brains. I believe water not only captures and transmits that energy but can also store it. I believe this bog may harbor many memories."

At first thought, this seemed ludicrous, and I almost told him so, but I could tell by the look in his eyes he believed it to be true.

"What harm can come of trying?"

I took a deep breath, prepared to argue, then thought better of it. I unbuttoned my sleeve and rolled it to my elbow, then knelt at the water's edge. "Dip it in anywhere?"

"It should not matter."

I took a deep breath and slipped my hand into the icy water. I was not prepared for what happened next.

A surge shot through me; I can think of no other way to describe it. It began at my fingertips and quickly raced through every inch of my body, causing my muscles to go taut. Blinding white light obscured my vision, then went to black, as my sister and Vambéry disappeared from sight, replaced by a murky oil, a viscous filth that swirled all around me.

Then I felt her—and with a connection far stronger than what I remembered. This was no cord binding us together; it was a chain. For this moment, she wasn't a separate person, but an extension of me, and I of her, and together we shared not two minds but one. My thoughts were hers, and hers were mine.

Then I saw the bog.

I saw Ellen crouching on the shore of the bog, a large wooden trunk at her side. It was night, as it is now, but not this night. Then she was in the water, I was in the water. Not on the surface but standing on the bog's mucky bottom. Creatures of all sorts slithered past, maneuvering through the water in search of a meal. They paid little mind to me, this person standing in their world. Ellen raised her hands, stretching out her arms and fingertips until they could extend no more. Then I heard her speak, a voice emanating from nowhere and yet from all around me. "Come to me, my love."

The words echoed through the water, reverberating off the shore and coming back to me. They held a strength unlike any other, and I realized they were not words but a command, a call. The bog floor vibrated at my feet and I felt her eyes, my eyes, look to the muddy earth and watch as something pushed through before us. The dirt and peat washed away, and I realized it was a leg, a full human leg. It drifted from the bog floor to the surface, rising inches from my face. To our left rose an arm, then another leg, a torso, a head—hair swirling all around, all of them floating past. Then I stood at the bog's edge again, we stood at the bog's edge, and I watched as Ellen reached for each of these limbs, these fragmented body parts, and took them gently from the water, placing them within the large wooden trunk.

When the link severed, when the bond between Ellen's and my memories broke, I found myself lying at the edge of the bog, my head cradled in Matilda's lap, with Vambéry kneeling at my side.

"You must tell us what you saw," he said in a hushed voice.

. . .

14 AUGUST 1868, 1:42 a.m.—We rode quietly in the coach back to Thornley's house. The episode at the bog—and I thought of no other way to describe what had occurred—had drained me. I felt as if I could sleep for days.

I told Vambéry and Matilda what I saw, Ellen somehow standing at the bottom of the bog, summoning body parts that then floated to the surface, where she loaded them into a trunk. In my dream state, this scenario had seemed perfectly logical, but now, granted the leisure to reflect, it seemed more the product of a fevered dream, becoming less real with each passing second.

Matilda sat beside me, my hand in hers as she attempted to comfort me. My transgressions of earlier finally forgotten with the frightful moment. Until moments ago, I shook furiously, but that had finally calmed. Across from us, Vambéry wrote all in his notes. He asked me to describe the trunk, and I did as best I could.

"It was a dark-stained wood with a flat top and silver hinges and locks."

"Silver? Are you sure of this?"

"They were silver in color, but I cannot be certain as to the actual metal."

"What about the dimensions? How long and how wide?"

I thought about this question for a minute, my mind picturing Ellen placing a leg inside the trunk, with plenty of room to spare. "At least four feet long and about two feet tall. Probably two feet wide as well."

"Any identifying marks or labels?"

"Not that I noticed."

"But there may have been some?"

"Possibly."

Through all of this, Matilda remained silent. She appeared to be writing in her own diary, but when she held up her sketchbook, I realized she had been drawing instead. "Did it look anything like this?"

She had drawn the trunk in painstaking detail, and when I saw the image, I recognized it immediately. "Exactly like that."

Vambéry reached for Matilda's sketchbook. "May I?"

I leaned forward and studied the drawing. "There was an intricate pattern stenciling the trunk, something carved into the wood, the same image repeated over and over again. But only on the outside; its interior was plain, lined with felt or maybe velvet."

Vambéry made note of this, then returned his gaze to me. "This is important, Bram, so I wish for you to close your eyes and think hard. Think of the interior of the trunk first, since that is your strongest memory; picture it in your mind, every last detail."

I did as he said and forced my mind to focus on that horrible image: Ellen placing body part after body part within the trunk.

Vambéry went on. "When you see the interior clearly in your mind, I wish for you to turn your attention to the outside of the trunk. The mind is a wonderful instrument, capable of so much more than we understand. You do not have to take in these images as a passive observer; if you concentrate, you can pause them. You can step closer to that trunk, so close that you can touch the wood with your hands and feel the patterns with your fingertips."

Vambéry's voice grew melodic, soothing. He spoke to me in a deliberately flat cadence; he would later explain he had subjected me to hypnosis, a phenomenon Professor Dowden had introduced to me at Trinity. When I heard his voice again, he sounded distant. I saw the trunk again, but this time Ellen was frozen, her hands about to place the torso inside, a male torso. She held it there so effortlessly, even though it probably weighed eighty to ninety pounds. I took a step closer to the trunk, then another, until I stood in front. I noticed the weight of its contents caused the trunk to sink slightly in the soft earth, and I couldn't help but wonder how Ellen would move it from this place. She looked radiant in the moonlight, her face frozen in this memory, framed by her long hair, still wet from the bog. Her eyes were blue on this night, a deep blue, reminding me of the ocean at the moment the sun dipped beneath the horizon and night took hold. This was the Ellen I recalled from childhood, unchanged and vibrant. Concern filled her face, though, an urgency as she went about this business.

"The trunk, Bram, focus on the trunk," Matilda said, and I suddenly felt her beside me, the warmth of her hand again in mine.

I turned back to the image of the trunk and leaned in hard.

I imagined my fingers slipping over its surface, the engraving feeling as real as if I were kneeling right beside it. The pattern rendered was small and intricate, and I couldn't decipher it. A series of grooves, really, each no more than half an inch long, one after the other. The entire outside was covered, not a single inch going untouched. "Crosses," I whispered. "Thousands of tiny crosses."

My eyes snapped open, Matilda still beside me.

The coach came to a stop just then as we arrived at Thornley's home.

14 AUGUST 1868, 2:18 a.m.—Thornley had the door open and had rushed us inside before our feet touched the cobblestones of Harcourt Street.

"Hurry," he said. He held a revolver and carefully scanned the trees and bushes surrounding his property. "It's still out here; I'm not sure where it went."

"What is still out here?"

"Just get in the house, all of you," he ordered, locking the door behind us.

Thornley went to the window next to the door, peered out for a moment, then crossed the hall to a window in the library and pulled back the curtain. His eyes were fixed on the blackness outside.

"What are you looking for?" I prodded, stepping to the window.

"I thought it was a dog, but I think it might be a wolf. All black. I saw it the other night when I returned from the hospital, and it was out there again less than an hour ago—standing on my walkway, staring at the front door. My God, Bram, it was big. The biggest wolf I have ever seen. And do not tell me there are no wolves in Ireland. I know exactly what I saw and it was a wolf."

"Your first instinct, that it was a dog, is probably correct; most likely, it was only a dog."

"Nonsense. It was a wolf, I tell you."

I could smell brandy on my brother's breath, but I do not think he was drunk.

"Thornley, where is Emily?" Matilda asked. She was standing at the foot of the staircase, examining the fingers of her right hand. Holding them up to the light, she saw they were red. "There is blood on the banister."

I turned back to my brother. "Thornley, may I have the gun, please?"

Thornley glanced down at the weapon in his hand. Then his eyes jumped from me to our sister. "What is it you think I've done?"

Through all of this exchange, Vambéry remained mute, but I spied him moving slowly around to Thornley's side, his hand tightening on the knob of his cane.

"Give me the gun, Thornley." I said this as a command, holding out my hand to him.

Thornley placed the revolver in my hand. I quickly removed the bullets and dropped them in my left pocket, then secured the revolver in my right.

Matilda raced up the stairs.

"Wait!" Thornley shouted, before running after her.

I heard Matilda scream as I bounded up the steps behind my brother, Vambéry following.

Matilda was standing at the foot of my brother's bed. Emily was lying atop its sheets, her arms and legs securely tied to the four bedposts, a gag in her mouth. Her chin and neck were covered with dried blood, as were her hands, her arms, and her clothing as well. She stared up at us just then and screamed, her voice muffled by the gag.

"What have you done?" Matilda shouted at Thornley, reaching for the rope securing Emily's left wrist.

Thornley pushed past me and shoved Matilda aside. "You mustn't untie her!"

"Is she hurt?" I asked, taking in all the bloody evidence. I didn't detect any sign of a wound, however.

"It's not her blood you're seeing," Thornley said, standing between Emily and the rest of us.

"Whose blood is it, then?" Vambéry demanded.

"She's not well. She hasn't been well for some time now. She doesn't understand what she's done. I doubt she even remembers what she's done."

Vambéry took a step closer and leaned in towards Emily's face. "What, exactly, did she do?"

Emily twisted and strained in the bed, testing the strength of her bindings. The bed frame creaked as she tried to sit up. The bindings held, though, for now at least. Her face flushed with anger at this, and she tried again.

Thornley pulled a syringe from his medical bag on the nightstand and plunged it into Emily's shoulder. She turned to him and again tried to sit up, tugging at the ropes with enormous strength, but her efforts quickly ebbed as the drug took effect. She fell back into the mattress and drifted off to sleep.

"Laudanum," Thornley said. "It seems to be the only thing that works. Although I'm finding it less and less effective. I had been putting it in her wine; now only injections have any effect. The dose I gave her would normally keep a man my size out for six to eight hours; she'll be awake again in less than one."

Vambéry carefully pulled back Emily's gag so he could inspect her teeth.

"What are you doing?" Thornley said.

"How long has this been going on?" Vambéry said, peeling back her lips from the gums and leaning in yet closer. Her breath reeked of rot, even from where I stood.

My brother turned away from us in an attempt to conceal the tears in his eyes. "Weeks now, but tonight is worst of all. She has never done . . . this." He spread his hands, gesturing at the bloody gore.

Thornley told us how he had found her in the basement. He told us of the mice. I nearly became ill at the thought. Matilda, too, had turned a pale white. Only Vambéry seemed to be unfazed. He studied the mark on Emily's neck. "What about this? When did you first notice this mark?"

"A few days ago," Thornley replied.

Vambéry pulled a chain from around his neck, a cross dangling from the end. "This crucifix is of the finest silver. It was given to me by a priest at a monastery I visited about four years ago in a small town called Oradea on the border between Hungary and Romania."

He removed the chain and held the cross by its base. With a careful motion, he pressed the silver talisman against the back of Emily's right hand. Her body jerked on contact with it, and smoke rose from the place the cross touched. I smelled burning flesh and watched in horror as her skin became red and blistered.

"Stop!" Thornley cried out, batting Vambéry's hand aside. "You are hurting her!"

Matilda and I stood by in stunned silence.

"Has she been near this Ellen Crone?" Vambéry asked, looping the chain, the crucifix reattached, back around his neck. "Perhaps Ellen has afflicted your wife as some kind of warning, meaning to frighten us away, to keep us from investigating further. Has she ever been in contact with Ellen Crone before?"

"Not that I am aware of," Thornley told him. He reached for his wife's hand and held it tenderly in his own, his fingers caressing the wound. "Can you help her?"

Vambéry let out a deep breath. He glanced at me and quickly averted his eyes, something not lost on me. "These undead, they spread their illness by bite. Once bitten, once this disease enters the blood, there is little that can be done. Much depends on the number of times she has been bitten, just how much she has been exposed. We must allow her rest and fluids, as much as she is willing to drink, red wine most of all to replenish her healthy blood. We must give her body what she needs to force this infection out. There is also a need to ensure she is not bitten again. These creatures tend to return to the same victim; this helps to prevent their discovery. The one who has bitten her will return, and we must keep this creature from getting back to her at all costs."

"You've encountered these beasts before, haven't you?" Matilda said. "You speak of them as if from firsthand knowledge, yet you tell us so very little."

Vambéry appeared taken aback by this remark. I imagine he had never encountered a lady as forthright at my sister, and in truth, he may never do so again. For this, I was, as ever, grateful; she asked the questions that were on all of our minds.

I watched as Vambéry settled into a chair beside Emily's bed, his eyes warily watching my brother's wife as she slept. "There is little to tell, I'm afraid. Nothing of which has ever been proven by scientific measure, only what I pieced together over many years from legends and superstitions. The story we read from Ellen's book, her tale of the Dearg-Due, I can tell you it is not unique. I found similar stories in cultures throughout the world. These stories of creatures born of the Devil who sustain themselves on the lifeblood of others. As a younger man, I was skeptical of such things, but as I heard of them over and over again from all corners of the world, I began to believe. Isn't it logical to assume that even the wildest of fables found life in a buried truth? The evidence cannot be dismissed; you witnessed this yourself. They possess the power of necromancy; to manipulate the dead, they are, in fact, the dead themselves. Somehow cursed to walk the earth, unable to find true death. With this curse comes an unimaginable power, the strength of twenty men, a cunning far beyond most, the result of an existence spanning centuries. Much like bees, I learned there is a hierarchy. There are worker drones in a state much like young Emily here—those who only follow commands. And there are those who issue the commands— the ones who use the drones to do their dirtiest work. These are the ones we should fear most, these are the ones like your precious Nanna Ellen, the Dearg-Due, if her tale is to be thought of as fact.

"It is believed that the strongest of them can assume any form, be it bat, wolf, swirling mist, even human. They can appear young, old, or any age between. Some can manipulate the elements, producing fog, storms, crashing thunder. Their motives remain unknown, but one thing is clear: They leave a trail of death in their wake, thinking no more of a human life than we would the life of a fly."

I looked down at Emily in her bed, now sleeping soundly, at the punctures on her neck. I could not help but think of the marks on my wrist, which I dared not look at, not now anyway. "What are their weaknesses?" I asked, moving the discussion forward. "How do we put an end to them?"

Vambéry nodded at these questions. "As with the stories of their strengths, there are likewise stories of their vulnerabilities."

I watched as he stood and retrieved the looking glass from Emily's dressing table and brought it over to the bed, holding the mirror at an angle to her face. "Look closely. What do you see?"

Matilda, Thornley, and I all leaned in to look.

My sister gasped. "I see her reflection, but it is not complete! I can see through her, as if she were transparent!"

I saw, too, that she was transparent, and clearly Thornley saw it, because he drew back in horror and fell into the chair previously occupied by Vambéry.

Vambéry set the mirror down on the night table. "She has not completely turned, mind you; that is why we still can see her at all. The true undead cast no reflection; they cast no shadow, either."

"Then why would Ellen own a looking glass?" Matilda asked.

Vambéry shrugged. "Perhaps out of nostalgia, a reminder of the life she once had. But there is no way of knowing for certain."

"What else?" I asked.

"They cannot cross moving water under their own power, and, as with Ellen's story, they cannot enter the house of the living unless invited. Their powers are limited to the desolate hours of night. While they can walk about in broad daylight, they attempt to avoid the sun at all costs. It is during these bright hours that they are at their most vulnerable. And they can find rest only by lying in the soil of their native land. Because they are born of something unholy, sacred objects, such as crucifixes, communion wafers, and baptismal waters, are poison to them. They are repelled by garlic as well, although I have no knowledge as to why this is so. The same holds true for the wild rose—if a blossom is placed upon the tomb while the craven creature reposes, it will not be able to rise until that rose has expired utterly."

"Can they be killed?" my brother asked, his voice low, as he stared at the inert form of his wife.

Vambéry nodded. "They can be destroyed only by driving a wooden stake through the heart. Then the body must be decapitated and burned to ash, and then those ashes scattered to the four winds. Nothing short of this grisly solution will be effective."

Thornley lowered his head to his hands. "Why would Ellen do this?"

Vambéry shot me a sideways glance, then quickly turned away. "She is somehow attached to your family, but her reasons are known only to her. She must be tracked down and stopped. I fear that with another bite, your wife's heart will stop and she will turn into a vampire. Ellen will surely return to finish transitioning her and welcome her into the fold of the undead; we will stop her then."

"We need to get to Ellen first, in other words," I said under my breath. "Find her while she rests, while she is most vulnerable. Waiting for her to return here, when she is at her strongest, is foolhardy."

"I agree," said Thornley. "We need to take the offensive. I will not wait for her to cut us down one by one. We must find her resting place."

Vambéry considered this for a moment. "I know a man who may be able to locate her from the items we acquired from the grave, her possessions you recovered. I can bring him here."

For the first time in nearly a week, my brother allowed a smile. "I can give you something far better than some old trinkets." He reached into his pocket and pulled out the small lock of Nanna Ellen's hair and held it up to the light.

FROM THE NOTES
of ARMINIUS VAMBÉRY

(RECORDED IN CIPHER AND TRANSCRIBED HEREWITH.)

———————◆———————

14 August 1868, 4:08 a.m. —I dared not put pen to paper until certain it was safe to do so.

I must not let my excitement rule my words; it is important I document everything in a clear and concise manner. Nothing can be left out. All must be duly recorded.

This night continues to yield revelations and generate distress at a pace that has left me utterly exhausted. I must not sleep, though, not here, not in this house. Not while a creature of the night sleeps in the bed before me and another wanders these haunted halls, a guest welcomed by his own brother.

I instructed the others to rest while also insisting I remain in the room with Emily and Thornley for the duration of the night. Thornley is now sound asleep in a chair to the right-hand side of the bed while I occupy another chair beneath the window in the far corner. I inspected Emily's bindings myself and am satisfied they are sufficient in nature, at least for the night. The sickness is spreading within her, and with it a great strength is being realized. These thin ropes may be enough for tonight, but tomorrow I will insist on replacing them with leather straps, possibly silver chains. That is, of course, if she is permitted to live another twenty-four hours. Allowing her to turn would be an injustice to her mortal soul, one I am not certain I am willing to risk. Already, I see signs of the laudanum wearing off. She has been stirring and mumbling a bit in her sleep, both of which increased notably in frequency over the past hour. For now, though, she rests.

The others are silent now, too, and while I would hope they found sleep, I will not presume such to be the case. Bram, in particular, puzzles me greatly, and under no circumstance will I lower my guard in his presence. Earlier, when I had the mirror in hand to demonstrate Emily's decreased reflection therein, I took the opportunity to gauge Bram's capacity to cast a reflection as well. Although I had but only a second to conduct my experiment, I am certain his reflection was evident. I find this particularly perplexing, given what he and the others told me. If he has, in fact, been bitten by the undead, by this ghoul Ellen Crone, as often as he claimed, he should have turned many years ago. And to think, he has drunk of her blood, too! Earlier, he handled Crone's looking glass and brush without any sign of distress, even though both are forged of silver. I can only assume he has found some way to counteract the tests known to and utilized by me. The Devil is very crafty in his ways. Perhaps this is some kind of natural evolution, that he has developed an immunity to the weaknesses usually plaguing the undead. If such is the case, I am increasingly horrified, for at some point this immunity may become unstoppable. I plan to test this premise further, when given the chance. I am curious to see what will happen if Bram ingests holy water. I shall slip it to him without any advance warning to determine if these immunities are unconscious or if they require him to arm himself in advance.

I feel I am deceiving my friend Thornley Stoker, but these are things I must do. His judgment is compromised in all matters regarding his wife and his brother. The disease they carry cannot be allowed to spread, and if I must feign friendship with the afflicted in order to ascertain the weaknesses inherent in this disease—and then to destroy it and those infected by it—so be it.

I have no doubt this Ellen Crone is the key.

My driver has been sent to fetch Oliver Stewart. I have known Stewart for a number of years and I trust in him fully. As a practitioner of the dark arts, he has helped me in the past locate objects as well as people, and his discretion will prevent him from asking questions. I eagerly await his arrival.

There is—

THE DIARY *of* THORNLEY STOKER

———◆———

14 August 1868, 4:10 a.m. — I awoke to my sister screaming. It startled me, and I nearly fell from the chair alongside my wife's
bed as Vambéry raced past with his cane in hand, rushing down the hall
towards my guest room. Bram and I nearly collided as he bounded up
the stairs. We poured through Matilda's open door to find her standing
beside the window, her finger pointing towards the glass.

"He's outside!"

"Who is outside?" Bram asked.

Vambéry went to the window and peered into the inky night.

Matilda covered her pale face with her hands and shook her head. "It
was dreadful! I awoke to a tapping at the glass. When I went to the window, I saw Patrick O'Cuiv's face pressed against the pane. He smiled at
me and tapped on the glass again with his fingernails. His nails were
long and yellow, hideously so. Oh, and his teeth! He had these . . . they
were not normal. His lips were curled back like those of a snarling dog,
and his teeth were like fangs. He licked at his lips and said my name. He
said it so quietly, as if mouthing it, yet I heard him perfectly, as if he
were right next to me. God, it was horrid!"

"He is still out there," Vambéry said, looking out the window. "And
he is not alone."

Bram and I both went to the window and looked out, and there he was. Patrick O'Cuiv, the man who died not once but twice, the man whose autopsy I witnessed personally. He was now fully intact again and standing in the grass down below. I had no doubt Matilda had seen him at the window, even though we were on the second floor and there was no way for him to reach us from outside. But I also had no doubt that man could reach us as easily as I could reach my brother next to me.

"He cannot get in, not unless invited," Vambéry said. "I am more concerned about them."

I followed his gaze and felt my heart jump at what I saw. Not one but two large wolves, both black as night, stared up at us from the corner yard with ruby-red eyes. One wolf walked over to O'Cuiv and sat at his side, not once taking its eyes off us. "Where did you put my gun?" I asked Bram.

"Bullets will do little good here," Vambéry said. "Only one made of silver would serve any function, and only then if it pierced the heart. Anything less just slows them down, nothing more."

"Then what do we do?"

"Sunrise is an hour away. Until then, we wait behind the safety of these walls," Vambéry said.

Bram went to Matilda and wrapped his arms around her. "Do not look."

Another scream.

This one came from Emily down the hall. Oh, why did we leave her?!? Even for a moment!

Vambéry was out the door immediately, pulling from his cane a long silver sword as he ran. Bram and I raced after him, with Matilda behind us.

We found Emily sitting up on the bed, the ropes that bound her only minutes earlier lying at her side unraveled. Behind her stood the tall man in black I had encountered Tuesday night, his face a deathly pale, his eyes burning red. He held Emily up, with one arm around her; the other holding her head to one side. My eyes jumped to the thin streams of blood oozing from the puncture wounds on her neck, both of which had been newly reopened. The man had blood on his lips, which I could see clearly in the moonlight as the red contrasted with the stark white of his unnaturally long teeth.

He hissed at the sight of us. This was the warning of an animal, not of a man, and the look upon his face reminded me of a feral dog.

"Release her!" Vambéry shouted. He swung his sword through the air, the silver blade catching the light as the tip missed the man's face by mere inches.

With his free hand, Vambéry pulled the chain from around his neck, breaking the clasp and holding the small cross out in front of him. Again, the man hissed, an angry expulsion that catapulted bloody spittle across the bedsheets. With blinding speed, he released Emily from his hold and took a step back. Her unconscious body fell upon the bed in a limp heap.

Vambéry lunged, the tip of his sword targeting the man's chest.

In the instant before the blade made purchase, the man burst apart—there is simply no other way to describe it. He exploded from his center mass outward in a burst of black—thousands of tiny fragments rushing outward in all directions. My arm instinctively covered my eyes as these projectiles pelted my body, bouncing off of me, painfully stinging me.

"Bees!" Bram shouted. "He's transformed himself into bees!"

It was then that I heard the buzzing of drones, the room having gone from quiet to deafening.

As a child, I had been attacked by bees after disturbing their hive, and to this day I still recall the growing noise they made as they left the safety of their hive and pursued me—this faint buzz that grew louder until they were upon me. There was no build of that sound here—there was nothing, then in one instant it was as if I stood in the center of a hive.

I felt a razor-hot sting in my arm and swatted at the angry bee that had landed there. It then tore away, leaving behind its long stinger. Another bee stung my neck, feeling as if someone had plunged a knife into it.

I spotted the others swatting at the masses of yellow and black, Vambéry most vigorously. Somehow, the bees' numbers seemed to be growing, each bee dividing in two, then dividing again. The swarm became so thick I could barely make out the other side of the room. Through pinched eyes, I found the bedroom door and started for it, each step more challenging than the last. Behind me, Vambéry began to shout, a prayer of some sort, his voice fighting to be heard over the cacophony:

"Almighty God, grant us grace that we may cast out the works of darkness and put upon us the armor of light now in the time of this mortal life in which Thy son, Jesus Christ, came to visit us in great humility, that in the last day—"

His voice was abruptly cut off by a shout, this time from Matilda. I think a bee had stung her hand, but I couldn't see for sure. She was favoring her left arm while wildly waving her other.

Vambéry repeated the prayer, this time louder, and the rest of us joined in, our voices growing over the buzz. Almost as quickly as they appeared, the bees mercifully flew through the open window and disappeared into the night. The room fell into silence then, punctuated only by our labored breaths.

I went to Emily's bed.

She was unconscious but breathing steadily. Her closed eyelids were wildly a-flutter, caught in some dream. I pulled her legs out straight and positioned her head back on the pillow, then knelt down beside her, stroking her hair. I was oblivious to the pain of the half a dozen or so stings I had sustained. At this moment, there was only my love, my Emily.

Behind me, the others were carefully plucking stingers from their own skin and one another's.

"How is that possible?" Matilda, the first to speak, finally said. She was visibly shaken but was attempting to conceal her fear.

Vambéry sounded exhausted. "I have heard stories of them trans-forming into mist or becoming various animals, but to become thou-sands of tiny bees and attack as he did, to attack us as one mind while also being many . . . Such a feat would require extraordinary power."

"That was the man who followed me home from the hospital the other night, the one who was asking about Ellen, was trying to find her," I said. Emily's hand felt cold in mine; had she dipped her fingers in a bucket of ice, they would not have been this frigid.

"He is very old. He would have to be in order to wield such a skill," Vambéry replied in awe.

"How did he gain entry to the house?"

"Your wife must have invited him. If not tonight, at some earlier time."

There was a washbasin beside the bed. I reached for the towel next to it, wrung out the excess water, and used it to clean the wound on her neck. The two small punctures were no larger than before, but were clearly red and inflamed. Both were sealed, though, as if they had been healing for hours.

I pulled back her hair and inspected her forehead. "The cut on her cheek is gone. It was there only a few hours ago." I glanced at Bram and Matilda. "You remember? I showed it to you."

"I remember," Bram said, his hand covering the place he had pur-posely cut on his own arm.

Vambéry gently lifted Emily's hand and pushed back her sleeve. "The

place where the cross burned her has healed, too." He frowned worriedly. "We have not much time."

"Can this man be 'uninvited'?" Matilda asked.

Vambéry lowered Emily's hand back to her side. "It no longer matters. Her blood has mingled with his; they are one and the same now.
Her will is not entirely her own."

"After Ellen bit me the first time," Bram said, "I was able to hear her
thoughts, and she could hear mine. We need to be mindful of our words
around your wife, my dear brother. This man may be listening."

"And now?" Vambéry asked. "Do you still share this connection with
Ellen Crone?"

Bram shook his head. "Not like before. As a child, I believed I could
track her across the world, and that she could follow me. I sometimes
knew her thoughts as well as I knew my own. Something has changed
over the years."

"She can block you," Vambéry explained. "The fact that you no longer feel the connection does not mean that she cannot."

"I don't think it works that way. In order for her to see into my mind,
she has to open her mind to me—even if that door is opened for only a
second. I don't believe she can hide the connection from me. I felt her
the other night in Clontarf in the moments before I went to her, I am
sure of that now, as fleeting as that link may have been."

Vambéry pondered this revelation for a moment. "Are you able to
block her as she blocks you?"

"I don't know."

"This is important information. You need to try. If you are somehow
able to control it, we can use this to our advantage. If not, I am afraid
she may use you to divine our intentions. That is something we cannot
have," Vambéry said.

Emily's fingers tightened around mine, and her breathing grew shallow. Rather than taking long, deep breaths of sleep, she resorted to short, quick gasps. Her body tensed, and then her back arched.

"Hold her down!" Vambéry shouted.

I tightened my grip on her hand and placed my other hand on her shoulder. Bram and Vambéry both went for her legs. She knocked the three of us back as if we were some child's toys. Her eyes snapped open, and a hiss escaped her lips as she sat up in the bed so quickly that her movement was but a blur.

Vambéry had the silver crucifix out again and he brandished it in her face. Emily averted her glance and curled up into a ball on the bed. A moment later, she was still again, her breathing normal, as she drifted back to sleep.

"She is trying to fight the infection, but it is a losing battle," he told us. "She will turn soon."

"What can we do?" I squeezed her hand, and though I didn't think it possible, it was colder than before.

"Do you have garlic in the house?"

"Maybe in the kitchen or the cellar."

"Fetch it. A mixing bowl as well."

I ran downstairs and returned with a large bowl and braid of fresh garlic from the kitchen. He took the items from me and set them on the night table. I watched as he placed the garlic in the bowl, then retrieved a small bottle from his leather bag, along with a package wrapped in a green cloth. He held the bottle up to the light. "This is holy water from Saint Michael's." Vambéry made the Sign of the Cross, then uncapped the bottle and poured the contents over the garlic. I watched as he carefully unwrapped the green cloth.

"Are those blessed communion wafers?" Matilda asked.

Vambéry nodded. "The host, yes. Also from Saint Michael's."

These also went into the bowl.

Using the handle of a bowie knife, he crushed the contents until it became a white mash, added some holy water, and stirred it to form a paste. Vambéry carried the bowl over to the window, closed and locked it, then began spreading the paste along all the edges. "This should prevent that man from reentering. For now anyway." He took the remainder of the paste and spread it around the bed with his fingers, encircling Emily. "She should not be able to trespass this barrier, either. It is not permanent, but it will suffice in safeguarding us through the wee hours of the night."

I stared in awe at Vambéry, wondering what other secrets he harbored.

14 AUGUST 1868, 8:15 a.m.—The dawn crept in from the east and reached through my home with eager fingers. I would like to say I had found rest, but that would be a lie; I do not believe any of us did. Bram spent the night on the sofa in the library with Matilda curled up in the armchair at his side. She refused to go back to the guest room and did not want to be alone. Vambéry and I continued to keep our vigil over Emily. No other incidents took place; she slept soundly.

Vambéry's coachman returned shortly after first light with word that a man named Oliver Stewart would arrive after dusk. Matilda tried to argue against this delay, pointing out the entire day would be lost if we waited, but Vambéry told her Stewart's methods would not prove effective during daylight hours; Ellen was most likely at rest then and therefore could not be found.

When at last my brother returned to Emily's side, his eyes were red and his brow creased with the shadow of sleeplessness. I imagine I appeared no better.

Last night, after Vambéry mixed his concoction of garlic and the holy water, he fashioned cruel bindings from four of my leather belts found in my chest of drawers. He employed them to secure my wife's arms and legs to the bedposts in place of the rope I had previously utilized. When I asked if he thought the leather would hold fast, he informed me that yes they would, but his eyes shared a far different answer. Since the last incident, I also noticed his cane was always at his side. Although he returned the sword to the shaft, he had proven how quickly he could brandish the blade, and it was clear he would do so if threatened. What was not clear was whether he expected that threat to come from the window or from my wife, for he seemed leery of both.

While spreading the holy garlic mixture around the bed, Vambéry spilled some on Bram's hand—the same hand wherein Ellen bit him. While I am sure this "accident" was meant as some kind of test, the deliberateness of the act was not lost on any of us. Vambéry's hand tightened around the knob of his cane the moment he did it, and all of us turned to Bram to see what would happen. Bram thought nothing of it; he simply wiped the mess away and gave Vambéry a crooked smile. If Bram was infected, it was clear this disease impacted him to a far different degree than it had my wife.

Shortly after Bram arrived in the room, Emily's eyes fluttered opened, and five words slipped from her lips: "Did the monster go away?"

Upon hearing her voice, I fell upon the bed and wrapped my arms around her. I wished to never let her go. She felt so icy! When my cheek pressed against hers, it was as if I leaned against a windowpane on a wicked winter night. I did not pull away, though; she needed to know she was not alone in this, she needed to know my love. She spoke coherently yet recalled but little of the previous night's events. I had changed her bloody clothes some time earlier, and she made no mention of the mice, nor did we. Vambéry said it was good she spoke only of things that brought her strength and happiness, not those that would remind her of her illness.

Although we all knew she was ill, aside from her lowered temperature, there was little to remind us. In fact, quite the opposite was true. I had never seen her skin so perfect; she bore not a single blemish. Even her hair appeared fuller, with lively curls dancing throughout, and the color seemingly had deepened. If I hadn't known better, I would have thought she was ten years younger than her true age. I attempted to open the draperies, but Emily shrunk away from the light and claimed it hurt her eyes, so I closed them reluctantly. The room was grand in scale, but the walls seemed to move in on us a little more with each passing hour until I could bear it no longer and had to go outside and walk the grounds. The damp earth revealed no tracks—human, wolf, or otherwise.

At one point, Matilda brought my wife a tray of fruits and a pitcher of cold water as well as a cup of tea—chamomile, her favorite. Emily would have none of it. She insisted she had no appetite, but told Matilda to leave the tray beside the bed in case she changed her mind. It was then she also asked for her leather-belt bindings to be removed. Up until that moment, she had scarcely acknowledged them, and when she finally did, she did so in such a nonchalant manner I found it almost amusing. Vambéry pulled Bram and me into the hallway to confer about her request, and we decided it was best to remove the bindings for now, but they would be reinstated at dusk. Emily agreed to this proposition, even though she still had not shown any acknowledgment of the previous night.

We replaced the bindings as the sun began its descent. Emily did not protest. Although she slept most of the day, she grew more alert as night approached, yet she also seemed to retreat. She spoke less and seemed to sink into her own thoughts. I feared another episode was at hand. I could not bear witness to this eventuality, so I went downstairs to join the others.

As planned, the servants were dismissed early. There had been much whispering amongst them. None had been permitted to see Emily today, and while they knew my brother and sister, they eyed Vambéry with unease but did not ask me about him. I was not one to keep secrets from my staff, and recent events had clearly disturbed them.

Vambéry concocted more of his paste and again sealed Emily's windows, insisting that nothing could get in and that it would be safe to leave her to rest alone while we gathered downstairs.

Then Oliver Stewart arrived promptly at seven.

Vambéry let him in and led him directly to the dining room, where the table had been cleared in preparation for his visit. Rather than light the gas lamp, we set flame to candles and to incense all around the chamber so that it was filled with dancing light and an earthy, spicy aroma. Three of the chairs had been removed, leaving only five circling the round table. Stewart took this in and nodded. "This will suffice."

Stewart had not shaken hands upon entering the room. When Bram attempted to do so, Stewart shrunk away and placed his hands behind his back.

Stewart was an unusual-looking man. He was no more than five feet in height, and Vambéry informed me he wore lifts in his shoes to gain another inch, along with a tall bowler hat. His face was squat and full, as if someone had pushed on his skull as a child and forced it to expand sideways rather than lengthwise. If I had to guess at his age, I would place him in his fifties. He wore white leather gloves, which he refused to remove, and thick spectacles that caused his beady eyes to appear far larger than they actually were. His gaze darted about, taking in every inch of the space, while making scant eye contact with the rest of us.

"Mr. Oliver is very sensitive," Vambéry told us. "Simply touching another person can bring on an episode very similar to the one Bram experienced at the bog. It can be quite disturbing and disorienting. Therefore, please respect his wish to not come in contact with anything or anyone unless requested."

"It is nothing personal," Stewart said, his voice sheepish voice, his eyes riveted to the floor.

I remembered seeing this man before at the Hellfire Club on at least one occasion, but we did not speak. He had been in the company of

Vambéry at that time, too, and I recall the two of them rushing through the main hall to the back stairs. Stewart nearly hugged the wall, avoiding all those members standing at the center of the room. His hands had been in his pockets then, his eyes locked on the floor.

"Shall we get started, then?" Vambéry said. He pulled out a chair for Matilda and took the seat next to her.

Stewart's eyes lingered on Bram for a moment, then he, too, sat, taking the seat in the far corner. I took the chair beside Vambéry, and Bram found a seat between Stewart and me. Stewart produced a detailed map of Dublin and the surrounding countryside from his black satchel and unrolled it on the table. He then retrieved a small wooden box from the bag, unsnapped the latch, and carefully opened the lid, revealing the contents. "This is called a scry. I inherited this particular model from my grandmother nearly thirty years ago when she realized I possessed the sight. She received it from her grandmother. To the best of my knowledge, it is about two hundred years old."

"The sight?" Matilda repeated.

Stewart glanced at her for a second, then looked back to the item inside the small wooden box. "As Mr. Vambéry was so kind as to explain, I see things when I touch people or items that have come in contact with people. This may mean a quick flash of memory or possibly something entering their mind at that very moment. Other times, the vision is far stronger, and I am lost to it, unable to focus on my actual surroundings and taken over by the sight. Over the years, I have learned to direct it, to seek out the information I wish to possess, whether that be a secret locked away in one's mind or even lost in the subconscious. I have also learned to use this sight to pinpoint the exact location of a person or object, which I believe is the reason Mr. Vambéry asked me here tonight, is it not?"

"Yes," Matilda said. "You're here to locate our former nanny."

"Ellen Crone," I added.

"Ellen Crone, yes," Stewart repeated.

He reached into the small wooden box and extracted a device made of gold. The top was a cross consisting of two thin braces with a gold chain dangling beneath. Attached to the bottom of the chain was a weight in the shape of a teardrop, also wrought in gold, with its tip colored black. The weight hung about six inches below the cross portion he held in his hand. It reminded me of a marionette. He hovered the scry just above the table and let the weight swing to and fro. "The hair, please," Stewart said.

I was so enthralled by these unfolding events that I failed to realize he was addressing me. All eyes turned to me, and I reached into my pocket and extracted the small lock of Ellen's hair I had carried with me my entire adult life. I held it out to Stewart.

"Please place it on the table."

"Yes, sorry." I set the lock of hair down on top of the open map.

Stewart stared at it for a long while, his head tilting this way and that. Then he inserted his index finger in his mouth and removed the white glove with his teeth, dropping it on the table at his side. When his hand was free, he flexed the fingers and carefully reached for the hair, holding it in a tight fist.

His eyes closed and he exhaled, the air whistling between crooked teeth. His eyes fluttered behind his lids like someone in a dream state. With his left hand, he reached across the map, the scry dangling beneath his fingers. He mumbled some words in a language I did not understand and began to move over Dublin. The tip of the scry pointed down at the various roads and buildings, the chain taut but swaying. For the next ten minutes, he crisscrossed the map, moving from side to side, up and down, until eventually he passed over every square inch. Then he did it again, and again after that. Nearly an hour passed without any result, and all of us were becoming restless.

"Maybe she is no longer in Dublin," Bram said, apparently buying into this sideshow. I was beginning to think this exercise was a complete folly.

Stewart opened his eyes and set the hair and scry down on the table. "I will require additional maps."

At this point, the frustration took hold of me, and I stood from my chair with a huff, went to the library, and returned a minute later with Matilda's sketchbook, opened to the map of Ireland. "See if you cannot find her with one of these; I am going to check on my wife."

"Give it time, Thornley," Vambéry said. "This is not an exact science."

"Science? This is not science at all! This is a parlor trick at best."

"Perhaps I should leave," Stewart said. Probably the only thing he said of worth since his arrival.

"No, you must not," Matilda said. "We must keep trying."

"May I see the hair?" Bram asked.

I shrugged my shoulders. "Why not?"

Bram reached across the table and took the hair in his hand, closing his eyes much like Stewart had. "Where are you, Ellen?" I heard him say.

A storm was kicking up outside, and I went to the window as the rain began to fall. I half expected to find Patrick O'Cuiv and a pack of wolves on my front lawn, but this time there was nothing. Lightning flashed in the distance, followed by a clap of thunder strong enough to jingle the china in the curio cabinet beside me.

I had my back to the table only for a matter of seconds, no more. Of that I am sure. And when I turned back, I spotted Emily through the dining room door, standing midway up the staircase. I first thought I was imagining things, for she stood there perfectly still and completely naked. With one of the leather bindings still dangling from her wrist. When our eyes met, I watched in awe as she leapt from the landing and over the railing, somehow soaring across the foyer and hall to the dining room beyond. She executed this maneuver in utter silence, and it was not until she crossed the threshold of the dining room that the others even saw her.

Vambéry, shocked, pushed back from the table, toppling his chair. Matilda screamed. Stewart's eyes went immensely wide, but he did not move, frozen in fear. Only Bram acted, and he acted with swiftness. He seemed to snatch her midair and slam her down against the table in one fluid motion, pinning her there by the neck, her arms and legs flailing. Her foot caught me, and the power of it sent me crashing into the wall. I felt the plaster crumble and the lath snap upon impact, and a pain shot up my back. I forced myself upright as Vambéry pulled the sword from his cane and prepared to plunge the silver blade into my wife's heart.

"You cannot!" I shouted, diving across the table. I nearly caught the blade in my back, but Vambéry pulled back his thrust, missing me by only a fraction of an inch. Instead, I crashed to the ground at his feet.

"I cannot hold her much longer!" Bram cried out. He still had her pinned, by the shoulders now, but she was bucking beneath him, trying to break free.

Matilda reached over the table and snatched the scry from Stewart and held its cross-like scaffold above Emily's face. My wife instantly froze in horror, her head turning to the side and her eyes pressing shut. "Stop or I will press it to your skin!" Matilda said, but the threat was unnecessary; Emily's body had gone soft. Her senses seemed to return, for her flailing arms covered her exposed breasts and privates, and she pulled her knees in close to her chest as a child might do when seeking protection. The loud hisses that had been escaping from her throat ceased, and her eyes stared up at me pleadingly. "Oh, he is calling me! His voice is so beautiful!"

"Who?" Vambéry asked.

Emily ignored him. "He is searching for the Dearg-Due as well. His precious countess."

Grasping her shoulders, Bram shook her. "Who!"

"The tall man." Emily then smiled. "He wants to dance with me. I must go to him."

Stewart stood from his chair and leaned over her. "Where can we find Ellen Crone?"

Emily eyed him for a brief second, then her hand shot out and grabbed his. Stewart's fingers went white as she squeezed. His face registered the pain, but before he could scream, his head snapped back and his eyes rolled up, exposing the whites, as a vision took hold. Emily froze, too, as if the two of them were in some kind of communication. "I so love to dance," Emily said softly.

Beside me, Bram cried out. I turned to find him in terrible pain. He released Emily and tore at the buttons of his shirt, ripping the material open. His hand fell upon the chain around his neck and he ripped it free, hurling it on the table. It was *the* ring, the one he found with Matilda all those years ago. The metal glowed a fire red, a heat so strong I could feel it from where I stood.

"Whitby!" Stewart cried out, his face twisted in agony.

Emily released his hand and bounded from the table.

In an instant, she crashed through the enormous dining room window and disappeared into the thick of the night's storm.

THE JOURNAL *of* BRAM STOKER

————◆————

14 August 1868, 11:19 p.m. —My brother would have hurtled out the window after his wife if not for Vambéry holding him back. I clutched my burnt hand and chest and stared around the room in utter disbelief at what had just happened.

Matilda stood perfectly still in the corner of the room, her hands over her mouth, her face such the picture of fright that I half expected her hair to have turned white. Her eyes shot from the table to me, to Thornley and Vambéry at the window. Finally, they zeroed in on Stewart; the man was curled up on the floor, clutching his hand. Tiny sounds escaped from him—in truth, whimpers.

It was then that Matilda seemed to snap to full alertness. She crouched next to him on the floor and held his arms, careful not to touch the exposed skin on his neck or at his wrists. "What is in Whitby?" she asked him. This surprised me, for I thought she meant to comfort the man, but instead she only wanted an explanation.

"Do not touch—" Stewart said softly.

"You must afford him a chance to recover," Vambéry said from the window. "Emily came in direct contact with him and he was not prepared for it. I realize this may be vexing for you or me to comprehend, but when it happens to a clairvoyant as strong as this man, it can be quite traumatic, even dangerous."

"I am okay," Stewart mumbled. "But please, Miss Matilda, please back away. I mean you no disrespect, but you are far too close."

Matilda did as he asked.

Still at the window, Thornley was now sobbing. I went to him and looked out, surveying the night. There was no sign of Emily. If she had left tracks in the muddy earth, the rain had washed them away. But I sincerely doubted she had.

"She is out there all alone," Thornley said. "We must find her. She cannot care for herself."

"We will, I promise. Let me close these shutters; the storm is coming in."

Thornley glanced absentmindedly at the puddles collecting on his dining room floor, then waved a hand in my direction before walking back to the table and collapsing into one of the chairs.

I made one last assessment of the night, then closed the shutters and engaged the lock. When I returned to the table, Vambéry was there, holding my ring to the light. "What is this?" His voice had taken on an angry edge.

"That is the ring Matilda and I found in the palm of the hand we found in Artane Tower," I replied. "We told you about it already."

"You told me about the ring, yes, but you did not mention the inscription on it or that you still possessed it. Did you not think those details of importance?" Vambéry leaned in close to Stewart and allowed him to read the words circling the interior of the ring. "Would you care to hold it?" Vambéry asked him.

Stewart grimaced in obvious discomfort. He scrambled to his feet and reached for his glove. "I will do no such thing. I would like your coach to return me to my home immediately."

"You cannot leave yet!" Matilda stepped between him and the door. "You must tell us about Whitby." She scrambled for her sketchbook on the table and turned to the map of England, tapped at the mark next to the town of Whitby. "What is this place? What is this Whitby?"

"You would be best served to forget all about Whitby or ever finding your nanny," he replied. Turning to Thornley, he added: "And you should forget your wife. He has her now; there is no getting her back."

"*Who* has her?"

Stewart pushed past him for the front door. "I will tell your coachman to return here after he takes me home."

Matilda tried to go after him, but I grabbed her hand, shaking my head.

"Let him go," Vambéry concurred. "What do you know of Dracul?"

"Nothing. Aside from the inscription on the ring, I have never heard the name before," I said.

Vambéry gestured to the vacant chairs, and Matilda and I sat. He then picked up the ring and held it clamped between his thumb and forefinger. "This explains much," he said. "More than you will want to hear, but you must if you are to understand what we are up against." He took one of the remaining seats and set the ring on the table. "The Draculs are an ancient family born in the mountains of Wallachia; they rose from the peasant class to protectors of the people to ultimately rulers over the land, safeguarding the populace from numerous invaders, primarily the Turks, for centuries. It is said they did so with great might and fearsome battle techniques, and that they benefited from an unholy alliance with the Devil himself. It is said each member of this family traveled to the mountains near Lake Hermannstadt to attend the Scholomance, the Devil's school. Here, students were exposed to all the secrets of nature, to the language of animals, and to countless magic spells and charms, all taught by the Devil.

"Admittance was limited to only ten students per class, and at the conclusion of learning, nine of the students would be released and returned to their homes while the tenth would remain as payment to the

Devil. At least four of the Draculs are believed to have been selected for this honor over the centuries. The so-called Tenth Student becomes the Devil's aide-de-camp, his personal student, and is taught magic far darker than any other. They learn the ability to cheat death, to manipulate the minds of others, to transform their own bodies into anything they wish. They become gods among men, but the price is steep, for the Devil claims their soul, and the gates of Heaven are forever closed to their ranks, as their final test requires them to renounce God and embrace all that is unholy."

"This is a legend, right? Nothing more?" Bram asked.

"It is as real as the story of the Dearg-Due your nanny put to paper—what I firmly believe to be her past life. All legends, after all, find their basis in fact."

"So you believe this 'tall man' to be one of the Draculs?" Matilda asked.

Vambéry nodded. "I believe him to be the *voivode* Dracula, yes. I heard his name spoken of in legend throughout Eastern Europe, sometimes referred to as *stregoica*, *Ördög*, *pokol*, even *wampyr* in a German text shared with me in Budapest. The physical description is always similar: tall, dark hair, thick eyebrows, an aquiline nose. I have seen numerous drawings of the man, but he always appears a little different in each one. The similarities are there, though."

I recalled Matilda's attempted drawings of Ellen from all those years ago, how she was never quite able to capture her, each image different from the last. I caught Matilda looking at me; she was thinking much the same.

"The most common image," Vambéry went on, "can be found in an old pamphlet from Nuremberg published in the fourteen hundreds. Therein, he is known as Dracula the *voivode*, but I believe he has gone by many names."

"I do not care what name he is known by or what atrocities he committed in the past, this wicked man has taken my wife," Thornley said. He was again at the window, with the shutter open enough to see out into the storm. "I will chase him to the ends of this world to get her back. If Ellen is somehow with my Emily, I will put a blade through her heart, too, if that is what is necessary."

"To pursue him means death. Think about what you have seen," Vambéry said. "This man transformed from a singularly human form to a swarm of bees before our eyes. I believe we can assume he brought Patrick O'Cuiv back from the dead, not once but twice, the second resurrection after his body had been dissected in autopsy. This very act offers a glimpse at his malignant powers. He somehow has infected your wife with the vile disease that thrives in his own blood, making her a willing slave and turning her against you. If the story of the Dearg-Due is to be believed, your Ellen joined the ranks of the undead when she renounced God. The evil that created Dracul flows through her veins as well. You stand no chance against one; to take on both is ludicrous."

"How can he travel to England? You said they cannot cross water?" Thornley asked.

"I said they cannot cross moving water under their own power," Vambéry countered. "But Dracul possesses great wealth and with it he can procure the aid of others, people lacking scruples."

"We must see this through," I said quietly. "Whatever Ellen has inflicted on me, whatever this man has done to Emily, all of it is connected. This curse has haunted us since childhood; we must bring it to an end."

Thornley said, "How can we be certain Emily has gone to Whitby? What if we leave and she returns here to an abandoned house?"

I had picked up the ring again and gripped it tightly in my hand. "Emily has gone to him, and we know he has gone to Whitby. He came here tonight to spirit her away. We only served to slow him down."

"What about Ellen?" Matilda asked.

"Ellen is on her way there as well, of this I am certain," I said.

"How can you know?"

My arm was itching incredibly, and for the first time in many years that cord binding me to Ellen tugged at my imagination, the link I thought as a child I was only imagining.

"I just know."

But what I could not know was whether I was using this shackle to follow Ellen or if Ellen was using it to bring me to her, as an offering to this Dracul. Regardless, I was certain of one thing: answers were buried at the end of this path of questions.

Vambéry eyed me but uttered not a word. He was focused on my hand, where the burn had once inflicted pain but which festered no more and was now healed.

Thornley returned to the table and sat beside him. "Armin, you have been a tremendous help, more so than I could have ever hoped. I cannot ask you to come with us, that would be too much, you have given so much already."

Vambéry said, "Enough! Of course I will accompany you. If you are going to march to your death, the least I can do is bear witness. We will need supplies, though; I will begin gathering them at once. We should be prepared to leave at first light."

NOW

The man is glaring at him.

A shiver crept up Bram's spine, as if this dark entity had reached out and caressed his cheek.

At the man's feet, the coiled remains of the two snakes spasmed and twisted in the muddied grass. Bram watches in awe as the mucky mess surrounding them begins to bubble and the serpents are swallowed beneath the surface, the beady black eyes of one of the snakes locked on him still as its ugly head disappears from view.

A fog begins to collect then, rising from the still erupting earth like some ungodly steam. First it gathers only around the man, but then it spreads out from him, growing wider in a concentric circle configuration, fanning out until it reaches the tower and begins to wrap around it in some kind of embrace. Bram advances to the other window and sees that the soil has begun to bubble on that side of the castle as well, the grass simmering with steam, followed by the expulsion of fog. The mysterious mist hovers near the ground, rising no more than a foot or two, but within ten minutes the entire structure is shrouded.

The man's eyes never leave Bram, although he appears to be in deep concentration. He flexes his hands at his side, stretching his fingers out straight, his long nails pointing to the earth. Then, in a fluid motion, he lowers himself to the ground and plunges his fingertips into the dirt.

The fog stirs around him, swirling slowly then gaining speed. If a wind drives this, Bram does not feel it; the air inside the room lies still.

In an instant, the fog vanishes, as Bram watches it first sink to the ground, then disappear as it is sucked beneath by some unseen force, an inhaled breath.

All goes quiet, so quiet that when someone speaks from behind the door, Bram startles.

He is coming for you, it says in that little girl's voice.

With that, the boiling mud around the man begins to stir as snakes break the surface—thousands of snakes, of all colors and sizes, wiggling out from the hell below.

LETTER FROM MATILDA
to ELLEN CRONE,
DATED 16 AUGUST 1868

———— ◆ ————

My dearest Ellen,

I will not restate the occurrences of the past few days, for no doubt you already know. I can only assume the tall man, the one we refer to as Dracul, has informed you. I also believe that the link Bram shares with you allows you, in some way, to monitor him. You must know, therefore, that we are on our way to Whitby.

We boarded a ship in Dublin called the RMS *Leinster* and crossed the Irish Sea with little difficulty—unless, of course, you consider the two large trunks our Mr. Vámbéry brought in tow, a curious assortment of clothing and holy relics. Far more than the simple bag I brought. Bram and Thornley also thought it best to travel light.

The ship transported us to Liverpool, where we boarded the train to Whitby, by way of Manchester, Leeds, and York. We are expected to arrive within the hour.

Thornley has been understandably distressed yet subdued. He did not wish to leave his home and nearly stayed behind. Even after all that has occurred, he clings to the belief that whatever affected Emily dwells only in her mind and that she now is wandering the streets of Dublin in some kind of daze. He cannot bear the thought of her returning to their home to discover him gone. After much debate, Bram convinced him he would be right in joining us. He instructed his servants to leave all the doors and windows unsecured at all hours and, should Emily return, to notify him at the Duke of York Inn by telegram.

Bram tells us that you, too, are in Whitby, but he cannot tell us why. Did you travel with the tall man, this Dracul? Or is he following you there as we are? What could be the nature of your business in such a far-off place?

Why are you running from us? Or are you chasing us?

Is there no end to the roads you will travel?

Bram has been scratching at his arm. I don't think he realized that I noticed, but I did. He scratches at your bite mark all the way to his shoulder. This "itch" within him seems to grow as he draws closer to you, as we near Whitby. He talks little of it, but it obviously worries him so. Even now, as he stares out the train window at the English countryside rolling past, his mind is elsewhere, his mind is on you.

Affectionately yours,
Matilda

THE JOURNAL *of* BRAM STOKER

17 August 1868, 12:05 p.m. —After three days of travel, we arrived and settled into the little town of Whitby without incident. I must admit, I was fearful to board a ship and cross the Irish Sea. Something about the confinement I found deeply disturbing, also the rushing water all around us. The experience made me feel so small, so vulnerable. Had I not been so utterly exhausted, I may have spent more time worrying about these things, but instead I slept. I expected my dreams to be filled with images of Ellen and this quest before us, but they were not; there was only a blackness devoid of all sight and sound. I can only imagine death to feel this way; that is how I slept.

Upon arrival in Whitby, Vambéry summoned a coach to transport us to the Duke of York Inn, situated on the town's western-facing cliffs, where we took possession of our reserved rooms. Vambéry and Matilda occupied rooms of their own, while I shared a room with Thornley. I felt it best not to leave him alone in his current condition. He is asleep now upon one of the beds, but he is not enjoying restful sleep, it being fitful instead. He keeps becoming entangled in the sheets, and more than once he has been given to mumbling in his troubled slumber. Most cannot be understood, but I was able to pick out his wife's name, something about her feeding, and some nonsense about the police pursuing him for the murder of the guard at Steevens' Hospital. I know the man died in his presence, but he was in no way responsible; surely Thornley knows this, yet his mind seeks guilt. Perhaps it is because he did not report the crime, or perhaps the stress of all the events of late are simply manifesting themselves as guilt. Thornley is versed in the study of the mind, which I am not, but I must admit its workings are quite fascinating and intrigue me no end.

I have settled into an armchair at the window to record this entry, the sea breeze feeling quite exquisite bathing my skin. To inhale the salt air reminds me of Clontarf so many years ago. Whitby is a lovely locale, the little River Esk meandering through a deep valley, broadening as it nears the harbor. The houses of the old town, seemingly piled one upon the other, are all red-roofed. Overlooking the town is the abbey, a noble ruin of immense size. Between it and the town is the parish church— St. Mary's, I was to learn later—around which lies a capacious grave-yard, chockablock with tombstones. The grade of the hill is so steep over the harbor that part of its bank has given way and some of the graves violated. Vambéry had pointed to this sad development when first we arrived. "Many of those tombs are empty, the headstones there just to placate the loved ones of those lost to the sea." This explanation did not erase the image in my mind of the cliff breaking away and the bodies of the buried falling to the waves below.

To reach the graveyard from the street, one must climb one hundred and ninety-nine steps—no simple feat, considering how steep the hill is and how strong the winds are blowing off the sea. At the top of the steps stands the church and abbey.

I was drawn to the summit of this hill and its abbey.

Even before Vambéry left word for Thornley and me to meet him in the lobby of the inn, I knew we would be climbing those steps soon.

. . .

17 AUGUST 1868, 4:13 p.m.—"I have spent the past few hours in search of information," Vambéry told us, "anything my contacts might share that may be of use to us."

The four of us sat around a table at a small outdoor pub on Church Street, with the abbey looming over us in the distance. The blue sky of earlier was gone, replaced with one of dull gray and thick clouds. There was rain in our future, but none as of yet. A fog hung over the harbor, threatening to roll in.

"I would have gone with you," I said.

Vambéry waved me off. "You needed to get some rest, all of you, for what lies ahead. I got plenty of rest in my younger years and have little need for sleep now."

"You have friends here?" I think the question came across more skeptical than Matilda had intended, and her face reddened.

"I have friends everywhere, my dear. In my line of work, one can never have too many friends."

At this point, we all knew better than to ask him what that line of work was, so we said nothing.

"Ellen is very close, I am sure of it," I said.

"What about Emily?" Thornley asked.

"I don't know." This was the truth. While I could most definitely sense Ellen nearby, I had no connection to Emily. "Ellen feels as if she is sitting at this table with us. I believe she's watching us right now. The daylight is fearsome to her; it makes her feel vulnerable, so she stays within the shadows, but close, very close."

"What about the tall man, Dracul?" Vambéry asked. "Can you feel him?"

I could not, and I told him so. "But when I think about him, I believe Ellen can feel him. In fact, I *know* Ellen can feel him. I don't believe he is in Whitby yet, but he will be soon. She waits for him to arrive . . . yes, she is watching us and waiting for him." I said these words slowly, as they came to me. I couldn't explain this bond between Ellen and me, but it seemed to be strengthening, allowing me to reach out and pluck thoughts from her mind. I couldn't help but wonder: If she were doing the same, would I know?

"I want you to try something, Bram. I want you to think about Emily while focusing on Ellen as she thinks about Dracul. Think of Emily in Ellen's mind. Does she know where Emily is?"

My eyes closed, and Vambéry said these words in a soothing voice, a monotone; I found his tone put me in a dreamy state, on the verge of sleep. "Plant the thought in Ellen's mind, then try to capture the result."

I did as he requested, then said, "Yes, Emily is with the tall man. A dark, dismal place. Waiting. Anxious. No rest. Rocking. Rocking with the sea? Wait, no, not anymore. Coach. They travel by coach."

"Good, Bram, very good. Now this is important, so think hard. When did they leave Dublin?"

I forced the thought into Ellen's mind. If she resisted, I did not sense any pressure. The answer came back swiftly, plucked from a fast-moving current. "Saturday night, by boat, to Liverpool. Private coach then. Many horses. Fast. So very fast. Dark. She expects them some time to-night, late into the night."

"You are doing very well, Bram. I want you to attempt one other thing. I know you can do it, so just allow your mind to relax and accept that you can. This task will be no more arduous than looking from right to left or taking a drink of your tea, do you understand?"

"Yes." I heard my voice, but it sounded distant, like I was across the street overhearing myself respond.

"You said Ellen was watching us. You even said she was watching us right now. I want you to look through Ellen's eyes and tell us where she is. What is her view of us, from what direct—"

My eyes snapped open as a sharp pain sliced through my brain. It rolled forward and felt as if someone had squeezed my eyes in their hand with all their might. A moan almost escaped my lips, but I bit it back.

"Breathe, Bram, breathe," Vambéry intoned, his voice at my ear. "It is over now, relax."

I blinked back the light. Even with the storm clouds overhead, it seemed immensely bright. With my elbows planted on the table, I rested my head in my hands.

"She blocked you. Ellen caught you poking around in her mind and locked you out. This was to be expected. Did you learn where she was?"

I thought about this for a second. "No. Still close, but she might be in any one of these buildings." Hundreds of windows surrounded us from all angles, from storefronts to houses to our own inn and the abbey perched opposite it on the cliffs. I had no idea where she was.

"This is still good; we have learned much. I do not believe this is her first visit to Whitby. In truth, I think she has been coming here for some time," Vambéry said.

Matilda had rested her hand on my shoulder. "What makes you say that?"

Vambéry gestured towards the harbor. "For the past few years, there have been sightings of a phantom hound, large and black, prowling the moors. The locals claim the beast is far larger than the typical dog, wolf-like in its appearance. In the past few weeks, these sightings have increased in number and frequency. It was seen as recently as last night."

"And you think this wolf is Ellen?" Thornley asked.

"I have reason to believe so, yes. There is more." He nodded towards the abbey. "Another local legend tells of a woman in white seen in the windows of the abbey, high up in that tower. The keeper of the abbey assures me that this particular tower is inaccessible, yet even he saw her as recently as this week past. While the descriptions vary, I believe this specter, too, may be our Ellen Crone."

"I have been drawn to that place since we arrived here," I admitted. "I'm not sure if that is where Ellen is now, but there is a familiarity that cannot be denied."

"She used Patrick O'Cuiv's grave to conceal possessions; maybe she has done the same here," Matilda said. "For someone who has defied death, it seems fitting to hide possessions in some forlorn grave, some-place the locals have long forgotten and will never disturb. It would be an all too fitting refuge in which to hide her maps."

"But how can she enter there in the first place?" Thornley pointed out. "Is it not designated a holy site?"

Vambéry smiled at this assertion. "I asked that very question at the Whitby Library and learned a very interesting fact about the abbey's history. The first monastery was built more than a thousand years ago by King Oswy of Northumbria and sheltered both monks and nuns. A Saxon princess named Hilda served as abbess. In 664, a synod was convened—"

Matilda frowned. "'A synod'?"

"A gathering, a council," Vambéry explained. "One of the most impor-tant meetings in the history of the Church, called to reconcile the differ-ences between the Roman and Celtic churches in the British Isles. At this time, there were few sites considered holier. In the tenth century, the entire structure was destroyed by the Danes, and the current abbey was built to once again house Benedictine monks. It was an active mon-astery for nearly five hundred years, until Henry VIII ordered the dis-solution of all monasteries in 1539. That allowed the buildings and land to be bought by Richard Cholmley, a major land owner from Yorkshire. His family lived on the property until the eighteenth century, at which point it was abandoned. This is the part I found most interesting." He paused for a second, then leaned into the table. "Mr. Cholmley used stones from the abbey to build his house. As was tradition at that time, before he could dismantle a holy sanctuary, the structure was deconsecrated by the Church. Only then could pieces be used to build a private home."

"Are you sure of this?" I asked.

"Absolutely. The cemetery and remaining grounds no doubt stayed within the graces of the church, but the abbey did not; it is no longer holy ground. Many believe the lady in white to be Hilda, the original abbess, roaming the ruins of the abbey she loved, but like I said earlier, I believe this to be Miss Crone, and why not? If you are to believe the story of the Dearg-Due, what better place for someone who renounced God to hide than an abbey, which is now deconsecrated?"

"A place believed to be holy, but is not. Hiding in plain sight," said Thornley. "Truly remarkable."

Something caught Vambéry's eye just then and he stood. "Please excuse me for a minute."

I watched as he left the table and walked down the block to the corner of Bridge Street and Church, where a flower vendor had recently arrived and was setting up shop. She was unpacking her blossoms and spreading them out on a blanket along the side of the road. They spoke for a moment, then the woman pointed to her wagon and money exchanged hands. She handed Vambéry a basket, which he carried back to the table and set at its center.

"If we do find Miss Crone in the abbey, I would like to present her with this gift," Vambéry said. "There is nothing a woman likes more than fresh-cut flowers."

I leaned forward and looked in the straw basket. It was filled with large white wild roses.

17 AUGUST 1868, 4:58 p.m.—We climbed the steps to the abbey, commencing at Church Street, winding our way up the cliffside to the abbey above in a gently curving progression of steps. Earlier, Vambéry's

trunks had found their way safely to his room at the Duke of York Inn. He had retrieved specific items from them and filled four leather satchels, which he then divvied up amongst us to carry. While I did not look in the others' satchels, mine held mirrors and crosses of all different sizes. As Thornley walked in front of me, I could see the barrel of a rifle protruding from his bag. He had shown it to me earlier; a new Snider–Enfield Mark III, its barrel shortened to make for ease of travel. I also saw Vambéry place the roses in Matilda's bag. I am not sure what was contained in his own satchel, but whatever it was appeared to be hefty—he shifted the weight from one shoulder to the other every few minutes.

In just the last half hour, the sky had grown more woeful as storm clouds rolled in. I could see the harbor in the distance, the ships now returning to port. Those already docked were tying down in anticipation of the oncoming inclement weather. With each step we took ascending the steps, the air grew a little colder and the fog a little closer, until all we could make out was the fine mist surrounding us. The world below, the little town of Whitby, became hazy. I could not help but recall what Vambéry had said about Dracul manipulating the weather and I wondered if he was here now. By the time we achieved the halfway point up the stairs, Thornley was favoring his left knee—an old rugby injury—and Vambéry appeared short of breath. I reached for Vambéry's satchel and slung it over my other shoulder. "I will return it to you at the top," I told him.

Vambéry prepared to argue but granted me a quick nod instead. "My leg is a burden, particularly at a time like this," he said, now breathing through his mouth.

"The air is thin up here, difficult for anyone."

"Not you."

I said nothing to this, just kept walking. He was right, of course, I felt no fatigue whatsoever. I could have sprinted up the steps, had I so chosen.

"Do you sense she is up there?" Matilda asked.

I shook my head. "I've felt nothing since she blocked me earlier. If she is in the abbey, I cannot tell."

We passed only three other people as we mounted the steps farther, two older fishermen and a woman. All three eyed the sky nervously as they made their way down. When we reached the apex, we found ourselves alone in the sprawling graveyard, with St. Mary's Church to our left and the abbey in front of us, a large pond right next to it. The graveyard continued on over the hill towards the cliff, high above the water. The site was much larger than I had expected. "Where do we begin?"

Vambéry asked for his leather satchel, which I readily returned to him. From a pocket in the front, he pulled out an old map and unfolded it. Its weathered paper bore a drawing of the buildings and grounds. "We are here," he said, pointing to the steps snaking up from the town at the edge of the map. "Saint Mary's is still considered holy ground, so Ellen could not possibly be in there. Most of this cemetery is still consecrated, too."

"What about the graves of the suicides?" Matilda asked, studying the map.

"Yes," Vambéry said, "they can be found here and here." He indicated two spots on the map—one near the side of the abbey, the other perched precariously on what looked like the very edge of the cliff. "The suicides are not part of the church grounds but are on land belonging to the abbey."

Lightning filled the sky over the sea, three quick flashes. We all regarded it with trepidation.

"Perhaps we should split up before this storm strikes," Vambéry suggested. "Bram and I can take the interior of the abbey while the two of you search the suicide graves."

"Is that safe? Maybe we should stay together," Matilda said.

"If these creatures come out during daylight hours, they have no powers. They are less than mortals. If she is here, if any of them are here, they are most likely at rest," Vambéry explained. "We have four hours of daylight remaining; we must make the most of it."

Matilda reached out and squeezed my hand. "Do be careful."

"You as well."

Vambéry said to Thornley, "If you discover anything, come retrieve us. We are close by."

I watched Matilda and Thornley make their way past the ancient towering cross that marked the cemetery entrance and disappear amongst the large headstones.

Vambéry reached down and picked up his bag. "Come, my boy. Let us hurry."

Much of the abbey was a crumbling ruin, but that which remained was extraordinary—tall, intricately carved columns and massive stone blocks reaching for the swirling gray clouds of the heavens. The grounds were overgrown with foliage and weeds, all fighting to claim this structure, yet it was fighting back, unwilling to concede just yet. We passed under an apse and entered the abbey at the south transept. The remains of a staircase stood among a pile of rubble against a central wall.

"These cloisters follow the exterior walls," Vambéry informed me. "To the west, they lead to the nave, and the east end houses the choir, presbytery, and sanctuary. The round towers standing sentinel at all four corners are accessible by staircases; they are frequented by the locals, particularly on nights when ships are out at sea during a storm and a high vantage point is required to help guide them safely to port in the harbor."

"Where was the lady in white sighted?"

"She has been observed atop all four corner towers as well as at the apex of the central tower above us, in the keep behind the crenellations." He then looked upwards. There was a hole in what remained of the ceiling, and churning storm clouds were clearly visible through it.

"Most of the supporting structure for this central tower obviously has crumbled away. In fact, about thirty years ago this entire section was lost, including the stairs. The upper rooms were deemed unsafe and sealed off. If Ellen is anywhere, I think she would be there."

I stepped deeper into the crossing. The air was rank with mildew, small puddles of water stood stagnant. Weeds grew between many of the stones, forcing their way through the mortar. I ran a finger over the stone of the wall and it gave way under my touch. My arm tingled. A name came to mind. From where, I could not know, but I uttered it under my breath. "Marmion."

Vambéry stopped and turned to me. "I am sorry, what did you say?"

"Marmion."

"From where do you know that name?"

I shrugged. "I don't know. I mean, I don't recall. It just dawned on me."

Vambéry stared at me. "Is it from Ellen? Something you plucked from her mind?"

"Maybe. Again, I don't know. What does it mean?"

"Walter Scott wrote of the tragic legend—a nun who fell in love with Marmion, a knight, who would betray her love in the end. She had broken all of her vows to be with him, you understand. When the lovers were eventually discovered, she was bricked up inside the walls right here at the abbey," Vambéry said.

"Was she ever found?"

"No. If the story is to be believed, she is still here somewhere. Many have searched for her over the years, but no trace has ever been located."

I said, "If Ellen had the thought, what is the connection?"

Vambéry had no answer to this.

I ran my hand over the wall, my eyes drifting to the breach in the ceiling. "Can we get in through there?"

He shook his head. "That leads to the ward, an outer courtyard on the upper level next to the tower, but any doors have since been sealed with mortar and stone to keep people at bay."

The outer walls of the crossing were lined with niches, no doubt intended to hold statues or books while this place was still a functioning monastery. They were spaced about six feet apart. All now housed cobwebs and dislodged stones and sported copious quantities of dust. The remnants of a fireplace still stood proud against the far wall, the flames long extinguished. As my eyes fell upon it, I felt the tingle in my arm again.

I traversed the room.

The hearth was perhaps eight feet across, the firebox itself almost five feet wide and nearly as tall. I could hear nesting birds twittering far up the chimney. I am not sure if I saw the small pile of dirt in the left corner of the firebox first or if I smelled it, but the scent registered immediately, for it reeked of the same rotten soil we had found under Nanna Ellen's bed all those years earlier.

THE DIARY *of* THORNLEY STOKER

(RECORDED IN SHORTHAND AND TRANSCRIBED HEREWITH.)

---

17 August 1868, 4:58 p.m. —My sister moved through the graveyard with purpose and with dispatch, carefully stepping over the dead at our feet and scrutinizing each stone as we progressed. This sector of the graveyard held little interest for her; she was concerned only with the suicides' graves at the cliff's edge. As we approached, she continued to study the roiling clouds above. The air had taken on a chill in a matter of minutes, and I now felt the first drops of rain on my head.

We passed a large pond, the scent of which crept across the cemetery, mildewy, stale, and stagnant. The waters were still, save for the occasional ripple produced by the coming rain.

"Here," she said, stopping in her tracks. "See that small stone wall? We found a similar wall in Clontarf. It serves to delineate the ground that is sanctified and the ground that is not."

At this place, I noted a shift in the terrain itself. Just beyond the wall, the weeds appeared thicker, with vines rolling over tombstones and encasing them as if attempting to pull them down to the ground. And the stones themselves appeared much smaller; while the markers behind me rising from the consecrated plot were tall, anywhere from two to six feet in height, stones marking the suicide graves were squat. Many were flush to the ground, some bearing no inscriptions at all. This was, indeed, a land of the unwanted and forgotten.

"What are we searching for?" I asked my sister, my eyes darting from stone to stone.

Matilda knelt and cleared away the weeds from the face of a stone; her fingers then traced the lettering beneath, worn and faded with time. "It is difficult to say. With the O'Cuiv grave, the soil seemed like it had not been disturbed in years, yet we found Ellen's possessions inside. Vambéry said these creatures possess the ability to change shape, even transforming into mist. This ability applies to the items in their possession as well. If such is the case, she could enter and exit a grave through the smallest of holes, something so small we may not be able to detect it."

"That is not very helpful, my dear sister."

Matilda moved on to the next grave. "There may be a familiarity to the name, or possibly a symbol on the stone. If Ellen used the grave as a place of rest or to store possessions, I believe she would have marked it somehow. You start over there, and I'll go through these; keep working towards the outside of the yard."

I began moving through the graves, searching for anything of significance. The cliffside loomed precariously close, and I again noted how many of the graves were perched right at the precipice. This area of the cemetery was ripe for reclamation by the swirling sea.

Matilda screamed and jumped back.

"What is it?"

"A snake. It startled me, is all."

I had not seen a single snake until her outburst, then, as if on cue, a pair slithered past me. There were no snakes in Ireland, so I was not accustomed to seeing them. In truth, they made my skin crawl.

"The ground is moist here, primed for grass snakes. They're harmless, though; it's the adders you need to watch out for. They're not very aggressive, but if you step on one and it bites you, they have some of the most lethal—"

"Thornley?"

I looked up to find Matilda kneeling at a small headstone.

"I think I found something."

I walked over and crouched down beside her as she busied herself plucking away weeds. The inscription on the stone proved difficult to read, but was still legible, simply stating IN REMEMBRANCE OF BARNABY SWALES. There were no dates.

"I don't understand. What is the significance? I've seen dozens of headstones like this. Is the name familiar to you?"

Matilda shook her head. "It just reads 'In remembrance of . . .'"

"So do many of the other stones here," I replied. "A lot of these people were lost at sea; there would be no body to bury, so they mark the grave like this instead of saying something like 'Here lies . . .'"

"There is not a single grave amongst the suicides that says 'In re-membrance of . . .' save this one. They are all out there," she said, ges-turing towards the other half of the cemetery. "Why would an empty grave be amongst the suicides? That does not make sense."

She was right, of course. The purpose of a suicide grave was to bury a body considered to be unholy or unblessed by the Church, away from sanctified ground. One that could not be officially buried on Church property. The damned were meant to be forgotten, interred and lost, never to be mentioned again. An empty grave had no place here. "I'll get a shovel."

Above, the clouds could hold back the storm no longer, and thick drops began pelting us relentlessly.

NOW

───◆───

Bram watches in horror as snakes writhe out of the soil at the base of the tower and attempt to climb over one another—so many snakes that the ground itself disappears, lost beneath their squirming, coiling bodies.

At the center stands the man, his arms now outstretched, his eyes still closed, his fingers still twitching. Bram cannot help but think of a conductor and his orchestra, each instrumentalist following his baton. All of this activity is taking place in complete silence, Bram aware of nothing but the sound of his own breathing.

Behind him, the odor of newly turned earth drifts from behind the door. This rank perfume of the grave is all too familiar to him now and he can only imagine its source here. Then he hears the loud grunt of a beast of some kind followed by the shrill laughter of a little girl, both also coming from behind that door.

The last rose he placed there is now shriveled up and dead, and his basket is empty; he had placed the last two on the windowsills in order to keep the man, this Dracul, from entering. He considers moving only one, but knows that is probably exactly what this man wants him to do—free the window and allow him entrance into this place.

The odor grows worse, and Bram tries to shield his nostrils with the sleeve of his shirt.

Around the frame of the door, the last of the paste dries right before his eyes and crumbles to the stone floor. A dark muck begins to seep out through the crack between the foot of the door and the floor itself, a sour-smelling mess teeming with maggots and wiggling worms. Bram pulls off his coat and tries to stem the grotesque flow, but it somehow moves around his blockade, impossibly climbing over his coat, into every crease. Bram pulls away in disgust.

He returns to the window and looks down.

The man is watching him yet again, a broad grin on his face, the ground around him still alive with slithering snakes. He raises his long arms above his head and points to the open window.

The stone walls of the tower, covered as they are with vines and errant foliage, centuries worth of vegetation attempting to scale the ancient façade, become the snakes' destination as they begin to slip over the unfettered growth. First just testing, then becoming more bold, they slowly creep up the side of the structure. Where vines and foliage do not reach, the snakes, twisting and churning their bodies over one another, keep climbing, gaining inch after inch.

Bram tugs at the shutter, and the wood becomes dust at his touch, the result, he has no doubt, of some evil spell cast by the man below.

The man below closes his fingers into a fist, and the creature behind the door slams into the oak with a tremendous force. Filthy muck shoots out from all the edges, spraying across the room. Then it begins to drip from the top of the door, running down over the wood and the corroded metal lock.

Bram runs back to his leather satchel and dumps out its contents. He has no more holy water, no more blessed host. Nothing left with which to defend himself. He plucks one of the crosses from the wall and brandishes it in his left hand.

Outside, the snakes keep climbing, so close that Bram can hear their angry hisses as their thin forked tongues flick between their ever-ready fangs.

THE JOURNAL *of* BRAM STOKER

———◆———

17 August 1868, 5:12 p.m. —"What is it?" Vambéry asked from behind me.

I ducked deeper into the firebox and looked up. "There is a ladder here embedded in the chimney stones."

Vambéry squeezed in alongside me and he, too, glanced up. "I see nothing. Hold on—" He disappeared and returned with a lit candle in hand.

I reached up and gripped my fingers around the ladder's first rung. "Here, do you see?"

He raised the flickering candle. Stones protruded every few feet in a zigzag pattern from the top of the firebox to what appeared to be another fireplace on the floor above. The chimney was large enough to accommodate me standing up, and I rose to my full height. With the satchel slung over my shoulder, I began to climb. Vambéry handed up his cane, then followed after me, favoring his bad leg.

I crawled from the chimney into the firebox on this secondary level and found myself in a room much smaller than the one below. It, too, smelled dank, and while no footprints were evident upon the dirty floor, I noted this deficit with caution, remembering the complete lack of footprints in the tower at Artane or in Nanna Ellen's room.

Vambéry hoisted himself up behind me with a grunt and dusted off his jacket and pants. There was a small window to the east, and he looked out. "The sleeping chambers were on this level; this one most likely belonged to Lady Hilda." He cautiously inched forward. "Be careful where you step; this floor is brittle and can collapse underfoot." There was a narrow door at the far side of the room, and he went to it. "The tower keep is one more level up."

Beyond the small room, we found the remainder of the staircase adjacent to the ruined hallways running to the left and to the right. While the steps leading down below were missing and the shaft sealed, those leading up remained intact. Vambéry advised me to stay close to the wall and follow directly behind him, placing my feet where he placed his as he tested the steps ahead of us with his cane. This part of the structure felt very much like a house of cards that could fall with little provocation, and I pictured us both crashing through the floor and landing under a pile of stone and rubble.

The stairs ended at a large oak door that stood ajar, and a dark room beyond.

THE DIARY of THORNLEY STOKER

---

17 August 1868, 6:19 p.m. —We dug about three feet down before we discovered the old wooden box.

An old box of teak approximately three feet long and one wide. At first I thought it was a child's coffin, but as we unearthed the box, I quickly realized it was too small even for that.

A part of me believed we would find Emily buried within this grave. I pictured her sleeping soundly under this thick blanket of earth, waiting for the rise of night before she would somehow find her way past the smothering soil and tangled roots and busy maggots and worms to the land of the living. I then pictured her as she appeared that last moment before she bounded from our dining room out into the gloom, her eyes filled with fright, her lips so very red against her pale skin.

I cursed Bram and the others for putting these thoughts into my head, for making me believe my wife had somehow been transformed into a monster.

"Help me lift it out," I heard Matilda say.

I forced thoughts of Emily from my mind and reached down into the hole. I had to lie on my side and stretch out in order to make purchase with the box, forcing my fingers under one corner and tugging. It was heavy, far heavier than it appeared.

The rain was falling steadily now, and the bottom of the hole began to fill with water. When I pulled at the box, it lifted away from the mud with a sickening smack. I worked my hand beneath it again and carefully raised the corner until Matilda could grip it and pull it from its hellish hole. Even with both hands, she could barely lift it, and I had to assist her.

I sat up in the tall weeds and looked down at myself. I was a mess. I was soaked to the bone, my clothing was caked with mud. Matilda fared no better, her long hair sticking to her face, cheeks covered in dirt and grime. Had anyone seen us, we surely would have been arrested for vagrancy, possibly even for grave robbing. Were that to happen, we would fit right in with the common criminals, the frightful way we both looked. But Matilda did not seem to care—I watched her brush her hair aside with her hand, leaving a muddy trail across her temple.

The box was nailed shut, and I had to employ the tip of the shovel's blade to pry it open.

My heart stopped at what was inside.

The box was chockful of gold and silver coins, paper currency, faded documents . . . Matilda reached past all of it and plucked a stack of letters from the far corner, her face growing pale.

"What is it?"

"I wrote these letters to Ellen and left them in Patrick O'Cuiv's grave in Clontarf. We buried them there."

"How is that possible?" The earth around this grave had not been turned in years.

Rain pelted the paper in her hands, and the ink began to run. "Let's get this inside the abbey," I said, attempting to reaffix the lid.

Matilda stopped me and reached back inside. She pulled out what looked like a property deed. "This is for land in Austria; it's in the name of Countess Dolingen."

"Best to put it back inside," I said. "It will be ruined out here."

She finally nodded and returned the items, and I closed the lid. The two of us quickly carried the box towards the abbey.

With the rain the sky grew dark, churning black and thick with storm clouds blotting out the sun. Had I turned, I would have seen Ellen Crone rise up out of the pond behind us, with Maggie and Patrick O'Cuiv close behind. I would have seen them drift over the surface of the water towards us, towards the abbey, with sharp teeth gleaming white and eyes of red fire.

NOW

The snakes climb with unnatural speed, not as individual animals but working in unison, forming layers and weaving together in patterns that allowed the next group to climb just a little higher than the last. The hissing grows incessantly louder, topped only by the banging from behind the door, each hit sending more foul-scented muck through the air. Bram looks to the roses on the windowsill and watches in horror as they wilt and turn to black before his eyes.

The first two snakes appear directly in the room, and Bram hopes that is only because the creature behind the door somehow summoned them; he had hoped the roses would prevent the evil from entering from outside, a thin hope, but it was all he had. As the roses wilt and die, so do those hopes. He scoops up his journal and shoves it deep into his pocket, maybe it will be found on his body.

Back at the windows, Bram uses his bowie knife to cut back the vines, all he can reach. They are thick and coarse, but he saws through them one after the other. This slows the snakes, but only for an instant. They twist in and out of one another, forming their own path.

The first snake comes over the sill on the opposite end of the room, and Bram runs to it, stomping on its head with his thick boot the moment it strikes the ground. Another comes over the sill a moment later and springs out at him, appearing to fly through the air. Bram ducks aside and slices at it with the knife, watching as both halves hit the stone floor and somehow slither across to the other side. Two more come through the other window—Bram tries to get to them, but the moment they are on the floor they disappear into the shadows, one towards his bag, the other into the far corner. Three more come through the window behind him, and Bram moves just fast enough to dodge their bites, back to the other side of the room. He chances a glance out the window and spots more serpents than he can count, all on the verge of entering the room.

From the corner of his eye, he also spots Dracul. This dark man, this thing of evil, continuing to stare up at him from the ground, his black cloak fluttering around him as if it is alive, the air otherwise still. Standing beside him is his brother's wife, Emily.

Half a dozen adders pour in from the window and land at his feet, their loud hiss drowning out all else.

THE JOURNAL *of* BRAM STOKER

———◆———

17 August 1868, 6:19 p.m. ——Vambéry was first into the room, but only after freeing his silver sword from his cane. He pushed through the door with speed I wouldn't have thought possible, prepared to strike at whomever or whatever might be waiting on the other side. I followed quickly behind him, passing over the threshold with no weapon other than my wit. What I wouldn't give for the Snider–Enfield Thornley carried!

The chamber was dark, devoid of life.

But it was the rank odor that hit us first.

It was a scent I had grown unnaturally familiar with—damp earth and death, mildew and rot.

Vambéry quickly covered his nose and mouth while pivoting about, ensuring we were alone. "It reeks of a tomb in here. This must be where she rests."

Aside from a chair against the far wall next to a narrow window, the space was vacant.

"The tomb is not here," I said, "it's over there," pointing to a thick oak door at the back of the room. My arm had begun to itch incessantly, and I felt the tug of Ellen all around me. I glanced at the ceiling, expecting her to be tucked up in the wooden rafters, but she was not there; the only life was the hundreds of tiny spiders clinging to the ghostly maze of webs adorning the ceiling.

Vambéry went to the door. "Are you sure? Is she in there now?"

I couldn't tell, and I told him so. I felt her touch, her breath, the slow beat of her heart all around me, surrounding me. If I closed my eyes, it was as if she held me in her arms and pulled me to her chest in an embrace. A blackness swooned around me, and the room seemed to fade away until there was nothing but me and her.

"Bram!"

Hearing my name was like sustaining a swift kick to the chest, and my eyes snapped open. Vambéry was standing at the heavy oak door, glaring at me.

"Stay with me, Bram," he implored. "Do not let her take control."

Vambéry turned back to the door. The thick oak was sealed securely in place by a heavy iron lock built directly into the center, with bolts branching out to both the left and the right into the frame, not unlike the one I remembered from the tower in Artane. He knelt down and peered into the large keyhole for a second, then dropped his leather satchel at his side and began rummaging through one of its pockets. From it he retrieved two thin blades and soon began tinkering with the lock.

A pain shot through me, and I fell to the floor, my knees cracking against the cold stone. Ellen's presence squeezed me, and all at once I felt the heavy weight of fear. Fear for myself, fear for Vambéry, and fear for—

"Matilda and Thornley." I had blurted out their names without realizing it, and Vambéry glanced up at me, then went back to work.

"What about them?" he mumbled, twisting one of the blades in the lock. The mechanism began to give.

I struggled to breathe, sucking in air.

It was then that Patrick O'Cuiv appeared in the doorway. He was larger than I remembered, an imposing presence that blocked any possible chance of exiting the room. His skin was as white as a blank sheet of paper, his eyes were glowing an unnatural shade of red.

I dove for the sword at Vambéry's side, but before I could get my hand around the grip, Maggie O'Cuiv was in the room, her movements so fluid she appeared to float rather than run. She was but a blur as she crossed the space and kicked the blade away from me while lifting my body like a rag doll from the floor with her small child hands and pinning me against the stone wall, her feet somehow leaving the floor. I felt her icy breath at my neck.

I saw Ellen then. I saw Ellen Crone as she came in from the hallway, moving with the same ease Maggie had, moving so fast she didn't seem to move at all. One moment she wasn't there; then she was, her red eyes glaring at Vambéry.

"Away from that door!" she shrieked.

17 AUGUST 1868, 6:54 p.m.—Vambéry jumped aside; then Ellen was upon me, only inches from me, her burning red eyes fixed on me. I was brought back to my childhood, to the moment she dropped from the ceiling. I could not move, I could not breathe; I did not make a sound. When her fingers reached up and pressed against my temple, my world went black. The room around me faded away, and I was in another place, another time. Ellen's mind opened to me, her thoughts, her memories, revealing the true fate of the Dearg-Due, revealing to me the true life of the woman before me.

I AWOKE FROM DEATH for a second time three years after my beloved pierced my heart with a dagger and buried me in a grave covered with stones and with a white rose placed atop in hopes of bringing some peace to my tormented soul.

My tired eyes had fluttered open and peered into the gloom of what could only be the interior of a castle, a chamber so similar to the one my terrible husband locked me in a lifetime ago. I thought it had all been a dream, a horrid nightmare that had commenced when I was but a child, that perhaps my father, or even my beloved, would rescue me, but then I saw him, this tall man, bending over me in the dim light, suspending a rabbit by its leg over my mouth. Its neck had been sliced open, and blood flowed freely from the wound to my willing lips. I tasted every sweet drip; I felt its warmth racing through my muscles and tissue and limbs. It seemed to impart life in me as if it were something new.

"How can that be?" I heard myself say in a hoarse voice, a voice that had not uttered a word in a long, long time.

The man said nothing at first, still clasping the rabbit with one hand, his free hand squeezing the carcass to release every last drop of blood. When he did speak, I found his voice to be deep and rich, thick with an accent I could not quite place. "I have woken you from a deep sleep. I have brought you back to life."

I tried to sit up, but I was so weak that simply lifting my hand to his face was quite the feat, but I did so nonetheless. I touched his cheek and felt a coldness not unlike my own, dead flesh that somehow was still living. "How long?" I forced myself to ask.

"How long have you slept, you mean?"

I nodded weakly.

"Three years have passed since you were sealed in that grave."

At this revelation, I did sit up, the rabbit's blood further awakening my limbs with each passing second. "Only three years? My beloved, then, he lives still?"

The dark man finished with the rabbit, licking at the wound in the poor creature's neck before tossing it across the room. "If by 'beloved' you refer to the man who plunged a dagger into your unsuspecting heart and buried you behind his house, yes, he lives. I allowed him to live because I thought you would wish to kill him yourself for what he did."

I shook my head violently at this assertion. "Kill him? I could never do such a thing. He is all I have ever loved."

I realized now I lay in a large wooden box filled with the dirt of my earthly grave. I still wore the same white dress I had at last memory, which bore a hole in the fabric above my heart, now encrusted in stiff, dry blood. My fingers went to the spot and probed the flesh beneath. I found it perfectly mended; not even a scar remained. "He only wished for me to find peace in death."

The dark man, now sitting in a chair beside my box, leaned forward and ran his hand through my hair. "Mortals cannot be expected to understand us, and you should pay them no mind. They are no more to us than that hapless hare," *he said, gesturing towards the corner where the carcass lay. "They are akin to flies buzzing about our heads, pests, perhaps sustenance, nothing more."*

"But he is my true love."

The dark man smiled. "He is no more your true love than beefsteak is to a sailor returning from a year at sea."

I tried to stand, tried to exit the box, but my legs were still wobbly. "I must go to him."

"You will do no such thing."

"Am I a prisoner here?"

To this query, the dark man responded not at all. He simply rose and went to the door, pausing but briefly to say, "Rest," before leaving the chamber. I then heard the door's heavy lock engage. And I was alone.

When I finally stood up and got out of the box, I quietly went to the window, taking careful steps, and looked out. I did not recognize the countryside. There were mountains and rolling hills, nothing of the Ireland I was familiar with. I turned my gaze to the stars above and saw that the constellations were all wrong. I understood then that he had taken me to a distant place—where, exactly, I knew not.

———————

I SLEPT AFTER THAT—for how long, I could not be certain. When I awoke, I was again in my box, the soil of my homeland comforting to me, its texture and scent welcoming. *A peasant girl was in the room with me. I tried to speak to her, but she found my tongue unfamiliar. She just sat there, smiling at me nervously and pointing to a fresh basin of water on the table in the corner. Next to it was a note—*

> Refresh yourself, then join me in the dining
> room when you are ready. The girl is for you.
>
> —D

THERE WAS *a large four-poster bed in my room and lying atop it was the most beautiful gown I ever laid eyes upon. The royal blue fabric was soft to the touch, with a dark lace trim woven throughout in an intricate pattern. Next to the gown was a necklace with sparkling diamonds encircling a sizable red ruby. I could not even begin to calculate the worth of such a necklace, for the stones it displayed were larger than any I had ever seen or even could imagine existed.*

The peasant girl just then approached me from behind, and I felt her untying the laces of my white funeral dress, now brown, grimy with dirt and blood. It dropped to the floor and was pushed aside. She undertook the tedious task of washing me with a cloth from the basin. When I was finally cleansed, she assisted me into the blue gown. It fit perfectly. I wished I had a mirror, a habit I had yet to break, but there was none available, not that it would matter. She reached for the diamond-and-ruby necklace and secured it around my neck, then took a step back to admire her handiwork. A smile inched over her lips, and she bowed gently. I thanked her, fully aware she did not comprehend a word, then made for the door. She stopped me before I could leave and held up her wrist. There was a series of tiny bites evident along her forearm, marks I knew all too well.

At the thought of her blood, a need grew within me, an urgency. I had hoped this sick desire had passed after all the death I left in my wake, but it came over me stronger than ever as I looked down upon this poor girl's wrist, at the throbbing vein just beneath the surface of her skin. I would not take her, though; as I longed for a taste of her life, I could not take her.

I shook my head and turned away, pressing my hand to the door.

She understood this, and a look that mixed offense with relief crossed her face. She opened the door and led me down a narrow hallway, through a small octagonal chamber with no window to speak of, and into a large dining room. The dark man sat at the far end. A plate sat in front of him, but it was covered with years' worth of dust. I could not help but wonder if this room had ever seen any use.

"You are stunning," he said, gesturing to the empty chair at the opposite end of the table. "Please be seated."

I crossed the room and sat down.

He sniffed at the air, then said, "You did not drink of her? That is too bad. The blood of her family is amongst the purest of this land."

"And where, exactly, is this land?" I asked, trying to prevent the hostility I felt from coloring my voice.

"You are at my home deep within the Carpathian Mountains, near the Borgo Pass. You are safe here."

"Carpathian Mountains? Transylvania?"

He nodded.

"I wish to go home. I wish to leave immediately," I told him.

His face remained as rigid as stone at this request, his expression revealing nothing. Nearly five minutes passed before he spoke again. This pause was not unusual for us; time was of so little consequence, as I would later learn.

"I have saved your life and opened my home to you. I cared for you and provided nothing but love, yet you rebuff me. Had I not already been familiar with you and that which happened to you, I would take offense at this. But you have been through much, and I am patient; I can forgive such hostilities."

"I wish to leave," I said again.

The dark man leaned back in his chair. "You have not even asked me my name."

"I have no desire to know your name."

Again, we stared at each other for a long while. Next to me, the heartbeat of the young peasant girl began to quicken; I could see the vein pulsing at her neck. She, too, wished to leave and could not. I think this man somehow knew my thoughts had drifted to her, for he raised his hand and summoned her to his side. She walked around the table with trepidation, her heart quickening still.

At first, he did not acknowledge her presence beside him; his eyes remained fixed on me, then he reached for her hand, taking it slowly, deliberately slow. He raised her arm to his nose and smelled her, taking in her scent, her essence. When his lips curled back, when his teeth pierced her skin, the girl tried to remain strong, to appear brave, yet I knew better. The fear coursed through her.

He then drank of her blood.

The girl tensed yet did her best to remain still. Within a few moments, her eyes became heavy, her skin pasty. I feared he may drain the life from her—a queer thought, considering how many lives I have ended without regard, but a thought that occurred to me nonetheless. Just when I was about to tell him to stop, he released her. The girl stumbled backwards until she found purchase with the wall, where she slid to the floor and lost consciousness.

"You belong amongst your own kind," the dark man said, ignoring the small drop of blood trailing down his lip. "It may take time, but you will someday understand that."

He reached for a bell on a table to one side of him and rang it. An older woman appeared from a door at his left. She glanced down at the girl on the floor and quickly turned away.

"Please return the countess to her room," the dark man instructed.

"The countess?" I exclaimed aloud.

A small grin played at the corners of his mouth, but he said nothing to this. The older woman bowed and took me by the arm, leading me back to my room. The door locked behind me, and again I was alone.

I found pen and paper and wrote a letter to my beloved, the first of many. I knew they would never reach him because I had no means of posting them, but I took comfort in writing the words to him, in knowing he was out there.

When the sun began to rise, I removed the gown, put my stained white dress back on, climbed into the box, and slept until the following night.

———

I AWOKE TO A THIN VOICE. The young peasant girl from the previous night was standing over me.

"Countess Dolingen? The master has requested your presence."

The girl seemed to have recovered from the blood loss. She was still a bit pale but otherwise seemed normal.

"He is not my master," I replied.

She said nothing to this response, only offered a hand to help me step from the box that became my bed.

Again she led me to the dining room.

Again he sat at the head of the table.

Again I sat opposite him, our nonexistent meal laid out before us on the empty table. "I was dead; how did you bring me back?" I blurted this out before he had a chance to speak.

It was clear this man was not accustomed to someone challenging his authority, defying him, and he seemed taken aback by the thrust of my words, then slightly bemused. "Your killer stabbed you in the heart, this is true, but he stabbed you with a knife made of steel. Not even silver, mind you, steel. All he accomplished was to stun the heart until the blade was extracted, nothing more. Had he employed a wooden stake, you would not be sitting here this evening. But you were fortunate. His incompetence saved your life."

For this man to say something so harsh about my beloved, I wanted to dive across the table and rip out his throat. The anger that motivated me to slay so many when I was first reborn surged through my body—I forced it back, I forced it away. I did not want to be that hateful person, not anymore.

The dark man's eyes narrowed. Could he read my thoughts? I began to believe that he could. If he could, he must know I was so—

"You must eat," he said. "The rabbit's life may have sustained you, but only human blood will help you fully heal. You grow weaker by the hour."

At this admonition, the young servant girl came back into the room and stood beside the table. She was joined by a youth of no more than twelve. He came in behind her and stood tentatively at her side, his eyes turned to the ground.

"Choose," the dark man said.

"I choose to return home to my beloved; I want nothing more from you."

"Choose, or I will drain them both."

His eyes grew dark at this, a deep red the color of burning embers. The urge to take advantage of either the boy or the girl swelled within me. The blood coursing through their veins—I could see it, taste it. Still, I did not make a move.

The dark man slammed his fist down on the table and crossed the room in a blur. He lifted the boy by his neck and pushed his head aside. I heard his teeth tear into the flesh a moment before the scent of blood filled the room and yet I remained perfectly inert. When he finished his macabre meal, he threw the boy's limp body at me. The corpse landed on the table and slid across it, coming to a stop mere inches from me. The boy's glassy stare reassured me he was, indeed, dead.

The dark man crossed the chamber and picked me up by the neck, as he had the boy, and dragged me from the dining room down a series of hallways and staircases. I kicked at him as we went, but he was too strong for me. He carried me like I weighed nothing into the deepest heart of the castle. He carried me to a dungeon and tossed me inside. I scuttled to the far corner and cowered like a broken dog. I wanted to stand up to him, I wanted to show him I was not scared of him, but in that very moment I most certainly was afraid.

Without a word, the door closed and the lock was engaged, and I found myself in utter darkness. At least a week passed, possibly two, and then the door was finally opened again, and an older woman was pushed inside with me. She fell to the floor at the center of the room, and again the door was locked. When she recovered from this rough treatment, when her eyes adjusted to the gloom, she discovered me in my corner. "My blood is your blood," she said in a whisper.

"I will not," I told her. I was so weak; I needed it badly. I refused to hurt her, though; I would die before I hurt another.

"My blood is your blood," she repeated. "If you do not, he will kill one more of my children. I cannot bear to lose another."

Two more days passed. When I woke on the third day, the old woman was looming over me with a knife. "Do not let him hurt my children," she said, before plunging the knife deep into the artery at her neck. Her body collapsed on top of me, and my mouth went to the wound and I drank. I drank until there was no more.

When I was allowed to return to my room, my wooden box had been replaced with a stone coffin. The soil of my homeland filled the bottom, and I found this to be a welcome sight. A dozen other dresses hung in the armoire now, all tailored perfectly to fit my body. I washed myself at the basin, changed into a new dress, sat at the desk, and wrote another letter to my beloved. I wrote until nearly dawn, before climbing into my new coffin and allowing sleep to wash over me.

———

SIX MONTHS PASSED LIKE THIS, always the same ritual. I marked time by counting the letters I wrote to my beloved, all of which were hidden beneath a loose stone in the floor. I awoke on my hundred and eighty-third night to find the stone pried aside and my letters gone. The door to my room stood open, the first time since I arrived here, and I went down the hallway alone. I found the dining room empty. Another door to the right of the dining room stood open; on all my previous forays, it had been closed and locked. I stepped inside and found myself in a library of sorts, with thousands of texts in varied languages, and most appearing extraordinarily old, lining the shelves. Tapestries, thick with dust, hung on some of the walls. On a table at the center of the room were all my letters to my beloved in a neat stack. Beside them stood another stack, this one all legal documents—deeds and trusts, property transferred to the name the man had given me, one Countess Dolingen.

I wandered the halls of the castle and found no one. I considered leaving by way of one of the windows, but I had no place to go and little knowledge of where I was; the risk was too great. Instead, I searched room after room. I located the man's chambers, and many others as well, most undisturbed for who knows how long. Some housed nothing more than broken furniture and shredded draperies, others were filled with riches, more gold than I ever conceived possible. There was no sign of the dark man or the few servants I had seen since arriving at the castle. The only sign of life was the rats scurrying about, the incessant tick, tick, tick of their tiny nails on the cold stone floor. I would end up drinking the blood of a number of these unsuspecting rats before the dark man finally returned.

I AM NOT SURE HOW LONG he was gone, but on a night shortly after the leaves of fall began to turn color I woke in my coffin to the sound of a scuffle outside. I went to my bedchamber window, which overlooked the castle's courtyard, and found the man standing beside a coach drawn by a team of six large black horses. He looked up at me and smiled. "Ah, my lovely countess. Please join us. I have something for you!"

He pulled a man from the coach and dropped him at the ground by his feet. His head was covered with a black sack, and his hands were tied behind his back. I did not need to see his face to know who he was; I recognized his scent even from where I stood.

I launched myself through the open window and landed in a crouch on the cobblestone below.

"That is impressive!" the dark man said. "I usually climb down."

I started towards him, and he raised a hand. "Stop!"

In an instant, he had a blade pressed against his captive's throat.

"Do not hurt him!"

The dark man pulled the sack from the man's head, and my beloved looked back at me, seeing me for the first time in years. I knew I had not changed in his eyes, I had not aged even a minute since he last saw me, and I heard his heart beat wildly in his chest as he regarded me now. His blond hair had grayed a little, and his face appeared a little harder, but otherwise he had not changed much, either. I would not have cared, in truth, if he had aged into an old man, crippled and near death. The love that coursed through me burned, and I wanted to go to him, to hold him, to never let him go.

"Is this the man you have been writing to? The man who owns your heart?"

I could not help but nod, and even with a knife pressed to his throat, I saw a sparkle in my beloved's eye that told me he felt the same about me. He loved me now, right now, more than ever before.

The dark man frowned. "But how can that be? He left you in that castle as you were tortured for years. When you finally returned to him, he plunged a knife into your heart and buried you beneath a pile of rocks, left to rot into the earth. How can you love such a man?"

"My heart belongs to him; it always has, it always will," I said softly, holding back the tears that clouded my eyes with a red mist.

The dark man scoffed at this. "I saved you from death. I give you everything you could possibly desire, yet you feel nothing for me. You and I are of the same kind and we belong together, not you and this man—do you not realize that? He will be dead soon, just a pile of bones, while you and I will live on. Together, there is so much we can do; you only need to open your eyes and see it. Open your heart and let me in."

He never said such things to me before; and, until that very moment, I thought of myself as nothing more than his prisoner. The idea of loving such a man filled me with dread. I could not do it.

As this thought passed through my mind, the man's eyes narrowed, and he let out a ferocious scream, one so loud it echoed off the mountains around us.

The howls of a thousand wolves answered him, so loudly I heard nothing else. In an instant, he raised my beloved to his feet. It was then that I realized just how weak my beloved truly was, how sallow his skin appeared. It was then that I saw the marks upon his neck and realized the dark man had drunk of him, had drained his blood nearly to the point of death.

The dark man raised his own wrist to his mouth and tore it open with his sharp fangs, then pressed it to the lips of my beloved. I froze in horror as he drank, for I then knew this was not the first time. They had made this exchange a number of times on the trip back from Ireland to this forsaken place; more of the dark man's blood flowed through his veins, in fact, than his own. My beloved drank until he could drink no more. Then the dark man released him, letting his body crumple to the floor.

The loss of blood weakened the dark man, but only for a moment. He forced himself to stand erect to his full height and snapped his long, bony fingers. A dozen men appeared—Szgany, I was to learn later, gypsies from the local area. Four came up behind me and bound me with ropes laced with silver. I tried to break free, but the silver somehow held me still, and where it touched my skin it burned. I struggled, but they were able to hold me, each tugging their rope taut so I was held captive in the middle of them, unable to reach any one of them. I cursed the fact that I had drunk nothing but rat blood for so long. With human blood, I might have been able to overpower the Szgany, but now I was too weak. I was a prisoner once again.

I watched my beloved turn.

I watched as the last of the life left his body and the blood of this man took over. For much of the night, in truth, I could do nothing but watch. All the while, the dark man stood over him while the Szgany continued holding me still.

When my beloved finally awoke and looked out upon the world with reborn eyes, the dark man removed one of his rings and slipped it onto my beloved's finger. "This is in case anyone should wonder to whom you belong," he said.

The dark man stood over him and again snapped his fingers. The Szgany unhitched the horses and positioned them in a circle around my beloved. Then they began to tie their silver ropes to my beloved's limbs and around his neck, the other ends fastened to the horses' harnesses, and I realized what was about to transpire and cried out, but my protest fell on deaf ears. The dark man held on to my beloved until the ropes were secured and he was now at the center of this pinwheel of horses. I cried out to him to try to break free, but he was still lost, groggy and disoriented, unaware of the predicament he was in. The Szgany stood at the ready beside the horses.

"Please, do not do this," I pleaded.

"You have done this to yourself. You brought this upon him." The dark man snapped his fingers again, and each of the Szgany brandished a small dagger and plunged it into his horse's flank. As if one, the horses screamed in pain, lunged forward, and began to run.

I watched in horror as my beloved was torn to pieces, his arms, legs, and head separated from his torso with sickening snaps. The gypsies had closed the gates to the courtyard, so the horses had no escape. After a few minutes, they stopped their wild run to nowhere, and the pieces of what used to be a man littered the ground around us.

The dark man walked over to my beloved's violated torso and plunged his hand into the chest, pulling out the still-beating heart. He held it out to ensure I saw what he had done.

I could say nothing at this point, my voice silenced. I would not have been capable of hearing anyway over the screams reverberating in my mind. I collapsed to the ground and cried as the Szgany kept me held fast with their silver ropes.

The Szgany gathered the remains and deposited them into wooden boxes, then loaded the boxes onto the floor of the coach. My beloved's heart was placed in a box all its own, a small red oak box with gold clasps, also loaded onto the coach. When they were finished, the horses were harnessed again and the dark man gave instructions to the driver and sent him on his way.

At this point, the Szgany released me, too. It mattered little; I could not have moved even if I had wanted to.

The dark man came over and knelt at my side. "My men have been ordered to bury each piece of him in a separate cemetery, never to be found. His body will never die. His soul will suffer for eternity as a member of the legions of the undead. All of this brought on by you. If you wish to hate me, so be it; now you have good reason."

He stood up and started for the castle door, adding, "It will be light soon; return to your room. Tomorrow, I have commissioned someone to paint your portrait. I wish to capture this moment forever."

———

THE FOLLOWING DAY, an artist did arrive, and the dark man made me pose for the artist, just as he said he would. I was too distraught to argue and did as I was told. I even wore the diamond necklace with the ruby at the center. Shortly after we began, the dark man presented me with a belt with a brooch at its center with a depiction of a dragon; I wore this trinket also. The painting was atrocious, looking nothing like me

The word hate does not begin to describe my feelings for this man, this awful creature, this beast. I loathed him so, but there was nothing I could do. I was his prisoner, both in body and in mind. Yet he spoke not once of his atrociousness, of the dreadful things he had done to my beloved. After this day, he acted as if the brutal events had never taken place. He expected me to love him! He wished to make a wife out of me! Of course, I could not love him, could not consent to be his wife, not ever, but my protests did not dissuade him. At every opportunity, he professed his love for me. He lavished gifts upon me—priceless jewels and properties and every luxury he could imagine. I had escaped from one prison only to be imprisoned once again. I graciously accepted these offerings, but offered no love in return. Instead, his gifts were strategically hidden around the castle.

Hundreds of years would pass like this. Fluid and fast, seeming like months. The two of us existed in the castle, with no one else in attendance other than a constant flux of revolving servants. They came and went, as they aged over time—daughters would become mothers, who would then become grandmothers, and their ways would pass to the next generation, but the dark man and I did not age. I refused to learn the servants' names or anything about them. I also refused to reveal to the dark man a single thing about which I cared that could be held as ransom over my head. I spoke to him only when spoken to, and only because I knew others would suffer if I did not. He had no qualms about killing these servants and he did so at every opportunity.

I knew he read my thoughts, and in time I learned to read his, too, and soon words became of little use to either of us. I found I was able to shield my thoughts from him by concentrating, and although he did the same, he slipped occasionally. I utilized these lapses to venture into his mind, to search. I found that when he rested, I could venture even further, so I began to awake earlier than he and go to his coffin and sift through his sleeping brain. I eventually learned the whereabouts of my beloved, where the decapitated head and each ripped-away appendage had been buried. The man had had him scattered all over the continent, but I was able to determine the locations and made notes on the maps I scavenged from the dark man's library.

I was patient.

The years taught me patience.

I waited for—

"BRAM!" Matilda screamed. "Let go of him!"

My eyes fluttered open, and I was once again standing in the small chamber atop the central tower of Whitby Abbey. In reality, only seconds had passed. Matilda and Thornley were trying to push past Patrick O'Cuiv, but he kept them from entering the room. Vambéry still crouched at the large oak door. Ellen was still inches from me, her fingers resting against my temple. There were tears in her eyes and a sadness so deep I began to weep as well.

"You escaped?" I managed to say.

Ellen nodded. "In 1847, after hundreds of years as his prisoner."

"So when you came to us, to our family—"

"I hid in your house; he wouldn't think to search for me amongst humans. I didn't believe so anyway."

Our minds were still strangely linked, and words passed seamlessly between us, entire conversations, years of memories, in what seemed only a matter of seconds. "You've been searching for the remains of your beloved?" I inquired softly. "You came to Clontarf to find his arm, buried amongst the suicide graves at Saint John the Baptist, the place so marked on your map. You didn't mean to stay with us for so long; you put us in danger, which you didn't want to do, but you did nonetheless. What you did to me—"

Ellen placed her finger on my lips and hushed me. "I never meant to hurt your family; I never would. You were such a sickly boy, only days from death; I could not watch that happen. I couldn't watch them treat you with such primitive methods, knowing it did no good, knowing I could help. I had to help. So I gave you my blood." Her eyes fell to the floor. "Penance, I suppose, for all the lives I took years past, when I first turned, before I realized the true value of life and love."

"And you've visited me again and again since that night," I said.

"I have watched over you, yes. You must know, Bram, there is no permanent cure. Without my blood, your illness will return to claim you. I've never let that happen. I will never let it."

My eyes widened as another thought entered my mind. "Your beloved's name, it was Deaglan O'Cuiv! The great, distant ancestor of Patrick O'Cuiv, their family and blood." More thoughts rushed in, and I had to close my eyes to concentrate, to sort them all out and make sense of them. "Patrick O'Cuiv did not kill his family; this dark man, this Dracul, did—when he came to Ireland in search of you!"

Ellen sighed and closed her eyes, as if just hearing this explanation brought her pain. "That poor woman and the children, he killed them all. I had no choice but to turn Patrick and Maggie; he would have returned for them, too. I turned Patrick while he was in his cell; that is how he survived a mortal's death. I turned Maggie shortly thereafter, knowing it was the only way to protect her. Can you not see? I had to leave your home after that; I had to draw him away from there before he came for your family. He was so close."

I said, "It took him fourteen years, but he did come for us. And he took Emily."

Ellen's eyes dropped to the floor. "Time is of little consideration for him. He wants you now, too. He wants you more than anything. Because my blood flows within you, you escaped death; because of my actions, you walk the earth today. He will not rest until he takes all that is dear to me. He knew taking Emily would draw me out, and you as well. He simply took her to bring both of us to him."

"And what of your beloved, Deaglan O'Cuiv?"

At this, her gaze went to the thick oak door at the back of the room.

NOW

Bram stares at what remains of the last white rose, now shriveled and dead at the foot of the door, its once-beautiful bloom now nothing more than dust covered by muck and filth. Snakes slithered through these dregs, leaving their trails behind them, their fangs gleaming in the pale light as they circle, then prepare to—

Bells!

Bram hears church bells.

The bells of St. Mary's Church, adjacent to the abbey.

Loud bells, above all else.

With the bells come the dawn, a thin strip of sunlight cutting through from the east and burning away the shadows of night.

The banging on the door ceases.

The hissing of the snakes dies.

All goes quiet.

His back against the wall, Bram's arm continues to slice through the air even after the snakes disappear, wielding the bowie knife at nothing more than phantoms in the gray light.

Gone.

All of them gone.

Bram finally falls still and slides down the wall to the floor in utter exhaustion.

He wants to stand up and look out the window, but he does not have the strength. No matter, he knows the man is gone. He knows Emily is gone, too. They both vanished with the first light of dawn.

No SLEEP.

Not yet.

He pulls the journal from his pocket and turns to a blank page.

It will only be a matter of time before the others return. He has to finish writing.

THE JOURNAL *of* BRAM STOKER

———❖———

17 August 1868, 8:22 p.m. — "Bram? What is happening?" It was Matilda. She was still trying to push past Patrick and Maggie O'Cuiv. She gasped at the sight of Ellen.

"It's okay, Matilda. I'm okay."

From the corner of my eye, I saw Vambéry glance at his sword, and I gently shook my head.

"Ellen is not the enemy," I said. "And they are not the enemy," I added, gesturing towards Patrick and Maggie O'Cuiv. "We've got this all wrong."

"They are undead!" Vambéry growled. "Of course they are the enemy!"

I picked up Vambéry's sword and inserted the blade back in the cane, holding it out of reach. "Let them in," I told Patrick O'Cuiv.

He looked to Ellen for approval, then stepped aside.

Matilda ran to where I stood and wrapped her arms around me, her eyes locked on Ellen. Thornley stepped in behind her, lugging what appeared to be a very heavy box. He set it down just inside the door, watching me with a wary eye.

"Please tell them what you showed me," I instructed Ellen. "Tell them all of it."

For the next hour, she did just that.

. . .

I LISTENED IN SILENCE as she revealed the entire story, trying to hold back the emotion as she did so, but it was painfully obvious that she loved Deaglan O'Cuiv with all her heart, as she did his relatives, his blood. I watched Maggie and Patrick O'Cuiv as Ellen spoke, I watched the emotions flood their pale faces, I watched Maggie cry tears of red as Ellen explained how the dark man had punished him, punished her. Then Ellen told us how she spent the last seventeen years seeking out each part of Deaglan O'Cuiv's body—buried in suicide graves around the continent, with the exception of his heart. After recovering them, she had hidden his body in numerous places over the years, from the tower at Artane Castle to the waters of Ireland's bogs, ultimately bringing them here and locking them behind the door in this very room.

"The hand we found in Artane Castle belonged to Deaglan O'Cuiv," Matilda said softly to no one in particular.

"It was alive," I told her. "We both saw it move."

"I thought we imagined it, all these years . . ."

"He cannot die, nor can his body," Ellen went on. "Not like this. Perhaps if he were burned or his heart pierced with a wooden stake, but as long as his soul is trapped within that cursed body, he lives. In this weakened state, his mind is not his own; he belongs to Dracul, to the man whose spoiled blood circulates in his forlorn flesh."

Ellen's gaze fell to the floor. "I've tried to speak to him, but he is in such agony. His every thought is manipulated by Dracul. Anytime I sense my beloved, Dracul snatches him away."

Vambéry snickered, his eyes longing for his sword. "You've been trying to speak to a box of body parts? This is preposterous!"

Ellen turned towards him, the anger and frustration burning in her glare. "It's Dracul's blood that makes him so! If his entire body can be brought back together, it will heal, of this I'm certain. Deaglan will come back to me."

"Where is his heart?" I asked, ignoring Vambéry's outburst.

Ellen sighed. "I only recently learned its true location. Dracul hid the heart well in a small village outside of Munich. He guarded this position most of all, but he let it slip two nights ago; I found the location in his thoughts." She paused for a second. "His guard fell when he took Emily, and I plucked it from his mind."

"What does he mean to do with Emily?" Thornley asked, his voice thin.

"She's bait," I replied before Ellen could answer. "He wants to draw us all out. Everyone who knows of him. I don't believe for a second he let this location near Munich be known by accident. He wants us to go there."

"How do we know Deaglan's heart is even there? Maybe this is all a lie," Matilda said.

"It's there," Ellen assured her. "Of that I'm certain."

"Why are we even discussing this?" Vambéry blurted out. "Whatever is behind this door should be burned to ash. We need to release the souls of these undead; that is God's way, and it is the only way! Their plight is meaningless!"

Maggie O'Cuiv crossed the room with ungodly speed, her feet almost leaving the floor, seeming to float within inches of Vambéry and looking him square in the eye. "We are all that stand between you and him. He will hunt each of you down one by one, and when he is done with you, he will go after your families. He has nothing but time."

"If we are so frail, then why do you need us?" Vambéry replied. "Surely you do need us or you wouldn't be informing us of these details. You would have killed us already."

Ellen placed a calming hand on Maggie's arm and turned to Vambéry. "You are right, we cannot do this alone."

"What do you mean?" I asked.

"'This place where he has hidden Deaglan's heart, the locals call it the Village of the Dead. Legend has it that hundreds of years ago nearly everyone in the village died by some unseen cause and after being buried, sounds were heard coming from their graves. A few of the graves were opened in the light of day and the bodies therein were found to be rosy with life and their mouths fresh with red blood.'"

"More *strigoi*," Vambéry muttered.

"*Strigoi?*"

"Vampire, the undead," Vambéry said.

"Dracul did this when he hid the remains of my beloved Deaglan."

Matilda looked to me and I knew she had this realization at the same moment I had, but I was first to speak. "When he brought Deaglan's heart to this place, he killed everyone in the village, turning them into undead to protect this hideous place."

Ellen nodded. "An army of undead, all at his command. We cannot enter that place, we are too far outnumbered."

"But we can if we go during daylight hours," Vambéry said softly.

"I don't understand," Thornley said.

Vambéry nodded towards both O'Cuivs, then towards Ellen. "Their abilities and strengths are great, but only under the cloak of night. During daylight hours, they are no stronger than us—weaker, even. Most of the undead rest when the sun comes out; they hide, they are too vulnerable during that time. You saw this with Emily. If we come upon this place during the day, we can enter and retrieve O'Cuiv's heart with little to no risk of intervention."

"Dracul will surely be there; you can strike him down while he rests and rid yourself of his threat," Ellen added.

I saw Vambéry's eyes brighten at this, at the thought of destroying this source of evil.

"What about Emily?" Thornley asked. "What would that mean for her?"

"She could be saved. If Dracul dies, the hold he carries over Emily dies with him," Vambéry explained. "She will be of his blood no longer."

"What of Deaglan O'Cuiv," I said. "Would this not kill him?"

"Not if his body has been made whole again. I can sustain him," Ellen replied with certainty. "I will give Deaglan my blood before you kill Dracul. This is the only way to ensure he is released from Dracul's grip."

Matilda went to Ellen and took her hand in her own. "If no one else will say it, I will," she announced boldly but softly, drawing in a deep breath. "We will help you; we will help one another." Her gaze fell on me, then on Thornley and Vambéry in turn, lingering perhaps a moment longer on the latter. "We will help you find the heart of your beloved. We will reunite you with the man who brought you the only happiness you have ever known, and you will help us to free Emily, to bring her back to Thornley, so we may end this nightmare. Then together we shall all rid the earth of Dracul. We will triumph or we will fail together."

Ellen squeezed Matilda's hand, her eyes glistening. "The happiness brought to me by Deaglan can only be eclipsed by the joy I experienced with your family. I have, and will, do everything I can to keep you safe." Ellen looked to me as she offered this last promise. I could not help but wonder if there was a deeper meaning underlying her words.

"WE SHOULD NOT STAY HERE, not all of us in one place." This came from Patrick O'Cuiv and took us all by surprise; I realized I hadn't heard his thick Irish brogue since I was a child. He crossed to the window and looked out over the abbey grounds, past the cemetery, and to the forest beyond. "Some should remain to guard Deaglan while the rest make preparations."

Something crashed against the inside of the large oak door. Matilda let out a cry, and we all turned towards it. Another loud bang followed the first.

"He's awake," Maggie said.

Vambéry stepped back from the door. "Who is awake? You said he was nothing but body parts in a box."

Ellen raised a finger to her lips. With her free hand, she reached out and grasped my forearm. I heard her voice in my head:

DRACUL CAN SEE AND HEAR *by utilizing Deaglan as a conduit; they are of the same blood. As long as my beloved remains locked in that room, isolated, Dracul cannot tell where he is. He is blind, and the location unknown to him. If he knew, he would surely come for Deaglan, for us. We must not speak of the locale or our plans, not aloud, not here. Dracul is near, though, so very near. Deaglan cannot be left unguarded, not now.*

HAD I UNDERSTOOD what was to come, what sacrifices would need to be made, what cost would be incurred by us all, I might not have volunteered to stay overnight in the Whitby Abbey tower keep and watch over Deaglan O'Cuiv's remains while the others prepared for our journey—not with Vambéry, maybe not at all.

17 AUGUST 1868, 9:30 p.m.—It is important to note that it had to be me who stayed behind. I did not trust Vambéry alone, none of us did after his outburst, and he insisted on staying. If given the opportunity, Vambéry would probably open the door and set Deaglan's remains afire. He would rain down destruction upon us no matter the penalty. Patrick O'Cuiv must have harbored similar feelings because he insisted on remaining in the tower as well. Thornley and the others left to book passage and settle our bill at the inn. They would then wait there until

morning. We all agreed that it would be best to leave at first light, when Dracul and the undead were at their weakest and most vulnerable.

I was right to worry about Vambéry, for the moment the others left he announced, "Whatever is inside this room is evil, Bram. It cannot be allowed. We need to end it."

He said this with no regard to Patrick O'Cuiv, who was standing at the window, an unmoving sentry.

Vambéry's cane leaned against the wall in the far corner, out of his reach. I felt ill at ease around this man, friend to Thornley or not; he regarded me in much the same way he did Patrick. Part of me expected him to wield that sword to try to strike us both down. Thornley insisted such was not the case. Vambéry was a reasonable man, he said. But, still, I could not help but distrust him.

"You heard what Ellen said. The man behind this door is not our enemy."

"What lies behind this door is not a man at all," Vambéry replied. He had brought our bags into the room and was shuffling through their contents. "I do not trust your Ellen or her traveling companions any more than I trust Dracul. I think you are blinded by some childhood allegiances and memories. You and your brother and sister are not thinking rationally, so I must do the thinking for one and all."

He pulled out a large crucifix and held it up to the lamplight.

Although Patrick O'Cuiv's back was turned, he somehow sensed the cross's presence. He turned around and faced Vambéry. "Put that away!" he hissed.

"I will not. If our purpose here tonight is to keep *strigoi* out, then I plan to do just that. Perhaps you should wait outside."

O'Cuiv gave me a weary look, then moved past us both in an instant, finding a place in the hallway just outside the room.

Vambéry pulled out a hammer and nails and affixed the cross to the wall next to the door. He then retrieved a second crucifix, followed by a third. "Perhaps you might help?" he said.

I located a second hammer in Vambéry's bag and started on the other side of the room. When we ran out of crosses, we hung mirrors, all that we had in our possession. The better part of an hour elapsed before we finished. Vambéry nodded at my bowie knife. "Carve crosses into all open surfaces; leave nothing unmarked. The mirrors tend to confuse these beasts, if only by multiplying the number of crosses."

As I went about this task, Vambéry placed garlic and holy wafers into a small bowl and crushed them with the handle of his knife, he then added water and stirred the mixture until it formed a thick paste like he did at Thornley's home. Then, using the blade, he forced it into the space where the thick oak door met the surrounding stone. "*Strigoi* can become mist and pass through even the tiniest of cracks. This will prevent anything from getting in or out. The water is holy."

The scent of the paste was strong, and Patrick O'Cuiv shuffled uncomfortably out in the hallway when he smelled it.

Vambéry began to sweat. He paused for a moment, steadying himself against the door.

"Are you all right?"

Vambéry nodded, but he did not appear well. I thought it was his anger boiling up inside him, but this reaction was something else entirely. He finished applying the paste, then retrieved one of the white roses from the basket he purchased earlier. He invoked a prayer in a whisper, stumbling over the words, then placed the blossom at the foot of the door. "No *strigoi* can leave his grave if he must pass such a rose, and most assuredly the chamber behind that door is nothing short of a tomb."

These last words were forced out with no small effort on Vambéry's part. His eyes rolled back in his sockets, and I managed to reach him just before he collapsed and was able to ease him to the ground. His skin was cold and clammy.

I sensed something behind the door, a presence. Something stronger than anything I had ever encountered.

"Arminius?"

The man's eyelids fluttered, and his mouth moved as if to speak, but he said nothing.

"What is going on in there?" Patrick O'Cuiv said from the hallway, no longer able to look into the room now filled with crosses and mirrors.

"Vambéry passed out."

"Not Vambéry," O'Cuiv replied. "There is something happening behind the door."

"I . . . I do not know." I felt it, too, though. Whatever it was grew stronger, pulled at me in much the same way Nanna Ellen had when I was but a child. I wanted to open the door, wanted to wipe away the paste Vambéry applied there and stomp the rose to dust. I wanted to open the door and let it out. I felt it reach for my mind and wrap around my skull, these shadowy fingers groping, kneading at my thoughts.

I look forward to meeting you, Bram.

Vambéry mouthed this greeting, but not a sound escaped his lips; instead, I heard the words in my imagination only. He was unconscious, of this I was positively sure, yet his mouth moved again.

I learned so much about you from Ellen. She thinks so highly of you. Your sister as well. And your brother. Such a resourceful family. I can smell her blood in your veins, her sweet blood. And she so loves the taste of your blood. I cannot wait to sample it myself, Bram. In all these years, do you realize I never fed on your Nanna Ellen? I never had her blood on my lips. To know that, soon, I will taste not only hers but yours . . .

Vambéry's pulse was racing, and he was breathing in quick, short gasps. Too, every muscle in his body had contracted and tensed. His fingertips were extended so far, they appeared to bend back towards the top of his wrists. He continued to mouth the words I heard only in my head.

Poor Deaglan O'Cuiv, only half a man living in a box. Why do you not let him out? Let him breathe. Let him enjoy the night. He has been imprisoned for so long, I think he deserves that, do you not?

"Do not open that door, Bram! Dracul speaks through your friend somehow and it is trickery. You cannot trust your eyes and ears." Patrick paced with frustration in the hallway, unable to so much as peek into this room.

Is that Patrick O'Cuiv I hear? Come to put his great-great-great-grand-uncle back together again for our lovely Ellen? Please thank him for his hospitality; I so enjoyed spending time with his wife and children. I am sorry I could not stay longer, but I suppose I stayed long enough. His little boy cried out for him moments before I took his life. He expected his father to save him; so naïve and sweet—Sean, I believe? Oh, and little Isobelle! She thought I was her father when I reached down into her bed and brought her little body to my lips. The young can be so trusting. In all my years, I found nothing to compete with the blood of a young child, always so fresh and clean, free of the pollutants most adults allow their bodies to ingest. I only wish I could drain her veins again and again. Then there was Maggie! That Maggie was a clever one, to hide from me. Now that Ellen has turned her, perhaps I will take her as a child when this travail is all brought to a conclusion. She and the lovely Emily can come back with me when our little game has ended and the lot of you are being feasted upon by the worms.

A loud bang resonated through the tower, and I realized Patrick had struck the wall. Dust flickered down from the ceiling, raining upon the floor.

I noticed Vambéry's hand, then, his palm covered with an inky, sticky substance. Something had oozed out from under the door; he must have touched it while applying his holy paste. I realized this thick liquid had created a bond between him and Dracul. The bond through which Dracul now spoke.

You will wait for me, won't you, Bram? Right there on that very spot? I can be there soon. You only need to tell me where you hide. Why don't we take a look? Get our bearings?

At this, Vambéry's eyes snapped open, and he sat up perfectly straight, taking in every square inch of the room. His head pivoted from side to side, then up and down. He broke from my grasp and raced to the window before I could stop him. He gazed up at the stars, then down at the grounds, at the town, the graveyard, the forest, and the ocean beyond.

Ah, yes, of course, his voice said through Vambéry's lips. *Where else?* Then silence.

Vambéry fell to the ground at my feet and mumbled soft, incoherent words. Then his eyes fluttered open, his breathing returned to normal.

Patrick spoke from the hallway. "We must get him out of here. As long as he is near that door, Dracul can reach him and make use of him again. You and I are protected by Ellen's blood; he is weak and therefore open."

I knew he was right, and even before Vambéry had fully recovered I carried his limp body out to the hallway and handed it to Patrick O'Cuiv. "Take him back to the inn, to be with the others, away from here. I will guard the door until morning." I showed him the stain on Vambéry's palm. "Wash away this blot on his hand thoroughly."

Patrick eyed me worriedly but knew I was right. "I will return to help you."

I shook my head. "Stay with the others, protect them. He cannot get in here, I'll be fine."

I gestured to the crucifixes and looking glasses on the walls—a futile effort, admittedly, for he could not gaze upon them. That very fact proved my point. I retrieved Vambéry's cane and handed it to Patrick. "When he wakes, return this to him. Perhaps it will help muster trust between you and he. Although you may not believe so, we will need him, his expertise."

Patrick took the cane in his other hand.

"Now go before Dracul tries to invade his body once again."

With that, he was gone, hoisting Vambéry up as if he weighed nothing and disappearing back into the bowels of the abbey.

And then I was alone in the room, my eyes fixed on the door, the presence lurking behind it crowding my every thought. I pulled the rifle from Thornley's bag and sat in the chair.

I now faced the long night ahead.

PART III

It is not a mere fabrication of theologians that Hell exists, for it is right here on earth. I have personally stood at its border and seen the devils carry out their work.

—Bram Stoker, *Makt Myrkranna*

NOW

ARMINIUS

Arminius Vambéry, lying upon a soft bed at the inn, awakens with the first light of morning, remembering nothing of how he got there, nothing beyond being in the tower keep of Whitby Abbey with Bram and Patrick O'Cuiv.

Matilda is hovering over him, a warm, damp cloth in hand. "He is awake," she says to someone behind her.

Thornley.

The two of them help Vambéry sit upright. Every wretched bone and muscle in his body aches.

"Are you able to stand?" Matlida asks. "To walk?"

"I believe so."

"You must," Thornley announces most impatiently. "Our train awaits, and we need to retrieve Bram—he is still in the Whitby Abbey keep."

There is no sign of the undead; Ellen, Maggie, and that monster Patrick no doubt are deep in slumber.

Vambéry, weak and disoriented, is in somewhat of a haze when they exit the inn, but climbing the one hundred and ninety-nine steps to the abbey for yet a second time cures him of that. At the top of the stairs, however, his bad leg is throbbing. The events up to this point seem but a dream, by his reckoning, but now are beginning to take on a decidedly realistic quality as the three of them make their way through the abbey, climb the ladder hidden in the chimney, then ascend yet more stairs to the tower keep.

They find Bram lying in the corner of the chamber, nearly unconscious due to exhaustion. He grasps his journal in one hand, the other hand resting on the stock of the trusty Snider–Enfield rifle. He looks as if he has aged a good ten years in the span of a single night.

"Dracul knows we are here," Bram says. "*He* was here, but I kept him at bay."

Matilda goes to Bram and tenderly runs her hand through his hair. "Patrick told us. You were such a brave fool to stay here all alone," she whispers at his ear. "I should kill you myself, knowing you wish for death so heartily. We tried to come back last night to help you, but Ellen would not allow it. They kept watch over us at the inn and insisted you would be safe."

Thornley and Vambéry assist Bram to his feet, help steady him. It is then Bram pats the leather cover of his journal and nods at Vambéry. "This will help you to understand all," he offers weakly.

The damp room reeks of death. The floor is muddy and covered with tiny stones that resemble the coiled fossilized remains of serpents. The crucifixes and mirrors on the walls are either broken or twisted out of shape, and any number of them have crashed to the floor.

"What happened here?" Thornley asks.

In response, Bram only raises his hand and shakes his head. "Later . . . What about the train?"

"We leave in an hour," Matilda replies.

It takes Bram a moment to comprehend what she has said. "Ellen?" he finally inquires.

Matilda glances at Vambéry and, lowering her voice, says, "She and the others have already been put aboard the train."

Vambéry can picture them, the undead trio, sealed in their crates and sleeping upon beds of soil, more vulnerable now than at any other time. They must be in one of the cargo cars, but he has no way to know which. His fingers tighten on the knob of his cane, which he found on the floor next to his bed.

Thornley nods towards the heavy oak door at the far reaches of the room. "We need to make haste."

Bram is staring at the door, and Vambéry sees hesitancy in his eyes, fear.

"We promised," Matilda says.

He thinks about this for a second, then nods. Reaching into his pocket, he pulls out the tarnished brass key Ellen had given him and goes to the door. He slips the key into the heavy lock at the center and twists it; a loud click echoes through the room as the bolts on either side retract.

Bram reaches for the handle and pulls open the door.

If the room in which they stood smelled of death, the room beyond the door reeks of a tomb. Flakes of dried paste fall from the edges of the door, and the mud that covers the floor gives off an odor so noxious it seems to push back at them. The three squint and cover their noses before stepping inside.

The chamber isn't very large, only about eight feet in diameter, with no window or other means of egress. At the center of the room stands a wooden trunk about two feet deep and four feet long—no larger than one would use to transport clothing for a long trip. The same trunk Bram saw in his vision of Ellen at the bog—every inch of the exterior covered in tiny crosses carved into the wood.

The lid of the trunk is ajar.

They approach and peer inside.

Lying in the trunk, with soil loosely tossed overtop, are the remains of a man. Vambéry sees there is a leg and two arms protruding from the soil, along with part of a torso. On the far end, a man's head; only the eyes and the tip of a nose visible of the face, his eyes closed as if in slumber. As Vambéry understands it, the man died hundreds of years ago, but his remains are remarkably preserved. Vambéry tries not to look at the torn flesh on the neck, where the head once was connected to the man's torso.

"Deaglan O'Cuiv," Thornley says.

Vambéry watches as Bram reaches through his open shirt collar and pulls out the ring he is wearing on a chain around his neck. He lifts the chain over his head, removes the ring and slips it on one of the fingers protruding from the soil. "This belongs to you."

The finger twitches.

"Remarkable," Vambéry says softly. He reaches inside and brushes some of the dirt from the man's face. "The flesh is cold, yet there is still life."

Deaglan O'Cuiv's eyes flutter, and his mouth distorts in a soundless scream. Vambéry snatches his hand away.

"To spend eternity in such pain . . ." Matilda says, leaving the thought unfinished as O'Cuiv's eyes slowly close again.

The man's torso is barely visible, but Vambéry sees the wound where the man's heart had been yanked from his breast, the void left behind now filled with soil. How any of this is possible, he does not know, yet here it is. "I cannot look at this anymore," he says, reaching for the lid of the trunk and shutting it.

The old brass latches clatter together, and Thornley secures each, then turns to Bram and Vambéry. "Ready, gentlemen?"

Bram takes one end of the trunk, Thornley and Vambéry take the other, and, with Matilda in the lead, they carry it out into the main chamber. As they leave the room, Vambéry cannot help but notice the long scratch marks evident on the inside surface of the door. From top to bottom, and stained with dried blood, the oak has been clawed and splintered in what appears to be a failed attempt at escape. He also takes note that the box of gold and documents is gone, most likely already on the train.

Together, they transport the trunk down the abbey steps to an awaiting coach. It is then loaded onto the train to Hull, where they will catch a ship to Amsterdam. From there, they are to board another train to Rotterdam, Düsseldorf, and Frankfurt, scheduled to arrive in Munich in approximately three days' time.

Once settled into their seats aboard the train, Thornley gives Vambéry Bram's journal, another diary in Thornley's own hand, and letters written by Matilda to Ellen, asks him to read all as they pull away from the station, Whitby lost at their backs.

Vambéry carefully reads it all, doing his best to place all the pages in some semblance of order, flipping back and forth, adding his own notes as he goes.

Several hours later, he finishes the final page scribbled in hasty script by Bram that previous night while trapped in the abbey tower. He closes the cover of Bram's journal. All these recorded moments weighing heavily on him—this boy, this family, caught in something so horrendous for so long.

He leans back in his seat as the train bounces along, the English countryside rolling past the window.

He has much to think about.

MATILDA

Matilda wakes aboard the S.S. *Hero* to what she thinks is someone speaking her name. It comes to her in her sleep, a whisper across some great distance. She sits up in her small berth and glances around the stateroom. She spies nothing. She had left the porthole open, but only because there is no deck nearby, the only view being the sea, but also because she welcomes the sound of the waves lapping against the hull of the ship and the equally comforting sound of the sails steadily flapping in the wind, filling the otherwise quiet void of the night.

Matilda.

This time she is certain she hears her name. From somewhere outside, as impossible as that may be.

Matilda rises and slips a cloak over her nightclothes, then goes to the cabin door. She opens it, half expecting to find someone on the other side, but there is no one, the hallway is deserted. Matilda has been aboard ships such as this before and she is aware that at this hour most of the passengers would have retired to their staterooms, leaving only the crew silently scampering about the vessel performing their duties. But the crew does not know her name, and, anyway, she sees no one, crew or otherwise.

Bram and Thornley occupy the cabin to her left, and Vambéry is on the right. She considers waking her brothers, then thinks the better of it. They both need the rest more than she does, with Bram, in particular, exhausted after his ordeal in the tower.

Matilda pulls the hood of the cloak over her head and holds the garment securely at her neck, then follows the hallway to the flight of stairs that will take her up to the main deck. There, the salt air fills her lungs, wintry and briny, and she embraces the scent. It reminds her of their home all those years ago. As she crosses the main deck, a crew member shuffles past, muttering something in a language she does not comprehend, before disappearing around a distant corner.

There is another standing on the starboard side near the forecastle—slender and still, also in a dark cloak. Matilda recognizes her immediately. She crosses the deck and goes to her, standing at her side.

"Hello, Ellen."

Ellen continues standing stock-still, staring out at the water.

"You should not be out here alone. I fear Vambéry will not hesitate to kill each of you at the first opportunity."

"I am not worried about Arminius Vambéry."

Matilda knows that Ellen and the O'Cuivs were spirited aboard the ship inside wooden crates, each filled with the soil from their graves and nailed shut. Those crates had been stowed deep within the hold of the ship and surrounded by other crates on all sides. None of it would be accessible until reaching Amsterdam and the cargo was unloaded on the dock. Yet here was Ellen, standing before her now. Matilda recalled how Dracul turned himself into a swarm of bees at Thornley's house, and how Vambéry had told them the undead also could transform themselves into mist and access the smallest of places. All of this had seemed like a fairy tale to her—until now.

"Where are Patrick and Maggie?"

"Resting. To wake aboard a ship can be frightful, surrounded by all this water. We cannot cross water on our own except when the tide is at its slackest, but, be that as it may, we still are not capable of swimming even if we could swim in life. Patrick learned this almost fatal lesson all too well in Dublin when he fell overboard and was given up for dead."

"We saw him—his body—in the morgue in Dublin."

Ellen nods. "I know, I read your letters."

Matilda stares down at the water, at the waves cresting against the hull. "Did you kill the guard?"

"I would not do such a thing," Ellen replies. "I have not taken a single human life in more than two hundred years."

"Dracul, then?"

"Dracul," she says. "He found Patrick O'Cuiv in much the same way you did: those hideous scars. He hoped Patrick would lead him to me. He had been following Patrick since the day he fell off the boat in Dublin. Patrick hoped to lose him by boarding a ship, but Dracul has no such fear of water. In truth, I am not sure he fears anything anymore. He gave chase. Patrick panicked and tumbled over the side. I beat Dracul to the morgue by mere minutes, was able to replace Patrick's heart and revive him. Then we escaped, with Dracul on our heels. He killed the guard because the guard saw his face, no other reason but that."

"Did he kill Thornley's coachman? I thought it was Maggie."

"Maggie has never taken a human life, and I doubt she ever would. She may possess a temper, one that sometimes gets the better of her, but a murderer she is not. I'm sure it was him." Ellen falls silent for a moment, then goes on. "Dracul has no regard for human beings. When I escaped his castle, he killed every servant, vowing never to allow another human in his home again. Mothers, fathers, children—he killed them all out of nothing more than spite. He reveled in their suffering."

Ellen finally turns to Matilda, who truly is able to look upon her for the first time since childhood. Her eyes burn the brightest of blues with such energy that they nearly glow. Her pale skin is perfect, free of age, much as it had been fourteen years ago. Her flowing blond hair is pulled back and hidden under her cloak, but Matilda knows it has not darkened. This is the Ellen she remembers, the Ellen she will always remember.

Ellen steps closer and places her cold hand on Matilda's. "I cannot allow you and your brothers to continue pursuing this quest with me, it is far too dangerous. The only reason Dracul allowed you to live this long is because he knows he can use you against me, you and Thornley both. With Bram, Dracul's reasoning is far worse. He is fascinated by Bram, by the fact that my blood healed him and gave him abilities he would not otherwise possess."

"The way he heals?" Matilda ventures.

"Yes, the way he heals. Increased eyesight, the enhanced hearing. His strength, his energy, his mind. And his link to me. How long will he live? Longer than most? Not as long? How many of these attributes are truly his and how many are born of my blood? He was expected to die as a child, and he would have died had I not intervened. But he is living on borrowed time."

"He owes you a debt of gratitude," Matilda allows. "We all do,"

"You owe me nothing. I am leading you to your death. I spent so many years trying to keep you safe, keep you away from me, and yet here we are together."

"We are all here by choice. What he did to you I find it unimaginable. If we can somehow help reunite you with your true love and repay you for all you have done for us . . . There is no question why we are here. We are here for you. You are part our family."

Ellen considers this assertion and squeezes Matilda's hand. "Thank you for your letters, Matilda. Thank you for keeping me in your thoughts."

The boat rocks as the waves increase in size, and an icy wind blows in from the east. "There is a storm brewing."

Ellen sighs at this, her mind otherwise lost to thought. "You should return to your cabin," she finally says.

"You should rest, too."

"I'm afraid this is the last rest I will find for a very long time."

At one point in her life Matilda was very fond of Ellen's smile, of the warmth it expressed. She hopes to see one of those smiles now, but it does not come. Instead, she takes both of Matilda's hands in hers and leans in close. "When your brother awakens, tell him that what he saw in that room, the things that came from behind the door—they were not born of my beloved Deaglan O'Cuiv. It was Dracul acting through him. The fact that they share blood allows for that. My beloved would never say those things, do those things. I hope one day soon that the three of you will meet him and come to know the man I love."

"Yes, one day very soon," Matilda reassures her.

She leaves Ellen standing there on the deck, her cloak flapping in the sea breeze, and wonders if this is the last time she will see her alive. She wonders if by this time tomorrow she and her brothers will still be alive.

BRAM

Amsterdam is but a blur as they disembark from the S.S. *Hero* and make for the train station. Thornley attends to their luggage while Bram and Vambéry ensure the three wooden crates and the trunk in their possession are carefully extracted from the cargo hold. A customs agent approaches, but after a few words with Vambéry, and an exchange of funds, the agent waves them through. Bram secures a carriage, and the crates and trunk are loaded onto the back and transported to the station to be secured inside one of their train's many boxcars. As the crates and trunk slip away into the murkiness of the dark car, Bram cannot help but wonder who is in each crate, there being no markings to speak of.

Within an hour of arriving in Amsterdam, they are off, as the train picks up speed and heads for Rotterdam, Düsseldorf, then Frankfurt. They arrive in Munich in the morning shortly after the clock strikes eleven. From the station, Matilda, Vambéry, and Thornley make their way to the Hotel Quatre Saisons, where rooms await them. Bram follows shortly thereafter, choosing to ride with the crates and trunk. As the heavy carriage rolls over the cobblestones, Bram places his hand on each of the three crates and closes his eyes until he determines which holds Ellen.

He arrives at the hotel to find Vambéry waiting out front. "I arranged for transport, but it was no easy feat; nobody wishes to go anywhere near this region. They have all heard stories since childhood of hauntings and the dead and they want no part of it. They say that on Walpurgisnacht you can hear the screams even here. The maître d'hôtel directed me to a gentleman from Bethany Home who was willing to rent us a suitable carriage and a team of six horses, but he could not spare a driver. He said even if he wished to do so, none of them would go. We'll have to drive the carriage ourselves."

Bram nods on hearing this information; he had expected as much.

"Ah, here he is."

A rotund man with a thick gray beard pulls into the drive behind the first carriage in an open-bed wagon being drawn by six horses. The horses have all seen better days, their swayed backs and prominent withers revealing their age all too readily, the eyes of the two wheelers are cloudy, showing some degree of blindness, yet all six are animated, showing real enthusiasm for the task before them.

Bram and Vambéry glance at each other but say nothing.

The man climbs down and shuffles over to where they stand, removes his hat, and scratches at the remains of his white hair. "I know they are not much to look at, but they're all strong and broke; they won't give you any trouble. Some of my younger steeds are as fearful of that place as my men. My son took one out there last year, and the horse turned around at the midway point and galloped home without once breaking stride. The animal did not seem to notice that my boy nearly fell off; it didn't stop until it was standing with its head over the stable door."

Bram notes the man's English is very good, although heavily accented, and comments on it.

"I went to school in New York," the coachman says, "then came back here when my father took ill. That was thirty years ago. Always meant to go back but have never had the time."

"What can you tell us of this place we are going?" Bram asks.

The man crosses himself. "Black plague, I think. Wiped out the entire village. Very fast. Most succumbed to sickness, others fled. From what I've been told, the tables of some of the houses are still set with plates and silverware for dinner. There is a cemetery, but they ran out of room, the last people to leave the village resorted to burying bodies anywhere they could find flat ground. Not sure why they didn't burn them; from what I understand, that's how they dealt with the plague in other parts."

Vambéry generously tips the workers at the hotel and instructs them to transfer the crates and trunk from the carriage to the wagon.

"When can I expect you back?" the man asks, eyeing the load.

The man didn't ask about the contents, Bram notices. He wonders what Vambéry told him.

"Hopefully, by nightfall."

They all seem to realize this is a lie but say nothing.

The man strokes the neck of the nearest horse. "They've all been fed and watered. If any one of them gives you grief, it will be this young gelding. But he should be fine here in the middle of the team."

With that, the man is off, walking back the way he came.

Matilda and Thornley appear at the hotel entrance, then the four of them climb aboard the wagon, Bram and Vambéry riding in the back with the cargo while Thornley takes the reins.

SIX HOURS UNTIL NIGHTFALL

When they leave the hotel, the sun is shining brightly, but once the town is at their backs a chilly northern wind takes hold. The blue sky disappears behind thick gray clouds, the air grows moist with an incoming storm. Bram turns his gaze from the sky back to the crates, pressing his palm to the wood and closing his eyes. When he locates the one containing Ellen, he reaches out to her with his mind. She assures him they are heading in the right direction.

They come upon a crossroad, and Vambéry asks Thornley to stop.

When Thornley pulls back on the reins, the horses obediently come to a halt, the wheelers and swing pair helping to steady the leaders, who would have been perfectly happy to keep trotting along.

Vambéry climbs down from the wagon, favoring his bad leg, and goes to a stand of cypress trees, snatches away some weeds flourishing around one of the trees' trunks. "Here!" he says, his hands uncovering something.

Bram gets down from the wagon and approaches him. Vambéry has found a small wooden cross, once painted white but now brown and splintering. "A grave?"

"The Germans bury their suicides at crossroads."

Bram thinks about this for a second, then retrieves a shovel from the wagon.

Vambéry places a hand on his forearm. "The ground is undisturbed here, nothing has tampered with it."

Bram shrugs him off and plunges the blade of the shovel into the earth. "O'Cuiv's grave didn't seem like it had ever been touched, either, yet look what we found inside."

"Same with the one we found at Whitby Abbey," Matilda adds.

Bram continues digging. "It makes sense. Suicide graves are never in blessed ground, and they often remain undisturbed for hundreds of years. For their kind, they are the perfect place for storage or even rest while traveling. You yourself said the undead can become mist. Why not hide in such a place?"

The tip of the shovel's blade strikes something, and the two men look at each other, then drop to the ground and begin digging with their hands.

The condition of the coffin is even worse than the cross, the wood so rotted that Bram's hand punches right through the lid. He is relieved to find there is no body inside.

"Is there anything there?" Vambéry asks.

Bram has his arm inside the coffin up to his shoulder, feeling around. "No, nothing, I think it is . . . Wait, I think I've got something."

He pulls his arm out of the casket, and he is clutching an envelope in his hand that is sealed with red wax. Bram dusts it off and holds it up.

"It is addressed to you," Vambéry says under his breath.

Thornley and Matilda have climbed down from the wagon at this point and have come close as Bram tears the envelope open and unfolds the single page it contains:

> I welcome you to this lovely land. Bring them to
> me. Bring them all to me.
>
> —D

Bram crumples the letter up and tosses it into the bushes. "He is toying with us, trying to slow us down."

In the distance, they hear the howl of one wolf being answered by the howl of another. The horses stomp their hooves nervously in response.

"We should keep moving," Thornley tells them.

Bram quickly fills the grave, and they all climb back into the wagon. Thornley urges the horses on again and they reluctantly obey, moving at a speed a little slower than earlier.

Above, dark clouds churn and roll towards them, bringing a breeze that seems to carry ice; then the sun reappears, pushing it all back. Bram fears the storm might win, though, for the light loses strength with each volley. He pictures Dracul summoning these clouds, the thunder and lightning becoming audience to what is to come.

They press on.

Every now and then, the horses toss up their heads and sniff the air, but then continue on without incident. The Isar River flows to the west, where the ground is littered with sweet chestnuts. If allowed, the horses might stop and eat the nuts, but today they show little interest. Instead, they plod along, chestnuts crunching under hoof and wheel. It is only when they are asked to stand that they paw the ground with their hooves.

They cross a small stone bridge, then continue uphill, the road narrowing as the wagon somewhat awkwardly reaches the plateau at the top. Thornley pulls back on the reins and brings the team to a halt. "Is that where we're to go?"

He is pointing at a path that breaks away from the main road and seems to dip down into a little winding valley, the floor of which is lost in the forest.

Again, Bram places his hand on the crate containing Ellen. A moment later, he nods his head. "Not much farther now."

Thornley maneuvers the heavy wagon onto the narrow road and drives on.

"Do you see someone?" Matilda asks nearly an hour later, breaking the silence. "Down there, near the crest of that hill. Is that a man?"

Bram follows her gaze and sees him, too. A tall thin man standing off to one side of the overgrown road. He remains perfectly still as he watches them watching him.

"Is that Dracul?" Vambéry, squinting, inquires.

Bram shakes his head. "No, I have never seen this man before."

The man is attired in a white shirt tucked into baggy, dirty white trousers, and he is wearing a cowboy hat. There is an enormous belt cinched around his midsection studded with brass nailheads. His black boots come nearly to his knees. A thick black mustache bisects his face, and his hair is long and black.

Bram's arm begins to itch, and he reaches out and touches the edge of Ellen's crate.

"What is it?" Matilda says.

"He's not alone. I think they've been following us for some time now. A dozen of them, maybe more."

Vambéry reaches into the satchel at his feet and wraps his hand around the stock of the rifle without removing it.

Bram closes his eyes, his mind listening to Ellen. "They're only watching; I don't think they intend to hurt us."

"They do not look like locals," Vambéry points out.

"I don't think they are."

"Are they undead?" Matilda asks.

Vambéry shakes his head. "Not if they are out in the daylight."

The man is gone when Bram opens his eyes, having vanished into the woods. But Bram can still feel his presence, though, him and others all around.

They continue forward, the hours passing in silence, the cypress and yew trees growing dense by the foot. Tall and thick, the old trees sway with the increasing wind and bitterness of the approaching storm—a storm that moves slowly, seeming to follow them rather than passing overhead.

"We must be getting close," Vambéry says, pointing at the ground. Bram glanced over the side of the wagon and sees the remains of a stone foundation of an old building long lost to the elements. Another building, smaller in size, stands about a hundred feet farther down the road.

They pass the place where they saw the man and find no sign of him. No footprints, no trampled weeds, nothing.

Another wolf howls in the distance, much closer than the last. The horses begin to strain and rear, but Thornley speaks to them soothingly and they quiet down.

The road winds through the trees, and soon they come upon a low stone wall and follow it down to the floor of the valley.

The remains of the village appear before them. One moment, there is nothing; then they turn a corner and the ruins appear from behind a wall of tall cypress. Old stone structures, the thatch and wood roofs long since rotted away, dozens of them, all clustered together. The name *Dreptu* pops into Bram's mind, probably from Ellen. He knows it isn't a German word, and it isn't the name of this place, yet it is there, now known to him.

At the middle of what is probably the village green stands a black coach and four horses, their coats glistening and dark as coal.

THREE HOURS UNTIL NIGHTFALL

"Is that his coach?" Matilda asks, her eyes fixing on the black vehicle sitting silently in the center of the village ruins.

"Where's the driver?" Bram asks. There is no sign of whoever drove the coach here. The windows are covered in dark velvet, holding back all light—Bram can't see inside. He might be in there or he might be somewhere else in the village. He may be watching them right now.

"There's someone lying on the ground," Thornley says, climbing down from the wagon. Vambéry and Bram follow.

The weeds around the coach are tall, and at first Bram can't see anyone. Then he does, a body lying near the front right wheel. Unmoving. Bram starts towards the coach.

Vambéry grabs his shoulder. "Wait."

Vambéry retrieves the rifle from his satchel. He also retrieves three wooden stakes, the ends sharpened to wicked points. He hands a stake to Bram, another to Thornley, and retains the third for himself.

"I see at least three other corpses," Matilda tells them, standing in the back of the wagon. "Two behind the coach, the legs of another around the other side."

Bram sniffs the air, confirming that the bodies around them are, indeed, all dead.

He crosses the village green with the other two men at his back. As he approaches the coach, he again tries to peer inside, but the curtains are not only pulled tightly shut but are tacked to the frames of the windows. If someone is in there, Bram cannot tell.

The body beside the coach is dressed in the same garb as the man they spotted on the road earlier. His eyes and mouth are open, locked in an expression of extreme fright. There is a small tear at his neck, still sticky with drying blood.

"This happened recently," Bram says. "No more than a few hours ago."

Vambéry shakes his head. "That is not possible. The *strigoi* do not hunt during the daylight hours; they lack the strength. Look at the size of this man. He could have overpowered Dracul easily if his life was threatened. Dracul would never risk such a confrontation."

Thornley next kneels beside the two bodies behind the coach. "These two are the same, drained of all blood. Their bodies are still warm."

Bram is now at the fourth corpse, his fingers slipping over the two small punctures at the neck. "What if they died willingly?"

"What do you mean?" Vambéry frowns, puzzled.

"What if these men gave themselves to Dracul, allowed him to drain them in order to give him strength for whatever is to come? He knows we travel with three undead."

"If he fed," Vambéry says softly, "he has the upper hand."

Bram nods.

"What about the one we spied on the road?" Thornley points out. "Is he with them, too? If such is the case, how many *living* men does Dracul command out here?"

Bram tightens his grip on his wooden stake and goes to the door of the coach.

"Wait!" Vambéry calls out.

Bram does no such thing. Even though the lock is engaged, he twists the handle with such force that the metal snaps with a pop. He tugs the door open, flooding the interior with light.

Vambéry is at his side in an instant, his stake held high and the rifle dangling from his shoulder.

The coach is empty.

The black horses whinny at this encroachment, and the coach lurches forward, the front wheel running over the arm of one of the dead men before returning to a halt.

Bram stares at the interior; his arm begins to itch again.

He was here.

Dracul is close, even now.

But how can that be?

Bram turns to the sky, at the threatening clouds churning above, blotting out the sun. "Is that enough to protect him?"

Vambéry thinks for a moment. "He would not risk remaining in the open for very long. But a storm could offer concealment and distraction."

"So if he arrived during daylight, perhaps a few hours before us, he wouldn't stay in the coach out in the open because that would be suicide. He would find someplace to rest until nightfall," Bram says, surveying the surrounding village.

Vambéry's focus is now on the cemetery behind the few remaining structures of the village. "He would seek out a grave, which would be freshly dug since he would have to be buried during the daylight hours. And we know he has other men out here to accomplish the deed."

Thornley rounds the coach. "We need to find him and kill him while we can. You said that was the only way to save Emily. Drive a stake through his heart and end his hold over her."

"This may be what he wants," Bram says. "We should be searching for Deaglan O'Cuiv's heart, not Dracul. We have less than three hours until sunset; that isn't much time."

"My only concern is saving my wife," Thornley tells him. "We kill Dracul, Emily is saved, and we then have all the time in the world to find Deaglan's heart."

Vambéry shakes his head. "If we truly intend to save Deaglan O'Cuiv, that will not work. He will become mortal the moment Dracul dies. If that happens before he is whole, before his heart is beating within his chest again, it will surely mean death."

"We will try to do both," Bram says. "Search for Dracul while we try to find the heart. Then we strike him down the moment we are able. We have no other choice."

Thornley and Bram start back for the wagon. Vambéry drops to his knees beside one of the dead men.

"What are you doing?" Bram asks.

Vambéry pulls a curved blade from the sheath at his hip and begins sawing off the man's head.

"Arminius!"

"If we do not remove their heads, they could become *strigoi* with the coming night. Then we would be outnumbered for sure. This is the only way to save their souls. If we are to hurry, you must help me."

Bram glances at Thornley. Vambéry's request seems extraordinary, but they simply cannot risk the four becoming *strigoi*. The two brothers do as they are told. When they are done, Vambéry stuffs the mouths of the severed heads with garlic and rolls them under the coach.

Back at the wagon, they again scrutinize the village, the decayed, collapsing structures. "Where to begin?"

Bram climbs into the back of the wagon. "We must wake Ellen."

TWO AND A HALF HOURS UNTIL NIGHTFALL

Bram climbs up into the wagon and removes the tarpaulin covering the crate containing Ellen. "Hand me the hammer."

Thornley roots around in one of the satchels, produces a hammer, and hands it to his brother.

"Be mindful of the trees. We do not know how many of Dracul's men are out there or where they hide, but I am sure they are nearby," Vambéry says, the Snider–Enfield rifle at the ready.

Bram edges the hammer under the lid of the crate and tugs. The nails give with a loud squeal. He works his way around until the lid comes free, then sets the hammer at his feet and eases the lid to one side. Ellen's face is concealed beneath a thin layer of soil, her body buried deeper in the crate. He brushes the dirt from her eyes and pale cheeks, then quietly says her name.

Ellen's eyes open with a start; red, piercing. Bram is reminded of a memory from childhood: *What color would they be today?*

All of them watch without a word as she sits up, the soil crumbling away from her. She turns to the sky, realizing night has not yet fallen, then reaches back and pulls the hood of her cloak over her head, shielding herself from the muted sun.

"Should we wake the others?" Bram asks, eyeing the two other crates.

"No, they must rest," she replies. She is weak, and her entire body is trembling.

"Are you able to do this?"

She slowly takes in her surroundings, her red eyes darting over every surface. She freezes at the sight of the coach, the deceased surrounding it.

Bram tells her that it is empty, what they found.

"You were right to wake me; we haven't much time." She climbs out of the crate, more dirt falling away, and drops down from the wagon while Bram holds her arm, steadying her.

Ellen's head snaps up and she sniffs at the air, her gaze on the forest. "There are many eyes upon us."

"How many men?" Vambéry asks.

"Perhaps a dozen, maybe more."

She studies the decaying village, her eyes fixing on a house about two hundred feet to their left. Half the roof is gone, but all four walls still stand. "Bring Deaglan there."

Before Bram can ask why, she walks off towards the house and disappears inside.

Matilda climbs down from the wagon and trails after her while Thornley and Bram lower the trunk containing Deaglan O'Cuiv's remains to the ground and carry the box behind her, their leather satchels piled on top.

Inside the house, Ellen clears off a table, the empty plates of a meal long forgotten. "Set it there." She points at the floor beside the table.

Bram and Thornley do as she says, and she kneels before the box, carefully unlatching its clasps. She lifts the lid, and Deaglan O'Cuiv's unblinking eyes stare back at them through a film of dirt.

Exhibiting the gentleness of a mother with her newborn child, Ellen begins removing her beloved's body, one piece at a time, and placing him upon the table. She starts with his head, then his torso, then both arms and legs. Bram and the others watch all of this in silence, her eyes moist with crimson tears as the pieces she retrieved from all over the continent slowly come back together.

Bram cannot help but look at the junctures where this pitiful man was pulled apart. The ragged flesh at the shoulders and the thighs, the neck. The empty cavity in his chest where Dracul had punched through and pulled out his heart. Bram can't imagine the pain such an atrocity would have inflicted. And knowing that this poor man still feels that pain even to this day, hundreds of years later, it is almost too much to comprehend.

Ellen leans over the man's violated remains and kisses him gently on the lips. "Soon, my love. Soon you will be back in my arms."

TWO HOURS UNTIL NIGHTFALL

"Someone must stay with him," Ellen says, covering the body with the tarpaulin from the wagon. "He's not safe with those men out there."

"I need to find Emily," Thornley says, already looking out the empty window at the deepening storm. "And what about Patrick and Maggie?" he asks. "They're still on the wagon."

"Bring both in here as well," Ellen instructs.

Thornley nods at Vambéry and Vambéry reluctantly follows after him.

Bram turns to his sister. "You need to stay here with Vambéry."

"I will not."

Ellen is shaking her head. "I don't trust that man to be alone with them."

"I need to go with Ellen, and Thornley will never agree to stay; that leaves the two of you," Bram tells Matilda. "I need you to stay, to watch over the O'Cuivs. Please."

"Vambéry will attempt to kill them all the moment they are alone," Ellen insists.

"I don't think so—and certainly not with Matilda there."

Matilda nods tentatively. "Bram's right, I can keep in his favor, if not with charm then with force of might. He is only a man, after all."

Bram goes to one of the satchels and fishes out a Webley revolver, checks the chamber to ensure it is loaded, and hands it to Matilda. "At any trouble, fire a shot, and we will come running."

Vambéry and Thornley return with the first crate, then fetch the second, placing them side by side in the corner of the room. "If Dracul's men are out there," Vambéry says, "they are not making their presence known."

"They're out there," Bram says, sensing them as Ellen had, their eyes no doubt locked on the small house.

Bram tells Vambéry he is to stay and Vambéry agrees after some persuasion. Vambéry tries to hand the rifle to him, but Bram tells him to hold on to it. He has his bowie knife and a stake.

Vambéry gives Thornley the curved blade he used on the men outside, along with a small bag of garlic. "Look for a fresh grave; that is where he will be resting. He arrived while the sun was up, which means he could not turn himself into mist to enter the grave, he would have been buried, I am certain of this. If you find him, you must drive a wooden stake through his heart and sever his head from his body and place the garlic in his mouth, like we did the others."

ONE HOUR AND FORTY-FIVE MINUTES UNTIL NIGHTFALL

Bram, Ellen, and Thornley step out of the house and return to the village green. Although the sun is now lost behind thick clouds, Ellen appears weak. Her skin has taken on a grayish cast, and her eyes are hazy, no longer bright red, as when she woke, but a dull, faded blue-gray. She pulls the hood of her cloak out over her head once again and disappears in its shadows.

Bram feels the men around them, human beings, lurking in the trees and behind the ruins, but he cannot see them. These men will not be seen until they want to be, but they are there, everywhere. Bram quickly comes to the realization that they are there only to observe— for now anyway. If they planned to attack, they would have surely done so by now. Whether they are in the evil thrall of Dracul remains to be seen.

Ellen falls still, her eyes fixed on the ground.

When Bram looks down, he understands why. Amongst the weeds, beneath the twisted vines and overgrown foliage, the earth is littered with splintered and broken crucifixes.

"How are you able to stand among them?"

"This place is unholy, the whole lot of it," she replies. "They were buried, but the graves were never consecrated. These relics are unblessed."

"These are graves?" Thornley asks.

Ellen nods. "When Dracul hid my beloved's heart here, he killed everyone, the entire village. He placed a curse upon the land. The few remaining survivors buried their dead and moved on; they left this place to rot away, to be forgotten."

"Not the plague," Thornley states softly.

"It was never the plague. People believe only what they can understand."

Thornley is surveying the village green, as well as the land between the buildings and the land beyond the village. Bram knows what he is thinking for he saw it, too. The crosses are everywhere; the bodies are everywhere. "How will we ever find the right grave?"

Ellen points to her left. "The original cemetery is beyond that hill. He would have hidden the heart there, before all these people died, not out here."

They cross the village green and mount the hill. As they come to the crest, a large structure looms into view: a great marble tomb surrounded by dozens of stone markers.

MATILDA

"I don't understand; why did she unpack the body?" Vambéry asks, staring at the tarpaulin on the table. "Would it not make more sense to get the heart and leave this place as quickly as possible? Go somewhere away from Dracul, someplace safe, then try to bring him back there?"

Matilda opens her mouth, prepares to argue, says nothing.

Vambéry continues. "Even if this works, and I am doubtful that it will, he can only be made whole again after sunset, probably with an infusion of large quantities of blood. Have you asked yourself where she is going to obtain that blood? At last count, her only viable sources are you and me or your brothers."

"She won't hurt us. She would never hurt us."

"No? Not even to rescue the man she loves? Someone she has loved for hundreds of years? She has known you and your family for, what, twenty years?" He fiddles with his cane. He twists the top and pulls out the silver blade. "We should kill all of them and leave here, come back for Dracul another day." He taps the top of the blade against the crate containing Maggie O'Cuiv.

"Put that thing away," Matilda says.

He ignores her. "For all you know, she has marched us all to our deaths to save the only thing she really cares about."

Thunder cracks outside, and Matilda startles.

Vambéry looks up through the hole in the roof. "If we leave now, we could probably beat the storm back to Munich. We could come back in the morning when we have the entire day to search. If you still wish to help her, that is."

"It took us the better part of a day to get here. We leave now, and Dracul will take the heart, and Emily, and hide them both somewhere else. Someplace far away. He will never allow us this close again. It must end tonight."

He taps his blade against Maggie's crate for a second time. "In a little more than an hour's time, these two will awaken, and we will stand no chance against the three of them—four, if you count Deaglan O'Cuiv. If we end this now, while they sleep, we can put their souls to rest. We can end this curse upon them."

Matilda tightens her grip on the revolver.

Vambéry's eyes widen. "You would shoot me? I am only trying to be the voice of reason. These decisions must be based on fact, not emotion."

Matilda pushes past him and goes to the window. "Shut up," she says. "I heard something."

BRAM

ONE HOUR AND TEN MINUTES UNTIL NIGHTFALL

The marble of the mausoleum is as white as the fog that shrouds Clontarf Bay, and the entire structure seems decidedly out of place here. There are only half a dozen or so tombs aboveground; all the others are traditional in-ground graves, their stone markers leaning this way and that at irregular angles and eroded with time.

Ellen goes down the hill and enters the cemetery without hindrance. If the ground here had once been sanctified, it is no longer. She goes to the mausoleum and stares at the epitaph above the door:

COUNTESS DOLINGEN VON GRATZ
IN STYRIA
SOUGHT AND FOUND DEATH
1801

The words are freshly engraved. Bram knows Dracul refers to Ellen as Countess Dolingen, but the meaning of the rest is unclear to him.

"Gratz is the capital of Lower Styria," Ellen says softly, knowing Bram's thoughts. "The man I was forced to marry, the one who left me for dead in that tower, he was from Gratz. It was customary for a wife to not only take a man's name at marriage, but the place he called home as well."

"And the year?" Thornley asks.

"That is the year I began planning my escape from Dracul's castle." She pauses for a moment, her words heavy. "He knew all along."

Beneath the inscription stands a large bronze door. There are no hinges or locks to speak of, and when Bram pushes on it, it does not give.

Thornley walks around the tomb to the other side and calls out to them. When Bram and Ellen round the corner, they find him pointing at some Russian lettering high atop the back wall:

Мертвые путешествия быстро

"What does that say?"

Although Bram cannot read these words, he knows Ellen can. She says nothing at first, but then when she does speak it is with restraint. "'The dead travel fast.'"

Bram looks at her, puzzled. "What is this place?"

"This is where the dead go to be forgotten, my dear Bram, where the dead truly die."

It is then the sky finally opens up, the thunderous clouds release a fury of rain.

And it is then that Bram hears Emily's faint cries coming from somewhere else in the cemetery.

MATILDA

ONE HOUR UNTIL NIGHTFALL

He doesn't so much step out of the forest as the forest seems to release him. Matilda is staring into the trees, the perfectly still trees, when the branches part and reveal a man standing within. Matilda knows at first sight this is the same man they spotted back on the road. Not because of the strange garb he wears, that is not unique—the bodies around Dracul's coach wore the same thick belts with dirty white shirts and trousers. Instead, it is his eyes, an unsettling expression Matilda recognizes from earlier.

He steps from the trees and stands in the clearing not ten feet from the window.

Matilda raises the revolver and sights on him, but she does not squeeze the trigger. She cannot kill a man outright, not when he has done nothing wrong. Yet she knows this man is here to inflict harm on her and those she loves.

"He must have followed us," Vambéry says in her ear.

"He knew where we were going," she replies, her eyes fixed on the man. "And he came here, too."

A large knife hangs from the stranger's belt, but he makes no effort to retrieve it. Instead, he only watches her with those unwavering eyes.

A second man steps out from the trees behind him, stands about five feet to his right. Three more follow. Within ten minutes, Matilda and Vambéry are surrounded, silent sentries encircling the house.

A thick rain begins to pour down, yet the men hold their stations, oblivious to the storm as the wind picks up around them, as lightning rages in the sky above, as thunder crashes all around.

"What do you want?" Vambéry shouts out at the first man, but the man says nothing in response. Water cascades from the brims of their hats, trickles down to the blades at their sides, puddles at their feet in muddy pools that submerge the crosses and set the dead leaves afloat.

"They allowed us into this village, but they have no intention of letting us leave," Matilda tells him. "That is why they are here."

Vambéry crosses the room and retrieves his rifle, then finds a box of cartridges in their supplies. He returns to the window and loads the Snider–Enfield.

"I count ten of them out there but there may be more. That rifle is a single-shot, but we have my revolver, which chambers six rounds. If they storm the house and we start shooting, we will cut down half of them, provided every shot finds its target, before they are on us with those blades. Those are not very good odds," Matilda says without looking up, her gaze still locked on the first man.

"What do you suggest?"

She nods towards the two crates. "We wait until dark, then let Patrick and Maggie take them."

Vambéry glances at his sword.

"Forget it," Matilda tells him. "You might be able to strike down one or two with that thing, but not enough to matter. We need to sit tight."

Suddenly, the men outside, as one, all take a step closer to the house.

BRAM

ONE HOUR UNTIL NIGHTFALL

"Did you hear that, too?"

Thornley and Ellen both nod.

"It came from over there," she says, pointing deeper into the cemetery, towards the far corner.

The three of them push through the weeds, careful not to step on the stones and crosses, making their way towards the sound as heavy raindrops slap the ground around them.

A muted scream, this one much closer.

"That was Emily. I am sure of it!" Thornley cries out, his eyes frantically searching, his hands pushing through the overgrowth.

Bram is first to notice the headstone.

The surface is smooth, its once-sharp edges now rounded and dull. It is about three feet in height and leaning hard to the left, and whatever memorial had been inscribed in the stone has long since been worn away by the elements, leaving behind nothing but faint lines and curves. It is not the original inscription that the three of them stare at now; it is the fresh writing, the block letters scrawled across the stone's face in what could only be blood, beginning to run with the rain:

STOKER

The grave itself is a stone vault, partially aboveground, partially buried, nearly invisible under the dozens of large rocks stacked on top. This activity is recent, Bram is sure of that, for the stones don't have the dull pallor of the other rocks lying along the ground—some of them still have a layer of dirt on one side where they were removed from the earth and stacked here, stacked atop this grave.

At the very crown of the heap sits a single white rose.

Again, they hear Emily's muffled cries.

"The sound is coming from beneath the rocks! From within the grave!" Thornley drops to his knees and begins pulling the stones away, lifting the heavy rocks one by one and moving them aside.

Bram reaches for the white rose and holds it up, carefully avoiding the thorns along the stem. Beneath the cover of her cloak's hood, Ellen shies away with a soft hiss. As he holds the flower still, the white petals grow gray, then black around the edges. The petals shrivel, then twist upon one another, then crinkle to dust. Even in the falling rain, they become dry and flake away, detaching from the stem and riding away on the strengthening wind.

"Help me!" Thornley says breathlessly.

Bram releases the stem, and it, too, disappears, picked up and carried away by the growing storm. Then he drops to the ground and begins pulling rocks away from the grave at his brother's side

Ellen watches the stem vanish, then she joins them, too. Though the sun cannot be seen, she remains void of strength. Still she lifts rock after rock and rolls them to the side, the cries of Emily Stoker growing louder with each passing second.

Nearly thirty minutes pass before all the stones are cleared away. The final three are so heavy Bram and Thornley have to move them together. With grunts and groans, they push the last of them aside, the surface of the tomb finally exposed.

The lid is five inches thick and solid granite. Bram expected it to look like all the other graves they have violated of late, as it appears to be sealed and presumably untouched for years. But there is a fissure evident along the seam and deep scratch marks on the lip of the lid. Evidence that it has been recently breached.

"He put her in here during daylight hours," Bram says.

"Maybe with the help of those men back at the coach, but not alone." Ellen runs her fingers over the heavy stone.

"I do not care how or when he entombed her here," Thornley says. "We need to get her out!" He calls out to his wife, but she does not reply; instead, more screams, raw and full of fear, pour forth.

Bram presses his palms against the lip of the granite lid and pushes. Thornley and Ellen push, too, but the stone holds fast. It is not until Bram sits on the ground and pushes with his legs, his back braced against a tree, that it finally gives and slides open.

Emily's screams become piercing, eclipsed only by the rumble of thunder.

MATILDA

THIRTY MINUTES UNTIL NIGHTFALL

"There's more of them back at the coach—they found the bodies," Vambéry says. He has the door cracked and is looking out at the village green.

Matilda takes her gaze off the man at the window for a second and turns towards the front of the small residence. Vambéry opens the door just enough for her to see.

Two of the men are dragging the bodies around the coach and lining them up in a straight row in front of the house. They pick up the severed heads and place them atop the matching bodies. They leave the wooden spikes impaled in their violated chests. Matilda would have expected a lot of blood, but there is surprisingly little, nothing but the stains upon their shirts, and the rain is making quick work of that. What had been a deep crimson before was now diluted to pink. It drips to the ground where the thirsty soil soaks it up.

Four other men emerge from the woods and join these first two, the six now surrounding the black coach and its team of horses. Another man nonchalantly walks over to their wagon and unhitches all six of their steeds, leading them towards the trees.

Seventeen men now in total.

Matilda turns back to the first one. He continues to watch her with a blank stare, icy rain dripping down his face.

BRAM

———— ◆ ————

The heavy lid of the tomb slides away and falls to the side, Emily's cries now pouring out—penetrating, haunting. She is buried beneath a thin layer of soil, and Thornley works to brush it away from her face.

"Cuts like blades and needles all over my body!" she wails. "Needles and blades and pins slicing into me, peeling away my skin!"

"I see nothing!" Thornley says frantically. "What is it?"

He has her face uncovered—Bram has never seen her with so little color to her complexion. Her eyes snap open, and Bram expects them to be red, but instead they are muted green. They flit back and forth, taking in the three of them hovering over her. A large roach scurries across her face and disappears inside her filthy blue gown; she pays it no mind.

"Emily, tell me, what did he do?" Thornley says. "What has he done to you?"

Dirt has gotten into her mouth, its grime now running down her lips and chin, mixed with red saliva, dripping down her—

"My God, there is a body under her," Bram breathes.

"It feels like he is sticking pins and needles into my skin, under my nails, in my eyes—pins and needles everywhere!"

Bram looks past his sister-in-law to the bones beneath her, ancient bones, the original occupant of this tomb. But there is something else beneath the sorrowful remains, glistening.

Thornley reaches inside the coffin and cradles Emily in his arms, lifting her out as she shrieks, "Pins and needles everywhere!" her arms are limp at her sides, covered with burns and welts.

"What has he done to you, my love?" Thornley pulls her close, embraces her, muffling her cries in his chest.

"There is more in there besides bones," Ellen says, "beneath the dirt." She has noticed it, too, the shimmering.

Bram leans in closer. The skeleton is wrapped in tattered cloth, no doubt the remains of clothing long since rotted away. He reaches in and carefully moves the bones aside, his eyes locking on the shiny metal. His fingers brush over it, wiping away the black soil—a cross, a small silver cross of the type typically worn around the neck.

Ellen draws in a deep breath and turns away.

Bram digs deeper into the dirt and finds more crosses. His fingers come up with a dozen chains. "The coffin is filled with them."

Emily screams, her cries so loud they echo off the trees, throughout the valley. They are answered by the howl of a wolf from somewhere distant in the forest. The burns on her arms—they are from the crosses, where they had come in contact with her flesh.

"Pins and needles! Pins and needles!" Emily shouts.

Thornley runs his hand through her hair, trying to soothe her, trying to hush her.

"Pins and needles, under my skin!"

"Emily, please stop—"

"Needles and pins! Needles and pins! When a man marries, his troubles begin!" she taunts, this time accompanied by a cackling laugh. She lifts her face to her husband's, then leans in as if to nuzzle him.

Thornley gasps and pushes her aside. His hand immediately goes to his neck, comes away bloody. "She bit me!"

Emily is smiling now, a thin trickle of blood at the corner of her mouth. Her tongue flicks out and laps it up. "It is almost time to play," she teases. "Won't you stay and play with me?"

She leaps from Thornley to the muddy ground beside him, again laughing. A thin, girlish, chilling laugh, as if she harbors a great secret and is bursting to tell.

Thornley stares at her in horror, his hand pressing the wound on his neck. He reaches over and snatches a handful of crosses from Bram's fingertips and holds them towards his wife.

Emily shies away, scuttling back across the muddy ground. The rain washes the remainder of the blood and dirt from her face, and Bram can see her teeth now, long and white, the cuspids ending in sharp points.

"She's gone completely raving mad!" Thornley says.

"She belongs to him now," Ellen tells him. "Once she has fed the hunger with human blood, there is no turning back . . . I am so truly sorry, Thornley."

"No, this cannot be." Thornley stares at his wife, now curled up on the ground like a baby asleep, her face shielded by her outstretched hand.

"No more needles and pins. None. No more." She says this over and over again. Her fingernails have grown sharp, and she lashes out at Thornley's hand, attempting to knock the crosses away. But for now he is still too fast for her to make purchase.

Bram notices the waning light, dusk is nearly upon them. He plunges his hands back into the casket and begins shuffling through its rank soil. In addition to the silver crucifixes, he uncovers small wooden ones, many now decayed and frail, splintering at his touch. He digs deeper and feels movement—a dozen roaches erupt through the soil and scale his arm. Bram brushes them away and keeps digging.

"What are you doing?" Ellen asks, her eyes carefully avoiding the crosses all around.

"No burial rite would include all of these crucifixes as part of the ceremony; they had to have been placed here for good reason. And they were put here a long time ago—not with Emily but hundreds of years earlier."

"When he hid Deaglan's heart?"

Bram looks at her. "Don't you see? These crosses, they are a shield. Even if you knew his heart was hidden at this very spot, you would not be able to reach inside and take it out."

"Is it in there?"

Bram's fingers find it then, the corners of a small box, buried deep in the coffin. He reaches in with both hands and pulls it out. A box of red oak, its gold hinges now tarnished black. He carefully sets it beside the tomb and works the latch. At first, it does not budge, but after a bit of prodding it pops open. Bram lifts the lid, and the three of them stare down at the heart of Deaglan O'Cuiv. Dark and small, shriveled with age, yet still beating—only once every minute or so, yet still beating.

"My God."

"But why would he lock Emily in with it, mark the grave the way he did? He led us to it," Thornley said. "We would have never found it here."

"He wanted us to find it," Bram agrees.

A gunshot rings out. It came from the small house.

FIFTEEN MINUTES UNTIL NIGHTFALL

Bram is first to climb the hill and spot the men surrounding the small house, more than a dozen of them, all attired in the same strange garb as those men they had found dead around Dracul's coach.

"He calls them Szgany," Ellen tells Bram under her breath.

"Who are they?"

"Mortal men sworn to protect and serve Dracul. They go where he cannot and keep him safe during daylight hours. As you have witnessed, they will sacrifice their lives for him. In turn, Dracul provides wealth for the families they leave behind. To die in his service means their kinfolk will never know poverty or famine. They gladly comply with whatever he commands."

Thornley stumbles up the hill behind them, bearing the curved dagger in his hand. Emily is nowhere to be seen.

"You didn't?"

Thornley follows his gaze to the blade and quickly shakes his head. "No, no, I could never. I reached for her arm and tried to bring her with me, but she pulled away and bolted off. I lost sight of her amongst the graves."

"Nightfall is nearly upon us," Ellen says. "She will gain her full strength then. You must be wary of her. If she tries to bite you again, there will be no escape. Make no mistake, she is no longer your wife now that his blood flows freely in her veins, she is a servant of the Devil."

Thornley lashes out. "Odd words coming from the likes of you." He reaches into his pocket and pulls out the lock of Ellen's hair and tosses it at her. "If not for you, this fate would not have befallen her. You had no business coming into our lives. You've brought nothing but pain."

Bram could see the hurt in her eyes, Ellen utters nothing in response. Her fingers coil around the lock of hair.

A second gunshot rings out, and the three of them turn back towards the house. One of the Szgany is pointing the smoking barrel of his discharged pistol towards the sky.

They watch as their frightened horses, unhitched from the wagon, run towards the forest and disappear in the trees. The horses at Dracul's coach seem unfazed by the noise—they stomp their feet and harsh, white breath escapes their flaring nostrils in the growing cold as they stare to the west, watching the sun settle behind the churning storm.

The Szgany with the gun falls back into position, and they tighten their formation around the house.

"They will not let us pass."

"You can make them, Bram. You have it in you."

Bram turns to Ellen. "What do you mean?"

"I have no abilities until nightfall, but you are not bound by this limitation. My blood may flow in your veins, but you are not undead, you are still human, something special. You only need to try," Ellen tells him, then places a cold finger upon his cheek.

It is only then that he sees, that he understands.

Bram places the palm of his hand against the muddy earth and digs his fingers into the ground.

MATILDA

TEN MINUTES UNTIL NIGHTFALL

Matilda's eyes never leave the first man, even as it happens. Whether from fear or shock, she continues to stare at him down the barrel of the Webley.

She watches a roach scurry from the mud and climb the man's leg. Not until it runs across his neck to his face does he swat the bug away. This doesn't seem to matter, though, for the moment the roach hits the ground, it is joined by a dozen more, and they all climb the man, a number of them crawling into his boots and the cuffs of his pants. At first, he remains still, as do the others, but when he realizes what is happening, when he sees these filthy creatures upon him, he begins to swat at them. But for each that falls back to the earth, fifty more mount his boots and begin to climb.

The ground swarms with them, a rolling mass of brown and black as roaches appear from the mud and crawl over one another, climbing until they find his legs. The man before her is covered with them in seconds, thousands of these insects crawling over his every inch—she can barely see the white of his shirt, the fabric of his pants. His arms flail and he cries out something in a language she does not understand. As he does so, three of them crawl into his mouth. He spits them out and claws at his face, brushing them away, but there is no end to the bugs. His hat falls away and it is gone in an instant as the roaches climb over it in search of higher ground, these black and brown little creatures glistening with the rain. A shiver races over Matilda's body as she watches the man fall to the ground and roll around under a blanket of bugs, his cries muffled by the lot of them.

When Matilda is finally able to tear her eyes away from where the poor man had been moments before, she realizes the roaches have engulfed not just this one victim but the other hapless men as well—more than a dozen in number—all writhing in agony on the ground.

Only then does she remember to breathe.

"Hurry! Get inside!" Vambéry cries out, holding the door open wide.

Thornley is first into the house, followed closely on his heels by Ellen, and then Bram, who clutches a small wooden box with both of his muddy hands.

BRAM

FIVE MINUTES UNTIL NIGHTFALL

The roaches parted as they ran towards the house, clearing a path in the carpet of writhing insects as men scream all around them.

Vambéry hastily slams the door of the house once they are inside.

"What the hell was that?" Thornley demands, retreating in the far corner of the room just inside the door, his eyes darting to Bram.

"I . . . I don't know," Bram stutters. He is breathing heavily, his heart pounding in his throat. He sets the small box down on the table and leans over it, steadying himself with both hands.

Matilda is staring at him, too, unable to speak, as rain pours in through the hole in the ceiling.

"We must hurry," Ellen says, reaching for the box.

Bram watches as she unhooks the tarnished latch and gently lifts the lid, revealing the heart inside.

"You did that," Thornley says. "You commanded those . . . those things?"

Bram says nothing. When he catches Matilda's eyes on him, he turns away.

Ellen reaches inside the box and takes the heart in hand, her fingers brushing off the dust with care, even tenderness. Her thoughts become lost in the task, oblivious to the others in the room. Folding back the tarpaulin over Deaglan's body to reveal the gaping hole in his chest, she returns the heart to its cavity.

Bram is not sure what he expects to happen next, but nothing does.

The body of Deaglan O'Cuiv remains inert, nothing but the pieces of the man he used to be assembled in loose order on a table.

Thornley crosses the room to Ellen. "You said Dracul's blood is evil. You said anything born of him is evil. What will happen if you wake this man? Should he be restrained somehow?"

Vambéry is there then, his silver sword in one hand and a wooden stake in the other. "I think we have let this go on long enough."

Ellen hisses at him and he backs away.

Thunder rumbles outside, followed all too quickly by Emily's peals of laughter. Bram and Thornley go to the window. Emily is standing at the top of the hill overlooking the cemetery, her long blue gown whipping in the wind and rain. She takes a step, then another, a sort of childish skip from one end of the hill to the other. "Come out, come out, my love! Dance with me in the rain! Thooornley . . . why are you hiding from me on such a beautiful night?"

Bram watches as she goes back and forth. There is something off about her steps, the flowing nature of them. It isn't until she makes her second pass that he realizes what it is—she is no longer touching the ground, but floating slightly above it. The icy rain seems to miss her, the drops rolling away before they contact her. The burn marks on the backs of her arms, the cuts, are all gone now, her skin healed. She laughs again, and Bram hears it in his mind as clearly as he hears it with his ears.

The storm breaks for a second, but it is long enough for him to realize the sun has left them, disappearing behind the horizon as night takes hold.

Emily dances atop the hill as the storm churns, swirling thick raindrops pounding at the newfound night. All but Ellen stand at one of the windows, watching her, watching as she finally stops and glares down at them from the hill. She raises her arm and points at the small house, at them, then turns her palm to the falling rain, somehow catching it in her hand although she remains dry. She calls out in a singsong voice, "Girls and boys, come out to play. The moon doth shine as bright as day. Leave your supper and leave your sleep, and come with your playfellows into the street!"

"She is absolutely mad," Vambéry says softly at Bram's side.

She sings this again and again. When she sings it for a fifth time, the wind and rain come to a sudden and swift stop. Emily laughs aloud and spins in a circle, the hem of her dress riding the wind.

A thin mist comes forth from the ground at her feet and curls into the air, spinning for a brief second before growing solid and taking the form of a man, a man none of them have ever seen. He wears strange clothing from another place and time and his blond hair is ruffled, hanging down over his red eyes. He seems confused at first, unaware of where he is; then his eyes find the small house, find them standing at the window, and he smiles.

Another mist sprouts from the ground, then another, and yet another after that.

"Vampires, the whole lot of them," Vambéry says. "They are rising from their graves."

A dozen more, both men and women, adults and children, come up the other side of the hill behind Emily, stopping when they reach her. More behind them.

Bram watches in revulsion as these ghouls begin to arise all around. He thinks of all the defiled crucifixes tangled in the weeds, the graves throughout the village, hundreds of undead all resurrecting on this dreadful night—all those poor victims Dracul drained and enslaved when he hid the heart of Deaglan O'Cuiv in this godforsaken place, all drank of his blood. He turned every last one of them; he controls them all.

Behind them, Maggie and Patrick O'Cuiv rise from their own graves, from the crates inside the house, their slumber over. They rise and stand beside Ellen, looking down at the body of Deaglan O'Cuiv, at the heart beating slowly within his chest.

Outside, Emily comes down from the hill and goes to the black coach. She strokes the neck of each horse in turn as she passes, their skin flinching and quivering, endeavoring to evade her touch, but, still in their harnesses, unable to do so. The undead stand all about, parting their ranks as she approaches.

A swirl of white mist rises out from under the coach, and, even before it assumes a solid form, Bram realizes where Dracul has been hiding all along. Had he studied the coach with a more discerning eye when they first arrived, he may have discovered it then, but he did not. Instead, he walked right past it, as they all did. Built into the underside of the coach, fashioned to blend into the woodwork unseen, was a coffin.

IT TAKES SHAPE not at Emily's side but halfway down the hill, between her and the house in which they all are gathered. The crowd of undead parts once again creating a void at their center and it is here the cloud of mist from beneath the black coach becomes a man.

He appears no different than he had at Whitby Abbey, Bram thinks.

Dracul stands there for a moment, regarding all around him, his long inky cape fluttering in the storm's violent breath. His deep red eyes gaze out over the legion of undead, up at Emily next to the coach, then finally settle upon the small house.

He smiles.

A number of the undead hungrily spy the inert bodies of the Szgany lying around the house, now abandoned by the marauding cockroaches, and they eagerly converge. Like a pack of wild dogs, they drop to all fours and fall upon the Szgany, hunkering over them, the Szgany disappearing under a frenzied cacophony that Bram will hear echoing in his brain for the rest of his life. Emily's laughter rings out once again, but Dracul continues to look at the house, his gaze unfaltering.

Matilda, still leaning on the windowsill, suddenly lets out a shriek and jumps back. An old man is there, his face stenciled with the lines of age. A tangle of white hair, disheveled and dirty, limply hangs over his brow. His clothing appears to be in ruins, torn and stained. He smiles at her, his teeth yellow and gummed with grime. Two of the teeth extend down over his cracked lips, the tips sharp. He runs a pink tongue over them and smiles again, reaching for Matilda with a gnarled hand. She raises her Webley and aims it at his chest. "Back!" she commands.

This warning does nothing but incite him further; he appears more amused than frightened.

Vambéry pulls a crucifix from one of their bags and shoves it in the man's face. He shrinks back with a hiss, spittle flying from his lips. Vambéry then hands the cross to Matilda. "Keep this displayed in the window. Do not let them get close." He tosses another cross to Thornley. "You—watch the front."

Bram's eyes are locked on Dracul; he has moved to the foot of the hill. "I don't think they can get in, not unless invited," he says softly.

"I am not sure I want to test that theory," Vambéry replies. "There must be two hundred of them out there, maybe more."

At Bram's back, Ellen pushes past, and he turns around. The tarpaulin that had covered the body of Deaglan O'Cuiv has been folded down to his waist, revealing the large cavity in his chest, his severed arms and head all lying in grotesque repose around the torso on the table. Patrick and Maggie O'Cuiv stand alongside him.

"Can you do something?" Bram asks.

Ellen says nothing in return. Instead, her eyes lock with Patrick O'Cuiv's. They are communicating, of this Bram is most certain, but he is not party to their thoughts.

Patrick O'Cuiv nods, then goes to the door. He pulls it open and steps out into the masses of undead.

"No! You mustn't!" Vambéry shouts. He races to the door with a crucifix of his own in hand and tries to pull it shut. Maggie O'Cuiv reaches for his wrist and yanks him back, her eyes avoiding the talisman he holds.

Bram watches Patrick O'Cuiv step out into the clearing. He approaches the remains of the Szgany, reaches down, and lifts one of the bodies by its arm, pulling it from the undead feeding upon the flesh. The body is riddled with bite marks, a gash in the neck runs with blood.

A small child, a little girl, watches this spectacle with lustful eyes. Then she springs at him, traversing a distance of no less than ten feet, and lands upon the Szgany's body, her lips pressing to the open neck wound. Patrick swats her away, as one would swat away a mosquito, and carries the body into the house. Maggie slams the door at his back.

"They drained him nearly dry," Patrick says in his thick Irish brogue. "The others fared no better."

Maggie moves in a blur; one moment she is standing at the door, the next she is behind Vambéry, restraining him with his arms pinned behind his back. The crucifix he is clutching clatters to the floor. "We should use this one," she says.

Vambéry tries to pull free, but she is too strong.

Bram moves towards her, drawing his bowie knife.

Ellen frowns. "We will do no such thing; release him."

Maggie hesitates for a moment, then does as she is told. Vambéry snags the cross from the floor and backs into a corner, holding it up before him.

Ellen takes the body of the Szgany from Patrick and carries it over to the table. She drapes it over Deaglan's remains, then turns to Bram. "I need your knife."

Bram hesitates for a second, then hands the bowie to her.

In a series of swift motions, she slices down the length of the Szgany's arms, legs, and body—a number of long slashes through his clothing and flesh. The man lets out a soft whimper, and Bram is surprised to see he is still alive, although barely. His clothing is riddled with tiny red blotches where the undead had attacked him, and the edges of Ellen's cuts quickly turn red as blood begins to run freely, dripping over the body of Deaglan O'Cuiv. Bram considers trying to stop her, to spare this man, but he knows it is no use. He won't survive his wounds; he'd either join the undead or meet his end with great suffering. This is merciful.

Then, above them all, soars the voice of Dracul.

"You amuse me," he says, "your little quest, my lovely countess, so full of purpose and defiance."

"I am not your countess," Ellen says under her breath.

"You will always be my countess."

Bram goes to the window and stands beside Thornley. He watches as Dracul turns to the sky, to the churning storm clouds, and with the wave of a hand brings hail to the rain, the storm growing more wicked at his touch.

"The castle has been so cold without you, so lonely. I had to dispatch the servants after you took leave, and I have yet to replace them."

"You killed the servants, every last one of them. Do you think I would not learn of this?"

"Their blood is on your hands, my dear."

"My God in Heaven," Vambéry breathes.

Bram turns to find him staring down at the body of Deaglan O'Cuiv on the table, now saturated in blood from the Szgany lying atop him. Ellen is carefully circling the table, her eyes glued to them both.

Deaglan O'Cuiv, Ellen's beloved, is somehow healing.

The tendons and veins of his severed head and limbs have been re-connected, and when Bram inspects them closely he can see blood puls-ing through the repaired appendages. Far from whole, to be sure, but they are regenerating.

The Szgany is clearly dead at this point, the last of his life drained. Maggie yanks his remains from the table and discards the body in the corner of the room much as one would discard trash. "He needs more."

It is then that Deaglan's hand flies out from his side and snatches Bram by the wrist.

DEAGLAN'S FINGERS SQUEEZE Bram's wrist with such strength that his long nails dig into the skin and draw blood. He pulls Bram close to the table, tugging him down with unnatural force until Bram's neck is at his mouth. "I have died a thousand deaths, felt the pain of each and every one of them, yet the only thought to have passed through my mind every second of every minute, every day of every year, was of this hunger . . . the sweet blood that would satisfy it and the wonder of whose it would be."

Bram feels a sharp sting at his neck, and the dry, chapped lips of this former man, this undead, as he sucks the blood from his vein. He tries to pull away, he tries to beat his fists against Deaglan's chest. His empty hand, longing for the wooden stake he held just moments earlier but is now gone. There is nothing he can do, though; he is held fast in Dea-glan's merciless embrace, his body paralyzed, his mind swimming in a daze.

From the corner of his eye, he sees Maggie O'Cuiv, first at his side, then behind Matilda. It is as if she has traveled there in a blur, and when she falls still she is standing behind his sister with Matilda's arms clamped behind her back, held fast in Maggie's vice-like grip. Maggie is shrieking with laughter, knowing this was the plan all along, and she grins at Bram before biting down on Matilda's neck.

Bram watches helplessly as Matilda's shoulder and dress grow red with blood, as it drips from the wound and out from between Maggie's hungry lips to the floor at their feet. Matilda tries to scream. Bram sees the pain and fear in his sister's eyes and knows it wants to escape in a loud fury, but instead only a whimper leaves her mouth, followed by a gasp as the air leaves her lungs. He can do nothing as his sister grows deathly faint and collapses into Maggie's arms where Maggie drinks still. She drinks until not a drop remains, she drinks until his sister is nothing more than this dead thing she cradles.

Behind him, Thornley cries out, and Bram is able to twist his head just enough to witness Patrick O'Cuiv snapping Vambéry's neck and tossing his spent body aside. It strikes the floor with a hideous thud. Patrick is on Thornley then, his terrible teeth tearing through Bram's brother's neck, spraying the room with hot blood even as Thornley screams—not the screams of a grown man but the screams of a child. All goes silent then but for the sound of Patrick O'Cuiv quaffing down every remaining drop.

All the while, Ellen stands in the corner of the room, lifeless, watching. A thin smile across her ruby lips.

Bram breaks free from Deaglan's hold, feeling a great pain as his flesh is torn away, and dives for Vambéry's sword, glimmering on the ground alongside its owner's lifeless body. With every ounce of energy in his body fighting the desire to pass out from his loss of blood, he comes up with the blade, the sharp edge finding Ellen's neck—

"Bram, no!" Ellen shouts. She wraps her arms around him and pulls him to the corner of the room, away from the table, away from her beloved. "It was a vision! Only a vision!"

The silver blade burns against her skin; Bram hears it, smells it, tastes it in the air.

Bram's eyes dart frantically around the room. He sees Matilda standing opposite him, her eyes locked on him. Maggie beside her. Thornley, Vambéry, and Patrick O'Cuiv standing motionless on the other side of the table, all watching him.

He sucks in a deep breath and releases the sword. It falls to the floor with a clatter and slides under the table. Vambéry snatches it back up.

Alive.

All alive.

It was like back in the room at the abbey, the visions from behind the door. Only now the body is right here, right next to them, in the same room—

"Dracul's blood flows through him still; he can use that," Ellen whispers at his ear. "He will use that until Deaglan is free. It is all right now, you are safe. It was not real. You are stronger than he."

"He is strong, my countess!" Dracul's voice rings out over the churning storm. "The strongest yet! How kind of you to bring him to me! Him and the others!"

Bram shakes off the remains of Ellen's loose hold and goes to the window. The undead are all around, their fiery eyes watching the house with unfettered lust. Above them, something runs across the remains of the roof, tiny little footsteps, quick and fast, followed by another pair. Others scratch at the walls. At the foundation, he can hear them digging, slowly digging under. Awful sounds, the undead everywhere.

"They cannot get in, not without being invited," he hears Ellen say. "Bram was right about that." The others hear her, too, but that does not put an end to their uneasy stares.

Dracul moves closer, only twenty feet or so from their door now, Emily at his side. "Bram, if you truly believe Ellen will spare your family and friend, you are laboring under a delusion. Why else bring you here? Someone will find your wagon in due time, but nothing else. Most likely, they will blame the wolves. How else for a group of foreigners to disappear in the woods?"

As if in response to this, Bram hears the wolves again, the howls of a dozen or more of them from amongst the trees of the forbidding forest.

Dracul waves a hand. "Some of my children have not eaten for a generation. Tonight they find joy, for a feast is at hand!"

Bram is not certain if he is making reference to the wolves, to the undead, or to both.

Emily advances to the little house, drifting down from her place next to Dracul and leaving no tracks behind in the muddy earth, the undead part for her allowing her access. She raps on the door, three slow knocks.

"A knock, a knock at my husband's door, will he kiss me evermore?" Emily's voice chimes out in a singsong. "A knock, a knock at my husband's door, my wish to join him, I implore. This last knock, this final knock, at the door, will he hold me, nevermore?"

Emily giggles at this, her childish rhyme. "Join me, Thornley! It feels so lovely and free! You cannot imagine! I want you with me so."

Thornley has picked up one of the wooden stakes and is absentmindedly rolling it around with his fingers, his free hand scratching her bite marks on his neck. He reaches down and pulls open the door. Matilda grabs at him, her hand latching onto the collar of his shirt.

Emily stands there, her skin aglow. She looks more ghost-like than human now. Her eyes glow a deep green, and her skin is as pure as that of a newborn child. Bram had always thought of her as beautiful, but she is breathtaking now, enchanting. "We have not lived, Thornley, not yet. But we can live now. It is not too late. Let me in and I will show you, I will show you everything."

"You cannot," Vambéry says in a hushed tone. "And you cannot go out or we will lose you, too."

Bram reaches down and takes the stake from his brother's hand. "We will find another way."

Thornley's gaze remains fixed on his wife, his eyes lost in hers.

Behind them, the body of Deaglan O'Cuiv jerks on the table, his hand grabs at Vambéry's arm and with a sharp spasm tightens around it.

Vambéry cries out in pain.

When Deaglan releases him, Vambéry thrashes about and stumbles back into the wall. His eyes roll back in their sockets and go white, a guttural moan crawling from his throat. Then he screams. The scream sharpens and tapers away until he falls quiet, his eyes jumping from person to person but seeing no one.

Bram is the first to get to him, catching him as his legs give out.

Vambéry turns to the now-still body of Deaglan O'Cuiv, then to Patrick, then back again, struggling the whole time to break free of Bram's hold.

Then Bram suddenly understands. "What did he show you? It's not true, none of it. It's—"

When Vambéry's glare bears down on Patrick O'Cuiv, all the muscles in his body tense. "I banish you from this house!"

"No!" Bram cries out. But there is nothing he can do.

Some unseen force reaches into the small house, takes hold of Patrick O'Cuiv, and rips him from it. The large man flies through the door and out into the night on a soundless wind. He crashes to the ground, and before he can stand, the other undead are upon him, their sharp fingernails and teeth tearing him to pieces in a feral feast.

Maggie shrieks and tries to run out the door, but Ellen catches her and pulls her back. "You can't go out there! Not like this! He is trying to turn us all against each other. Twisted manipulations and visions, nothing more!"

Ellen holds Maggie close, the girl sobbing. She glares at Dracul through wind and rain. "Is there no end to your madness?"

"They plan to kill us all," Vambéry tells Bram. "Do you not see? We are an offering meant to buy her freedom." He gestures towards Ellen. "Her and the lot of them."

Ellen takes a step back, her eyes pleading. "That is not true. I would never—"

"This is why she brought us here. Why else?" Vambéry glares at Ellen. "I banish—"

Bram punches him in the jaw, and the man crumples to the ground. "Enough! Mind games, all of it! You must be stronger!"

Maggie swipes at Vambéry with razor-sharp nails as he falls, but Ellen holds her back. The girl's eyes burn with fire, glaring down at him with fevered anger.

Matilda, who had remained mute through most of this, aims her revolver at the head of Deaglan O'Cuiv on the table. His head and limbs are fully reattached now. Fresh skin has grown over the muscle, veins, and tendons, still raw and pink but restoring him to a whole man.

Dracul steps to the door. "Pull the trigger, and I will grant you safe passage from here; you have my word."

"You kill him, and we are all dead," Ellen counters, Maggie still squirming in her arms.

Matilda pulls back the Webley's hammer. "Maybe there is no way for any of us."

"No more."

This came from Deaglan O'Cuiv, his eyes now open. He peers at them weakly. "No more death in my name."

Ellen releases Maggie and is there at his side in but an instant.

Matilda takes a step back, the gun still pointing at Deaglan's head. Then she spins around and fires at Dracul, who stands in the doorway. Round after round, she fires, then kicks the door shut when the weapon comes up empty.

And, from somewhere outside in the pelting rain, Emily laughs.

. . .

"THE BULLETS ACCOMPLISHED NOTHING," Thornley exclaims. He is standing at the front window, looking out. "They passed right through him, unchecked."

"We can stay in here until first light. He can do little but deliver threats as long as we remain in here," Bram says.

Vambéry staggers to his feet, eyeing Ellen and the O'Cuivs, rubbing his jaw. "With them?"

"Yes, with them." Bram insists.

Vambéry scoffs, braces himself against the wall, his legs uncertain.

Ellen has Deaglan's hand in hers, holding his palm to her cheek. The wrist of her other hand is pressed to his lips, where he drinks. Words pass silently between the two. How long this has gone on, Bram is unsure.

Maggie pushes past Vambéry and takes Deaglan's other hand.

Deaglan O'Cuiv might be awake, but he seems far from well. His skin is nearly translucent. Bram swears he sees the blood pulsing beneath the thin flesh, slowly forging new vessels where none had been only minutes earlier—regenerating, albeit very slowly—Ellen's blood now flowing through his veins.

"Do you understand what must happen?" Ellen asks him.

Deaglan nods weakly.

Ellen draws her wrist from his mouth. "There is no other way."

"I know."

"Can you stand?"

Again, Deaglan nods, and together the two women help him swing his legs over the side of the table, help him to his feet, wrapping the tarpaulin around his waist. There is a ragged scar on his chest at his heart, but otherwise the wound has healed.

"We are coming out!" Ellen shouts over the rain.

Bram's heart sinks. What is she doing?

Maggie reaches for the door and pulls it open. Just outside, Dracul stands with Emily at his side. As Thornley said, the bullets left not a single mark.

Dracul tilts his head at the sight of Deaglan O'Cuiv. "My blood has served you well. How resilient you have become!" He then turns to Ellen, displaying a crooked smile. "Are you still prepared to make the trade we discussed?"

Ellen first looks at Bram, then Matilda and Thornley. "I am."

"You can't do this!" Bram shouts at her.

"Fortunately for you, my friend," Dracul says to him, "this decision does not fall to you. It was made for you some time ago." Dracul turns to Ellen. "Shall we?"

"I have your word?"

"You do."

Ellen takes a deep breath, then strokes Deaglan O'Cuiv's cheek. "I love you with all my heart, and I always will. Find peace. Somehow, find peace. It is for you I do this."

"And I you," he said softly. "I will be with you at every moment, now and forever."

She releases him and leans to Maggie's ear. "Keep him safe. Always."

Maggie says nothing, only nods, her eyes empty as she gazes upon the spot where Patrick O'Cuiv had fallen. Then she leads the limping Deaglan O'Cuiv out, past Dracul and Emily, past the undead, and, untouched by anyone, disappears into the shadows of the dark forest.

At the door of the house, Ellen watches them retreat, her eyes filling with tears of red.

Thornley slips a stake into Bram's outstretched hand. Bram wraps his fingers around it, feeling its heft. He could not kill them all, but he is certain he can get to Dracul before—

Ellen glances down at the stake. "Leave it here, there is no need for it." She studies the other faces in the room, particularly Matilda and Thornley, before turning back to Bram. "If you come with me, you will be safe. But the others must remain here."

"I am not going anywhere with you." He tightens his grip on the stake.

"Take me instead," Thornley says. "I want to be with my wife. Even if only for a few more minutes. Take me and I promise I will not be any trouble."

For the first time since arriving here, Dracul appears confused. Then: "Oh! You have not told them?" This seems to thrill him. "Did you believe the outcome might somehow be different? That your little group could somehow battle all my children and emerge unscathed, the heart of your paramour intact, that all would be well? Why would I stand for such an outcome? You are so naïve, the whole lot of you. The only reason any of you are still alive is because I have need of you, no other reason. The day that my need ends is the day you must fear most."

Vambéry produces a bottle of holy water—from where, Bram does not know—and holds it behind his back, his fingers fiddling with the cap.

Amused, Dracul waves a hand at him, and the sacred liquid in the small vial begins to boil. Vambéry drops it at his feet, cursing.

Dracul continues. "Bring the boy and let us be on with it, before I grow bored and burn this little shack to the ground and end all of them."

"Bram, please," Ellen pleads. "You must come."

He stands firm, just inside the door.

The anger within Dracul burns. "Enough of this nonsense!" He snaps his fingers, and lightning strikes a nearby cypress tree. The undead surrounding it jump back as a branch cracks and bursts into flames. Dracul retrieves the burning branch and holds it inches from the wooden beams of the tiny house.

"Don't!" Bram cries out. Whether or not it will burn in the rain, he doesn't know. But he can't chance it. "I'll go! I'll go."

And before the others can object, Bram drops the wooden stake at his feet. He steps through the door of the house into the raging storm.

THE UNDEAD FALL IN behind Bram, blocking any possible retreat. There is no turning back now.

Dracul drops the burning branch in a puddle, the flame fizzling out. Then he turns and starts ascending the hill, leaving the small house behind.

Bram tries not to listen to Matilda's cries, her shouts, his name on the wind. He can only hope that Thornley will hold her and Vambéry can keep them all safe until the morning.

Ellen reaches back and takes Bram's hand in her own. He allows her this gesture, although he is not certain why. Ellen's skin is cool yet dry to the touch, untouched by the rain, as are Dracul and Emily. He himself feels every drop, though, icy pricks against his skin. His shoes produce a sloppy sucking sound in the mud as they climb the hill—his shoes alone, for the others make no purchase with the ground and leave behind no tracks.

There is no moon out tonight, and Bram knows it is Ellen's blood in his veins that allows him to see at all, the life she has bestowed on him, this gift of time.

All around them, the undead stand. Unmoving save for their eyes, which serve as witnesses to what is about to come.

They cross over the hill, and the cemetery comes into view, the large white mausoleum and a hundred crooked tombstones. Ellen squeezes his hand, his arm itches, itching more than it ever has before.

If Bram is now marching to his death, so be it. He has been granted years that did not otherwise belong to him. Ellen has seen to that gift, regardless of her motives. Without her, that seven-year-old boy would have died in his little attic room, the world beyond his window remaining unknown to him.

At the foot of the cemetery, Dracul waves his arm and blue flames burst forth all around, flickering just above the ground. There is no evidence of anything actually burning to produce the flames, only the flames themselves hovering over the soaked soil. Bram is reminded of the strange candles that lit their way as they climbed the stairs of Artane Tower all those years ago.

They walk through the headstones, around the graves, and come to the entrance of the mausoleum. Dracul places a hand against the heavy bronze door. *"Deschis!"* he commands.

The door swings open, revealing an empty tomb within. A bier stands at the center, but there is no casket resting on it as there should be, only a flat stone surface awaiting its prize. A long iron stake rises from above the bier, jutting out through the roof.

At that sight, Bram's eyes flash back to the inscription carved above the entrance:

COUNTESS DOLINGEN VON GRATZ
IN STYRIA
SOUGHT AND FOUND DEATH
1801

And he understands. "This is to be your tomb."

"It is."

"But why?"

Ellen turns to him then. She wants to appear strong, but there is no hiding the tears in her eyes, the red-stained trails they leave on her cheeks and dress. "To keep your family safe, to keep the O'Cuivs safe, to free my beloved Deaglan, this was the only way. Dracul knows he will never fully possess me, not in his heart, not the way he truly desires. At best, he can only possess my physical body. I will allow that much if it means the rest of you remain untouched."

Dracul scoffs. "Why you care about these people, I will never know. They do nothing but devote each day to rehearsing for their deaths."

"They are the only family I have left, the only true family I have ever known," she tells him. "Now leave us for a moment so we may speak in private."

Bram fully expects Dracul to deny this request, but he nonetheless crosses the cemetery with Emily in tow. The other undead had not entered the grounds; instead, they stand in witness along its perimeter.

Ellen speaks quietly, words only Bram can hear. "I have told you that my blood within your veins will not last. How long you have before your illness returns, I do not know, but be certain that sickness will come back to claim you. I only hope you get the opportunity to live out much of a life before that day comes."

"We'll come back for you and free you. We'll come in broad daylight, when there is nothing he can do."

She is already shaking her head. "You will never be able to find this place again. Even if by some miracle you do, freeing me will bring an end to the agreement that I struck with him. It will mean death, not only for you and your family but for Deaglan and Maggie O'Cuiv as well, both of whom deserve the opportunity to be free. Do not let Patrick's sacrifice be for naught. You must promise me you will not try to find me. You will leave me here; this is what I want. As long as Dracul walks the earth, there can be no other way."

At this sorry truth, Bram can only nod in resignation.

She takes his other hand in hers, and Bram feels something press against his palm; she has slipped him a piece of paper. He shoves it deep within his pocket.

"You must never try to come for me *as long as he lives*," she says, her eyes locked on his. "Do you understand?"

Again, he nods.

Thunderclaps above, and Dracul is beside them again. "It is time for you to take your place, my countess."

Ellen releases Bram's hands, and he knows this moment is the last he shall ever feel her touch.

Soundlessly, she enters the mausoleum, climbing onto the cold stone bier and lying flat. Emily draws up alongside Bram but says nothing. A number of the undead come up behind them.

Dracul steps into the tomb and runs his hand through Ellen's long blond hair, rolling it between his fingers. "You will learn to love me," he tells her. "We have all the time."

With that, his other hand wraps around the iron stake, and he pulls it down with such force it pierces her breast, her heart, and embeds in the stone beneath her.

Ellen lets out a loud cry, a cry so reverberant it hurts Bram's ears. Her voice echoes through the valley and pierces the night, slicing through the storm. She ceases to move, and Bram thinks her pain is finally over; he thinks she has finally found rest, but he is terribly wrong. There is a blinding flash as lightning finds the iron stake and rides the metal from the top of the mausoleum to its very foundation in the earth. Ellen's body snaps up in a moment of agony, her screams lost behind an immense thunderclap; then she slams back down against the bier, sobbing uncontrollably.

Another bolt of lightning follows.

Dracul closes the large brass door, sealing her inside, muffling her wails.

"How could you?" Bram shouts at him. "You claim to love her, then subject her to this?"

"I love her more than you could ever know. But she must pay for her sins if she is ever to be forgiven. I am a patient man. I can wait for her, just as I will wait for you." Dracul runs one of his long nails under Bram's chin, over his neck, to his ear, scratching a thin red line in his skin. "Her blood flows through you, granting a life that was not meant to be. Like sin, such borrowed time must also be repaid. Upon your death, I will come for you; I promised to wait until only then. Your soul will be mine to possess for the rest of eternity. You will join all of my other children of the night," he says, gesturing across the cemetery at the undead surrounding them. "With the final beat of your heart, you will take your place at my side."

Bram opens his mouth to object, but before he can utter a word, Dracul glares at him with haunted red eyes. *"Codail, mo mhac."*

And all goes dark.

LETTER FROM MATILDA
to ELLEN CRONE,
DATED 22 AUGUST 1868

—————◆—————

My *dearest Ellen,*

I do not know what to make of the past days. Most of this time was spent in a sleepless haze while the rest felt like a waking nightmare. The kind of nightmare where you are being chased and can only run slower and slower as the predator gains ground at your back, grasping for your neck.

I woke this morning in a bed not my own.

I woke this morning in the same clothing I wore yesterday, covered in dirt and grime and soaked to the bone in an unfamiliar bed in a room I vaguely recognized but could not place upon first opening my eyes.

Then I recalled our trip to Munich, I recalled our travels to date, and I sat up with a start.

How I got here, in my room at the Hotel Quatre Saisons, I do not know, for the last thing I remember is being in that small house at the edge of a forgotten village surrounded by nothing but death.

I remembered you, my brother, and my dear sister-in-law walking off into the night on a death march that did not include a single look backwards, not one. If you had looked, you would have seen Thornley trying to rush out after you; you would have seen Vambéry bringing him back; you would have seen the swarm of undead standing all around, unwilling to let us go farther no matter how many bullets I fired into them.

Is there something to be said for ignorance? My brother believes it has its merits.

When I found Bram this morning, also asleep in the hotel room next door to mine, he was in a state more disheveled than mine. If not for his screams, I am not sure I would have found him at all, even so close by, but scream he did, and he did not stop until I had my arms around him and soothed him with words of love, family, and the safety of knowing all of this was close. He did not speak for the longest time, and when he did, I want you to know the first word he uttered was your name. He said it in a single breath, and it pained him so, for whatever thought passed through his head at that very moment caused him to burst into tears. I asked about the disposition of your fate, but he would not tell me, saying only it was something so terrible he could not imagine sharing it with anyone. Perhaps in time this attitude of his will change, but for now I decided not to push him. He has experienced enough already.

In truth, we have all been through enough already.

When his tears finally dried and his wits returned, he said he remembered something of grave importance and began rooting through his pockets. He retrieved a small folded sheet of paper with his name written at the top in your hand. He refused to let me read the contents, however. All in good time, I suppose.

Vambéry is tending to him now. That man—how I so wish to rid our lives of him.

It was Thornley I found most peculiar of all. As with Bram, Vambéry, and me, he awoke alone in an unfamiliar hotel in an unfamiliar room lying upon an unfamiliar bed two doors down from Bram, only he was not alone. Lying in the bed next to him was his wife, my dear sister-in-law, Emily. She did not awaken with the rest of us and, to the best of my knowledge, she still sleeps even as I write this letter. She is not well, of this we are all certain—her skin so pale and icy—but she is back, and she is with Thornley, and that is what matters most. Did you orchestrate her return from Dracul? I suspect as much.

How we arrived at the hotel, nobody is certain. Vambéry inquired at the front desk, and none of the staff recall us returning from our trip yesterday. There is no sign of the wagon we hired or the team of horses. The night manager swears he had not left his post at any time, yet we would have had to walk right past him upon our return. Our rooms are on the third floor, lacking balconies or any other form of exterior access. Unless, of course, you consider the large windows overlooking the square. I do not know about the others, but mine were open when I roused this morning, and my room retained the chill of the night; they had been open for some time—take from that what you will.

We leave for Dublin in three hours, then all of this will be behind us. I have four days' travel time to decide what I am going to tell Ma and Pa, if anything at all. Perhaps they will be satisfied just knowing I journeyed with my brothers. Perhaps that is all they need to know. In the end, all that really matters is family. Is that not so?

With that final thought, I must prepare to take my leave. Much has transpired, and I need time to absorb it all, to process it all, to understand what I have seen, for every thought becomes stranger as I attempt to unravel and interpret my memories. I will leave you, though, with one silly little question, one that just popped into my head. Although it may seem like a lifetime ago, only ten days have passed since I wrote you my first letter, and I find myself asking the same question I did then—

Where are you?

I feel like I should be closer to knowing the answer, but instead the truth feels further away than ever before.

> *Affectionately yours,*
> *Matilda*

TWENTY-TWO
YEARS LATER

———◆———

THE JOURNAL *of* BRAM STOKER

2 August 1890, 7:23 p.m. —I placed Matilda's letter atop the walnut box in which it had rested for the past twenty-two years and settled back into my squeaky chair to take in the whole of it. When I first stuffed that box full of our various letters, journals, and diaries, I arranged all of it in chronological order, as best I could, along with the maps from Matilda's sketchbook. At the time, I believed I had everything, but who was to say? Even Vambéry surrendered his notes, although with much reluctance and much coaxing on my sister's part. By the time we emerged from Munich and returned to the familiarity of Dublin, none of it seemed real anymore; it was more like a horrible nightmare shared by our small group, and although we had all documented our thoughts, none of us were particularly comfortable with sharing them, not even with one another.

It is peculiar, I suppose, how a group such as ours can come together over an event, then come so completely apart upon its conclusion. That is precisely what happened, though. Thornley immersed himself in his research and work, teaching and practicing medicine. He is held in high regard throughout the United Kingdom—quite renowned not only for medical and social work but also as a patron of the arts. Matilda was married last spring to a French diplomat; I do not know how much he knows of all this. Her devotion to art has been rewarded, her work now hanging in galleries of note, and her Celtic illustrations and essays have been featured in *English Illustrated Magazine* and other periodicals. For better or worse, Arminius Vambéry has been a constant in our lives, albeit intermittently so. I have gone years without contact with him, and, I must confess, I have been most grateful for those reprieves; then he will make an appearance for a handful of days, as if no time has elapsed at all. He will only tell me he works for the government— I have yet to pin him down as to which government—secretive work best left unmentioned, that is all that is clear. One night after many pints, he let slip that he spent more than a year in pursuit of Maggie and Deaglan O'Cuiv but turned up nothing. Wherever they wandered off to that particular night, they lost themselves to the world. He told me he gave up the search, but he was not convincing, not in the slightest.

I hope they travel fast. I fervently hope they remain out of his reach.

Me? I have made three trips to Munich over the past decades and have been unable to locate that small village, Ellen's resting place eluding me as well, as she said it would. What was found so easily at the time now able to hide with purpose.

In my professional life, I have muddled on through.

I published a few stories, in addition to my theater reviews, nothing particularly memorable, but the added income has allowed my wife, Florence, and me a few niceties that would otherwise have been hard to come by. We have a son, Noel, who is now eleven years of age.

I devote most of my time here at the Lyceum Theater tending to my good friend Henry Irving. We are coming off a strong run of *Macbeth*, and we've discussed an adaptation of *Henry VIII* as a next project.

I developed a life here in London, although I am able to return to Ireland quite often. I am happy, content.

I am rambling, of course. Easier to do that than to write about the true reason I put pen to paper this day. The reason that prompted me to pull this walnut box down off the shelf and examine the contents after twenty-plus years.

I received a visitor today.

A woman.

A woman I never met before, yet one who, in just fifteen minutes, has somehow managed to turn my life upside down and shake it.

I was at my desk, tending the receipts from last night's performance, when her steady knock at my door broke my focus.

"Mr. Stoker?"

I glanced up to find a slight woman of no more than five feet tall, with shoulder-length brown hair, and fashionable dress consisting of a pleated bodice with a high collar and a comfortable skirt, not unlike something Matilda might wear. The latest fashion, I suppose, not prone to the frivolous tendencies of older generations but styled with comfort in mind. I placed her in her mid-twenties, but her age was difficult to ascertain; she possessed, shall we say, a timeless beauty. A tiny wild white rose was pinned to her lapel.

I set down my pen and smiled up at her. "Yes?"

"Might I have a word with you? My name is Mina Harker."

I stood up and cleared a chair for her, then took my place back at my desk. "What can I do for you, Miss Harker?"

"*Mrs.* Harker—I have recently wed."

"Well, congratulations." I smiled again. "Well then, Mrs. Harker, how may I help you?"

She smiled back, but it was forced, and I could easily see she had much on her mind. This was a woman of deep thought, and I could tell she had carefully planned this visit, mentally organizing that which she planned to say, unwilling to be distracted or derailed.

Mrs. Harker reached into her bag and extracted a sheaf of papers, neatly typed and bound. She placed the manuscript on my desk and pushed it across to me. "I believe we have a common enemy. Arminius Vambéry said you are one to be trusted."

She did not wait as I read these pages, only said she would return at the same time tomorrow. Then she was gone.

At the mention of Vambéry's name, I think I knew what this was about, but I did not want to believe it. Even as I began to read, as I flipped through each and every page and took in her words, I did not want to believe. After all, it has been so long.

On the final page, she had scribbled two sentences in hasty script:

Vambéry said you know where this beast hides? Where he goes to lick his wounds?

I considered these sentences for a moment, then turned the manuscript over and found myself staring at the first page, at the two words written dead center:

COUNT WAMPYR

I picked up a pen and drew a line through WAMPYR, and replaced it with DRACUL, then added the letter A at the end, for I had learned that and much more before locking everything away in the back of my mind all those years ago.

The papers then went into my leather satchel. I would not be here when Mrs. Harker made her return tomorrow, perhaps for the best. I was bound for Whitby in the morning and I would read her words again in more detail during the journey. Some would say it was chance she found me now, as I am about to take my leave and begin work on a new novel, a new novel about something very old—an evil amongst us, a truth of the most incomprehensible sort. Coincidence, others would say.

I would disagree with both, for I believe in neither.

. . .

PEN IN HAND, I wrote:

She stood in front of me, right in the moonlight, and I cannot remember ever to have seen a girl of such breathtaking beauty. I am not going to provide a detailed description, as words can do her no justice, but she had golden blond hair, which was bound in a chignon. Her eyes: blue and large.

Our Ellen. My Ellen.

Those eyes again, they are just the same.

I coughed into my handkerchief, my favorite, for some time ago Mother had embroidered it with delicate purple flowers, reminding me of the wild orchids that grew in the fields we roamed near our old home. The white cloth was riddled with stains of crimson, both old and new, signs of death unwilling to come out in the wash. When I coughed into it again, my red spittle glistened. No longer Ellen's blood but now solely my own. Her blood gone from my body over the years, its healing properties gone with it. I felt the aches and pains of my childhood illness creeping back, waking from a patient slumber.

The time, the gift, that Ellen gave me drawing to an end.

Dracul had said he would return for me upon my death, and I believed him. Yesterday I made arrangements to be cremated immediately upon passing, a final checkmate in this game of ours.

I promised Ellen I would never come for her, not while he lived. This promise burns at me each of my borrowed days.

Not while he lives.

The walnut box sat upon my desk and I went back to it; I dug to the very bottom, shuffling through the pages, until I found what I was looking for—the small folded piece of paper Ellen had given me in those final moments.

I carefully unfolded it and smoothed the edges, now yellowed and crinkled with time's careless caress. I looked down at her writing, faded but still readable:

END HIM

LATITUDE 47

LONGITUDE 25.75

My arm has not itched in some time, but today it has, and the itching has not ceased. For after Whitby, I knew where I was to go next, my path decided for me long ago. My words the only bread crumbs I leave behind.

It was finally time I paid Dracula a visit, long overdue, the sharpest of stakes in hand.

—*Bram Stoker*

EPILOGUE

———————

PATIENT # 40562
CASE RECORD
WM. THORNLEY STOKER, M.D.

———————◆———————

17 October 1890—The walls bleed water; that is the cause of the musty odor and stink in the air, of that I am fairly certain. At least that is what I tell myself whenever I take the stairs down to this level and traverse the halls, a walk I undertake religiously every Tuesday and Friday, and have for more than twenty years now. Years that have not been kind to me, for I feel them with every ache and pain in my bones. Today, this festering comes from my right leg—a bit of gout, I am afraid, but it is too early to tell.

I brought her dinner with me. Perhaps this is the real purpose of my twice weekly visits—knowing only I can bring her dinner. Of course, plates of food are presented to her daily by the hospital staff, but they are rarely touched; it is my dinners that sustain her.

Her door is at the far end of the hall, a large, heavy monstrosity with only a small slit to pass the tray through at the very bottom and a simple wall vase mounted to its center holding a single wild white rose. I pluck out Tuesday's blossom, now dry and quite dead, and replace it with a fresh one from the garden I maintain. The walls of her room are constructed of thick stone, with no windows to speak of.

She has not tried to escape for some time, but I take comfort in knowing that the white roses seem to keep her contained, although I will not pretend to understand how.

I slide the tray under the door through the slit. She grabs it quickly and pulls it through. This action is followed by a thin slurping I wish not to hear. When she finishes, she speaks to me, her voice so clear and perfect an angel could sound no better. "I have something to tell you, Thornley. Something best told in a whisper. Let me out so I may find your ear?"

I lean against the door, placing my hand on the wood. I long to touch her, to feel her touch on me, the tenderness of her kiss. And yet I know it can never be.

"You know I cannot."

"But I long for your touch."

"And I for yours."

She slips her fingers through the slit, and I lower myself to the floor so I may rest my hand on hers. She is cold, always so cold, but this is my Emily, and I care nothing about that; it is the contact I long for.

You can tell much by a person's hands, the smoothness or roughness of them, the color of their skin, how they groom their fingernails. As I glance down at our hands intertwined on this stone floor, the differences between us glares back at me. While admittedly I do not possess the hands of a worker but those of a surgeon, time still shows upon them. My skin has taken on a patchwork of colors, the start of age spots and thick veins. My fingers have grown plump. They are not my father's hands, and I sometimes wonder if they are even my own, they have changed that much over the years.

Emily's finger twitches in mine; she likes to do this when we hold hands, her fingers rarely still, perhaps her way of letting me know she is still there, thinking of me. Her finger twitches, and I look down upon it, so smooth and soft, the skin of a child untouched by time.

It is when we hold hands like this I see the years between us grow, the distance between us lengthen. We will grow old together, our hands ever entwined, but only mine will age.

"Will you stay with me for a while?" she asks softly.

"I will stay with you always."

AUTHORS' NOTE

For many of us, *Dracula* is a formative novel. A book we pick up as children or young adults and revisit as the years pass, a constant on the bookshelf, an old friend. In fact, it might be so familiar that the question of the story itself, how it came to be, hasn't occurred to us. Yet, like Jonathan Harker's journey in the classic novel, the events that led to publication are ripe with mystery. When Bram Stoker first brought his manuscript to his publisher in the United Kingdom, Archibald Constable & Company, he opened the conversation with one simple line.

This story is true.

From the original preface of *Dracula*:

> The reader of this story will very soon understand how the events outlined in these pages have been gradually drawn together to make a logical whole. Apart from excising minor details which I considered unnecessary, I have let the people involved relate their experiences in their own way; but, for obvious reasons, I have changed the names of the people and places concerned. In all other respects I leave the manuscript unaltered, in deference to the wishes of those who have considered it their duty to present it before the eyes of the public.
>
> I am quite convinced that there is no doubt whatever that the events here described really took place, however unbelievable

and incomprehensible they might appear at first sight. And I am further convinced that they must always remain to some extent incomprehensible, although continuing research in psychology and natural sciences may, in years to come, give logical explanations of such strange happenings which, at present, neither scientists nor the secret police can understand. I state again that this mysterious tragedy which is here described is completely true in all its external respects, though naturally I have reached a different conclusion on certain points than those involved in the story. But the events are incontrovertible, and so many people know of them that they cannot be denied.

Bram also clearly claimed that many of the characters in his novel were real people. The preface goes on to say:

All the people who have willingly—or unwillingly—played a part in this remarkable story are known generally and well respected. Both Jonathan Harker and his wife (who is a woman of character) and Dr. Seward are my friends and have been so for many years, and I have never doubted that they were telling the truth; and the highly respected scientist, who appears here under a pseudonym, will also be too famous all over the educated world for his real name, which I have not desired to specify, to be hidden from people—least of all those who have from experience learnt to value and respect his genius and accomplishments, though they adhere to his views on life no more than I.

BRAM STOKER did not intend for *Dracula* to serve as fiction but as a warning of a very real evil.

Worried of the impact of presenting such a story as true, his editor pushed the manuscript back across the desk with a single line of his own: *No.*

Otto Kyllman, his editor at Archibald Constable & Company, went on to tell Bram that London was still recovering from the horrible murders in Whitechapel—and with the killer still on the loose, they couldn't publish such a story without running the risk of generating mass panic. He would have to make changes.

At that point, Stoker nearly pulled the book, knowing compromise would mean his message might get lost. But at the same time he knew that without a publisher, his message wouldn't be seen at all. Ultimately, he relented, and over the coming months Stoker worked with Kyllman to reshape the novel, the two often butting heads over what should stay and what could not. Even the title of the book was changed from *The Un-Dead* to *Dracula*.

When the novel was finally published, on May 26, 1897, the first 101 pages had been cut, numerous alterations had been made to the text, and the epilogue had been shortened, changing Dracula's ultimate fate as well as that of his castle. Tens of thousands of words had vanished, the preface reduced to:

> How these papers have been placed in sequence will be made manifest in the reading of them. All needless matters have been eliminated, so that a history almost at variance with the possibilities of later-day belief may stand forth as simple fact. There is throughout no statement of past things wherein memory may err, for all the records chosen are exactly contemporary, given from the standpoints and within the range of knowledge of those who made them.

WITH THAT BEGAN A GAME, a mystery we've only begun to unravel more than 120 years later. Today, general practice has the author submitting a copy of his novel to his publisher in his home country, then that publisher, or the author's literary agent, distributes it to the rest of the participating publishers worldwide. Essentially, all publishers work off the same original draft. In Bram's time, such wasn't the case. Bram personally mailed a draft of the novel to each of his publishers around the globe. When he agreed to Kyllman's changes, he did so knowing those changes would impact *only* the U.K. edition; to other publishers, he could send his original story.

So Bram had found a way to tell his tale.

Throughout *Dracul*, you will find references to *Makt Myrkranna*, the recently translated Icelandic version of *Dracula*. *Makt Myrkranna*—which means "Powers of Darkness"—is not the *Dracula* known to us. The changes go far beyond simple variances in translation. There are different characters, different locations, different story lines. While both novels begin in a similar fashion, the endings could not be further apart. Dracula had a love interest, a woman his equal in many ways, a woman he knew as Countess Dolingen von Gratz—whom Bram believed to be Ellen. When one reads *Makt Myrkranna*, the tale we thought we knew as *Dracula* becomes less concrete, unsettlingly fluid. The sensation of reading it is Bram whispering in our ears, telling us there is far more to the story.

What was in those missing 101 pages? Bram left a trail of bread crumbs, and you only have to know where to look and be willing to follow them. First editions worldwide appear to be the key to discovering the entire tale he wished to tell.

Bram also left copious notes. He was rarely seen without a journal in his pocket. He documented everything from story ideas to family

Image © Noel Dobbs, Bram Stoker Estate

["I once knew a little boy who put so many flies into a bottle
that they had not room to die!!!" quoted in Part II of *Dracul*.]

anecdotes to the weather. Portions of *Dracul* came from his journals, and as we searched through them, Bram's words were resurrected.

Early on, Bram detailed what vampires can and cannot do. Missing from his list? Sunlight. Bram felt vampires could go out during the day but did so without their powers. The deadly effect of sunlight on a vampire did not get tacked on to the legend until the film *Nosferatu* in 1922.

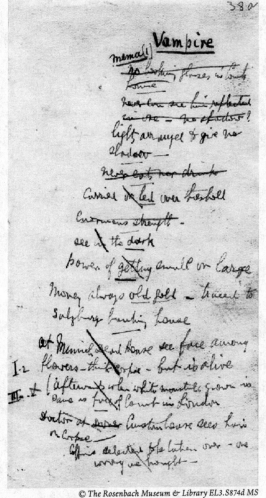

["Vampire

Memo

no looking glasses in Count's house

never can see him reflected in one—no shadow?

lights arranged to give no shadow

never eats nor drinks

carried or led over threshold

enormous strength

see in the dark

power of getting small or large

money always old gold—traced to Salzburg banking house

At Munich Dead House see face among flowers—think corpse—but is alive

III Afterwards when white moustache grown is same as face of Count in London

Doctor at Dover Custom house sees him or corpse

Coffins selected to be taken over—one wrong one brought"]

And what about the true origin of Bram's monster?

Although most believe Dracula to be Vlad Dracul, there is no mention of Vlad the Impaler in any of Bram's notes. They are the same in surname only.

This connection between Vlad the Impaler and Dracula was not made by Bram; instead, it was a conjecture put forth by two professors from Boston College, Raymond McNally and Radu Florescu, in their book *In Search of Dracula*, published in 1972. The "Vlad the Impaler" story line was also advanced by Francis Ford Coppola in his 1992 feature film, *Bram Stoker's Dracula*.

Bram's monster was far older than Vlad the Impaler. In fact, he was a product of the Scholomance as detailed in the first line of this note:

.["Scholomance = school in mountains where Devil teaches mysteries of nature. Only 10 pupils a time and retains one as payment."]

That "one" was Dracul.

And as for how Bram first became fascinated by

© *The Rosenbach Museum & Library EL3.S874d MS*

monsters? It began when he was a child, when his Nanna Ellen told him the tale of the Dearg-Due.

LIKE *Dracula*, *Dracul* finds its roots in truth. A few dates have been changed and events condensed, necessary when telling a story such as this. For a full, carefully researched history of the Stoker family, visit www.bramstokerestate.com.

By all accounts, Bram was a sickly child, unable to walk, at times near death, bedridden until the age of seven—when he was miraculously healed. By the time he entered Trinity College, he displayed no residual effects from his childhood illness. In fact, he excelled at athletics: rowing, swimming, gymnastics, rugby, and racewalking. The extended Stoker family included a number of physicians, including Dr. William Stoker (1773–1848), an expert on fevers and bloodletting, and his son, Dr. Edward Alexander Stoker (1810–1880), who treated Bram. When he was well enough, Bram was entertained with tales of banshees, blood-sucking fairies, the legend of the Dearg-Due—and his mother's personal horror story. At fourteen, Charlotte survived a cholera epidemic in Sligo, which she later relayed to Bram. At his request, Charlotte wrote the stories down for him. Her graphic account, written in 1873, was in Bram's surviving papers.

Charlotte and Abraham Stoker, Sr., lived in a town house at Marino Crescent from before Thornley's birth in 1845 until they moved to Artane Lodge sometime before their third child, Tom, was born in 1849. A short distance away stood Artane Castle, a ruin by the time Bram was well enough to roam the area freely.

Thornley was one of Ireland's most renowned surgeons. He held many positions, including visiting surgeon to Swift's Hospital for Lunatics, where it was said he performed surgeries so new that they had not yet been named.

Thornley's wife, Emily, in fact was locked away in an asylum for the last years of her life, the reason known only to him, the man who institutionalized her. Though no one knows why, Thornley kept a lock of hair on his person for most of his adult life—a lock that belonged to Ellen Crone, who served as nanny to the Stoker family for many years.

Matilda was an artist from her earliest days. She was educated at the Dublin Art School, and was a member of the Royal Hibernian Academy. She studied painting and ceramics, and as children she and Bram both won awards for their art. She and her younger sister, Margaret, went abroad with their parents when Abraham Sr. retired, first to France, then to Switzerland, then to Italy, where Matilda continued to study art. Matilda moved to London soon after her father died and lived first with Bram and Florence, then with her brother George and his wife, Agnes. In 1889, at the age of forty-three, she married Charles Petitjean, eleven years her junior.

Tom served in a variety of posts during his long career in the Indian Civil Service, notably as Chief Secretary to the Government Secretary. He returned to Blackrock, Dublin, to marry Enid Bruce in 1891. She accompanied Tom back to India where they lived until he retired in 1899.

The village of the damned exists today, as it did in Bram's lifetime, hidden, not far outside Munich.

In 1868, Whitby Abbey boasted a center tower, at the top of which was the room where Bram had his standoff in *Dracul*. During World War I, the German navy shelled and destroyed this tower, along with much of the abbey.

Although Bram felt the need to protect the identity of Van Helsing, many believe him to be Arminius Vambéry, a friend of both Thornley and Bram's with a colorful past who was known to frequent the Beefsteak Club attached to the Lyceum Theater. Bram drops a hint in the text of *Dracula* as to Vambéry's identity when Van Helsing refers to "his friend Arminius of Buda-Pesth University."

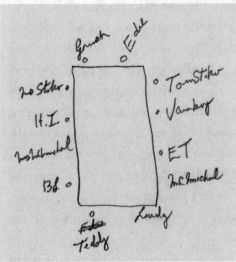

Seating chart of a dinner at the Beefsteak Club (clockwise): Bartholomew Grunszt (former private secretary to Lajos Kossuth/ Governor-President of Hungary), Edith Wardell (Ellen Terry's daughter), Tom Stoker (Bram's brother), **Arminius Vambéry**, Ellen Terry (celebrated actress), Mr. McMichael, Harry Loveday (set designer, Lyceum Theater), Teddy (Edward Gordon Craig, Ellen Terry's son), **Bram Stoker**, Mrs. McMichael, Henry Irving, Florence Stoker (Bram's wife)

Image © Dacre Stoker

Bram wrote the actual location of Dracula's castle, indicated by latitude and longitude, in his private journal, reversing the numbers as a form of protective code, and guarded that location for the remainder of his life:

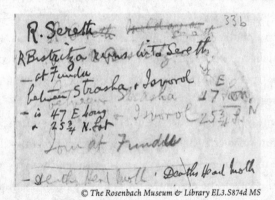

© The Rosenbach Museum & Library EL3.S874d MS

Through his notes and journals, both published and not, through hints purposely left behind in first editions of his masterpiece, Bram found a way to tell his story. He led us to *Dracul*.

In March of 2017, Paul Allen, the cofounder of Microsoft, invited us to view the original *Dracula: The Un-Dead* manuscript, which he purchased at auction some time ago. This rare opportunity allowed us to verify many of our findings. Although we were asked to sign nondisclosure agreements prohibiting us from discussing much of what we saw, we can confirm that the short story "Dracula's Guest" was most certainly excised from the original novel. We can also confirm that the manuscript in Allen's possession begins at page 102, crossed out at the top and renumbered as page 1, the first 101 pages missing. Throughout the manuscript, we were able to find passages cut from the final draft, referencing the text from those first 101 pages, the text that would later become this novel.

There were many times when we felt Bram's eyes peering over our shoulders, reading our words as they filled the page, reading his words brought back from texts long forgotten. We like to think he was smiling, handing us his notes as we went along, telling us where to look next.

Bram Stoker once said, "There are mysteries which men can only guess at, which age by age they may resolve only in part." *Dracul* is a first step in understanding the mystery he laid out for us. Perhaps, as other first editions of *Dracula* are translated worldwide and compared to the original published by Archibald Constable & Company, we will learn the rest.

Did Bram Stoker truly believe that Dracula, this monster that had haunted him since childhood, would come for his immortal soul upon death? We may never know. You have to wonder, though—why did he leave instructions to be cremated immediately upon death at a time in history when it wasn't commonplace to do so? Perhaps he saw something in the shadows that gave him pause—a reminder, the whisper of a story told to him in his childhood. Or maybe he simply read a long-lost note from his nanny and realized that not all monsters go away with time. In fact, some don't leave you at all—they wait. They're a patient lot. And no matter what it takes, you have to keep ahead of them, an inch outside their grasp will do.

Dacre Stoker & J. D. Barker

Photo © E. Willis

DACRE'S ACKNOWLEDGMENTS

I first would like to thank the many people who attended my "Stoker on Stoker" presentations over the last ten years and encouraged me to publish the stories I shared with them. This could not have been done without my co-author, J.D. I appreciate his genius in shaping a story; working with him in this free-flowing collaboration has been a genuinely rewarding experience.

The Stoker family records and lore, in many ways the novel's historical underpinnings, are a credit to my wife's hard work, eye for detail, and world-spanning network of family genealogy contacts. I owe Jenne more than I am at liberty to divulge. Thanks also to my son, Parker, for his welcome feedback and editing assistance.

After reading an early draft of *Dracul,* my mother, Gail, reminded me of Charlotte Stoker's note to Bram on *Dracula*: "It is splendid, a thousand miles beyond anything you have written before . . . Well done, Dacre." My mum's support has always meant the world to me.

A special thanks to Kristin Nelson, my agent, and Mark Tavani, executive editor at Putnam, for helping us to bring Bram and his family to life on these pages.

J. D.'S ACKNOWLEDGMENTS

With a book like this, there are always so many people to thank, I invariably always miss one or ten. For that, I apologize in advance.

Kristin Nelson, my wonderful agent and friend. Thank you for finding this book a home. Mark Tavani and all those at Putnam, *thank you* for welcoming us into that home.

Dacre Stoker and family, thank you for inviting me into your world, for pulling back the curtain on a childhood treasure. Thank you, Bram, for leaving your words behind. The world knew your nightmare; maybe now they know you, too.

Finally, my favorite person, my wife, Dayna. I may have a headful of tales, but our story always tops the heap. Thank you for being you.

DRACUL

DACRE STOKER *and* J. D. BARKER

Discussion Guide

A Conversation with Dacre Stoker and J. D. Barker about DRACUL

BOOK
ENDS

PUTNAM
— EST. 1838 —

DISCUSSION GUIDE

––––––◆––––––

1. If you read Bram Stoker's *Dracula* before reading *Dracul*, how did it shape your expectations? Has reading *Dracul* changed how you see the original story?

2. *Dracul* is the story not only of Bram Stoker but of his sister Matilda and their older brother Thornley. Did you identify with one of these protagonists more than the others? How did each contribute to solving the mystery?

3. The novel is inspired by real notes and texts that Bram Stoker left behind. Discuss the interplay of fiction and history in *Dracul*. How did your sense of the story change after reading the Authors' Note?

4. How is *Dracul* shaped by its setting? How do the customs and expectations of its place and time affect the way people react to the supernatural threat at hand?

5. *Dracul* moves between two time frames, one detailing the terrible things Bram saw as a child, the other bringing the reader into the tower to face the horrible being that hunts him. How do the authors use this two-tiered structure to create anticipation? How do the scenes set in the tower change the way you read the chapters about Bram's childhood?

6. The text known as *Dracula's Guest* was excised from the original *Dracula* manuscript and later published by Bram's widow, Florence, as a short story in 1914. Have you read *Dracula's Guest*? How does it bridge the gap between *Dracul* and *Dracula*?

7. There have been countless adaptations of Bram Stoker's *Dracula*—other books, TV shows, movies, radio dramas, and stage presentations. What original ideas or narratives did *Dracul* add to the larger *Dracula* legend?

8. In this novel, Ellen Crone is both a monster and a prisoner. How did learning about her past change the way you perceive her? How did it change the way you look at *Dracula*?

9. The final entry of Bram Stoker's journal gives readers insight into the lives that the characters come to lead twenty-two years after the events of the novel. What do you imagine will happen to the siblings?

10. Upon reading the Authors' Note, do you believe that there is any truth behind the events that Bram Stoker detailed in *Dracula* and the first 100 unpublished pages that *Dracul* is based on?

11. What did you find to be the most terrifying moment of the novel? What is it about the *Dracula* legend that has made it so enduringly frightening?

A CONVERSATION WITH DACRE STOKER AND J. D. BARKER ABOUT *DRACUL*

⸺ ◆ ⸺

Why did you decide to write this novel together and what was the process of writing as a team? How was writing Dracul *different from your previous work?*

Dacre Stoker: I had an idea in mind for a story about Bram's life leading up to his writing *Dracula*, but knew I would need a coauthor to best tell the story. I met J. D. at the Horror Writers Association annual conference (I had read his book *Forsaken*, loved the writing style, and in particular, one of his characters), and, after spending a few hours with him at a signing table, we hit it off with sharing ideas. I knew that we were compatible to work together. I provided a lot of historical information and a timeline about the Stoker family, and we blended those with J. D.'s ideas of suspense and horror. We spent a long weekend together in North Carolina laying out the plot for our story . . . I would send blocks of text to J. D. and he would use some and not use others. It was a wonderful collaboration.

J. D. Barker: I first read *Dracula* as a child and it's been a fixture on my bookshelf throughout the years. It's one of the few novels I've revisited often enough, I've lost count. When Dacre asked me to take part in such an iconic project, I was flattered. He offered a peek behind the curtain, and I simply could not resist. We quickly settled into a rhythm, with the sense Bram Stoker was near to check our work. In order to match Bram's voice, I immersed myself in his published material, notes, and journals. I also listened to the *Dracula* audiobook on a loop for the duration. I've worked with coauthors before, but this is the first time the loudest of those voices belonged to a man long since passed.

What kind of research did you do for the book? While researching, did you travel to all the locations the story takes place in?

DS: We needed to include real events in Bram's life while weaving them together in a fictional manner to create a narrative that would hold suspense. We created a timeline of actual events and merged in fictional events in a way that the reader would have a difficult time telling the difference. We dissected Bram's notes for *Dracula*, the *Dracula* typescript, the short story *Dracula's Guest*, and *Makt Myrkranna* (an early version of *Dracula*). I spent time in Dublin and Whitby visiting all the significant locations that we used in *Dracul* (of course some of them no longer exist). We felt that to be true to Bram's style of writing in *Dracula* and to properly portray a sense of realism—we needed to be historically and geographically accurate.

JDB: My wife and I have a ten-month-old baby girl at home, so my travel is currently limited to late-night diaper runs. Having visited, Dacre was instrumental when it came to describing many of the places in the novel. Others required substantial research. While the locations may exist today, they are far different than they were in 1868. A location central to the story was destroyed by the German navy in World War I—we had to piece together its condition in Bram's day.

Do you believe Bram Stoker really thought of Dracula *as a true account?*

DS: I believe that Bram was a master at making his readers feel that he believed the story was real. Remember, *Dracula* was written in 1897, a time when the occult was in vogue, mesmerism was an emerging science, and the supernatural was . . . well, felt to be quite possible. There are two lines in the novel *Dracula* that I believe sum up how Bram felt:

"I want you to believe, to believe in things which you know to be untrue," and "There are mysteries which men can only guess at, which age by age they may solve only in part." In addition, I am reminded of a line in the 1992 film *Bram Stoker's Dracula*; J. V. Hart included in his screenplay a similar thought: "The strength of the vampire is that people will not believe in him."

JDB: For any author, fiction works best when those lines blur. If permitted, a character can graduate from a simple sketch on the page to a living, breathing being. Someone with the singular desire to tell you their story. In other cases, fictional characters aren't so fictional. When reading *Dracul* and *Dracula*, it's impossible to not draw correlations between the people in Bram's story and those in his real life—his family, friends, and acquaintances. During his earliest years, Bram Stoker experienced some horrific events at a time when his imagination was most susceptible. You can't help but wonder how that shapes a person's thoughts as they grow older. Did he believe in monsters? We may never know. But I can comfortably say he hedged his bets just in case.

What is the significance of the instructions Bram Stoker left for the disposition of his body upon his death?

DS: Bram left verbal instructions with his wife, and he was clear that he wanted to be cremated. He did not give a reason, but I believe that he wanted to insure that he was able to rest in peace.

JDB: Ha. This is where Dacre and I differ. My mind loves to take a leap. When someone selects cremation at a time/place in history when it isn't commonplace, the only logical answer is that he's hiding his immortal soul from the vampire staking claim, right?

Bram Stoker wrote the actual location of Dracula's castle in a coded diary entry and guarded that secret until he died. Did you visit the secret location?

DS: Bram wrote a note with coordinates of longitude and latitude, but they were "coded" or altered in a way to hide the actual location of where the two points converged. He switched the two numbers: as written, they point somewhere in the Gobi desert, but when ordered correctly, the coordinates intersect right on an extinct volcano in the Carpathian Mountains of Northern Transylvania, Mt. Izvorul Câliman-ului. This was the location for his Castle Dracula, in what is now Romania's Câlimani National Park. This past summer I hired a guide and, together with my son Parker and a few other friends, hiked up Mt. Izvorul and had quite an adventure. We made it to the top and left a sealed capsule commemorating our visit to the peak. We also met with the park officials, who agreed to create a special trail and erect a plaque memorializing the location of Bram's Castle Dracula.

JDB: Not only were the first 101 pages of *Dracula* removed from the manuscript prior to publication, but the ending was altered as well. In the original, the mountain on which Dracula's castle stood erupts in a fire-filled blast. From the original: "From where we stood it seemed as though the one fierce volcano burst had satisfied the need of nature and that the castle and the structure of the hill had sunk again into the void." It can't be coincidence that Bram would write the longitude and latitude of a volcanic peak in Transylvania in his notes, one matching the description in his novel so accurately. The fact that he never revealed this as the location of Dracula's castle publicly has left the door open for others to stake claim as the Count's home. I'm not sure how Bram would feel about that.

In his early preface Bram says that there are several well-known people who appear as characters in Dracula *whose names he has changed to protect their identity. Who are these people and why is their inclusion significant?*

DS: Bram states quite clearly in his early preface to *Dracula* that Jonathan Harker, his wife and Dr. Seward are friends. He also suggests a familiarity with the scientist, thus changing his name (van Helsing). "All the people who have willingly—or unwillingly—played a part in this remarkable story are known generally and well respected. Both Jonathan Harker and his wife (who is a woman of character) and Dr. Seward are my friends and have been so for many years, and I have never doubted that they were telling the truth; and the highly respected scientist, who appears here under a pseudonym, will also be too famous all over the educated world for his real name, which I have not desired to specify, to be hidden from people. . . ." By using these real people in his novel, Bram makes a compelling case that his story was real.

JDB: In my mind, it's clear Arminius Vambery was the inspiration for van Helsing. I personally see many similarities between Thornley Stoker and Dr. Seward, Matilda Stoker and Mina Harker, even Bram himself and Jonathan Harker.

What is the significance of the Makt Myrkranna and why is it referenced in Dracul?

DS: *Makt Myrkranna*, which translates as "Powers of Darkness," was published from an early draft of *Dracula*. Although *Makt Myrkranna* was published in 1901, it represents a version of Bram's story before it was edited by his publisher (Archibald Constable, London) and ultimately released in 1897 as the *Dracula* we all know. We believe this early version of the story was considered too realistic—on the heels of the Jack the Ripper murders, it would have been too unsettling for London readers.

JDB: In many ways, *Makt Myrkranna* represents the story Bram wished to tell. It varies greatly from the *Dracula* tale familiar to us all and begs the question: Who made the changes and why? In today's publishing world, when we write a novel, we send a single copy to our editor. Our publisher then sends it off to the various other publishers around the world. In other words, they all work from the same draft. In Bram's time, that wasn't the case. He personally mailed his manuscript to each publisher and in doing so, left breadcrumbs behind—hints at his original story removed from the English version. *Makt Myrkranna* was discovered when an Icelandic first edition of *Dracula* was translated to English. It's impossible not to wonder what other secrets may still be hiding out there. What will be found when other first editions are translated? Perhaps Bram's greatest secret has yet to be revealed. For now, it only sleeps and waits.

Photograph of the author © Todd Lista

DACRE STOKER is the great-grandnephew of Bram Stoker and the international best-selling co-author of *Dracula: The Un-Dead*, the official Stoker family–endorsed sequel to *Dracula*. He is also the co-editor of *The Lost Journal of Bram Stoker: The Dublin Years*. He currently lives with his wife, Jenne, in Aiken, South Carolina, where he manages the Bram Stoker Estate.

Photograph of the author © Peterson Gallery

J. D. BARKER is the internationally bestselling author of *Forsaken*, *The Fourth Monkey*, *The Fifth to Die*, and *The Sixth Wicked Child*. He was a finalist for the Bram Stoker Award for Superior Achievement in a First Novel and winner of the New Apple Medalist Award. His works have been translated into numerous languages and optioned for both film and television. Barker currently resides in New Hampshire with his wife, Dayna, and daughter, Ember.

VISIT DACRE STOKER ONLINE

[f] dacrestoker.com
dacrestoker
[o] dacrestoker
[y] @stokerdacre

VISIT J. D. BARKER ONLINE

jdbarker.com
[f] therealjdbarker
[o] jdbarker_author
[y] @jdbarker